PROBING

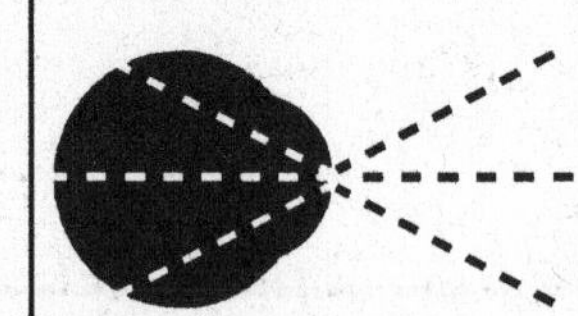

This Large Print Book carries the Seal of Approval of N.A.V.H.

CYCLE THREE OF
THE HARBINGERS SERIES

PROBING

LEVIATHAN BY BILL MYERS
THE MIND PIRATES BY FRANK PERETTI
HYBRIDS BY ANGELA HUNT
THE VILLAGE BY ALTON GANSKY

THORNDIKE PRESS
A part of Gale, a Cengage Company

Farmington Hills, Mich • San Francisco • New York • Waterville, Maine
Meriden, Conn • Mason, Ohio • Chicago

Thorndike Press® Large Print Christian Mystery.
The text of this Large Print edition is unabridged.
Other aspects of the book may vary from the original edition.
Set in 16 pt. Plantin.

LIBRARY OF CONGRESS CIP DATA ON FILE.
CATALOGUING IN PUBLICATION FOR THIS BOOK
IS AVAILABLE FROM THE LIBRARY OF CONGRESS.

ISBN-13: 978-1-4328-4549-0 (hardcover)
ISBN-10: 1-4328-4549-7 (hardcover)

Published in 2017 by arrangement with Bethany House Publishers, a division of Baker Publishing Group

Printed in Mexico
1 2 3 4 5 6 7 21 20 19 18 17

CONTENTS

In this fast-paced world with all its demands, the four of us wanted to try something new. Instead of the longer novel format, we wanted to write something equally as engaging but that could be read in one or two sittings — on the plane, waiting to pick up the kids from soccer, or as an evening's read.

We also wanted to play. As friends and seasoned novelists, we thought it would be fun to create a game we could participate in together. The rules were simple:

Rule #1

Each of us would write as if we were one of the characters in the series:

Bill Myers would write as Brenda, the street-hustling tattoo artist who sees images of the future.

Frank Peretti would write as the professor, the atheist ex-priest ruled by logic.

Angela Hunt would write as Andi, the professor's brilliant but geeky assistant who sees inexplicable patterns.

Alton Gansky would write as Tank, the naïve, big-hearted jock with a surprising connection to a healing power.

RULE #2

Instead of the four of us writing one novella together (we're friends but not crazy), we would write it like a TV series. There would be an overarching story line into which we'd plug our individual novellas, with each story written from our character's point of view.

If you're keeping track, this is the order:

Harbingers #1 — *The Call* — Bill Myers
Harbingers #2 — *The Haunted* — Frank Peretti
Harbingers #3 — *The Sentinels* — Angela Hunt
Harbingers #4 — *The Girl* — Alton Gansky
Volumes #1–4 omnibus:
Cycle One: Invitation

Harbingers #5 — *The Revealing* — Bill Myers
Harbingers #6 — *Infestation* — Frank Peretti

Harbingers #7 — *Infiltration* — Angela Hunt
Harbingers #8 — *The Fog* — Alton Gansky
Volumes #5–8 omnibus: *Cycle Two: The Assault*

Harbingers #9 — *Leviathan* — Bill Myers
Harbingers #10 — *The Mind Pirates* — Frank Peretti
Harbingers #11 — *Hybrids* — Angela Hunt
Harbingers #12 — *The Village* — Alton Gansky
Volumes #9–12 omnibus: *Cycle Three: Probing*

There you have it — at least for now. We hope you'll find these as entertaining in the reading as we did in the writing.

Bill, Frank, Angie, and Al

LEVIATHAN

BILL MYERS

Chapter 1

"You okay?"

Daniel said nothing. No surprise there. Just kept starin' out the window of the plane. But the workout he was givin' the napkin in his hand said somethin' was up.

I motioned to the hills across the city. "Check it out. That's the Hollywood sign over there."

Nothing. Vintage Daniel.

We were a minute or so from landing, so I capped my pen and closed the sketchpad. I'd been drawing some sort of octopus thing. In the old days it would have been for somebody's tattoo. Not now. Now the stuff I see in my head has nothing to do with tatting somebody's future . . . and everything to do with our group's assignments.

The plane shuttered and jerked. Not a big deal. 'Cept I'd be more comfortable if Daniel hadn't muttered something.

"What's that?" I said.

He stayed glued to the window and repeated it. Something like *Leviathan,* whatever that means.

The plane bucked harder. I sucked in my breath. Me and flying aren't the best of friends. Though you wouldn't know it by the free miles I've been racking up.

None of us knows who's footing the bill for these flights or paying the expenses when we get there. But we got ideas. For starters, they're the good guys. Least that's what we hope. And they're fighting off what we think are the bad guys — something called The Gate, a group that's got lots of nasty ideas and nasty dudes . . . some who aren't so human.

'Course we got some unearthly types on our side, too. Seems more than just our world is interested in what's going on down here.

The plane leaped again and dropped — this time a couple seconds. Enough for people to shout and scream. 'Cept Daniel. He just kept lookin' out the window. Only now his lips were movin' a mile a minute. I can't hear words, but I know he's prayin'. Or talkin' to his imaginary friends (who we're findin' out aren't always so imaginary).

Another drop.

"Daniel!"

He reached out and took my hand. A nice, sweet gesture . . . before we die.

More bucking and falling. The screams became nonstop.

Out the window I saw a freeway with cars — so close we could touch 'em. The plane's engines revved hard, throwing me back into the seat. The pilot was gunning it, trying to reach the runway.

The whole plane banged like we hit something. But we were still picking up speed, folks screamin', some cryin' out to sweet Jesus for mercy. A second later, we slammed onto the ground. I got thrown forward, seat belt digging into my gut. The engines shrieked, reversing thrust. The plane shook and shimmied like a car with bad brakes.

But we were down. And in pretty good shape — 'cept for the weeping and swearing . . . and the smell of vomit across the aisle.

Daniel leaned back into the seat and closed his eyes.

I took a swallow and turned to him. "We good?"

He nodded. Took a deep breath and blew it out.

I did, too.

The pilot came on, all apologies. Something about wind shears that may or may not be true. Who knows? Who cares. I stole another look at Daniel, his face all wet and shiny, but he seemed relaxed.

I let go of his hand, wiped my palms, and took another breath. Long and slow.

Just another day at the office.

Chapter 2

"Brenda!"

I braced myself as Cowboy, aka Tank, aka Bjorn Christensen, threw his grizzly-bear arms around me. (I'm as fond of hugging as I am flying.) We'd had plenty of talks about boundaries, but the big fellow could never quite seem to get it. And to be honest, with our last few assignments, I felt less and less inclined to remind him. I was changin'. Guess we all were.

"You're late, Barnick," the professor barked. He's also part of the team. But if he's changin', he's doing a lot better job at keeping it hidden.

"Professor, you can't blame them for the airline being late." That's Andi Goldstein. If the professor was the team's Eeyore, Andi, his bubbly, redheaded assistant, was our Tigger. But a whole lot smarter — 'specially when it comes to computers and in seeing patterns just about everywhere.

The man grunted and headed for the doors. "Limo is waiting."

I turned to Andi. "Bad day?"

She shrugged. "With him, who can tell?"

We headed out of the terminal. After Mr. Toad's Wild Ride on the plane, what I wouldn't give for a smoke. But we were late and there was no way the professor was going to wait.

Outside it was typical LA — noise, busses, taxis. And people. Way too many for my taste. It's not that I'm anti-social it's, well, let's just say the sun ain't the only reason I like livin' in the desert.

We followed the professor to a stretch limo waiting at the curb and climbed inside. Memories of our last gig, the one with the fog creepies in San Diego, came to mind. Needless to say, I hoped this mission would be a lot safer.

"So what's up?" I slipped off my backpack as the driver shut the door. "And why all the urgency? They gave us less than twenty-four hours this time."

No one had an answer, which was pretty typical. 'Course we could refuse and decline any time we wanted, but they (whoever "they" were) knew we wouldn't. The mystery and excitement were just too much for us. Like it or not, we'd become adventure junkies.

We always complained. But we never declined.

I glanced at Daniel. He'd already settled in, making himself comfortable playing one of his blow-'em-up app games.

"You know that will rot his brain," the professor said.

I ignored the man. A good tactic when I could pull it off.

Andi read from her tablet. "This came in just before you landed: 'Today, 2:00 p.m., Everbright Studios invites you and your party to be our guests for a VIP viewing of the final rehearsal and taping of the new reality TV show *Live or Die: The Ultimate Reality.*"

"A television show?" I said. "We've come all this way for a television show?"

Andi kept reading. "Following rehearsal, after a gourmet dinner with cast and crew, you will be escorted to front-row seats for the 7:00 p.m. taping."

I frowned. "And our purpose?"

She shook her head. "This is all we have."

I threw a glance to the professor. I now saw why the resident control freak was a bit cranky.

"And this limo?" I asked.

"The show's executive producer" — Andi glanced back to her tablet — "a Mr. Norman Anderson, ordered it for us."

"But why?"

Always the optimist, Cowboy chimed in. "Guess we'll just have to wait till we get there to find out. But a TV show, that'll be kinda fun, right?"

Fun wasn't exactly the word that came to mind. Like it or not, I was already catching the professor's negativity — something I wasn't thrilled about.

"Hey, check it out." Cowboy scooted to the closest window. "Look at them cool pillars."

Outside there were a bunch of big plastic pillars along the roadway. All different sizes. Even in the afternoon sun, you could see they were lit inside by colored lights that were changing from purple . . . to green . . . to red.

"The LAX pylons," Andi said. She went back to tapping on her tablet.

Cowboy pulled out his cell phone, made a quick pan across our faces, and began videotaping the pillars out the window.

Andi found a link and began to read: "Originally constructed in the year 2000, the pillars range from twenty-five to sixty feet tall. They were designed to give the feeling of taking off in an airplane. They culminate in a circle of fifteen one-hundred-foot columns that represent the fifteen city council districts, while simultaneously bringing to mind ancient sights such as Stonehenge." She paused and looked out the window. "Pretty neat art, huh?"

I didn't know what to say.

The professor did. "How much?"

"What's that?"

"The price tag. What was the expenditure for this 'neat art'?"

She glanced at her tablet. "Fifteen million dollars."

He looked back out the window and muttered, "Welcome to Los Angeles."

A moment later the TV monitor in the back blasted on. It was a scene from the first *Superman* movie. It only lasted a couple seconds, then went off. I glanced to Daniel. Then to Cowboy. Nobody had touched the controls.

"Well," the professor said, "that was certainly —"

The TV came on again. This time it was one of those old *Rocky* movies.

"Andi?" the professor said.

It went off.

"I'm on it." She scooted to the control

console and examined the glowing buttons.

The monitor came back on again. Longer. It was that weird Leonardo DiCaprio movie with the spinning top.

Then off.

"Andrea!" the professor repeated.

"I don't —"

Then back on. Some British sci-fi thing with a flying telephone booth.

And off.

Cowboy and Daniel moved over to help her.

Then on. I recognized this one immediately. It was a scene from the first *Hunger Games.*

Then off.

The professor grabbed the limo phone and spoke into it. "Driver, will you please —"

Back on again, drowning out his voice. It was some cartoon with talking ants.

And off.

"— but surely you have a master control up there that —"

And on. Another *Rocky* movie. Newer.

Andi scooted from the console and rummaged through what looked like a silverware drawer.

The *Rocky* movie went off.

The professor kept speaking to the driver.

"I find your ignorance comparable only to your —"

And on. Back to the *Superman* movie.

A moment later the professor slammed down the phone. The TV switched back to the first *Rocky* movie.

Andi pulled a steak knife from the drawer and slid back to the console. She began attacking its tiny screws with the tip of the knife.

The spinning top movie came back on.

"Andrea!"

"Patience, Professor. Patien—"

Then we were back to the British sci-fi thing.

She kept working on the screws until she was able to pull out the control panel, guts and all. But the TV still kept playing.

The Hunger Games was back on.

She stared dubiously at the attached wires.

The ant cartoon came on.

Then the newer *Rocky* movie.

She sighed, then gave the control panel a good yank, ripping out all the wires. The television went off. This time for good.

We sat in silence. Blessed silence. Except for Cowboy, who was never able to endure any silence for too long. "Well, that was weird, huh?"

None of us disagreed.

CHAPTER 3

"Hold positions, please. Camera Three, that's your hero shot. Two and Four, stay wide."

"Got it."

"Staying wide."

We stood way in the back of some state-of-the-art TV control room. A dozen people in headsets with faces lit by twice that many monitors and a long board of glowing lights and flashing buttons. Techno-geek heaven.

Andi loved it.

The fact that we got headsets to listen in made it all the better.

A couple hours earlier, our limo had pulled into the studio lot. We were greeted by a perky blonde, complete with Barbie figure and brilliantly white, glow-in-the-dark teeth.

"Hi there," she said as we climbed out and stretched our legs. "My name is Ashlee. I'm so glad you could make it. So how was your flight? Terrific, I hope."

"Howdy, I'm Tank," Cowboy said, giving her his good-ol'-boy grin. "Me, Andi, and the professor here, ours was great. But Brenda and the little guy, I guess theirs wasn't so hot."

"Oh, I'm sorry to hear that," Ashlee said.

I reached back inside the limo to grab my backpack.

"Oh, don't worry about that." She blinded us with another one of her smiles. "We'll have that delivered to your hotel."

"Right." I lugged the pack out and onto my shoulder. "I'll just hang on to it." Old street habits die hard.

"Rehearsal has already started," Ashlee said, "but I'm sure we can slip you into — oh, here's Skylar now." She motioned to an approaching clone of herself. Different hair, same teeth, and anatomically impossible figure. "She'll escort you through the studio and up to the control room."

"Hi there." The clone smiled. "My name is Skylar. I'm so glad you could make it. So how was your flight? Terrific, I hope."

I traded looks with Andi. Can anybody say *Stepford Wives*?

Cowboy didn't notice. "Hi, I'm Tank. Ours was great. But Miss Brenda's and Daniel's, here, theirs wasn't so good."

"Oh, I'm sorry to hear it."

"So, Skylar," Ashlee said. "We're running a bit late. Would you mind escorting our guests to the control room?"

"Why, I'd love to, Ashlee. If you'll join me and walk this way, please." She turned and we started toward what looked like a giant airplane hangar.

The professor sped up and joined her. "Excuse me, miss?"

She turned her perma-smile on him. "Yes?"

"What exactly is our purpose here?"

"Oh, that's easy. You're here because our executive producer, Norman Anderson, invited you. Didn't you receive his e-vite?"

"Yes, we did, but he failed to mention why."

"Oh. Because we're taping his new reality show, *Live or Die: The Ultimate Reality.*"

"I appreciate that, but the question still remains — why?"

"Because you're his invited guests."

He took a measured breath and tried again. "I understand the name of the show and I understand we are his invited guests, but you have yet to address the question of *why*?"

She looked at him blankly. Then apparently guessing he was hard of hearing, she raised her voice. "Because we're taping his new reality show, *Live or Die: The Ultimate Reality!*"

The professor opened his mouth, then closed it. It was obvious he didn't know how to communicate with her species.

When we got to the main entrance, Skylar turned to us. "Now we'll have to be very quiet." She looked to the professor. "As Mr. Anderson's *invited guests* you are being allowed inside the control room. That's quite an honor, but it will require that you turn off your cell phones and remain completely silent. Is that understood?"

Everyone nodded except for the professor.

She repeated louder for his benefit, *"Is that understood?"*

"Yes." Andi stepped in before he could respond. "We understand."

Skylar flashed one last smile and opened the door. We stepped inside and were struck by a wave of coldness. The edges of the room were dark, but you could see it was huge — a couple hundred feet wide and forty, fifty feet tall. In the center was a big oval sandpit. It was surrounded by a fake stone wall and fake stone bleachers — eight, maybe ten rows high.

"Welcome to the Colosseum," Skylar proudly announced. "It's like the Roman

Colosseum — you know, the one they have in Rome, Italy? Only it's not as big. It's a lot smaller because it's not as big. It's a miniature version."

"Of the one in Rome, Italy?" the professor asked. We all caught his sarcasm. Well, most of us.

"That's right!" Skylar beamed.

"Exactly." We kept walking.

As we approached the side wall I could see half a dozen TV cameras mounted around it. Another one hung from a cable over the pit, and two more were manned by live operators inside the pit. Each and every camera was focused on two people: a young man and a young woman. They pretended to fight, but in slow motion.

"Are those the stars?" Cowboy whispered.

Skylar shook her head. "They're what we in the business call 'stand-ins.' They're to help the director find the best camera angles for when the real fight begins this evening."

"Which brings me back to my original question," the professor said. "Why have we been selected to —"

"Oh, there's Brittani." Our guide waved to another perfectly proportioned assistant waiting at the top of the bleachers. She stood next to a large black room with mirrored windows on the front. Skylar started up the steps and we followed.

Andi leaned over and whispered to me. "Don't these girls ever eat?"

"If they do," I said, "it all goes to their boobs."

We arrived and the new girl flashed her mandatory grin. "Hi there. My name is Brittani. I'm so glad you could make it. So how was your flight? I hope it was terrific."

Now, for over an hour, we'd been standing (as in not sitting) inside the back of that big black room watching and listening to some overweight Jabba-the-Hutt director firing off instructions to his camera crew. Other than us, the only person standing was some lean, older guy with a buzz cut. By the way he paced, chewed gum, and sipped his grande Starbucks, you could tell he was in charge. I'm guessing he was the mysterious Norman Anderson.

"Hold right there," the director said into his headset.

On the monitors, the two stand-in actors froze. Since we'd been there, they'd gone from slow-motion punching to slow-motion swordplay, to slow-motion battle maces, to slow-motion lances. If it had been real, it would have been way too gross for Daniel. But everything was fake . . . including the fake blood smeared over the guy's face when he was fake stabbed in the eye before it was fake gouged out.

For the past few minutes, the girl was supposedly getting the worst of it. Her hand had been fake cut off by a cleaver — same fake blood, only now it spurted from a pump in her sleeve. And a few seconds ago, her ear had been fake sliced off.

"Beautiful," the director said. "Okay, Sean, take the butt of your sword and slam it into Jillian's face."

The actor nodded and, in slow motion, spun around and pretended to hit the girl's face.

"Jillian, drop to the ground. You're dazed."

She lowered to her knees and rolled over.

"Fantastic. Cameras Two and Three, don't forget to go for cleavage. With all that rolling around I want plenty."

The assistant next to him asked, "What about wardrobe malfunction?"

The director chuckled. "Let's hope."

The others laughed as if on cue.

"Okay, Sean, grab the axe off the back wall there, and come after her. Camera One and Two, go tight but give him room."

The images on the monitors shifted as the actor scooped up the axe and came toward the girl.

"Slower . . ."

He slowed.

"Raise it over your head."

He did.

"Everyone check your marks. This is the kill shot." He turned to Anderson, who paced behind him and nodded. He turned back to the monitors. "Alright. Gore lights, please."

The lights in the arena turned deep red.

"Strobe."

They began flashing.

"Camera Two, go for the money shot. Extreme close-up. I doubt he'll stop at one blow, so stay in there, nice and tight for spurting blood. We'll have the cameras watertight by tonight." He laughed. "Make that 'blood-tight.' "

Smiles all around.

"Alright, people, let's wrap this puppy and go on break."

Both actors nodded. Sean slowly brought down the axe until it hovered an inch from the girl's face.

"Good. And repeat."

He raised the axe and brought it down again.

"Good."

"What if it flips?" the assistant asked. "What if the girl wins?"

"Then we'll adjust. This is just practice."

He spoke back into the headset. “Okay, Sean, keep hacking. Don’t stop until I call.”

The stand-in nodded and pretended to hit Jillian again, then again, and —

Suddenly all the monitors flickered. For a second another show came on. Not a TV show, but a scene from the *Superman* movie. The same one that had come on in the limo.

The director shouted, “What the —”

The monitors all flickered to a *Rocky* movie. The same part we’d seen in the limo. Then the Leonardo DiCaprio spinning top.

We all traded looks.

Anderson slammed his Starbucks cup down on a console near us. “Engineering!”

“On it.” Some shaved-headed guy moved into action.

Next, we saw the show with the flying telephone booth. Then the scene from *The Hunger Games.*

The director swore — worse than me on a bad day.

The scene switched to the ant cartoon. Then the newer *Rocky* movie.

It was exactly like our limo ride. Except for one added bonus: The grande Starbucks beside us? No one touched it. No one was near it. But, suddenly, for no reason at all, it exploded.

Chapter 4

"And we're here because . . ." One thing about the professor — he's as persistent as he is obnoxious. At least this time we were with someone whose teeth didn't look Photoshopped and who actually had answers.

Norman Anderson was eating dinner with us and the rest of his crew in the studio cafeteria — if you call a "cafeteria" someplace where they serve prime rib, salmon, and plenty of veggie things for the vegheads.

Anderson barely glanced up from his steak to answer the professor. "You're kidding, right?"

"Do I look like I'm kidding?"

The lean fifty-something sized up the professor, then went back to eating. "You're here because I'm a man who can't say no to his daughter."

We traded looks. Clueless as ever.

He glanced back up and saw our expressions. "What? Helsa didn't tell you?"

The name stopped us cold.

"Helsa . . ." Cowboy said.

"Yeah. She and my daughter are, like, best friends." He spotted a waitress who didn't quite measure up to Team Barbie and signaled her to refill his water. Perrier, of course.

He turned back to Cowboy, who still had his mouth open. "You're the football player, right?"

"Was," Cowboy corrected. "But how do you —"

"And Helsa, she's your niece or something?"

Before Cowboy could correct him — little details like they were totally unrelated and Helsa was just a friend sent from a parallel world to sometimes help us — the professor cut him off. "Yes, she's his niece."

"Professor," Cowboy protested, "that ain't exactly the —"

"Close enough." The professor turned back to Anderson. "It's a rather long and boring story."

The man didn't notice or care. He went back to his steak. "So for months she's been telling my kid that you and your pals here have been dying to come onto a real Hollywood set. You know, see how things are done."

We traded more looks.

He took a sip of his water, stifled a burp, and set the glass down. "And since you were already in the area — vacation, is it? — I figured, why not? I mean, if it makes my daughter happy."

"Are they here?" Andi asked, glancing around. "Helsa? Your daughter?"

"Right," he scoffed. "Like I'd let them see a show like this. I sent them with the wife to Maui for the week." He turned back to Cowboy. "Cute kid, your niece. Strange, but cute."

It was about then I noticed the water in Anderson's glass rippling. Like someone bumped the table. But when I looked at the other glasses they were perfectly still.

It was the professor's turn to scoff. "You refuse to expose your own child to the violence of your show and yet you are perfectly willing to present it to the entire nation?"

Anderson gave him a look. It was obvious they weren't going to be friends. "Do you know anything about network ratings?"

"Not a thing."

"If you did, you'd know that everything's

in the toilet. Nothing's making money these days."

"So you're producing this type of barbaric ilk simply to make a —"

"This is the real world, Professor. Not some Ivy League hothouse. People here have to work to eat."

"Even if it means prostituting themselves?" The professor kept pushing buttons, one of his specialties.

"If someone's got the money and is willing to foot the bill, yeah, I'm willing to help them spend it."

I glanced back at Anderson's water. It was rippling harder.

Always the peacemaker, Andi cooled things down by asking, "When you say, 'foot the bill,' are you referring to the network? To your sponsors?"

"For starters."

"Starters?"

"There are other players. No one talks much about them; they prefer to avoid the spotlight. But we all know they're there and that they've got major bucks. Truth is, every year they're investing a bit more."

"Into programs as uplifting as yours," the professor said.

"The show was not created in a vacuum."

"Meaning?"

"They came to me. Not with every detail, of course. They trust my creative genius. But the initial concept was theirs."

"And you took their money for services rendered."

"I wasn't thrilled about it, but look at the country. You'd have to be an idiot not to see this is where programs are going. This is what people want for entertainment, so this is what they'll get." Anderson returned to cutting his steak, none too gently.

After a moment I asked, "These other people, with the money, they got a name?"

"Like I said, they like to be anonymous."

"But you know who they are."

"I've seen a contract or two."

"And?"

He looked up at me, then to the others. Obviously figuring it didn't matter, he returned to his steak. "They call themselves The Gate."

If we'd been surprised about Helsa, we were downright stunned about this.

Anderson didn't notice and kept eating. After a moment, he quoted, " 'For better or worse, the influence of the church, which used to be all-powerful, has been usurped by film. Films and television tell us the way we conduct our lives, what is right and wrong.' "

"They said that?" Cowboy asked. "The Gate?"

Anderson shook his head. "George Lucas. But they quote it. They're big fans of using the media to 'educate' and 'enlighten.' "

"By reveling in sex and violence," the professor said.

Anderson had had enough. He laid down his knife and fork and shoved away his plate. Leaning toward the professor, he said, "It's called entertainment. We give the people what they want. No one takes it seriously."

"Actually —" Andi cleared her throat as she pulled out her tablet and snapped it on. "There are over three hundred studies directly linking TV violence to social violence. More studies than link smoking to lung cancer."

Anderson turned to her, unsure how to respond.

"She's kinda smart," Cowboy said.

Searching for a link, she continued, "In fact, a 1992 article in *The Journal of the American Medical Association* concluded" — she kept looking — "ah, here it is: 'Long-term childhood exposure to television is a causal factor behind approximately one half of the homicides committed in the United States, or approximately 10,000 homicides annually.' "

Anderson frowned.

Cowboy grinned. "Told ya."

She kept reading. " 'If television technology had never been developed, there would today be 10,000 fewer homicides each year in the United States, 70,000 fewer rapes, and 700,000 fewer injurious assaults.' "

I glanced to Anderson's glass. The ripples had grown so strong the water was sloshing back and forth.

"Right." He grabbed his napkin, wiped his mouth, and started to rise. "Well, like I said, it's a living."

"Pretending to kill people?" the professor said.

"Pretending? *Pretending?* No, my friends, what you see tonight will not be pretend. It will be the real thing. *Live or Die: The Ultimate Reality.*"

"You mean you're gonna kill someone right there on TV?" Cowboy asked.

"We'll have disclaimers. Viewer discretion, late-night viewing, the usual."

"But —"

"The actors have signed waivers. Everyone knows what they're getting into."

"And you seriously believe people will tune in to watch?" Andi asked.

"Just like they did in the Roman Colosseum," he said. "Just like we do at freeway accidents. Sure, we wring our hands when we pass by, say we hope no one got hurt . . . but we slow our cars, hoping against hope that we'll see something awful."

No one had a comeback.

He turned to leave.

But I had one last question. "And your live audience? You think they're just gonna sit around and watch someone get snuffed?"

He turned back to me. "I wouldn't worry about that, miss. They're going to have a little help."

"Help?"

He didn't bother to answer. "So you don't miss any of the action, you'll have front-row seats. Now, if you'll excuse me, I have a few hundred fires to put out before the show — which you just might find entertaining . . . in spite of yourself."

He turned and walked away just as his water glass toppled over on the table, then crashed to the floor.

Chapter 5

What I saw next was pretty violent. So if you want to skip over this part and go to the next, no hard feelings. I'll fill you in later. 'Specially if you're like under seventeen or something. I'm serious. Fact is, if I wasn't part of all this, I would have skipped the whole show. But like someone somewhere said, "If you're gonna fight evil, sometimes you gotta look it in the eye."

That was the very argument we had about going back inside and seeing the show. I'd seen enough violence in my life. I don't need no more.

The others might have agreed with me . . . if it wasn't for the professor. As strange as it sounds, he was the one who kept insisting we go.

"Why's it so important to you?" I demanded.

"What it is to me is entirely irrelevant. But it's abundantly clear The Gate is behind much of this. Equally clear is the fact that we have been sent here, at no little expense, to deal with it."

"And don't forget Helsa," Cowboy added. "She's in on this, too."

"Yes." The professor cleared his throat. The girl was never one of his favorite topics. "The point is, great pains have been taken to arrange this encounter. It would be both illogical and irresponsible for us to simply walk away from it."

He looked at me for a comeback, but he had a point. I hated to admit it 'cause it was getting to be a habit.

He continued. "But not young Daniel here. You can load him up with all the vile video games you want, but I will not allow him to see this."

"Oh, *you'll* not allow him?" I said. "What, are you his guardian now?"

"I could do no worse than you."

He was right . . . again. Two for two. I let it go, hoping I wasn't losing my touch.

An hour later, one of the Barbies was babysitting Daniel somewhere else on the lot while the rest of us sat in the front row of the arena. The place was packed. Three hundred spectators waiting for the show. They had no idea what it was, but it was free, so here they were.

"Where's Andi?" Cowboy asked. "Why isn't she — oh, there you are."

"Where have you been?" the professor asked as she took her seat.

She motioned to the control room up behind us. "Checking their equipment. Looking for that glitch."

"And?"

"We couldn't find a thing. But they did offer me a job."

"They *what*?"

"Relax, Professor. I didn't take it. Though their equipment is breathtaking. Real state-of-the-art." She opened a small plastic case and took out what looked like fancy ear-plugs. There were four sets. "Here," she said, passing them out to us.

"What are they?" Cowboy asked.

"They're like noise-cancellation head-phones, but smaller. They go inside the ear."

"It's gonna get that loud?" Cowboy said.

She shook her head. "It's not about the volume. It's something else. Some sort of filtering device. All the crew wear them."

The professor looked at his doubtfully. "And what exactly do they filter out?"

Andi motioned back to the control room. "The engineer says it's some sort of high frequency they'll be broadcasting through the studio. Something about —"

"Ladies and gentlemen . . ." The announcer's voice echoed through the building. "Welcome to the world premiere of . . . *Live or Die: The Ultimate Reality!*"

The applause signs flashed overhead, and the crowd clapped and cheered.

The contestants were introduced. Not the stand-ins, but the real people: a perfectly cut, shirtless piece of eye candy in shorts, glistening in oil, and his opponent, some chick, an obvious supporter of the steroid industry, with skimpy shorts and a halter so tiny you wondered why she even bothered.

They stood at opposite ends of the arena, huffing and puffing, getting themselves all worked up . . . right along with the crowd . . . and me, just a little. Seriously. I mean I knew better, but it was like their enthusiasm was contagious.

The announcer continued, "Each of you have your weapons. Choose what you wish, any time you wish. And remember, there are no rules! Anything and everything goes!"

The crowd cheered, hooting and hollering their approval. And I felt myself getting pulled right along with them. Not much. But enough.

"You have no referees. No scorekeepers. The only way to win is to be the last one standing . . . the last one whose heart is still beating!"

The cheering grew louder.

"Because ladies and gentlemen: This *is* . . . THE . . . ULTIMATE . . . REALITY!"

Lights flashed, music blared, and I was clapping along with everyone else. Well, almost everyone. Andi, Cowboy, and the professor sat there like lumps on a log.

"Come on!" I shouted to them. "It's only a show!"

An air horn blasted and the fight began.

The kid was the first to attack. He grabbed a battle-axe off his wall of weapons and raced toward the girl. But she was no wimp. She grabbed a broadsword from her wall and spun around just in time to block him. The clang of steel filled the arena. He swung again and she blocked again. Then again. You could literally see the sparks.

The crowd behind us was on their feet. There was something so real. So honest and brutal.

Blow after blow came. First he had the advantage. Then she did. They went from weapon to weapon. What she lacked in strength, she made up for in speed. What he lacked in agility, he made up for in raw power.

They were so equally matched that at first

there was no blood. But as they wore each other down they got tired, sloppy. The first real wound came when they were both using swords. She managed to get a good one right across that handsome face of his. I gasped along with the crowd, then joined in the applause.

It got even more interesting when he attacked her with a short lance. She countered, holding him off with the sword once, twice. Then she misjudged. He sank his spear deep into her thigh. If she screamed, you couldn't hear over our shouting.

Then, to everyone's amazement, she broke the spear. Snapped it right off, leaving a piece still in her leg. More cheers. But that was nothing compared to when she reached down and yanked out that remaining piece. Blood gushed everywhere. The crowd went wild. It got even better when she ripped off her glove and stuffed part of it into the wound to stop the bleeding.

She limped back to her wall and grabbed the broadsword . . . then came at him with everything she had.

"Yes!" I shouted. "Go! Go!"

She swung hard. The kid barely dodged it. She missed his chest, but as the sword came down, she did manage to cut off two of his toes. More blood. The crowd went nuts.

"Yes!" I shouted. "Yes!"

"Brenda . . ."

I looked down to see Andi tugging at my arm. I shook her loose.

Now it was the kid's turn. He limped to his wall and grabbed one of those iron balls on a chain with spikes. He turned and staggered toward her.

But the girl wasn't backing down. She'd lost a lot of blood, and was still bleeding, but there was no way she was gonna run.

He came at her, swinging the ball. She ducked, the pointed spikes barely missing her. He swung it around again. This time she wasn't so lucky. The spikes missed her neck, but caught her arm, digging into the flesh.

She screamed, staggered backward, fighting to stay on her feet. But it was obvious things were coming to an end.

The crowd began chanting. "Kill! Kill! Kill!"

He came at her again, swinging. She ducked. Then, half running, half stumbling, she threw herself into him. He didn't see the blade she had hidden in her shorts. But he sure felt it as she sank it into his belly.

What a sight!

He stumbled backward, gasping, looking at the wound, then up at her, as surprised as the rest of us. She was gasping hard, too. They stood a moment, bleeding, trying to clear their heads . . . as we kept shouting and cheering them on.

Then, with an energy from who knows where, the girl scooped up her broadsword from the sand and raced at him, shrieking like a crazed animal.

He tried to spin, to dodge, but she slammed it down into his left shoulder so powerfully you could hear the joint crack and separate. And blood. So much we thought, we hoped, he'd lost the whole arm. But it was still there. Barely. It didn't matter. He was exhausted, overcome, and fell to his knees.

That's when the lights in the arena went red. That's when we resumed chanting. "Kill! Kill! Kill!"

The girl staggered toward him, barely able to walk. He looked up. Too weak to move. To care.

"Kill! Kill! Kill!"

"Brenda . . ." It was Andi yelling at me.

I didn't look at her. I couldn't. Not now. The strobe lights began flashing. The girl screamed, fighting to raise her sword. She nearly fell from the pain and fatigue.

The arena shook with our voices. "Kill! Kill! Kill!"

She finally got it over her head.

"Kill! Kill! Ki—"

"NOOO!"

I turned to see Cowboy leap from his seat and race toward the arena.

"Cowboy!" I shouted.

He jumped over the wall and dropped into the pit. Security guards streamed down the aisles.

"Cowboy!"

"STOP IT!" he shouted. He ran straight for the girl. "WHAT ARE YOU DOING? STOP IT!"

The crowd began to boo. But he didn't hear. Or care. He grabbed the sword from her. She was too dazed and confused to put up a fight.

"WHAT ARE YOU DOING?"

A dozen security people were clambering over the wall and dropping into the pit. The booing got louder. Cowboy threw the girl's sword to the ground. The lights came up. He turned to the kid who'd passed out, fallen face first into the sand. Bleeding out.

The announcer's voice boomed, "Remain in your seats! Please remain in your seats!"

By the time Cowboy kneeled to the kid, security guards were all over him.

"Remain in your seats. The show will resume shortly. Please remain in your seats."

The booing continued. And for good reason. Cowboy had ruined everything. The show was heading for its big climax, and he ruined it.

And that's what shocked me. Not his actions, but my thoughts. *Ruined?* Really? Cowboy was trying to save someone's life. And I resented him? What was I thinking? What was going on?

"Brenda . . . Brenda . . ."

I turned to Andi, confused and feeling more than a little guilty.

"Your earplugs," she shouted.

"What?"

She pointed to her ears. "Your earplugs!"

I looked down at my hand. I was still holding them.

"Put them in your ears! Put the earplugs in your ears!"

It made no sense. But she looked so serious. I turned to the professor. He was pointing to the ones in his own ears. I frowned, then nodded and put them in. The guilt and confusion grew even stronger. What had happened?

Suddenly, I heard the crowd gasp and I looked back to the arena. Cowboy was helping the kid to his feet. There was still plenty of blood, but no more was coming from his arm. His stomach was in bad shape. So were his toes. But the gash in his shoulder, the one that had nearly severed his arm and bled him out?

It was gone. There was no sign of the slightest injury.

CHAPTER 6

Our hotel looked just like one of those Hollywood postcards. Everything pink, big pool, lots of palm trees. The rooms were huge — kitchen, bar, big-screen TV, white carpet, tub with Jacuzzi.

And mirrors. Everywhere mirrors.

'Course, none of us could sleep after the show. Most of all me. So we were meeting in Andi's room.

I sat there sketching — the same monster as on the plane, only now I was making its tentacles stretch around something that was supposed to be the world. Daniel was out on the balcony playing his apps. Cowboy was watching some football game. Andi had gutted one of those earplug things and was studying it. And the professor had his face stuck in a newspaper.

"So it was all in my head?" I said. "All that stuff I was feeling?"

"Yes and no," Andi said. "The signal

broadcast throughout the auditorium lowered your inhibitions by restricting activity in a specific area of your frontal lobe."

The professor spoke without looking up. "Not entirely dissimilar to the fungus that attacked Andi and myself in Florida."

"But we killed all that," I said. "With that blue light."

"As far as we know," Andi said.

"Then how could —"

"Seriously?" The professor folded up his paper. "You don't think they could have found a different transporting mechanism by now? Something far more elegant?"

I added, "And more subtle. I didn't become some crazed zombie like you and Andi. I didn't think I was part of a universal mind."

"Nevertheless, your resistance toward violence was dramatically decreased."

"More than decreased. I really wanted to see that kid killed."

Andi nodded and quoted, " 'The outlook on any morality can be changed through TV viewing.' "

"Another study?" I said.

"J. L. Singer. Yale University."

"And those earplugs?"

She pushed them aside, taking a break. "They were designed to cancel out the signal. We all wore them . . . except you."

"So they plan on broadcasting that signal into every home in America?"

She shook her head. "The frequency is too high for the bandwidth assigned to television."

"Then, why —"

"Aw, shucks."

We turned to see Cowboy drop to his knees. He grabbed his Coke can, which had fallen and was spilling all over the white carpet. "I didn't even touch the thing. It fell over all by itself."

Before we could respond, the big-screen TV flickered and switched to that clip from *Superman* we'd seen before. It only lasted a second before going back to Cowboy's game.

"Oh brother." Cowboy sighed. "Again?"

Another flicker. This time to the *Rocky* movie. Then to the DiCaprio spinning top.

Cowboy pressed the remote again, then again, but nothing changed. "What's with the TVs in this city?" he complained.

Another flicker. Now we were watching that flying telephone booth show. Another flicker and it was *The Hunger Games.*

"It's identical to what we witnessed in the control room," the professor said. "And the limo ride."

Now we were watching that cartoon with the talking ants. Then the newer *Rocky* movie.

"Same order, too," Cowboy said.

"Are we certain of that?" I said.

"Here, let me check." Cowboy pulled out his smartphone as the TV repeated itself, starting with the *Superman* movie. "I was videoing them pillars, remember?" He brought up his recorded video and crossed over to us. "Hang on."

He fast-forwarded through us sitting in the limo, then the pillars, until he finally came to the first clip. It was the *Superman* movie. He pressed pause and waited for the same clip to reappear on the big-screen TV. Once it did, he hit play and we watched his phone and the TV as the cycle began again. In perfect sync.

Andi picked up a pencil and paper and began writing.

"Do you believe there is some sort of pattern?" the professor asked.

She shrugged. "Only one way to find out."

Cowboy's phone stopped, but the TV repeated itself.

"Then please," the professor sighed, "do us a favor and at least put that on mute."

Cowboy obliged. But the images kept appearing and reappearing. I glanced over to

Daniel on the balcony. He couldn't care less. Just kept on playing his game. Andi kept working, filling up one sheet, ripping it off, and starting another.

"Maybe they're like years or dates," Cowboy said. "Some secret code, like when you put all the numbers together they say something."

"To what purpose?" the professor said.

Cowboy shrugged.

"Or maybe it's not a pattern at all," I said.

Andi answered without looking up. "Everything's a pattern. Whether it's useful or not, there are always patterns."

Cowboy looked longingly at the screen, obviously not thrilled about missing his game. "Maybe I should call the front desk. See if they got another TV."

"Not yet," Andi said.

Cowboy slumped back into his seat. This was some kind of link. We all knew it. And the sooner Andi figured it out (and we all knew she would), the sooner we'd know what was going on.

I waited another cycle or two before I grabbed my pad and went back to sketching. The professor picked up his paper. And Cowboy eventually got up and joined Daniel on the balcony.

The TV never stopped repeating itself. It

was back to the spinning top for the thousandth time when there was a knock on the door. We all looked up. Another knock. More impatient. I went over to answer, hesitated, then opened it to see Norman Anderson, the producer.

"What are you doing here?" I said.

He just stood there, staring down at his cell phone.

"What?" I repeated.

Without a word he turned the phone to face me. It was playing the same video Cowboy had shown us — starting off with brief shots of us in the limo, followed by the airport pillars, and finally the flickering clips on the limo's TV.

Cowboy stepped back into the room. "Hey, that's my video," he said. "I filmed that."

"You sent it to him?" I asked.

"Nobody sent me anything." Anderson did not sound happy. "It's playing all by itself. Has been for the past ninety minutes." That's when he spotted our big-screen TV playing the same images. Without an invitation, he stepped inside.

"Oh brother," Cowboy said. He'd pulled out his own phone and was staring at it. "This doesn't make sense."

"Now what?" the professor said.

"My video. I didn't touch nothing, but now it's gone. Erased. All of it. Now I just got this." He turned his phone around so we could see that the screen was filled with a single word in bright red letters: *SINCERELY.* And below that a capital letter *S.*

Anderson looked down at his phone and swore. If he was unhappy before, he was downright livid now. He turned the screen back to us. It had the same word, *SINCERELY,* in the same red letters. And, at the bottom, the same capital letter, *S.*

I felt my own phone vibrate and frowned. Six people in the world have my cell number. (I like my privacy.) And half of them were in this room.

I pulled it out and, sure enough, there was the word *SINCERELY* followed by an *S.*

"Who's S?" Cowboy asked.

Nobody had a clue.

"This is all a bit too melodramatic for my taste," the professor said. "If the party wishes to leave us a message, they should at least have the courtesy to give us his or her name."

"Unless . . ." Andi stared at her latest sheet of paper.

"Unless what?" I said.

"Unless he didn't want his identity to be traced."

"Who?" Anderson said. "What are you talking about?"

Andi motioned to the big-screen TV. She waited for the *Superman* scene to come around. When it did, she simply said, *"Superman."*

"I was hoping for something less obvious," the professor said drolly.

Andi ignored him. "I don't know why I didn't see it earlier."

"A pattern?" I said.

She nodded. "And the professor is right, it is obvious." She turned to the TV screen and waited for the cycle to begin again. When it got there, she said, *"Superman* begins with the letter *S."*

The screen flickered and switched to the *Rocky* movie.

"Rocky, R."

The screen switched to the spinning top.

"*T* is for top," I said.

"Perhaps. But if we're naming movies . . ."

"Inception," Cowboy said. "That's from *Inception."*

Andi nodded. *"I* is for *Inception."* The screen switched to the flying telephone booth. "And this is the British TV series *Doctor Who."*

"D," Cowboy said. "For *Doctor Who."*

The image switched again.

"The Hunger Games," I said. *"T."*

"Except most people drop the first word when it's as common as *the,"* Andi said. "So let's consider this one an *H."*

Next came the cartoon with the talking ants. No one had a clue except the professor. "That's *Antz,"* he said. "My nephew loved that movie. Couldn't get enough of it. He's now an entomologist."

"A is for *Antz,"* Andi said.

The *Rocky* scene came back on. "And we're back to *R,"* I said.

Andi nodded. "But a different one."

"That's your pattern?" the professor groused. "Random letters?"

"Not so random." Andi looked back to the TV as the scenes cycled again, starting with the *Superman* clip. This time she called out each letter as the scene appeared: "S . . . R . . . I . . . D . . . H . . . A . . . R."

"That's not a word," Anderson said.

"Sridhar!" I half spoke, half whispered. "The kid from our first mission. The one at the Institute who did the psychic dreaming."

"Lucid dreaming," the professor corrected.

"He's doing this?" I turned back to Andi, waiting for her to answer. She didn't have to. Suddenly the TV fritzed out. Instead of movie clips we were back to watching Cowboy's football game. On the screen the crowd had leapt to their feet, cheering and clapping . . . as if someone had just scored an important goal.

CHAPTER 7

"So you've been fighting these supposed bad guys, this Gate, for how long?" Anderson asked.

"Long enough to know they don't play nice," I said.

"Such as?"

Cowboy answered, "Flying orbs, deadly molds —"

"And mind games." Andi sounded a little sheepish, no doubt thinking of her last encounter with them in Florida. "They're pretty good at those."

"No argument there," I said, thinking back to my own experience at the show.

We'd been sitting around Andi's hotel table for the last hour, explaining what we knew. Anderson listened carefully. He wasn't showing any of his cards, but you could tell he was interested. And concerned.

Finally he asked, "Why?"

"Why what?" I said

"What's their purpose?"

The professor answered. "That, my good man, is the million-dollar question. They appear to want some sort of control. World control. World dominance."

"Like in the end times," Cowboy said.

We looked at him.

"You know, like it says in the Bible."

Anderson turned to the professor, who said, "Not everybody is as gullible as our young friend here, but it does give one pause."

"And this Sridhar person?"

"A boy we tried to help. One who apparently feels compelled to reconnect."

"By jamming TVs, cell phones, and monitors?" Anderson asked.

"And maybe more," Andi said. "Do you remember what happened to your coffee in the control room?" She turned to me. "Or the water glass in the cafeteria?"

"Or my Coke can right here in this room," Cowboy added.

Andi nodded and pointed to the TV. "If he is indeed lucid dreaming, then maneuvering something with so little mass as electrons or as fluid as water would be the easiest way to impact our own world."

Anderson looked at her skeptically. "Lucid dreaming?"

"A technique first developed by the Department of Defense."

"*Supposedly* developed," the professor corrected.

Andi ignored him. "Select soldiers with psychic propensities were trained to send their souls out of their bodies while sleeping."

"To what purpose?"

"To spy on enemy facilities."

"You're not serious."

"It's documented."

"In part," the professor said.

"And it worked?" Anderson asked.

"According to the records. Though with some serious side effects."

"Like running into demons and stuff," Cowboy said.

Anderson threw him a glance and looked back to Andi. "And you think that's what this Sridhar fellow is doing, trying to get our attention?"

I spoke up. "The last time we saw him, Sridhar was being trained to work for The Gate."

Anderson nodded. He looked out the sliding glass door to the balcony, thinking.

"So why did you come here?" Andi asked him.

I added, "Other than irritation over some

cell phone malfunction?"

Cowboy interrupted. "If it's 'bout what I did at your show, I'm real sorry. But that boy, you could see he was hurt real bad. Like he was gettin' ready to check out."

"Which you may have noticed was the entire point of the show," the professor added drolly.

Cowboy looked down and shrugged.

Anderson stared at the big guy a long moment. Finally he spoke, quietly. "What you did tonight, that was some trick."

"Not his first," Andi said.

Cowboy tried again. "Like I said, I'm real sorry, but —"

Anderson held up his hand. "No, no. What I saw you do, it was a lot more substantive than anything we were doing. Than anything I've ever done."

"So why are you here?" Andi repeated.

He took a breath, then answered. "Those pillars at the airport, the ones on our phones? I believe they're connected to your Gate . . . and my show."

"Leviathan."

I turned to see that Daniel had entered the room. He stood in front of the table holding up my sketchpad. The one with the monster and tentacles. He repeated the word: "Leviathan."

The professor turned back to Anderson. "Explain."

Anderson nodded to Daniel. "I'm not sure about that. But there are some things you should know." He hesitated a moment, then continued. "I think it's best I show you."

Chapter 8

Forty minutes later, courtesy of another limo ride, we were at St. Bartholomew's Medical Center. It was pretty close to the airport. I stayed outside a minute or two to catch a smoke. When I joined the others, they were having coffee with some rich and entitled doctor barely out of puberty. I was not a fan.

"Yeah, June thirtieth, hard to forget." The doc took a sip of vending-machine coffee and made a face. Obviously not the gourmet roast he was used to. "Starting around one in the morning we had a huge rush. Stabbings, gangbangers, gunshots, rapes. You name it. And not just the usual minorities and lowlifes." He turned to me. "No offense."

I was liking him even less.

"And?" Anderson said. The kid looked at him and Anderson explained, "What you were telling me earlier. About the location."

"Oh, yeah. This was the crazy part. Every one of them had either been passing through LAX or lived near it."

We traded looks.

"These people," I said. "Any way we could talk to some of them?"

"That was nearly six weeks ago. Everyone's been released by now."

"What about addresses?" Andi asked.

"Doctor–patient confidentiality." He thought a moment. "But . . . we still have one with us. Least until we ship her off to happy acres."

"Pardon me?" the professor said.

"A nursing home. Soon as she gets out of here, her kids are sending her to a raisin farm."

My affection for him was not increasing.

"She'd been in an auto accident. Severe head trauma."

"Could we see her?" Anderson asked.

"Right now? No way."

"Right." Anderson nodded. "Of course."

We sat in silence. I was still trying to piece it all together. What did the violence have to do with The Gate? The pillars? I glanced at Daniel. With the leviathan?

Anderson wasn't quite done. "Listen," he said to Doc. "I got those new headshots of your niece."

"Yeah?"

"Getting prettier by the day. In fact, there's a pilot coming up that we just might be able to use her in."

"No kidding?"

"Of course there's a hundred other kids wanting the part, too."

"Right. Of course."

It seemed a strange topic to bring up now. But Anderson wasn't a top producer by accident. "About this older patient," he said. "You're sure there's no way we could wake her? Just talk with her for a couple minutes?"

The doc snorted. "They'd have my head."

Anderson nodded. "Right." He paused, then added, "Too bad."

Another pause. Longer. Cowboy, who hated any silence for over five seconds, was about to speak when I caught his eye and motioned for him to stay quiet. Something was up.

Finally Doc cleared his throat. "When did you say those auditions were coming up?"

"Hmm? Oh, next week."

He nodded.

Anderson took a sip of coffee, then added, "Sure is a cutie."

"Yeah," the kid said.

"Yeah," Anderson agreed.

Another pause.

"Listen." The doc rose from his chair. "Hang here a minute. Let me see what I can do."

"About?"

"The raisin."

"But you just said —"

"I know, I know, but if there's some way to help you out . . ."

"That would be great," Anderson said. "I mean if it doesn't jeopardize your position."

"This time of night? No one will know." He turned and started for the hallway. "Let me see what I can do."

He disappeared and I turned to Anderson. "You're good."

"Good?" he scoffed. "I'm the best."

"But what's that got to do with them pillars?" Cowboy asked.

"Hang on," Anderson said. "We just might find out."

Twenty minutes later we were on the third floor talking to an elderly Mrs. Whitaker. Eighty, if she was a day.

"Land sakes," she said. "It was the strangest thing. Sometimes when I can't sleep, which is a lot these days, I go driving. I was on Century Boulevard and this young fellow cut me off. Right in front of me. Didn't even look back. I think he was black." She turned to me. "No offense."

From her, I didn't mind.

"I didn't even honk at him. I just scowled. Real hard. Like this." She squinted, losing her eyes in folds of skin.

"And then?" the professor asked.

"And then he made one of those obscene hand gestures, like young folks do. And I got so mad. I can't explain it, but he really got my blood to boiling. Worse than I can remember in a long time. So I gunned it. And at the next intersection, when he slowed to make a turn, I slammed into him. Hard. *Bam!* And boy oh boy did it feel good. And I would have done it again, you know . . . if I'd still been conscious."

"You just sped up and hit him?" Andi asked.

"That's right."

"Couldn't help yourself?" the professor said.

"Oh, I'm sure I could. But I didn't want to. That's the strange part. I wanted to knock the stuffing out of him. So I did."

I couldn't help but nod. After what I went through during last night's show, I knew exactly what she was feeling. Only with me it hadn't been anger. It was the thrill of violence. I knew it was wrong. And I could have looked away and calmed down if I really wanted. But the thing is . . . I hadn't wanted to.

When we were done, we thanked her and started out the door.

"Young man?"

Cowboy, Anderson, even the professor turned around. But she was talking to Anderson. "The doctor tells me you're a TV producer."

"Yes, ma'am."

"Well, I did a little acting. In community theater, I mean. So if you ever need a feisty, go-get-'em gal who's middle-aged, look me up, okay?"

He smiled. "Middle-aged?"

"Or older. There's lots of things you can do with makeup to make me look older."

"Yes, ma'am. I'll keep that in mind."

We did our best not to smile as we turned and exited into the hallway. As we approached the elevators, Anderson looked to me. "So what she was feeling . . . sound familiar?"

I nodded. "Sure did."

"But what's that got to do with those pillars at LAX?" Cowboy asked.

We arrived at the elevators and Anderson hit the button. "It's about time you see."

CHAPTER 9

We were back in the limo heading for LAX. Anderson still wasn't playing all his cards. Not that I blamed him. Truth is, if he'd told us what he knew, we wouldn't have believed him anyway.

But we'd find out soon enough.

Meanwhile, Andi had found something on her tablet. "Hey guys, check this out. In the early morning hours of June thirtieth, Precinct 14 reported an unusual number of arrests — everything from DUIs to convenience store robberies, to date rapes, you name it."

"Precinct 14?" I said.

She nodded. "LAX is in that jurisdiction."

"It's just what the kid doctor said."

"And more." We turned to the professor. "If Andrea's information is correct, then crimes of rage weren't the only offenses being perpetrated."

Anderson agreed. "They were crimes of

impulse, lack of self-control."

I nodded. "I could have turned from last night's fight any time I wanted."

"But you chose not to."

"I knew it was wrong. I knew I shouldn't. But I didn't care."

"Because we were able to reduce the inhibition impulses of your brain." He took a breath. "At least that's what the tests showed."

"You've run tests on it?" the professor asked.

"Not us. An independent firm. One hired by an organization that likes to keep a low profile. Someone we've already discussed beforehand. Your friend and mine . . ." He let the phrase hang until Andi finished it.

"The Gate," she said.

He nodded. We all sat in silence, absorbing the information. A moment later he spotted something outside. "Here." He rapped on the glass separating us from the driver. "Stop here." The driver lowered the window, and Anderson repeated, "Stop here."

"But, sir, there is no parking —"

"Stop here!"

"Yes, sir."

The driver slowed and pulled to the side. Before the limo even stopped, Anderson was out the door. He crossed the four-lane road and headed toward one of the pillars. It rose from the grassy median, about twenty feet tall and glowing purple.

We got out of the car and followed. Even at three in the morning there was traffic — complete with honking horns and irate drivers motioning us to get out of their way. By the time we arrived, the pillar was turning a pale blue. I tapped its side. It was made of thick milky plastic. The color came from lights glowing inside.

Anderson knelt down at its base and pushed away some of the landscaped bushes. At the very bottom a metal box was attached. Rectangular, two by three feet. Camouflage green. A small amber light glowed on the top. Beside the light was a digital screen.

"And what precisely are we looking upon?" the professor asked.

Andi knelt to join Anderson as the man explained. "These are the same emotional generators we have stationed around the arena back at the studio."

"Emotional generators?" I said.

"Yes."

"That's what got Miss Brenda all worked up?" Cowboy asked.

Anderson nodded. "They are designed to

create and amplify the signal that reduces our inhibitions."

"The signal that those earplugs blocked," Andi said.

"Correct. They generate the signal, then cycle it from generator to generator, amplifying it until it is strong enough to direct at the audience."

"Like the old crystal lasers," the professor said. "Aligning and reflecting light frequencies back and forth until they're powerful enough to be released."

"If you say so. The point is, once they'd been thoroughly tested, my production company ordered six of the units."

"And?" I asked.

"We were charged for twenty-one."

"That's a big difference," Cowboy said.

"I put our production accountant on it and she said the other fifteen were donated to the Light and Luminescence Corporation."

"The who?" I said.

"The company in charge of maintaining these columns."

"Why would they need fifteen generators?" Cowboy said.

"How many columns do they have here?" Andi asked.

Anderson looked at her. "Fifteen."

The professor spoke up. "So your theory is that these generators are what affected the people in this area on June thirtieth."

Anderson nodded. "Lowering their inhibition and self-control."

"And this amber light?" Andi pointed to the little light on the box.

"It's in standby mode."

With effort, the professor stooped for a closer look. "Meaning what, exactly?"

"It's ready to transmit at any time."

"Now?" I asked.

"Or tomorrow, or the next day, or —"

Pointing to a toggle switch on the side, the professor interrupted. "Then I suggest we simply turn off the contraption and —"

"Professor, I wouldn't —"

Too late. He flipped the switch to the *off* position. Well, you'd think it should have been *off,* but the light turned from amber to bright green. At the same time the little digital screen beside it lit up with the numbers:

00:15:00

which immediately started counting down:

00:14:59
00:14:58
00:14:57

The professor swore, flipping the switch up, then down, then up again. Nothing.

00:14:56
00:14:55
00:14:54

I heard a quiet hum and looked up. Something like a miniature satellite dish, no bigger than a cereal bowl, was rising out of the top of the pillar.

"That can't be good," I said.

"Or that." Andi pointed across the way to the next column. A similar dish was also rising, pointing the same direction. And beyond that, another column with a rising dish.

"What is it?" Cowboy asked.

"Microwave," Andi answered.

"What are they pointing at?" I said. "They're all pointing the same direction."

Andi pulled out her cell phone.

The professor was still on his knees, fighting the switch. "Andrea!"

She pointed her phone up at the dish. "Triangulating now."

"What's going on?" Cowboy repeated.

No one answered.

"I'm too low," Andi said. "I've got to get a better angle. I've got to —"

Suddenly our cell phones chimed. All of them. I reached into my pocket and pulled mine out. On the screen was an old stone church.

Cowboy's must have shown the same. "A church?" he said.

I nodded and looked to the professor, who was also fumbling with his phone. "Professor?"

"Yes," he answered. "Mine is a church, as well."

"St. Johns," Anderson said. He was staring at his own phone. "The abandoned church on West Manchester."

"You recognize it?" Andi asked.

Without a word, he turned and started back across the street.

"You know this place?" the professor called.

Anderson shouted back. "It's six blocks from here."

I glanced at the digital clock.

00:14:18
00:14:17
00:14:16

We traded looks. Then started back through the traffic to join him.

Chapter 10

"And of all the churches in Los Angeles, how did you recognize this particular one?" the professor asked.

"The news," Anderson said. "It's been deserted a couple years now. Developers want to tear it down, but the city keeps blocking them. Very strange."

"What's strange about that?" Cowboy asked.

"The city of Los Angeles fighting to keep a church? You really aren't from around here, are you?"

We'd parked the limo a block away, Anderson's suggestion to draw less attention. The closer we got to the place, the creepier it looked. Weeds, ivy overgrowth, old stone walls. The steeple seemed a bit taller than proportionally normal. Other than that, nothing was unusual.

"So how we getting in?" I asked.

Anderson motioned to Cowboy. "With his

size and the condition of those doors, it shouldn't be a problem."

But it was a problem. From the sidewalk the doors looked like old, rotting wood. But when we got closer and checked them out, we saw they were actually metal — steel painted to look like old wood.

"Weird," Cowboy said.

I motioned to the small electronic box beside the doors. "Is that going to be a problem?"

Andi was already opening some program in her cell phone. "Shouldn't be." She grinned as she held the phone against the lock and it began beeping real fast. "One of my favorite apps."

We waited a half minute until the lock clicked and the beeping stopped. She pocketed the phone and pushed open the door. Immediately an alarm sounded, complete with flashing lights.

"Tank!" Andi called over it. "Will you take care of that?"

"Me?"

She motioned to the control panel on the wall not far from the door. He stepped up to it, gave it a good, hard look, then tore it off the wall with his bare hands.

Everything stopped.

He grinned back at Andi. "One of *my*

favorite apps."

The inside of the church was anything but a church. It had more monitors and walls of electronic junk than three or four of Anderson's TV control rooms put together. Geek heaven for Andi. She left us and began checking it out.

There was one thing we all recognized. On the bottom of each monitor was the same type of digital readout we'd seen at the airport:

00:09:01

"What does it mean?" Cowboy asked.

"I don't know," I said. "But I'm not liking it."

Oh, and there was one other thing we recognized. . . .

"Greetings."

We spun around to see a way-too-familiar guy in a three-piece suit. He'd just strolled out from behind one of the walls of computers.

"Dr. Trenton?" Cowboy gasped.

"Who?" Anderson said.

Trenton continued like he hadn't heard. "No doubt you've noticed you are on private property."

"Dr. Trenton," Cowboy repeated. "Remember us?"

"He can't hear you," the professor said. "I suspect he is a holographic image. As before."

And he was right. Trenton just kept on talking like he never heard a word. The guy pulled a pocket watch from his vest. "You have exactly fifteen seconds to remove yourself from the premises."

I turned to Anderson and explained. "He's from the Institute for Advanced Psychic Studies. A training ground for The Gate."

"Was," the professor said.

". . . we kinda destroyed it," Cowboy sheepishly admitted.

"Ten seconds."

Anderson took a step toward the hologram. "Fascinating." And then another step.

"Five seconds."

Anderson nodded. "He's simply a prerecorded display."

"Well, all right." Trenton closed his watch. "But please remember, you have been warned."

Suddenly, one of those floating orbs we'd seen in Florida appeared from behind Trenton. It was blue and the size of a softball.

Anderson took a step back. "What the —"

"Relax," I said, "it can't hurt you." More softly I added, "I hope."

Because I was the first to speak, it flew right at me and stopped three or so feet away. It hovered at eye level. I steeled myself, refusing to flinch. Hoping I sounded tough, I said, "And what do you want?"

A pencil-thin beam of light shot out and scanned my face.

"Andi?" I said. But she was out of sight, examining equipment. "Professor?"

A second later the beam stopped and Trenton turned toward me. "Well, Brenda Barnick, so good to see you again."

I glanced to the professor for help.

"Facial recognition," he said.

As soon as the professor spoke, the orb darted to his face and began scanning him. When it had finished, Trenton turned to him. "And Dr. McKinney. What a treat to see you as well."

"I'm sure you're thrilled."

Anderson turned to me. "What's going on?"

The orb flew to his face and began scanning. You could see the muscles in Anderson's jaw tighten, but taking his cue from me and the professor, he refused to back down.

Cowboy opened his mouth to speak, but I motioned for him to keep quiet. Daniel, too. I figured the fewer of us they knew were here, the better.

When the scan finished, Trenton stood a moment like he was thinking. Then his face lit up. "Well, hello there — Mr. Norman Anderson, the famous TV producer. Good to see you, sir. You've been so helpful to us these many years. However, and I don't mean to be rude, these grounds are private property and I am afraid you must leave. At once."

One thing I'd learned about Anderson, like me he wasn't great at taking orders. "And if I don't?"

Trenton gave no answer.

Anderson looked around the room. "What's all this about? And those extra generators at the pillars. The ones you've charged to my show's account. What exactly are you doing here?"

Trenton ignored him. "I believe there's somebody here who'd like to see you."

"Who? What are you talking about?"

Trenton just smiled. The floating orb shot back to him. He turned and disappeared behind the wall of computers with it following him.

Andi called from another bank of computers. "The generators are fully charged."

"They're what?" I said.

"The pillars have been building a charge.

They've begun transmitting it to these storage units."

"That doesn't sound good," Cowboy said.

"It gets worse. The steeple on top of this roof? It appears to be some sort of an antenna."

"To receive the charge?" the professor said.

"And to transmit it. From what I can tell, when the signal is strong enough — when the countdown reaches zero — it's going to beam the signal to a satellite in geosynchronous orbit overhead which, in turn, will broadcast the signal over a specific area of the nation. I believe it to be the central states of the Midwest."

Before any of us could answer, two eight-year-old girls suddenly appeared from behind Trenton's wall of computers. Hair tangled, faces dirty, shirts ripped and torn, they ran toward us. They were chained together, foot to foot. One was blonde, the other was —

"Helsa!" Cowboy cried. And he was right. The girl was our friend from the parallel universe.

"Daddy!" the blonde shouted to Anderson. "Daddy!"

"Sophia!" Anderson cried. "Sweetheart!"

"Daddy!" The girl stumbled and fell to

the floor, dragging Helsa down with her. "Daddy, help me!"

Anderson started toward her, but the professor grabbed his arm. "She's not here," he said. "It's a holographic image."

Anderson hesitated, then slowed to a stop.

"Daddy, you have to go!" the girl shouted. "You have to go *now* or they'll hurt us more."

"Hurt you? What have they done to you? Where are you?"

The girl didn't answer, only began to cry.

"Helsa!" Cowboy repeated.

But Helsa didn't answer, either.

"It's me. Tank," Cowboy said.

"She doesn't know you're here," the professor said. "The orb never saw you." To prove his point, he called out, "Helsa?"

Helsa turned to him.

The professor motioned to me and I did the same. "Helsa?"

She turned to me.

"Daddy, please!" the daughter cried again. "You've got to go!"

I frowned, trying to piece it together. No way did they know Anderson would break in. No way would they kidnap his daughter unless they knew in advance. But they couldn't know.

Daniel tugged on my arm. I looked down.

He was pointing at the girls. "Shadows," he said.

"What?"

He kept pointing. "The shadows. They're different."

I turned back to the girls.

He repeated, "They're different."

Then I saw it. The light hitting Helsa was coming from the right. The light hitting Sophia was from the front.

"Sweetheart," Anderson shouted. "Where are you? What have they done to you?"

"Daddy, please, you've got to go."

I called over to Anderson. "She's not there."

He answered, "Yeah, I get it, holographic image. But they've got her somewhere."

"That's impossible," the professor said. "The odds of them knowing you would be with us are —"

I interrupted. "Photoshop." They turned to me and I explained. "They grabbed a video of your daughter, probably off the Internet. They computer-generated her to talk and look at us, but they don't have her. She's not there."

"Daddy, please go."

The professor nodded. "Your daughter is safe and sound in Maui."

"And Helsa?" Cowboy asked.

"The same," I said, hoping I was right.

"Daddy! Daddy, you've got to go!"

Anderson looked from me to the professor, then back to the girls. He was a media guy. It should have made perfect sense. Then again, he was also a dad. He reached for his cell phone. "Well, there's one way to find out. I'll give them a call and see —"

Suddenly every monitor in the room lit up. Just one word. Two letters. Different fonts, different sizes, but the same two-letter word over and over again, filling the screens:

NO! no! NO! no! No! nO! NO! no! NO! no!
No! nO! NO! no! NO! no! No! nO! NO! NO!
no! NO! no! No! nO! no! NO! no! No! nO!
NO! no! NO! no! No! nO! NO! no! NO! no!

"What?" Anderson said. "What's going on?"

The words disappeared. They were immediately replaced by the same clips we'd seen so many times before:

Superman, Rocky, Inception, Doctor Who, Hunger Games, Antz, Rocky. Superman, Rocky, Inception, Doctor Who, Hunger Games, Antz, Rocky . . .

"Stop dialing!" I shouted to Anderson.

"It's —" I started to say Sridhar's name, but caught myself. "Our friend! He's telling you to stop!"

But the girl continued pleading. "Daddy, please. You've got to go!"

Anderson ignored me and went back to dialing.

The screens returned to:

NO! no! NO! no! No! nO! NO! no! NO! no! No! nO! NO! no! NO! no! No! nO! NO! NO! no! NO! no! No! nO! no! NO! no! No! nO! NO! no! NO! no! No! nO! NO! no! NO! no!

Anderson entered the last number.

"What did you do?" Andi shouted from her computers. She sounded panicky. "What did you just do?!"

I shouted back, "He's calling his daughter. Why?"

"His signal, it's overriding the satellite's signature."

"Meaning?"

"It intercepted the microwave. It's shifted it to his phone, to all our phones."

Anderson looked at me, then slowly disconnected.

"He hung up," I called.

"It doesn't matter — it's still receiving!"

"His?"

"Ours. They're all hot spots. Receiving and transmitting."

I threw a look over to the monitors.

00:04:27

"The clock says we've still got four and a half minutes."

"That's for the satellite uplink. But our own phones . . . every phone in this proximity is receiving the signal now. And transmitting it! It's happening now!"

Chapter 11

The professor smashed his cell phone onto the floor. It shattered into a half dozen pieces.

"What are you doing?" I shouted.

"If Andi is correct, I am destroying the transmitter device. Each of you must do the same. You must destroy your phones."

He reached for mine, and I pushed him away. "You can't be sure. These things are expensive."

"If you had a modicum of intelligence you would understand."

"I understand just fine."

He reached for it again, and I shoved him away harder. "You're not always right. What makes you so right?"

"Having more than a tenth-grade education increases my odds."

I shot him a glare.

"Or is it ninth grade, I forget."

He reached for my phone again, and I

punched him in the gut. It surprised me as much as it did him. But it felt pretty good. So I hit him again. That's when Cowboy grabbed my arm and spun me around.

"Stop it!" the big lug shouted. "Stop it right now!" I tried to twist free, but he was twice my size. "I'm so sick of you two fightin' all the time! You need to grow up!"

The professor righted himself, massaging his stomach. "Maybe if our resident bag lady could resort to a more civilized way of expressing her —"

"Shut up! Both of you. Just shut up!"

I stared at Cowboy. I'd never heard a mean thing come from his mouth. And the professor. Yeah, we had some mutual disrespect goin', but he'd never resorted to name-calling. And I'd never dreamed of hitting him.

"It's the generators!" Andi shouted. "They're affecting us."

"Well, fix it!" Anderson yelled. "You're supposed to be the electronic genius."

Cowboy let go of my arm and turned on him. "You don't talk that way to Andi. She's good, and smart, and sweet, and —"

She cut him off. "And not the slightest bit interested in you."

He turned to her, obviously hurt.

She continued. "Seriously, what do I have

to do to get through that thick skull of yours?" She turned to Anderson. "But you . . ." She smiled coyly. "You have the brains *and* the bod." Her voice softened. "Not to mention power. I like powerful men. If you ever feel you want a little companionship, intellectual or . . . otherwise, just let me know and I'll —"

"Please," Anderson sneered, "I'm not interested in children." His gaze shifted to me. "But real women — street-smart with experience — now that's something I could get into. Really get into."

"Dream on," I said.

"I'm serious." He stepped closer. "With all the bimbos around, it's been a long time since I've had myself a real woman. And, I'm betting, since you've had a real man." He took my arm.

I looked down at his grip then glared back up at him. He didn't get the message. I tried to break free, but he grabbed my other arm and pulled me toward him. I head-butted him. That message he did get. He staggered backward. But only for a second.

"Yeah," he said slowly, "a scrapper. I like that."

He came at me again. I threw a punch, but he grabbed my arm and pulled me into him, tight. I tried getting away, using my elbows and knees, but he had me in too close. I shouted. Swore. Turned to the others for help.

But the professor just stood there, arms crossed, smirking away. Cowboy was no better. Fact is, as he watched Anderson grab and grope, he got ideas of his own. Inspired, he turned and headed for Andi.

For the briefest second Anderson left himself open. I made my move. I jerked my knee into his groin. He groaned and stumbled away. He wanted a scrapper, he got a scrapper.

I threw a look to Daniel. He just sat on the floor, lost in the screams and explosions of his game app.

"Daniel!"

He ignored me.

"Daniel!"

He scooted around till his back was to me. He couldn't be bothered.

I spun back to the monitors.

00:02:28

"I told you," Andi said, "I'm not interested!"

I turned to see Cowboy had backed her against one of the terminals. He leaned over her awkwardly. "One little kiss ain't gonna hurt nothin'."

The professor laughed, and I shot him a look.

He shrugged. "Quite a show."

I might've hit him again, just for spite, if Anderson wasn't coming at me. He arrived just in time for me to land a good fist to his jaw. Probably broke my hand, but it sure felt good. Too good. Like hitting every man who'd ever hurt and abused me. Anderson swore up a storm. I answered by punching him again. This time his nose. It began bleeding. A real gusher. He backed up. Too bad, 'cause I really wanted to keep going.

And I wasn't the only one.

"C'mon." Cowboy hovered over Andi, practically drooling.

But she wasn't backing down. "What about *no* doesn't that hick brain of yours get?"

"Lotsa girls want me," he said.

She laughed.

"I'm serious. But I ain't ever given in."

"Trust me, your record's safe with me."

Another alarm went off. A piercing buzz. I looked back to the monitors. The numbers at the bottom had turned red:

00:02:00

The buzzer stopped just in time for me to hear Daniel shouting, "Yes! Yes!" I turned to see him hunched over his game, totally lost in it.

Off in the distance there was a police siren. More than one.

The professor chuckled. "Should be another busy night." I turned to him and he continued. "I believe Andrea said *all* phones within the proximity."

"Professor McKinney! Brenda!"

I spun back to the monitors. The digital readout continued at the bottom of the screen, but above it was a face I'd not seen in months.

"Sridhar!"

"Yes, it is I." He glanced over his shoulder, then back to the camera. "Please, you must put an end to this behavior at once."

"Where are you?"

"I have but only a moment. You must overcome your impulses and shut down the equipment in the room, and you must do so immediately."

"Actually," the professor said, "it's proving to be quite the entertainment."

"In just over a minute, the entire central portion of your country will be exposed."

"To what?" I said.

"To what you are now experiencing. The

loss of inhibition. People will become subject to their desires with little regard of the outcome."

"That's their problem," Andi said.

"Please," Sridhar said, "you must find the strength to restrain your desires. You must overcome your impulses and shut down the equipment."

The professor snickered. I grinned. We both knew the chances were next to none.

But the kid continued. "Andi, inside the panel to your left are several cables. If you would disconnect them —"

Andi cut him off. "Do you have any idea how sick I am of people always telling me what to do? Just because I'm brilliant I'm expected to fix everything at their command."

The professor countered. "Maybe if you had some backbone, people wouldn't feel compelled to take advantage of —"

"Shut up!" she snapped. "For once in your life just shut up!"

"Ooo." It was my turn to chuckle. "Look who's growing up."

"And you." She turned on me. "You think all that sarcasm makes you cool? Well, here's a little wake-up call for —"

The alarm went off again. Only this time

it didn't stop. The numbers below Sridhar blinked.

00:01:00

"One minute," Anderson shouted over the alarm. "This should get interesting."

As he spoke two other men showed up on Sridhar's monitor. They grabbed the boy and he shouted, "No! Let me go! This is not right! You must —"

"Sridhar!" I yelled.

"Let me go!" For a little guy, he put up quite the fight. "Let me go! You must not —" One of the goons slammed his head down onto the console. Hard.

"Sridhar!"

But it would take more than that to stop the kid. He was back up, blood streaming down his forehead, and shouting, "You must destroy that equipment. You must —"

The men yanked him out of his chair. He cried out until they hit him again. This time he went limp. Goon One dragged him off as Goon Two stuck his face into the camera. He fiddled with a switch and the screen went blank. Except for the readout below:

00:00:47

"This ain't good!" Cowboy yelled. I

turned to him in surprise. His face was twisted, like he was fighting something. "Sridhar's right," he said, "we gotta do something."

"Actually, it's really quite amusing," the professor said.

"No. It's gonna get real bad. Out there, everywhere. It's going to get real bad for everybody."

Anderson smirked. "And that concerns you because?"

"Because? Because it ain't right. Because they're people. Kids, moms, dads. Everyday people, just like you and me."

The sirens continued to approach.

Cowboy's face had grown shiny with sweat. Whatever was goin' on inside him was fighting hard. A real war. He looked to each one of us like we could help. Like we should want to.

"Are you telling me you don't want to see a little violence?" Anderson asked. "A little action?"

Cowboy closed his eyes, clenching his jaw, trying to drown out Anderson's words.

Anderson motioned to Andi. "You were pretty interested in a little action a second ago. I bet you still are."

The big guy looked to Andi. You could see the battle raging inside him.

Anderson continued. "I'm sure your God wouldn't mind. Just this once."

And that did it. Something inside Cowboy snapped. Switched on. The fight was still there, there was no missing it, but now there was something else. A tiny spark. A light that quickly grew. A strength. Brighter by the second.

Finally, he turned to Andi. "Those cables, where did he say they were?"

"You're not serious," she said.

Anderson agreed. "For the first time in your life you're free. Free to do anything you want. And you're trying to hold back, trying to hold us all back with some lame religious —"

"No, sir." Cowboy continued growing stronger. "I know what freedom is, and this ain't it."

I glanced to the professor. He was looking down, scowling. Whatever Cowboy was saying, whatever he was doing, was obviously having an effect on the old man.

But not Andi. She stepped closer to Cowboy. "Maybe you just haven't experienced enough freedom." It was laughable, hearing her pretend to come on to him.

But it worked.

Cowboy swallowed. He shifted his weight.

She continued. "Isn't that what you want,

Tank?" She stepped closer. "Isn't real freedom what we all want?"

He swallowed again. It looked like he was about to cave when, at the very last second, from who knows where, he found the strength to look away.

"Hey." She took his arm.

He ignored her and looked to the computers. "It's this panel here, right?"

I glanced to the monitors.

00:00:20

"Maybe." Andi stepped back in his way.

Cowboy took another breath. Then he reached out to her. As carefully as if he were holding an armed bomb, he took her shoulders and gently moved her to the side.

It was touching. And somehow, in a way I can't explain . . . inspiring. Enough for me to feel a little of my own resolve starting to return.

He stooped down and looked into the back of the computer.

00:00:14

"There's so many cables," his voice echoed from inside. "Won't you help me?"

Andi must have felt something, too. Like

the professor. Like me. Somehow his strength was feeding ours. She looked over to us. I didn't know what to say. And for once, neither did the professor. Andi frowned. She looked down at Cowboy. Then she knelt to join him.

00:00:09

"Could be those wires there," she said.

"These?" he asked.

"Yes."

00:00:05

"No! I'm wrong!" she said. "Try those. Those right there!"

He gave her a look.

She nodded.

He reached further inside —

00:00:01

— and gave a yank.

Nothing.

He yanked harder. Suddenly the console exploded with more sparks than the Fourth of July.

Everything went dark.

And there in the darkness, as embarrassment over our words and our actions washed through us, we started coming back to our senses.

Police lights flooded through the windows. A moment later, police officers burst into the room. But it didn't matter. It was over.

It was over and, somehow, some way, we had won.

Epilogue

The next day gave a new meaning to the word *awkward.* Yeah, the police showed up that night with lots of arrests around the area, including busting us for breaking and entering. And, yeah, Anderson had to pull some strings and do some fast talkin' to get us free. (Like he said, he's good at what he does.)

But the real truth is, it's like we all caught each other naked. Like we saw what we could really be like if you stripped away all our niceties. 'Course, we all apologized to each other, sayin' it really wasn't us. And, of course, we all knew we were lying. Because somewhere inside, some part of us really was feeling all that junk.

Anyway . . .

By late the next day, we were all loaded in the limo and headin' back to the airport, pretending everything was normal. Daniel was back to playing his apps, despite (or because of) the professor's criticism of my parenting skills. Andi was on the phone. I'd busied myself finishing up the sketch of that octopus monster thing. And the professor, as usual, was hiding behind his puffed-up intellect.

"A remarkable experience when you stop to think of it objectively," he said. "The possibilities when one's inhibitions are completely removed, when one is unfettered by moral restraint."

"Whatever it was," Cowboy said, "I didn't like it."

"You seemed fine with it for a time."

The big guy threw a nervous look to Andi, who was still on the phone. "God didn't make morals for us to go around breakin' 'em," he said.

"Yes, well, I'm afraid *God* had little to do with creating morality," the professor said. "Morals are merely the logical extension of man's attempt to keep our race from destroying itself — seeking what's best for the community rather than our own self-centered desires."

"I don't know about none of that," Cowboy said. "But I do know if it wasn't for God, I'd never have had the strength to do what was right."

"Maybe," I said. "But seein' what you did

sure helped the rest of us."

The professor agreed. "Witnessing proper behavior can, indeed, instill and promote proper behavior. While witnessing improper behavior can often —"

"Make folks do bad," Cowboy said.

The professor nodded. "Which is precisely why The Gate wishes to control the media."

"They want to show folks doin' bad so others start doin' it."

I pointed at Andi. "What was it she quoted? Any moral can be changed through the media?"

"Leviathan," Daniel said.

I turned to him. "What's that?"

He didn't bother to look up from his game.

"Leviathan," Cowboy repeated. "It's in the Bible. Some sort of sea monster."

"With tentacles?" I asked.

Cowboy shrugged.

"With arms that can slither undetected into every mind and household in America," the professor added.

Daniel's game blasted with another burst of gunfire followed by the usual screams and explosions.

I glanced to the professor. He gave the usual disapproving arch of his eyebrow.

"Daniel?" I said.

He didn't hear.

"Daniel?"

Still nothing.

I sighed. The professor had been right way too many times on this trip. But I had to give him another one.

I reached over and took the game out of Daniel's hands.

"Hey!"

"Leviathan," I said.

He reached for it. "That's mine."

"You've played enough for now," I said.

"That's not fair."

"Welcome to life."

He folded his arms and slumped into a sulk. I did my best to avoid the professor's eyes.

A moment later Andi disconnected from her call. "Well," she said, "that's encouraging."

"What?" Cowboy asked.

"Anderson has shut down the show."

"That's fantastic," Cowboy said.

"Good news," I agreed.

"And the LAPD is investigating the placement of all the equipment inside the church and the generators around those pillars."

"Will it do any good?" I asked.

She shrugged. "Norman says the news

channels have already gotten wind of it and —"

The professor chuckled. "Oh, Norman, is it now?"

I glanced to Cowboy, who pretended not to hear.

Andi continued. "Mr. Anderson casts a pretty big shadow in the town. More importantly, he has offered his services to us. He understands The Gate's influence, especially in its use of the media, and he's promised to do all he can to help stop them."

"That's great," Cowboy said, overdoing the enthusiasm a bit. "That probably means we'll see him again."

Andi nodded. "I hope so."

Cowboy looked out the window.

The professor took a deep breath. "And so, another battle has been won." Musing, he added, "Almost in spite of ourselves."

"But we still got the war," I said. "A big one. Seems there's nothing The Gate isn't messin' with."

Cowboy turned from the window. "But it ain't our job to worry about it, Miss Brenda." I looked over to him and he nodded at my sketchpad. "We just keep cuttin' off the tentacles that we find. That's all we can do."

"What's the old riddle?" the professor

asked. " 'How do you eat an elephant?' "

We turned to him and he answered, " 'One bite at a time.' " He looked back out the window as our limo pulled up to the curb. "That's how we shall destroy them." He repeated, as much for himself as for us, "One bite at a time."

We sat there in silence. Despite all we'd said and done to each other the night before, we'd never felt closer. Could be all the battles we'd been fighting together, the impossible enemy we were up against, or who knows what. Whatever it was, for that one brief moment, like it or not, we were family.

Finally, the professor opened his door and stepped out. The others followed. I lagged behind to get Daniel and all our stuff.

"Let's go, Barnick," the professor barked.

"Hang on." I turned to Daniel. "You got your hoodie? Those planes get cold."

He nodded and pulled out his sweatshirt. I checked the seats and floor for anything we might have left behind.

"Barnick."

"Hang on."

A moment later we crawled out. But the professor didn't let up. "Have you ever, for once in your entire life, been punctual?"

"You try lugging a kid around," I snapped.

"A kid?" He motioned to the nearby porter to handle his suitcases. "Don't tell me about children. I have four of them to look after. And there isn't a one of you who isn't more trouble than you're worth." He turned and started for the terminal. "Let's go, people. The plane's waiting."

I slung my backpack over my shoulder and turned to Andi. "And . . . we're back."

She grinned and took Daniel's hand. "It sure looks that way."

"Yes, it does," I muttered. "Yes, it does."

Soli Deo gloria.

■ ■ ■ ■

THE MIND PIRATES

FRANK PERETTI

■ ■ ■ ■

Chapter 1
A Broke Broker

Adrian Pugh, Wall Street broker, offshore investor, and one-time multimillionaire, paced nervously around his huge office, muttering, shaking his head in horror and disbelief. He turned and looked once again at the computer screen on his desk. The columns of figures and the totals at the bottom were still there. His first appointment was in ten minutes, and he would be eye to eye with one of the names on that computer screen.

After that, he'd be eye to eye with an arresting officer.

Outside the wall-sized windows, the skyscrapers of New York stood waist-deep in smog. The street was twenty stories below.

Twenty stories. More than enough.

Chapter 2
Andi the Pirate

Adrian Pugh's intent was to end his life, but an awning broke his fall. Still alive, he would have to explain how millions of dollars suddenly vanished — not only from his own portfolio but from the portfolios of his clients. When he could not explain, the task of finding that explanation trickled down via the usual mysterious channels to myself and my teammates. The fact that we basically liked but also could not stand each other had no bearing on the assignment we were given: to retrace Adrian Pugh's sailing vacation in the Caribbean on a forty-foot sloop.

McKinney here. James. Sixty, PhD, professor of philosophy and comparative religions, published, and so on and so forth, and no, do not be envious. Our sojourn on the crystal waters, verdant islands, and sugar-white beaches was strictly business, all eyes and ears to find a connection, if any, between Pugh's enchanting vacation and his precipitous loss. And let me add: A sailboat heeling in the wind with swanlike grace may appear romantic, but I assure you, the *Barbee Jay* was not roomy, especially with five aboard — especially *we* five.

Especially with Andi the Pirate at the helm, living in a world all her own.

"A stealin' scoundrel, a rogue I be,
from the Barbary Coast to the Caribbee,
to take in m'hand any gold I see,
with a hey, hi diddle and away!"

My red-haired youthful assistant, you'll recall. I believe she composed the ditty herself. It went with the outfit: full, white blouse; thick leather belt and toy cutlass; baggy, striped culottes, a red scarf on her head, and a huge gold earring she'd bought on the island of St. Clemens.

"Ahoy there, matey! So you be sprung from the brig at long last!"

I'd just returned to the deck from a nap in the aft state room, which was not much different than sleeping in a drawer. "I was reviewing Pugh's itinerary. And sleeping."

"And now you'll be wanting a hand at the helm, I'll lay to that."

"No, go ahead. You're having so much fun

— and what in the world are you singing about?"

She shrugged. "It's pirate talk."

Indeed. Adrian Pugh and family had taken in a raucous and touristy pirate show on St. Clemens, and so, keeping with our assignment, we took it in as well, and now . . . I could only snort with disgust. "Pirates! What sense does it make glamorizing criminals and reprobates?"

Andi looked up at the mainsail, curved and winging, and smiled as if seeing a vision. "Aye, but there lies the beauty of it. Stow away the rules and the makin' of sense and sail free!"

"Oh will you spare me!"

"What?"

"Armed thugs committing robbery on the high seas. Don't you see anything wrong with that?"

She wagged her head and rolled her eyes — as Andi, not Long John Silver, would do. "Ah, come on, it's the romance of it! Haven't you ever read *Treasure Island*? Or what about Peter Pan and Captain Hook? What about *Pirates of Penzance*?"

"What about 'stowing away the rules'? We're talking lawlessness here, aren't we?"

Oh dear. She gave me her studied look, a forewarning of debate. "Are you suggesting a transcendent morality?"

"You know I'm not."

" 'Don't I see anything wrong?' That is what you asked me."

"The limitations of language, I assure you. There is no transcendent law because that would presuppose a transcendent Lawgiver, and of course *that,* my young lady, is the stuff of folklore and mythology."

"So how can the pirates be criminals and reprobates if there is no overarching scheme of right and wrong?"

Enough of this. I checked the compass as if she hadn't. "I believe our heading should be 070. Andi?"

She didn't answer. The big sloop began to turn toward the wind.

"Hey, careful. The sails are luffing."

The boat kept turning lazily into the wind as the sails went limp, flapping like laundry on a line.

"Andi, you're —"

She was leaning on the wheel, her eyes blank and her head quivering. "Aardvark . . ." she said.

"What?"

"Aardvark Basil Crustacean . . ."

I jumped up and took hold of her before she fell, easing her down to the pilot's bench. "Andi? Come on now, come back to earth."

Brenda Barnick's voice came from the bow, "What's going on back there?" With the foresail majestically to one side, she'd been able to lounge on the foredeck in straw hat, shorts, and halter, reading a book and looking like a travel poster. Now, fighting off the rude slaps of the foresail, she was groping her way back. Irritation gave way to concern at the sight of Andi slumped on the bench.

"Aardvark Basil Crustacean," Andi muttered, her eyes still blank and glassy. "Aardvark Basil Crustacean, 233 997 417709."

Andi was given to numbers, patterns, formulae. "Andi?" I said, "What are you giving me — a phone number?"

"233 997 417709."

"Anybody writing this down?" Brenda asked as she stepped into the cockpit.

"Execute, execute," Andi said in a monotone.

"Tank!" I hollered. "Bring a pencil and paper!"

"Aardvark." Andi's eyes began to roam. "Basil. Crustacean." She drew a breath, propped herself up. "233 . . . 997 . . . 4177 . . ." Her eyes widened as she seemed to wake from a dream. "Zero Nine!"

She lunged for the stern rail and vomited over the side.

Tank came up the companionway to see the rest of us leaning over the railing. "Sick *again*?"

"Just Andi," I answered.

Ten-year-old Daniel was immediately behind Tank, all eyes as usual. Upon apprising the situation he backed down the steps into the galley, apparently to fetch something.

Brenda was still holding Andi, steadying her as she gripped the railing, gagging, coughing, gasping for breath. "Looks like a flashback."

"My fear exactly!" Andi's mind, so brilliant, so quick, had been sorely traumatized in our "fungus" adventure, hypnotized by a charlatan in Florida, and deluded by the "emotional generator" we encountered in Los Angeles. After all that, I assumed we were witnessing persistent damage.

"I'm — I'm okay," Andi said between coughs, spits, and swallows. She started to wipe her mouth on her puffy sleeve.

"No, baby, use this." With a praising smile, Brenda took a moist washcloth from Daniel's hand and gave it to Andi.

"Was it a flashback?" Tank asked. I noticed he had brought a pen and scratchpad.

"I wasn't having a flashback." Andi turned from the stern rail and rested on the bench, wiping her face and drawing in deep breaths of ocean air.

"I'm afraid you were babbling nonsense," I told her.

"I know what I was saying!" she protested, and wiggled her finger at Tank's scratchpad. He copied as she repeated quite lucidly, "Aardvark Basil Crustacean —"

"How do you spell *crustacean*?" he asked.

"Later. Fake it. Then there were numbers: 233 997 417709. That's A, B, C, and then some numbers, the same every time, even the spaces in between."

"But you were blanked out, as if having a seizure," I tried to counter.

She finished, "And then I said the word *Execute*. And then I said it again."

Now we all stared at her, waiting for the explanation. She only stared back.

"So what does it mean?" I asked.

"I haven't the slightest idea."

"How are you feeling now?" Brenda asked.

"Like I just puked. Where are we?"

"The Caribbean," I told her. "We left St. Clemens two hours ago. We were heading for St. Jacob. You were piloting the boat."

At that moment, Daniel squeezed around us and took the wheel, swinging the boat back on course. The sails filled, the boat gently heeled, and we started moving again. He also loved the role of sea captain.

"We were talking about pirates!" she told me as it came back to her.

"That's right."

"And debating a basis for right and wrong."

"Which we'll let rest for now."

She was coming fully around. She put her hand to her head. "Well, shiver me timbers."

CHAPTER 3
NIGHTMARE OF MURDER

The winds were steady and gentle when the *Barbee Jay* reached the island of St. Jacob and we dropped anchor in the harbor. To the west, just over a heavily jungled ridge, the lowering sun was setting the sky on fire, washing the rippled harbor and the little village of St. Marie with gold and crimson.

Brenda, Tank, Daniel, and I were on deck, all tempted to rouse Andi to see it all.

"Better let her sleep," I finally said.

As for Andi . . .

As she lay restless in the bow's V-berth, sleep became a theater of horrors as dark visions tumbled through her mind: the sea, dark and boiling; a pirate with red scarf and stubbly chin; the belly of an old ship at sea, rocking, the planks and timbers groaning; another pirate with a long black beard, laughing, the glint of gold in his mouth; the *zing!* of a cutlass being drawn; clashing blades.

Then came threatening faces emerging from the night. Cold, cruel eyes. A blonde, his face wrinkled, his hair thin. A big Asian man, all in black, wielding a knife.

"You really thought you'd get away?" said the blonde.

"This is no game," said the Asian, waving the knife blade closer, closer.

Banana Peel. The words bore no meaning, but they terrified her.

The men clamped onto her with a painful, iron grip. Terror. Choking. A slap across the face like a flashing, burning fire.

She kicked violently under the blanket, writhing, trying to get free. "No . . . no! Not me!"

The visions continued.

"Where is the money?" they asked. "Tell us or you will bleed."

Can't remember, can't remember!

"Then you will bleed. You will die."

The knife —

"NO!" She wanted to wake up but could not.

The visions coalesced into a nightmare. . . .

Grappling, breaking free, she ran down shadowy, empty streets, through alleys and archways in the dark. *Can't shout, can't call for help, no one must know . . .*

Footsteps behind her. The knife blade flashing in a patch of moonlight.

A long pier with boats on either side. The hollow *clump! clump!* of the planks under her feet, the hiss of surf.

Grabbed! An iron hand on her arm! Blows to her face! Striking back, lashing out, trying to get free.

Water, all around her. Stinging salt filling her mouth, her throat, her lungs.

Fire in her chest! FIRE!

With a muffled scream she kicked off her blanket and leapt from the berth, bounding about the main cabin like a pinball, banging her head on the ceiling, groping for a way out, yelling, screaming, thrashing her arms.

We collided with each other trying to get down the companionway. Brenda stopped short at the base of the steps while the rest of us piled up behind her, aghast.

Andi was like a trapped animal — crouching, fists clenched, throwing punches and kicking at enemies who weren't there. "Touch me and I'll take your hands for me trophy, by the powers!" She was still wearing her pirate costume, right down to the scarf and earring.

"Andi . . ." Brenda spoke in a hushed

voice, reaching out to her.

Andi planted a mean punch to her jaw, sending her into the galley cabinets. "I'll take you all like a man, and you scurvy scum!"

Tank got close enough to see into her eyes. "She's walking in her" — a foot to his chest sent him to the floor — "sleep!"

I took hold of her from behind. "Andi, you're going to hurt yourself — *oof!*" Her elbow rammed into my gut, and I lost my grip on her, my vision going dark.

"Nay," she said, "but *you'll* have me for shark bait if I know my own name!" She leaped up on the dining table, rubber cutlass in her hand. "I'll be free o' you all or under the hatches, you can lay to that!"

Brenda and Daniel blocked the companionway lest Andi find her way overboard. Tank grabbed one leg, I grabbed the other, and we pulled her down as she took to us with her fists. I saw stars, but somehow I held on.

With a free hand she yanked open the cutlery drawer.

I grabbed for that hand. I missed.

She let out a yell. "Take that, Banana Peel!" A knife sailed through the air.

Brenda ducked and the knife thudded into

the paneling right behind her. A perfect throw.

We pig-piled on top of her, even Daniel, and that seemed to arrest her madness. Or at least she ceased fighting.

Brenda, warily easing off the pile and shielding Daniel, called to her, "Andi? Earth to Andi, come in."

"You awake now?" Tank asked, side-glancing at the knife still quivering in the wall.

Andi was alarmed to find herself on the floor. "I was having a dream. Somebody was trying to kill me, and I ran away, and then they caught me and . . . they just kept wailing on me, beating me silly till I fell in the water and drowned."

Tank and I exchanged a look and slowly let her up.

The fight was over. We guided Andi to the dinette, where she sat down and, with a trembling hand, removed the scarf from her head. "I could see them. I could even smell them."

Brenda pulled the knife from the wall and placed it back in the drawer. Then she turned, arms crossed, and looked at Andi. We all studied Andi, so much it made her nervous.

"I didn't ask for this."

"Like . . . heck you didn't." Apparently Brenda was trying to be gentle with her words. "Playin' pirate with all that pirate talk and that getup when you got wires loose? Yeah, you were askin' for it."

"And you could have hurt yourself," I added. "You almost hurt us."

"Almost?" Tank said, discovering blood from fingernail gouges near his eyes.

I waxed fatherly, a role I hardly expected. "The pirate show on St. Clemens captured your imagination, and we don't fault that, but it's definitely time to put this fantasy aside."

"But —"

"But nothin'!" said Brenda. "How much is enough for you? You threw a knife at me! That's enough! That's plenty!"

"But . . ." Andi actually marveled. "I didn't do that. I mean, I did it, but . . . but I didn't do it really. I don't know how to throw knives."

"You do now," said Tank.

Awkward silence.

"Tomorrow we'll go ashore and just . . . vacation," I said. "It's what Adrian Pugh and his family did anyway, and it'll give you a chance to have some solid land under your feet. And please, doff that pirate outfit. Just be my bookish assistant for a change."

Andi removed her scabbard and rubber cutlass and placed them on the counter.

Brenda put out her hand. "And how about that earring?"

Andi's hand went to her ear. "Oh! It's still there!" She smiled, relieved. "I dreamed they tore it off."

"Who tore it off?" Tank asked.

"The guys who killed me."

Brenda still had her hand out. Andi removed the earring and, with sadness, handed it over.

"Tomorrow," I said, "we're getting off this boat."

Chapter 4
A Pirate at Breakfast

The next day dawned bright and clear, a perfect day to go ashore and repeat Adrian Pugh's itinerary: snorkeling, hiking, and a visit to a bird sanctuary. It seemed these benign, diversionary activities held little promise of a revelation, but at the very least they would be helpful toward reconnecting Andi's "loose wires."

When we sat at the table for breakfast Andi remained topside. When she finally descended the companionway, it was with a flourish. "And a top o' the mornin' to ya!"

"Good morning," said Brenda and Tank.

"Good m— what did you do?" I said.

As she sat at the table, she looked fairly normal in a sun suit and matching sun visor.

It was the beard and mustache she'd drawn on her lip and chin that struck us as a little odd — a thin, handlebar mustache with loops at each end, and a tight little goatee. "Am I not fit for your table now, as smart as a bright feathered cock and trimmed for the finest company!"

Our staring seemed to perplex her. She checked herself over. "Have I overlooked something? Begging your pardon!"

"You still doin' that pirate stuff?" said Brenda.

I gave a little signal with my hand and Brenda, much to be commended, put her lecture on hold. "Andi. You've drawn a mustache and a beard on your face."

She stared at us for a moment, then looked for something that would serve as a mirror. A shiny cream pitcher served the purpose. "Well — !" She touched her chin in wonderment, and then turned red. "All right, who did it?"

We went blank, still a step behind whatever was happening.

Which only fueled her anger. "Don't give me that innocent look!"

Tank ventured, "We didn't do anything. You did it to yourself!"

I corroborated, "That artwork on your face wasn't there until you went topside to fix yourself up."

Suddenly, with a different demeanor, she set down the cream pitcher, nodded grimly, and crossed her arms. Andi the Pirate spoke again, "Aye, so *that's* the way of it. Betrayal again, and by me own shipmates. If you cannot trust your chin to your friends, now where can you leave it, tell me that!"

We looked at each other. The trouble wasn't over.

Where to begin? "Andi, I think maybe you need —"

"I'll tell you what old Ben needs!" she spouted, pointing her finger at me. "Maybe just one day, nay, one little moment, when —" She stopped, staring at her pointing hand, rubbing her third finger with her thumb, looking at it as if she'd never noticed it before. "Blimey! Me finger's back on." We were nonplussed, so she explained, "Lost it, you see. Had a mainsheet wrapped around it and I weren't aware. A good gust o' wind come along, and *yank!* Off she went. Became food for fish, you can lay to that."

"You lost a finger?" I asked.

She gave me an impatient scowl. "Long you've been a mate of mine, Cap, and now you don't remember? Been touching the rum again?"

"Well . . ." I looked around the table, at every other set of eyes. "The food's getting cold."

We acted normal, passing eggs and French toast around, enjoying it as best we could, and talking about our plans for the day. Except Daniel. As Andi the Pirate stabbed her food with her knife, chewed rudely, and drooled, he couldn't take his eyes off her. He reached for his knife — and Brenda intercepted that whole notion before he could touch it.

But at some point I didn't notice, Andi resorted to her fork and wiped her drool with her napkin. "How far to that coral reef?"

Tank answered, "Just around the point, over on the west side."

"Gotta snorkel today. Can't miss it."

Andi again?

Brenda was ready for a retry. "What's that on your chin?"

Andi found the cream pitcher again and used it as a mirror. "Oh!" She laughed with embarrassment. "Sorry. I guess I got carried away this morning." She promptly went to the head — the washroom — to wash it off.

And so began a perfectly glorious day that ended much worse.

Chapter 5
Kidnapped

All day we enjoyed the pleasure of repeating the Pugh family's vacation: snorkeling, hiking to the top of the island's highest mountain, and exploring the closely arranged, meandering village of St. Marie to the sound of Caribbean music. We had dinner in a family-run seafood shop on the waterfront and could see the *Barbee Jay* through the front windows, rocking ever so slightly on the end of her anchor chain. Whether any of this had anything to do with the loss of millions in investors' money we did not discover.

As dusk approached and we sat on the wharf enjoying ice cream bars, Andi was restless. "Before we go back to the boat, how about walking the beach?"

The rest of us were tired, ready to call it a day. Daniel was already asleep, his head in Brenda's lap. Nevertheless, Andi was being herself, and anything that could help her remain in that condition suited me. I steeled myself against my own exhaustion and said, "I'll go with you. But we have to be back before sunset."

She jumped up. "Come on!" Before I could reach walking speed she'd run from the wharf to the sand below, sending the tiny sand crabs scurrying. True to her plan, she kicked off and carried her shoes.

I made my way along after her, staying close to the wet sand near the water for better firmness under my feet, and I left my shoes on, thank you. She slowed her pace, I caught up, and we walked together, stepping around tiny crab burrows and watching a pair of pelicans nabbing fish from the waves. Entirely therapeutic, or so I hoped.

As we rounded a point, Andi reached into her pocket, drew out her oversized gold earring, and looped it through her ear.

"Well now," I said, "where did you get that?"

"From Brenda's stash of stuff."

Wishing to avoid any further debate on right and wrong and whether or where a basis might be found for them, I didn't question her ethics. "But of course there's a risk involved, as we've observed —"

She abruptly stopped in her tracks and assumed a familiar roguish posture. "And from what tired old scow did you scrape that one? I've a right to me druthers, same's do you!"

I winced. *Oh no.*

She swaggered in front of me like bar scum wanting a brawl. "Learn if you can, laddie. There's no right or wrong in this world, only what a man makes for himself, you can lay to that!"

So we were into it again — whoever *we* were.

She turned her back on me and stomped away with a masculine gait. I followed, temper rising above discretion. "Andi — or whoever you are, I don't give a hoot — that will be quite enough!"

There was a snap and a rustle in the trees beside us. I saw something stirring, most likely an animal. But a large one.

"What are you looking at?" Andi asked.

"Nothing. Now you —" As I looked at her, she was Andi again. "Andi?"

Innocently, she answered, "What?"

"Andi?"

She replied impatiently. *"What?"*

I was stymied between three courses. What was I to be: her employer, her father, or her therapist?

"You are acting so weird," she said, wrinkling her nose.

I rubbed my forehead, admittedly to hide my eyes. "Wouldn't it be fair for me to know from moment to moment to whom I'm speaking?"

She looked around. "It's just us, Professor."

"So . . . Andi. May we talk about that earring?"

Her hand went nervously to her ear. "Okay, okay. Brenda's gonna be ticked off at me."

"You're quite right."

"But . . ." A slight sneer curled her lip. "I been through heavier storms than what she can bring, and I'll weather this one, too! Besides, didn't I tell ya there's no right or wrong in this world, no true or false, and that's the way of it?"

Since when did Andi agree with me on that subject? "Ben, I presume?"

A hushed voice came from the trees. "Aye, that's her!"

I saw no one, but someone was there. "We have company," I whispered urgently.

She pulled in close to me, crouching and wary. "Aye," she replied in a stealthy whisper, "and it's more than a creature afoot. I might know that voice."

I shot her a sideways glance. "You know who it is?"

Andi looked back at me. "Who *who* is?"

I gave up trying to talk to her. I just grabbed her hand. "We're getting out of here!"

With a barbaric scream, a filthy band of hairy, sweating scoundrels with muscular arms, sashes, pistols, scarved heads, flashing cutlasses, and grinning teeth burst from the jungle and hemmed us in against the sea, closing upon us like vultures upon carrion.

Pirates! At least a dozen. It was unreal. It was frightening.

Of course, I reminded myself, it had to be a paid prank — a bonus feature of the St. Clemens pirate show. Perhaps someone had put them up to this. I managed to fake a good-humored smile.

Andi didn't smile at all — she snarled, facing down an oversized caricature in a black leather vest and three-cornered pirate hat. "Rock, if it's a meeting the cap wants, he coulda sent a note!"

The caricature pointed at the earring and exchanged a nod with a bare-chested monster of superfluous muscle. "Aye, that's her!"

"Let's take her!" said the monster.

The other pirates burst into laughter and closed in on us like collapsing sandcastle walls.

Andi reached for a sword she was no

longer wearing, found nothing, and looked at me, awakened. "What's happening?"

The pirate Rock grabbed her. Three more pirates took hold of her arms and legs while a fifth threw a blanket over her. I spun about as pirates closed in, ready to inflict injury any way I could, but it was useless. The last I saw of Andi, she was writhing and kicking, wrapped in a blanket and tied with rope, carried by two laughing pirates. That was a millisecond before a blanket swallowed me and I, too, was helpless in a woolen cocoon and borne aloft.

I could still hear Andi's muffled screaming.

Chapter 6
The *Predator*

When our captors untied our bonds and lifted away the blankets, it was only because we were in a wooden boat and there was nowhere for Andi and me to run without the ability to walk on miles and miles of open water. Dead ahead, in silhouette against the red sky, lay our destination: a three-masted, square-rigged pirate ship right out of a Robert Louis Stevenson novel — or the pirate show on St. Clemens. Andi, now herself and immersed in the fantasy, drank in the sight. I could only hope Tank and Brenda had arranged all this. If not, they would have no idea where we were, and worse yet, these ruffians, whatever their game, weren't kidding.

Rowing with precision, our surly hosts brought the boat alongside. Andi scurried up the rope ladder and over the bulwark with no help. I climbed well enough, motivated by my preference for a larger boat over a smaller one.

The ship smelled of oak and tar and creaked with the swells in deep wooden tones. The rigging was stretched with spider-like precision, and the masts, yards, and sails, now furled, were worthy of a tour in themselves, but we were granted no time to gawk. Still prisoners, and treated as such, we were hurried along toward a door below the quarterdeck — the portal, I supposed, that led to the Captain's Quarters.

I was right. Inside, under the low-beamed ceiling, sitting at a map table under lamp-light, was the captain, a steely-eyed character from another age who had black curls down to his shoulders and a beard to his breast. I came within an inch of laughing, but thought better of it. He gestured with his hand and his men placed us firmly in two chairs facing him across the table.

He studied us a moment — mostly Andi — and then, of all things, began to sing what I guessed was an old sea shanty.

> "Haul on the bowlin', the fore and maintop bowlin' . . ."

And to my surprise, Andi gave the musical answer:

"Haul on the bowlin', the bowlin' haul!"

The captain rose to his feet for the next line.

"Haul on the bowlin', the packet is
a-rollin' . . ."

And Andi, eyes widening at her own knowledge, sang the response,

"Haul on the bowlin', the bowlin' haul!"

The captain cocked an eyebrow and exchanged a look with his men.

To which Andi took on a scowl that wasn't hers. "And what of it, Cap? Set your course with tremblin' or you'll stay in irons. The wind only blows when I whistle." Then she marveled and looked at me. "What did I say?"

"By the powers, it's Ben!" rumbled the monster, and the room filled with a tension that even I could feel.

The captain stared at Andi's gold earring, and then at her. "So, might you tell me where you are?"

She answered as if she'd known it all her life. "Aboard the *Predator*." She gasped, stunned. She looked around the room at the costumed cutthroats, and I saw recognition in her eyes.

So did the captain. "So you been here before, lass. You know these faces."

Of course, she had to have seen some of these thugs as characters in the pirate show, but we never heard their names. Even so . . .

She looked up at the oversized caricature in leather vest and three-cornered pirate hat. "Rock."

Rock snorted a chuckle and nodded.

"And . . ." She recognized the muscular monster. "Scalarag."

He gave a mocking bow. "M'lady!"

She stared, then pointed at the ship's token bald guy, the one with the bushy mustache and oversized saber. "Norwig . . . the Bean!"

Norwig cocked an equally bushy eyebrow and looked at the captain.

She named the other three: the mousy little raisin was Spikenose — he served as the ship's purser and cook; the morose man with the scar across his face was, naturally, Harry the Scar; the flamboyant Doug Fairbanks throwback was Jean-Pierre DuBois.

As for the captain: "And you're . . . Captain Thatch." She looked at me. "How . . . how did I know that?"

As if I had an answer. "I'm sure we'd all

like to know."

"You bought that earring," said the captain. "We were missing it, and there was talk around St. Clemens about you. The rest we tried guessing, and we guessed right." The captain extended his hand. "I'll take that earring now."

She shied back.

"Let him have it!" I advised, touching her shoulder to steady her.

She removed it from her ear and handed it over.

He smiled, a glint of gold in his teeth, and touched a button on an incongruous intercom. "We have it. We'll see if it talks." He tried putting the earring on his own ear but only grew impatient. "Here," he said, handing it to DuBois. "You and Sparks make an inquiry."

DuBois hurried out the door.

The captain gestured to Rock, who produced a three-cornered hat from a cabinet. "You want to be a pirate, lass, you need to look the part," said Rock. "See how this suits you." He placed it on her head.

A little big. She started to take it off —

The captain cautioned her with a wiggle of his finger to keep it on.

There followed an odd space of time, a

silence as if we were all waiting for something.

It finally came, though clearly unexpected: the horrible scream of a soul in agony from somewhere in the hull of the ship. It made us all start. The sounds of a commotion followed: shouts, pounding, more screaming. I could plainly read fear and consternation in the eyes of the men as they looked to the captain.

An electronic warble sounded from the captain's desk. He reached, pressed a button on the intercom. "Yes?"

"Captain!" came a voice. "You'd better get down here!"

With a muffled curse, the captain dashed out of the room. Through the door he left open we could see him dropping through the companion to the decks below.

I eyed the intercom. "Interesting device you have there . . . for the seventeenth century."

Any attempt at levity was lost on these men. They responded by tightening their circle around Andi and me, fingering their knives, swords, pistols.

We could hear no small row between the captain and someone else down below. That someone would soon be walking the plank, it seemed . . . or keelhauled, or flogged, or hung from the yardarm . . . or given a pink slip and a severance package, depending on the century.

The next thing we heard was the captain's boots thundering on the deck below and up the wooden stairs of the companion. He crossed the deck like an approaching thunderstorm, burst through the cabin doorway, and went directly to Andi, snatching the hat from her head and dashing it to the floor. "Seems it don't become you!"

Another volley of screams, this time muffled by a few more bulkheads, found its way through the door.

"Close that door!" the captain hollered.

Spikenose slammed it shut.

The captain fumed, paced, looked at his men, looked at us, and finally, with only slight control of his temper, told Andi, "Lassie, it looks like you and your father are going to be with us a while!"

"Uh, well, I'm not —" I stopped. At this moment, what could be less important? "If I may ask, just what do you want with us? I don't understand any of this, if you don't mind my saying."

The captain sat on the edge of the table and took a dagger from his belt. He played with it, stabbing it into the table and giving it a wicked twist. "Memory, Mr. . . ."

"McKinney. James McKinney, PhD."

He looked at Andi.

"Andrea Goldstein, assistant to Professor McKinney," she said.

The captain looked down the blade of his dagger as he continued to auger its tip into the tabletop. "Well, it matters little now who you are. What matters is what the lass remembers, and you'll be staying here, looking around, seeing our faces and seeing our ship until she does remember."

"Remember what?" I asked.

He gave the dagger a flip and caught it again by its handle. "Everything."

CHAPTER 7
THE TECHNO-LAIR

By the time Tank, Brenda, and Daniel grew concerned, borrowed flashlights from the seafood restaurant, and found the site of our abduction, the darkness had closed in and the tide would soon follow. Hurriedly, they examined the signs left in the sand even as the waves were steadily licking them up.

Brenda tried to count the different prints. "Man, I dunno . . . looks like six, maybe."

"This might be number seven," said Tank, pointing with his light. "Looks a bit smaller. It's got a different tread, you see that?"

"I see enough. We're in deep" — she noticed young Daniel nearby — "poop. Whatever we were lookin' for, it found us."

"So why'd they only grab Andi and the professor?"

Brenda shined her light in a nervous circle. "Who says they aren't after us, too? Daniel! Stay close!" Her beam landed on a clear trail of tracks leading from and back into the jungle.

"Hoo boy . . ." said Tank.

Brenda used the word she avoided the last time, and they all went in together, crossing the sand and stepping into the trees and the tangle, ducking under limbs, pushing aside vines. The dark under the jungle canopy was nearly total.

It was just as they began to question the wisdom of this exploration that they emerged on the other side of what was a narrow isthmus and found themselves on another beach.

Now Daniel, like a hound catching a scent, hurried over the sand, tracing the tracks toward the surf. Brenda kept her light on Daniel as they ran after; Tank beamed his light up and down the beach, knowing they were wide open and vulnerable.

"Tank!" Brenda called. "He's on it! He's found it!"

They hurried to where the child had halted, and there, in the beam of their lights, was a clear groove in the sand formed by the keel of a boat that was once there. Their lights would only reach so far over the surf, lighting up the closest waves breaking, and beyond that, nothing.

■ ■ ■ ■

In a way, we got our tour of the *Predator.* With Captain Thatch, Rock, and Scalarag as tour guides — to put it kindly — we walked the upper decks by the light of carried lamps and learned the locations and names of the forecastle, poop deck, and quarterdeck, the functions of the foremast, mainmast, and mizzenmast, and the sails affixed to each mast with their respective yards, the main, top, and topgallant. All of this was undoubtedly interesting, but Captain Thatch's main interest was Andi and trying to draw out what, by whatever means, she knew.

Which was a lot. She could already tell Thatch the names of the decks, the masts, the blocks, and rigging. She could name the cannons by the size of the balls they fired: twelve, twenty-four, and sixty-eight pounders. She blithely referred to the sixty-eight-pounders by their nickname — "smashers" — and when Thatch said the orlop deck was our next stop, she knew how to get there, leading the way down the companion steps, through several decks, and to the deck immediately above the hold, a dark, low-ceilinged space below the ship's waterline.

There, moving along a narrow corridor, she recognized a cabin, no bigger than absolutely necessary, in which there was a narrow cot, a minuscule desk, and an empty closet the size of a cupboard. She lingered at the door, inquisitive, but by now Thatch was so impressed by her that he hurried us along to another tight little space between bulkheads and decks.

Well. After all the touring in the seventeenth century, this room was a jarring change. It was lined and filled with twenty-first-century gadgetry: computers, monitors, servers, and banks of electronic gear with a dazzling array of blinking numbers and lights. Seated before it all was a half-pirate, I would say. He wore a striped shirt, red headscarf, and even a gold earring, but he was wearing Levis and canvas running shoes.

"This is Sparks," said Captain Thatch.

Sparks offered his hand — he was the first one on this ship to do so. I shook his hand, as did Andi.

"So now we're back in the real world," I quipped.

That was ill-timed. The captain grabbed a handful of my shirtfront and growled in my face, "It's all real, old man, as real as this fist under your chin! Out here, we have it our way, and our way is where you are." He cocked an eyebrow at me, expecting acknowledgment.

"You're the captain," I replied, convinced this man was no stranger to brute force.

Then, as if to heighten the tension, the same maniacal scream we'd heard before came through the boards below our feet, all the more terrifying for its proximity. We couldn't ignore it. With my eyes I questioned the captain.

"Pay it no mind," he said even as he glared at Sparks. "It isn't really there."

I was in no place to argue, but the scream did seem to bother him well enough.

Just as it bothered Sparks. He was clearly troubled by the scream and pled with the captain. "I can fix it. I just need some time to figure out Ben's programming."

Captain Thatch was more interested in watching Andi. "Look around you, lass. Seen it before?"

Andi's eyes were already locked on the computer screen, on the rows of numbers and code that I found undecipherable. "It looks so familiar!"

"Have a seat," said Thatch, nudging Sparks from his chair and offering it to Andi.

She sat before the monitor and studied it, hands on the keyboard, scrolling down, up again, looking surprised as if she knew what she was looking at. "Well . . . no wonder!"

The captain leaned in close, examining the monitor along with her. "Yes, my dear? What do you see?"

"The system is scrambled. It's . . ." She scrolled up and down, pointing at lines of code. "See here? It's an encrypted command in the program that engages if anyone violates the entry protocol. Instead of a sequential Brain Wave Authentication, the program inverts to Brain Wave Generation and then loops back on itself and self-scrambles. Which means . . ." She shuddered at a new awareness. "The particular Writer, W-902, would have Authenticated the wearer's brain, but then would have reloaded every brain pattern in cumulative layers of confusion. Pure madness!"

The captain took a gold earring — Andi's gold earring — from a hook on the wall, put on his reading glasses, and read a number from the earring's inner surface. "W-902." He cursed and railed at Sparks, "And you didn't notice? You didn't say a word before he put this on?" I caught him shooting a glance toward the hold below us.

"How was I to know Ben would scramble the system? How could anybody know?"

"Eh, he's done that and more, now hasn't

he? Made sure we couldn't track him and made sure the whole system was useless without him. A little insurance, I'll wager."

"But a lot of good it did him."

"And us! Instead of information we get a scrambled brain! And what about this Thursday with the big fish to catch?"

Sparks stared at the screen, wagging his head.

Thatch was getting dangerous. "I asked you a question!"

"I don't know!"

Andi piped in, "You need the entry code." She tapped some keys and a prompt appeared on the screen. Blinking. Waiting.

That got their attention. They halted their squabble and stared over her shoulder.

"Let's see . . ." she said, tapping the keys. "How about, 'Aardvark Basil Crustacean 233 997 417709'?"

The computer beeped, the screen went wild, lights came on, drives whirred to life, and a very attractive lady pirate appeared on the screen, presenting a menu of links and sub-pages.

Sparks was stunned. "We're in! We're operational!"

"Almost there," said the captain. "Well done, lass! Well done!"

The way these men whooped and high-fived each other, you'd think all wars had ceased for now and forever. *Did this give us any bargaining leverage?* I wondered. "I take it you're pleased?"

"Break out some grog," said the captain to Rock, "and let's have our dinner." He looked at me and Andi, and even patted Andi on the shoulder. "And two more places for our special guests!"

Well, we seemed to be on their good side, something I hoped to use to our advantage. Andi ventured a quick look at me, and with a similar look I agreed with her: Whatever else we didn't yet know, we could be sure we'd stumbled upon the very thing we'd been sent to find. We were right in the middle of it.

CHAPTER 8
PRISONERS

Brenda, Tank, and Daniel soon found that St. Jacob was not a good place for their friends to be kidnapped. There was no 9-1-1 system; there wasn't even cell service. The police station was a tight little cube of concrete with a dented Volkswagen Beetle for a squad car, and no one was there. They finally found the local police chief in his squat little abode next door. Tank and Brenda spilled their story in urgent fashion as he listened, absentmindedly wiping his mouth.

"So," Tank said, "we need help. We need cops and marshals and SWAT teams and stuff."

He weighed everything a moment. "You need to file a complaint."

He took a blank sheet of paper, took down all the pertinent information, then added his phone number. Having completed this single page to his satisfaction, he took a fresh piece of paper and began scribbling out a copy of the first.

"What are you doin', man?" Brenda asked.

He answered matter-of-factly, "I have to make posters to spread around."

"You don't have a copy machine?" Tank asked incredulously.

"Do I look like I'd have a copy machine?"

Brenda was flustered, to put it mildly. "Come on, there's got to be a better way than that!"

He finished making his first copy and began copying again. "You might try the TV station."

"You have a *TV station*?"

The police chief looked insulted. "Yeah. Channel Five. Sometimes the other islands can pick up the signal, depending on the wind."

"That'll work," said Tank.

"If you throw in some advertising," the chief added.

"What?" said Brenda.

He motioned for her to calm down. "Hey, no sweat. Margarita's owns the station. Cut a deal."

Andi and I had had our dinner shortly before being kidnapped, but under the circumstances we determined to enjoy the hospitality of our "hosts" and joined Captain Thatch, Sparks, Rock, and Scalarag for dinner in the Captain's Quarters. We raved about the beef, garlic potatoes, and broccoli, and even managed to choke down some kind of grog, all to keep things warm and humane.

The conversation trended toward the pirate life in a modern world, and so I asked offhandedly, "So it seems you've chosen a seventeenth-century reality over a modern one?"

Captain Thatch took a gulp of grog and replied, "Why not? Who's to say what's true but what there is on the *Predator*? No right, no wrong, no present, no past — just what is, and how we like it."

I gave Andi a side glance. "We were on this very subject not long ago, Andi and I."

"Of a certain. It's the talk these days. No truth, no shame, no God to draw the line."

I glanced at Andi again. "Yes, that is, after all, what it comes down to, and so here you are."

"And so here *you* are. Can't say we've done you wrong, now can we?"

Now Andi shot *me* a glance.

"Well . . ." I could hardly agree, but as Andi's eyes were telling me, what reason could I provide for disagreement? "That could depend on the recipient of the action, I suppose, whether the action would be in their best interests."

The captain laughed. "Their best interests? So now you've come up with a rule." Then he looked at me craftily, like a spider at a fly. "But them that makes the rules has their own interests, you can lay to that." He nodded toward Andi. "Like the pretty lass you have here, old man. Some real opportunity, I'd say, when it's you that pays her."

I hoped he was only pressing a point. "That would be unthinkable, of course."

"Unthinkable? *I* thought of it." He gestured with his fork. "So I'll wager so have you."

"If I were one to violate trust and honor!"

"Ha! Honor! Hardly a useful sentiment!"

"Quite useful in holding a ship together, I would think." I recalled a quote from C. S. Lewis. " 'We laugh at honor and are shocked to find traitors in our midst.' "

He scoffed at that, so of course I had to challenge him, and while we bickered over where such things as honor could come from and whether they existed outside of human choice and how they could be found in the absence of God — which was a moot point because, I argued, there was no God

— I noticed Andi picking up a banana and peeling it, gawking at it as if seeing a vision, oblivious to the debate.

"If there be no trust and no honor," said the captain, who was also watching Andi, "then there be left only the animal we are. . . . Am I right, Ben?"

Andi snapped out of her preoccupation and answered without pause, "Aye, Captain!"

The captain laughed and slapped the table in victory as his crewmen marveled. Andi was surprised, and then, I think, afraid for herself.

"So we're talking truth, are we?" said the captain, peering over the table at her as he spoke to me. "Well, for your truth you have a lovely assistant with joys to offer, but for my truth . . ." He pointed with his fork. "I think I might be talking to an old friend of mine." He addressed Andi. "Ben? You're looking a lot prettier these days!"

Andi shrank into her chair.

Sparks eyed her as if she were one of his computers. "The system's back online. We could try another download."

Thatch had to think about that.

"We'll just check for a signal, that's all," said Sparks.

Finally, the captain nodded. "Fair

enough."

Rock produced the same hat they'd placed on her head before and placed it on her head again as Sparks went out the door and then below decks.

The same eerie space of time passed — last time, it ended with a scream. I was afraid for Andi, angry with myself. Just when I thought Captain Thatch and I were, well, compatriots in opinion, I found I'd been foolishly letting him play a game with me, and now what would become of Andi?

The intercom warbled as before and the captain answered, "Well?"

"Nothing, Captain" came Sparks's voice over the speaker. "We can only load first-hand memory, not secondhand."

Thatch roared and pounded the table, his face contorted with a bestial anger I'd not yet seen. He bolted around the table, his hands going for Andi's neck. I reacted without hesitation, but had come only an inch out of my chair when Rock and Scalarag shoved me down with all their weight and held me there.

The captain's hands trembled around Andi's neck as if he longed to wring it but dared not. "You're . . . you're in there, aren't you? Hiding from an old friend. A *friend*!" He turned away, so angry he couldn't choose how to conduct himself; surely it was not with any dignity. "You turned on me, didn't you?" He turned and faced her again. "You sold me out!"

Andi was at a total loss. "Sir, I don't know what you're talking about!" She broke into tears. "I don't know what's happening to me!"

He took a moment to contain himself, then smirked at her. "Well I do, lass, I do, so we'll be keeping you a while." He let his cold, angry gaze dart between the two of us. "And give no mind to leaving the ship. Try to escape, and we'll sever the tendons behind your knees, roll you up in squid guts, and throw you to the sharks!" He looked at me as if looks could spit and ordered Rock and Scalarag, "Put this man in irons! Perhaps the lass will act in his . . . best interests!"

CHAPTER 9
THE SEARCH BEGINS

Margarita's, favored drinking establishment of St. Jacob, opened its doors at ten the next morning. The police chief, wielding a palm-sized handycam, waved Tank and Brenda to their marks on the beachside veranda, got some drinks in their hands — a margarita for Brenda, a grapefruit juice for Tank — and coached the customers to yuk it up in the background. "Okay, rolling."

As a TV personality, Tank was, well, a good athlete. He didn't know what else in the world to do than stare a hole through the camera. "Hi, I'm Tank."

Brenda, replete in fruit-basket hat and flowered halter top, blossomed as the finest of Caribbean beach bimbos, wielding her drink and swiveling her shoulders. "Hey, mon! I'm Brennnda! You lika me? I lika you! We got friends, you know?" She held up drawings she'd made of myself and Andi — quite good, actually. "They are missing.

Gone poof! You help us find them, no? They were on St. Jacob just last night, but where they are now, nobody knows! You know? You call us here at . . ." — she gave a grand air-headed flourish — "MARGARITA'S! The happiest place on St. Jacob!"

"Yeah," said Tank.

"Dos Equis on tap. Happy Hour at four!"

"Yeah," said Tank.

"And . . . cut!" said the police chief.

Brenda tossed the fruit-basket hat on a table and shook out her dreadlocks. "Okay, cool, we're on TV, and the cops are in the loop. Now let's get workin'."

Daniel, being a minor, was waiting outside.

He was wearing a Margarita's pirate hat. Brenda was about to ask —

"Part of the deal," said Margarita herself. "Cute kid."

Daniel held the hat on his head and met their eyes like it was something important. Brenda got it. "Pirates," she said. "It's got something to do with pirates. Andi had pirates on the brain."

Tank nodded, reading Daniel's eyes. "Ever since that pirate show on St. Clemens."

They came to the same conclusion: "We've got to get back there!"

But in the *Barbee Jay*? A sailboat was

slow, and they were novices at sailing.

"Hey, mon" came a voice. "Need a lift to St. Clemens?"

A jovial-looking fellow stood on the dock below Margarita's. He was . . . Jamaican? Native? Hispanic? Under that straw hat and behind that mustache he bore a remarkable resemblance to a cabby they'd met in Rome and another cabby Brenda had met in Florida. This guy had one foot on the dock and the other on a speedboat with not one, but two oversized outboards.

"How much?" Tank asked.

And there was that same grin they'd seen before. "Part of the deal."

The ship did have leg irons bolted to the mainmast where the recalcitrant could be bound in the sight of all, but a man so shackled would be unfit for swabbing the deck and so, free of chains and mop in hand, I labored under watchful eyes. Rock, perched on the forecastle and holding a crude leather flail, supervised. Norwig the Bean hauled up buckets of seawater to rinse.

"Move along, old man!" Rock hollered. "And work as fit as the young or feel the lash!"

I worked with "youthful" vigor while Norwig kept the deck awash before my mop. We were getting results — until the little raisin Spikenose came up from the galley with a pail of kitchen waste and faked a stumble, spilling the sour contents where I had just cleaned.

"Oops," he said, then turned and left.

"Ya scum!" Rock hollered at me. "Is that what you call a clean deck?" He hopped down, scooped up a sizable handful of fats and fruit peelings, and hurled them at me. I could have ducked, I suppose, but that wasn't the object, was it? They were out to humiliate me, and I thought it best to let them.

"What's that slop on the front of you?" asked Norwig as he promptly doused me with a bucket of seawater.

They laughed. Of course.

Temper, McKinney, I thought as I felt my face burn. *Master your temper!*

"Behold the man of great words!" Rock shouted, then looked at me with disdain. "But you can't talk the dirt off this deck, now can you? On this ship it's not words but work, and a man holds his own if he's a man."

"Aye, sir!" I replied, and with a bit of show I mopped the foul residue from the deck as Norwig splashed it along the bulwark and over the side.

Rock nodded, the mollified taskmaster. "So what were you back home, old man?"

He asked me in past tense, and so I answered from the past. "A priest."

His eyes grew wide — mockingly.

Before I saw it coming, a blow from his flail landed on the side of my face. I don't remember hitting the deck I'd just cleaned; I was too stunned to feel it.

I do remember him standing over me, flail in hand, delighted at the wretch he'd made of me. "So let's see you turn the other cheek!"

I was fearful for Andi, as she was for me, but we'd set our strategy with eye contact, expressions, planted phrases: we must cooperate, try to please, get things "human," and hopefully draw any information we could from our captors.

So, while I was up on deck getting humiliated and clobbered, she was in the cabin she'd seen earlier, desperate to recall anything the captain might find useful, trying to be of value. He was, after all, alone with her down there, and as he'd said, there was no truth or shame, no God aboard this ship to draw the line.

"This is Ben's cabin, isn't it?" she asked.

"That it is," said the captain. "Or, was."

She nodded. "My — *his* things are gone. He used to have a big case right there in that corner with all his documentation."

He placed his hand under her chin and turned her face toward him. "Ben. What were your plans?"

"By the powers, Cap —" She shook away the lingo that kept cropping up in her head and spoke for herself. "I, he, had to get off this ship. He had to get free and on his own before anything happened."

"What . . . anything?"

The words — and the terror — popped into her mind. "Ere we all get killed, and it be no wives' tale. As sure as I know m'name, they'll cut us and gut us and call it a pleasure!"

Chapter 10
Two Dead Men

Dr. Eli Torres was a general practitioner on St. Clemens, but it was his side job as St. Clemens' medical examiner that brought a powerful athlete, an urban female, and a ten-year-old child to the waiting room of his small practice. "A . . . drowning victim?"

"That's right, sir," said Tank. "We went by the pirate show, but they're closed because a member of the cast died in a drowning accident. We figured you'd know something about that."

Dr. Torres eyed the motley trio on the other side of the counter and wagged his head. "I really can't talk about it."

"Well," said Brenda, "could you just answer us this: Did the victim have a goatee and a curly mustache? Was his left earlobe torn from an earring being torn out? Was he missing the third finger of his right hand, and was he beat up before he drowned?"

With a furtive look around the waiting

room — it was empty at the moment so no one else saw them — Dr. Torres asked his receptionist, "What's our next appointment?"

She checked. "Well, it's —"

"Cancel it."

The doctor swung the clinic door open and urged them through. He led them into his office and closed the door. "Now. Start from the beginning."

"Pirates!" said Daniel, still wearing the pirate hat.

Dr. Torres looked at Brenda and Tank for confirmation.

Tank just said it. "Our two friends were kidnapped on St. Jacob, and we think it was by pirates, and so . . . we're looking for pirates."

Brenda jumped in. "Especially the one I described to you . . . I think." She was exasperated. "This is going to take a lot of explaining —"

Torres raised a hand. "Have you been to the police?"

"Yeah," said Tank. "On St. Jacob."

"And here, too," said Brenda.

Torres smiled. "And that's why you've come to me on your own."

"The cops are kinda slow," Tank admitted.

"We were hoping they'd jump all over this," said Brenda.

"No, this they're not jumping on," said Torres. "I suppose they told you one was an accident and the other was a suicide?"

"No," said Brenda. "They didn't tell us much of anything, they just — uh . . . what? The *other*?"

"Two drownings, back to back. I've got them both in the cooler right now, in there with some frozen fruit and a marlin. The first one's the victim you described. The other one's a shopkeeper who drowned soon after."

"A shopkeeper?" said Tank. "You mean, a guy who runs a little tourist store?"

"Like along the waterfront near the cruise ships?" Brenda asked.

"Like the Catch as Catch Can Emporium?" Torres filled in. Their wide-eyed reaction must have confirmed something for him. "So you know something about that, too." He took a moment, leaning back in his chair. "All right. Time out. Take a breath."

They took a breath. Several deep breaths.

Dr. Torres lowered his voice. "I like living here. I like my job. I like getting up in the morning knowing I'll live through the day and my family will be safe. If . . . some family members . . . want to help identify the victims, that's fine, that's part of my job, but whatever it is you know, and whatever you figure out from this moment onward, it's your business, not mine, and I don't know anything about it. You never came to see me and after today, I never want to see you again, and I sure don't want to be seen with you anywhere, any time. Are we clear on that?"

They nodded.

He sighed. "Maybe this will buy me a little favor with God." He went to the door. "I have them in the freezer in the back. The police didn't want them in the morgue; there'd be too many questions."

Brenda had Daniel sit in the waiting room with a child's book of animal adventures. She wasn't sure she'd be able to handle this herself.

When Dr. Torres rolled out the first victim and lifted away the sheet, she actually let out a cry, her hand over her mouth.

Tank said nothing. He just turned white and grabbed the edge of the table to steady himself.

"Ben Cardiff," said Dr. Torres. "He was a character in the pirate show. His captain came in and identified him the day after he drowned."

The dead man's face and body were pale and waxy-looking. The eyelids were only half closed, the eyeballs beneath dead and dry.

He had a tight little goatee and a mustache with curls on the end. His right earlobe was torn as if someone had yanked off an earring. The third finger of his right hand was missing.

"So . . ." Tank asked, voice weak. "How did he die really?"

"Really?" said Dr. Torres. "By drowning, yes, but as you can see from the bruises and cuts, he was severely beaten first. Beaten, then he either fell or was thrown off a pier. It was no accident — but I didn't tell you that."

Brenda drew near Tank because she just needed to. She didn't have to say anything; she knew he was having the same dreadful experience of seeing a face Andi had mimicked yesterday at breakfast. "And when did he drown?"

"Last Sunday night. And . . ." The second body was standing, wrapped like a mummy next to the marlin. Dr. Torres wheeled it out with a hand truck and uncovered the face. "Neville Moore, proprietor of the Catch as Catch Can Emporium."

Brenda and Tank cringed. Being drowned, left in the water a while, and then frozen had degraded Moore's appearance from the cheerful fellow they'd met on Sunday morning, right before they left St. Clemens for St. Jacob. Nevertheless, they could identify him.

"Yeah," said Tank. "We were in his store Sunday morning. He sold Andi that —"

"I don't want to know," said Torres. "I'm only letting *you* know."

"When did he die?" Brenda asked.

"Monday morning. The police told me it was a suicide — which is *my* job to determine, but they let me know what my findings were to be." He put Moore's body back in the cooler, then Ben Cardiff's. "You'll be interested to know that Neville Moore was stabbed through the heart with surgical precision and already dead before he was thrown in the water. Which, I hope, gives you fair warning that you do not have friends here on St. Clemens. Some other parties with tremendous influence got here first." He met their eyes. "You follow?"

Chapter 11
The Rule of Force

Having swabbed the whole deck from stem to stern, my next assignment was as kitchen boy under the authority of Spikenose. Though I expected far worse, the galley was clean, modern, well appointed, and Spikenose, when separate from the others, was easy enough to work with.

"The captain wants his afternoon tea," he said, setting out a tray with a silver tea service, quite nice for a pirate ship. I noticed it was tea for two. "Take this up to him. One quiet knock on the door, then enter, set the tray on the map table, cream and sugar on the captain's right."

I took hold of the tray handles, but having noticed the modern timbre of his speech, queried him with my eyes.

He caught my look, and as he dried a pan with a towel, replied in Pirate, "Aye, it's who's where on the ratlines, and Cap, he's the one at the top. I be the one slung near the bottom, and you, you're a barnacle on the keel." He smiled as if sharing a secret and spoke like a man from my century, "Sorry about the mess up there. Orders from Rock. It's how we test a man, how he finds his place. Keep it in mind, and be ready. There's no virtue on this ship, only muscle." He pointed to the tray. "Now away with ya, lad, or I'll add your nose to m'puddin'!"

I knocked once, quietly, then stole into the Captain's Quarters. Andi was there, seated across the table from the captain. Their conversation ceased abruptly upon my entrance. Thatch glowered at me. I delivered the tray according to Spikenose's instructions, noting in the process the cabinet from which Rock had produced the three-cornered hat the captain had made Andi wear. The cabinet door was open, and visible on shelves and hooks was a large and varied collection of hats, scarves, and earrings. Pirate accessories, one would think, but by now I knew they were more than that.

A theory confirmed, I believe, as the captain picked up his conversation with Andi, perhaps in defiance of my being there. "Ben, did you know you're dead?"

Andi was perplexed, being very much alive.

The captain poured her a cup of tea, but his tone was not cordial. "I saw you stiff and cold, you know. Went to the doc's office and there you were, like a side of meat. And someone tore the earring right out of your ear." He set the cup of tea before her and glowered at me again, my cue to back away respectfully and get out. "You remember that earring, don't you?"

Her hand went to her mouth. Something was coming back.

Thatch leaned over the table. "That earring belonged to me!"

Even as I was backing through the door, the memory struck her violently. She put her hand over her ear and let out a yelp of pain and terror.

"An earring?" the young shop assistant at Catch as Catch Can Emporium asked Tank and Brenda through the barely cracked front door.

"Yeah," said Tank. He indicated about a three-inch diameter with his thumb and index. "About that big around."

"You remember us?" asked Brenda. "We were in here Sunday morning. There was a red-haired girl with us and a stodgy old man, remember them?"

"Uh, well, sure, I guess," the girl said.

"And Andi — that's the red-haired girl — bought the earring, remember?" asked Tank.

"No. No, I'm sorry, I don't remember anything about that. Look, we're closed."

Brenda shot a glance at the store hours: nine to nine. It was five twenty. "Very sorry for your loss, of course."

"You have to leave."

"Well, may we leave you a phone number?" Brenda dug in her pocket for a scrap of paper and scribbled down her cell number and Tank's. She passed it through the narrow opening. "Excuse the doodles on the back. But these are our numbers if you want to talk at all."

The girl took the crinkled paper. "Okay."

"Let's eat," said Daniel.

Brenda asked casually, "Know of a good place to eat around here?"

"The Conch," she replied. "Great seafood." She stuck her hand out through the door just far enough to point the direction.

Brenda, Tank, and Daniel walked away, mingling with the tourists and island folk who crammed the narrow street.

"She's scared," said Brenda.

Spikenose's warning about the Rock's test

was none too soon.

Preparations for the evening meal produced the usual food scraps, and the mousy little chef piled them into the same bucket he'd spilled earlier, handing it to me to dump over the side. I never made it to the railing. The moment I emerged from the companion and onto the deck, a hairy leg jutted out to trip me. I stumbled and reeled along the deck even as a boot planted a blow to the bucket to knock it from my hands.

By some miracle, I recovered, neither falling nor letting go of the bucket, though some of the contents escaped and splattered on the boards.

Rock, Scalarag, and Norwig the Bean had been lying in wait just outside the companion, and now were having a good-ol'-laugh at my expense. Scalarag came at me, his eyes on the bucket, and . . .

What happened next would haunt me. Was it that leering face? The desperation of a prisoner with no alternatives? Within me, something *animal* overpowered reason and, with reckless power, I swung the bucket in a violent arc and struck the huge man in the face. The kitchen scraps splashed on him, on the deck, on everything; he reeled, hand to his face, and fell back against the capstan, blood trickling from his nose.

Rock and Norwig became stunned onlookers, suspended in time. Scalarag was quickly recovering, planting his feet, powering up his muscles, preparing for murder.

As for me, I considered myself as good as dead, and upon that conclusion, saw no point in timidity. I held the bucket out as if it were a weapon and said, "A word!"

Rock and Norwig looked at each other, amused.

"A *word,* says he!" said Rock.

"Aye," said Norwig, "more words. Be still me tremblin' 'art!"

And then I amazed — or rather, dismayed — myself. "If it be flesh yer hungerin' or blood yer thirstin', then step in, the lot o' ya, and be measured against me dyin' carcass, but you can lay to this: for every piece of me you take, be it nose or ear, I'll take for meself a piece a' you, so count it up and decide!"

There. Me dyin' words. Or so I thought.

Rock was the first to start laughing. Norwig came next and then, wiping the blood from his face with the back of his arm, Scalarag smiled and laughed with delight.

"So there be a man before us!" said Rock, exchanging a gleeful look with the others.

"Ask me," said Scalarag, regarding the

blood smeared on his arm.

"Give the man his badge," said Rock.

Scalarag took the red scarf from his head and approached me.

I tensed. What was this, a trick? A ruse? Hidden gadgetry?

Scalarag smiled, and the smile looked friendly. "Heave to, my man. It's only a scarf."

He stepped around behind me, and tied the scarf about my head as Rock and Norwig raised their fists in the air and cheered.

Scalarag came around and clapped me on the shoulders. "You're one of us now!"

I returned to the galley with emptied bucket in hand and a pirate's scarf upon my head. Spikenose noticed the scarf, of course, but only raised a knowledgeable eyebrow and went about his work.

I went back to peeling potatoes, my head a thicket of quandaries.

I was alive, and the muscular monster Scalarag was the only one injured. Astounding.

Nevertheless . . .

I had fallen to the level of an animal, yielded to temper, lashed out, abandoned reason for violence.

Nevertheless . . .

There could only be advantage in being

"one of them." Perhaps safety. Perhaps information.

Nevertheless . . .

I, a savage? A barbarian? Even though I could not argue against the ship's philosophy — No truth, no shame, no God to draw the line — I was ashamed.

Chapter 12
A Narrow Escape

The Conch was a nice place — three stars, perhaps. They even had a walk-around combo playing steel drums, bass, and guitar, and Daniel was just discovering that he liked calamari without encouragement from Brenda who didn't. Tank went for the mahi mahi because it sounded sophisticated, the polar opposite of hamburger. Brenda ordered sea bass.

"Pardon me," said a waitress. "Would you be Mr. and Mrs. Christensen?"

Brenda was nearly insulted. "Whoa! I wouldn't say that, girl."

"I'm, uh, Mr. Christensen," said Tank.

The waitress spoke to Tank. "You have a phone call from someone named Lacey."

Brenda and Tank exchanged a look. Brenda checked her cell phone. It was turned on.

"Uh . . ." said Tank, checking his own cell, "sure . . ."

"The phone's in the kitchen."

Brenda, Tank, and Daniel followed the waitress through the restaurant and into the kitchen, where she handed them a cell phone and left them alone.

Tank looked at the cell phone curiously. He put it to his ear. "Hello?"

"Hello?" came a female voice. "This is Lacey from Catch as Catch Can Emporium. Is this Mr. Christensen? Tank?" With the chefs and kitchen staff cooking and clattering, it was hard to hear.

"Yeah."

"Sorry to call you on another phone. I'm just afraid of hackers, you know?"

"Uh, yeah. Okay." Tank wanted to put the phone on speaker but he wasn't familiar with this make and couldn't figure out how. He held it just a little away from his ear so Brenda could lean close and listen. "Go ahead. Brenda's here, too."

"And the little boy?"

"Yeah, he's here."

"Please keep him close. I'm afraid for you."

Daniel was across the room, looking out the back window. Brenda signaled and said, "Daniel, get away from the window."

Daniel looked at her in alarm and pointed toward the street.

Linked at the ears with the cell phone between, Brenda and Tank moved through the kitchen hubbub and toward the window.

"Hello?" came Lacey's voice. "You still there?"

"Yeah, yeah," said Tank as he and Brenda looked wherever Daniel was pointing. "Go ahead."

"I need to tell you that . . ." Now there was traffic noise. They couldn't make out what she said.

"Uh, say again?"

Daniel was pointing to a woman hurrying away from the restaurant with a cell phone to her ear.

"I was saying that you could be in real danger. There's a . . ." More traffic noise, a loud truck.

At that moment, an old truck passed right by the lady hurrying away. She glanced sideways.

The waitress.

"Lacey!" said Daniel.

"Honey, that's not Lacey!" said Brenda as if seeing an omen.

"No," Daniel insisted, pointing toward a side alley, *"Lacey!"*

Tank and Brenda followed Daniel's pointing finger down a side alley, and there, running frantically their direction, was Lacey

— not on a cell phone. She caught sight of them through the window and gestured with flailing arms, screaming something.

"It looks like . . . *get down, giddy up . . .*" said Tank.

Suddenly a lady burst into the kitchen shouting, "Get out! Everybody out NOW!"

Daniel started tugging at them. "Get out!"

Tank got the concept. "Get out!" he yelled.

Brenda, Tank, Daniel, the kitchen staff, the lady, all ran, scattering, finding cover. Daniel tugged Brenda and Tank into the alley, around and behind a big dumpster. Lacey, huffing and puffing, piled in with them, shielding her head with her arms.

The explosion was deafening. They could feel it in the ground, in their guts. Bits of glass, wood, and masonry pinged and pummeled the alley walls. There were screams and shouts from up and down the street as debris rained down and after that, bedlam.

Scalarag ducked through the door to my small compartment with the evening meal on a tin plate. Though I'd been assigned to help prepare it, I was condemned to eat it in my quarters, my ankles in irons. The big man handed me the plate. I sat on my cot while he took the only chair. It seemed as if he might stay a while.

"Bless me, Father, for I have sinned."

What? This brute, now penitent? Our altercation must have made a deeper impression than I thought. Even so, having disgraced myself once through violence, I wasn't about to lie as well. "I'm sorry," I said. "I *was* a priest, but that was a long time ago."

"But you can still do the confession thing, can't you?"

He wasn't kidding. I told him, "Confession is always good for the soul, my son. I'm sure we can work something out."

He clasped his hands as if praying and looked mostly at the wall. "It has been . . . oh, ten, fifteen years since my last confession." Then he started confessing. It burst out of him. "My name isn't Scalarag, it's Tommy Bryce. I'm from Dubuque, Iowa, and I was a heavy equipment operator until I got in a fight and got fired and someone told me I ought to try out for the pirate show and so I ended up here. It started out being fun, all the pretending, the tourist show, the pirate ship. But you know, there's something about being a pirate. I mean, you start believing it, and then . . . there's just this wicked thing that happens."

"Like, for instance, an innocent tourist being locked in a cabin for reasons he doesn't know?"

Tommy nodded fervently. "Yeah, and ripping off the rich tourists. It's gotten out of hand, and now there could even be a murder."

There is *a God,* I thought — in jest, of course. "Ben?"

"Ben Cardiff. Seemed like a nice guy. He and the captain were like *that*" — he held up crossed fingers — "but they still didn't trust each other. Cap could run the old satellite system, but then Ben did an upgrade to all the wireless Internet stuff so he was the only one who knew how to run everything, all the Readers and Writers — but I guess I shouldn't say too much about that."

Oh, please do. "As you wish."

"But Ben had money problems and probably ended up being a traitor, trying to sell us out. He lit out Sunday night after our show, took all his stuff with him, and then . . . hey, if he made a deal with somebody, it went south. They say Ben drowned, but the cap saw Ben in the doc's freezer and he said somebody beat him to a pulp and tore the Reader out of his ear." He wagged his head. "It was bound to happen, that's what I'm saying. On this ship, the spoils go to the crafty, and every man makes up his own rules. And it's a tough bunch. Rock used to be a drug dealer. Norwig got busted for armed robbery."

"So how does the captain keep them all loyal?"

"As long as the takings are sweet they play along, but they're all looking for a better offer. Ben was, that's what we think." He leaned toward me. "Not that you and Cap are friends, but I wouldn't stand too close to him. You never know what might be coming his way."

"Good advice, my son," I said, laying my hand upon his head.

He waited, then finally asked, "You gonna give me some penance or something?"

"Just tell God you're sorry. And do what's right."

CHAPTER 13
LACEY AND DELILAH

Tank looked up and down the street. Folks were shaken, coated with dust, helping each other to their feet. A few were bleeding, but not seriously.

Lacey tugged his arm. "You've got to get out of here!"

"But people are hurt!"

"They'll live. You won't — not if you stay here!"

"But —"

"Let's go!"

She tugged and urged Brenda, Tank, and Daniel until they ran headlong down the alley and didn't stop running until they'd regrouped in the living room of a comfortable bungalow a few blocks inland. Lacey drew the shades, then cracked one aside to double-check the street.

"What . . . what just happened?" Brenda asked, settling into a soft chair, holding Daniel close.

"Somebody tried to kill you by planting a bomb in my mom's restaurant," said Lacey, finally sitting in another chair. "In the kitchen. It was set to go off at 6:01, and it did."

Tank figured the bamboo-looking sofa would hold his weight and sat, speechless.

Brenda shuddered. "But . . . how did you . . . ?"

"You ought to know," said Lacey.

The back door opened.

"We're in here, Mom," said Lacey.

In came the lady from the restaurant, the one who burst into the kitchen and told everyone to get out. She was bedraggled and dusty, carrying a shopping bag.

"You okay?" asked Lacey.

"I'm all right," the lady answered, brushing a lock of hair from her face. "Everyone's okay. The insurance rep will be by tomorrow."

"So what caused it?"

The lady gave her head a cynical tilt. "They say it was a gas explosion."

"Oh, I'm *sure*!"

"Purely accidental, just a leaky gas line and then a spark somewhere set it off. In a kitchen with flames and cooking going on everywhere, a *spark* set it off?" She collapsed on the other end of the sofa and looked Brenda, Tank, and Daniel up and down. "So just who are you people, anyway?"

"Mom, this is Brenda, Daniel, and Tank. Brenda, Daniel, and Tank, this is my mom, Delilah."

"Pleased to meet you," said Tank.

Delilah still stared, borderline glared, at them. "So what was that movie line? 'Of all the restaurants in all the towns in all the world, you had to come into mine'?"

"Mom . . ."

"And into *your* store," she said to her daughter. "So first it was your boss, and now it's my restaurant. Why'd you send them to *my* place?"

Lacey was mortified. "I didn't think —"

"No, you didn't." Delilah reached into her shopping bag and pulled out a half-melted wall clock, its glass face shattered. The hands indicated 6:01. "So how'd you know there was a bomb set to go off at exactly 6:01?"

Lacey pulled a scrap of paper from her shirt pocket — the paper on which Brenda had scribbled her and Tank's cell numbers. She turned it over to show Brenda's sketch on the reverse side: the very same half-melted wall clock with the glass shattered and the hands indicating 6:01.

Even Brenda was amazed. "I thought I was just playing around with a Salvador Dali kind of thing."

"I grew up looking at that wall clock in the kitchen," said Lacey. "And when I saw this I thought of what happened to Mr. Moore after you and your friends came into the store, and I called Mom. I was going to call you next, but time got really tight."

"So that waitress who said we had a call?" Tank asked.

"Never seen her before," said Delilah. "I was about to ask her what she was doing in my restaurant — and in my kitchen — but she ducked out, then Lacey called, then I put it together, and anyway . . . you saved my life and the lives of my staff — well, after putting us all in danger by walking into the restaurant in the first place."

"Mom . . ."

"So one more time, just who are you people? And who is it that wants to kill you and the rest of us over a stupid earring?"

Lacey explained to Brenda and Tank, "I didn't sell your friend the earring, but I saw Mr. Moore sell it to her, and then, Monday morning, after the pirate guy drowned, two men came into the store asking Mr. Moore about it: if he'd picked it up off the beach and if he still had it —"

Delilah broke in. "Neville used to go out with a metal detector and find things on the beach in front of the resorts: jewelry, money, anything valuable. Then he'd take it back to his shop and turn right around and sell it. Everyone knew he did that, so those two men could have found out real easy."

"Anyway," Lacey continued, "that's where the earring came from. Mr. Moore found it on the beach under a tree and brought it back to the shop and ended up selling it to your redheaded friend."

"What did the men look like?" Brenda asked.

"One was an older man, blond hair, dressed casual like a tourist. The other guy . . ." She cringed. "Big Asian guy. Looked real dangerous. They asked Mr. Moore to show them where he found it, so he went with them to show them, and the next thing we knew, Mr. Moore had drowned . . . just like the pirate."

"Ben Cardiff," said Tank.

Delilah nodded. "Which means you're in deep you-know-what."

Lacey explained, "Whoever those two men were, Mr. Moore told them about your friend — Andi, was it? — and where she and the rest of you were going. They know about you; they've probably been following you."

"You were lucky this time," said Delilah, "and I get a whole new kitchen if the insurance company pays up."

"But you don't know who they are?" asked Brenda.

Lacey exchanged a look with her mother and said, "Ever heard of The Gate?"

Delilah cautioned, "Shhh!"

Brenda and Tank could not conceal their shock. "We've . . . we've heard the name, yes," said Brenda, quite the understatement.

"It's the whisper around town," Delilah said guardedly. "With all the offshore banking that goes on here, a lot of money goes through this island, and a lot of dirty money, too, and a lot of shadowy people. But we don't talk about it, do we, Lacey? We mind our own business and make our living and stay out of the way."

"Well, we tried to," Lacey admitted.

"Until you people stumbled in and stirred everything up. Guess it had to happen, though. Nobody here's got the guts to stand up to the . . ." — her voice dropped to a whisper — "The Gate." Then she added at a cautious volume, "Whoever they are. Everybody's either bought or scared."

"But that's why maybe we should tell you

—" Lacey hesitated.

"Say it, daughter." She nodded toward Brenda, Tank, and Daniel. "You never know, they might be here for a reason. Maybe they're the only ones who can break this thing open. Maybe *God* sent them."

"Wow," said Tank. "Cool!" Then Brenda gave him a corrective stare. "Sort of."

Lacey leaned forward. "A strange little man came into the shop with his wife about a month ago. He looked at jewelry, he looked at watches, he looked at scarves. He just looked at everything, and he liked some of it, he didn't like some of it, he talked about the colors and the styles of things. But the funny thing was, he was blind."

"He did the same thing at the Conch," said Delilah. "He saw the menu, looked at the choices, could read right off it without looking at it."

"Turns out his *wife* was doing all the looking and reading, and somehow he could see everything she was seeing. She'd look at a scarf and he'd comment on the size and the color. She'd look at a watch and he'd talk about the features he liked as if he could see it. It was like he was seeing through her eyes."

"So . . . how did they do it?" Tank asked.

"Don't know, but here's the connection:

They were both wearing a big gold earring."

Brenda was fully alert now, spine straight. "Please say you have this guy's name, his number . . . something."

"He bought a watch and a scarf . . ."

". . . and a lobster and steak," Delilah added.

". . . and we saved the receipts."

Chapter 14
Zedekiah Snow

Wednesday morning, decked out in seaman's blouse and with a pirate scarf upon my head, I joined the crew, lending a hand and no small amount of muscle to hauling on the sheets and trimming the sails as the helmsman brought us about. While I had no intention of stooping to their level of savagery, it seemed my nearly breaking Scalarag's nose had at least broken the ice, and the crew was beginning to accept me, talking freely in my presence. The talk was we were heading back for St. Clemens to do a show the next day. What Thatch intended to do with Andi and me once we got there — or before we got there — was the foremost question of my day.

While I blended and sweated with the crew, Andi and Captain Thatch stood on the quarterdeck, still digging for treasure in her memory.

"It was a money deal," she recalled, wide-eyed at the recollection. "I . . . I mean, *Ben* . . . met with some people."

"Who?"

"Two guys, and they offered him a . . . Wow! A million up front, another million after delivery, all transferred into a secret bank account."

"HA! I can see it plain, the traitor!"

"Ben was trying to get out. They told him something like, 'It's all going to go down and you're going to go down with it unless you get out now. Get out, take the money, and disappear.' "

"Get out? Of what?"

Andi cringed as she shared it. "Whatever you pirates are doing."

"Two men? Who were they? Who were they working for?"

She shook her head. "I don't know."

The captain snapped his fingers. "Faces. Would you know their faces if you saw them?"

She closed her eyes. "I might. I remember an older guy, and some big tough guy like a hit man. I think he was Asian. . . ."

"Names?"

She shook her head. "Maybe they never told me . . . or Ben. But there was something else . . ." She winced, trying to remember.

"What, lass?"

"Something to do with a banana peel."

The receipts bore the name and signature of a certain Filbert Figg. A few discreet conversations among the St. Clemens merchants led Brenda and Tank to a shop owner who'd shipped some wind chimes to the same Mr. Figg. The shipping address was in Key West, Florida, the closely packed, miles-of-merchants tourist town that was once the haunt of Papa Hemingway. They caught a flight that morning and, after a cab ride through the busy streets and desultory throngs, found themselves at a row of houses crammed along the waterfront. The particular model of wind chimes hanging near the front door confirmed they'd found the right place.

Brenda and Tank suspected the name Filbert Figg was an alias, and they were right. The name they'd cross-referenced to this address was actually Zedekiah Snow, and it was his wife, Audrey, who answered the door. She listened patiently to their story, and when they described Andi's mysterious golden earring, she swung the door wide open. "Please come in. He'll want to hear this."

Zedekiah Snow was a small-framed, white-haired man in a baseball cap, his eyes crazily disoriented, his visage scarred from an old injury. He appeared to be in the middle of a strange Eastern exercise in the center of the living room, leaning this way, then that, hands holding an invisible bar of some kind, shifting his weight as if negotiating fierce rapids.

"Zed . . ." said Audrey.

"Not now!"

"You have visitors."

"Tell them to go away!"

Audrey looked out the front windows. Brenda, Tank, and Daniel followed her gaze and spotted a sailboarder tacking across the wind and jumping the waves. Then they noticed how the sailboarder and Zedekiah Snow were making the very same moves at the very same time.

"Their friend just purchased one of Ben Cardiff's earrings," said Audrey. "And now she's been kidnapped."

As one, the old man and the sailboarder lost their balance and fell, the sailboarder into the waves, the old man onto the floor. As the sailboarder paddled about in the waves, the old man paddled on the floor, going nowhere. "How can that — ? Oh, hold on!" He groped, then grabbed the bill of his hat, yanking it from his head and tossing it aside.

Now moving on his own, the sailboarder gathered up his board and started paddling for shore. Zedekiah Snow quit swimming and felt his way to a chair. He sat down and reached for a pair of dark glasses on the side table.

As he put them on, Audrey donned a pair of glasses from the kitchen counter and turned her gaze upon Brenda, Tank, and Daniel.

"Oh . . ." said Zedekiah, as if he were now seeing something through the glasses. "Looks like a family!"

Audrey introduced them as just friends.

"You're not from the government, are you?"

"No, sir," said Tank. "We're just —"

"I won't talk to the government. And I thought I was hiding. How'd you find me?"

"Ummm . . ." Tank began.

"Nevermind," he said. "Kidnapped? By whom?"

Tank and Brenda looked at each other. Daniel answered, "Pirates!"

Audrey looked down at Daniel. Zedekiah reacted. "Cute kid. Pirates? Yes, that would be Ben, all right. Large gold earring, was it?"

Brenda and Tank brightened. "Yeah," said Brenda.

"How'd she get it?"

"She bought it from a store on St. Clemens. The owner of the store was a scavenger and got it off the beach somewhere."

"Ha!" Snow must have been rolling his eyes behind those dark glasses. "So Ben's not as clever as he thinks."

"Sir, I'm sorry to tell you," said Tank, "Ben is dead. He was murdered."

Snow deflated a little, his hands plopping on the chair. "What about your friend? Did she wear the earring?"

"Oh yeah," said Brenda.

"Did she start behaving strangely?"

"She started acting like a pirate," said Tank.

"There *is* more to it. Better sit down and tell me the whole story."

When they'd recounted it all, including the kidnapping, the murders of Ben Cardiff and Neville Moore, and the bomb planted in the Conch restaurant, he took a moment to digest it, scrubbed his hands over his face, and said finally, "Well, your turn to hear my story, I suppose."

Audrey sat in another chair right next to him, looking at Brenda, Tank, and Daniel, as Zedekiah began. "You've gathered now that I can see you. Tank, the towering muscle man; Brenda, graceful carving in ebony; Daniel, the cherub with a special wisdom. It's coming into my brain through a Writer, a chip embedded in these glasses here." He tapped the dark glasses he wore. "And it's being sent from another chip, a Reader, in Audrey's glasses. She sees you, the image becomes brainwaves in her head; her glasses convert the brainwaves into a transmittable signal and send that signal through our translator system to my glasses. My glasses convert the signal back into brainwaves in my head, and my brain translates them back into the image she sees. Very simple concept."

The beachside door opened, and the sailboarder came in.

"Ah! My son, Jeremiah. No doubt you noticed our little experiment. We were sailboarding together. Jeremiah, how'd it go?"

The young man was wet and tired, but pleased. "Weird. Like I was you."

"And you were me!" Zedekiah laughed. To Brenda, Tank, and Daniel, he exclaimed, "The very first bi-directional mind feed! He sends me his sensory impressions through a Reader in his headband, I pick them up through a Writer in that billed cap over there and send back my rusty old skills in riding a sailboard. With bi-directional feed, we share the experience!"

"The problem was deciding just who was driving," said Jeremiah.

"That can be worked out with practice and mutual agreement. But you see how wonderful this could be? The blind can see through the eyes of their loved ones; the deaf can hear, the paralyzed can walk, and old blind cranks like me can even ride a sailboard through the mind and senses of someone else!"

"It's incredible!" said Brenda.

Zedekiah Snow sank back in his chair. "Mmm, and it's also dangerous, as you have discovered. Your friend Andi has experienced far more than she wanted . . . just as I feared would happen some day. Ben Cardiff and I were associates. Together we perfected the Read/Write system. It was Ben's idea to plant the Reader and Writer chips in head garments. It held great promise for the blind, the deaf, anyone else who might be denied a fuller life experience. But Ben was a moral weakling, and he came across a scoundrel willing to exploit that weakness: Horatio Thatch."

Tank and Brenda didn't recognize the name.

"*Captain* Horatio Thatch?" Zedekiah tried.

Their eyes widened. "The captain from the pirate show!"

"A pirate indeed," said Snow. "For the tourists and . . . a pirate of a very different kind when it comes to pirating the minds of rich tourists to gain access to their bank accounts and portfolios. Thatch wooed Ben away from me with promises of using our invention to get rich, and, I suppose, that's what's happened. Place a pirate hat or an earring or a scarf on a tourist to take a pirate picture, and while they're smiling and making a memory, all their bank information is downloaded directly from their brain. That's why Audrey and I were on St. Clemens a month ago — secretly, we thought. We were checking out what use Ben and Thatch were making of our Read/Write system. Now . . . oh dear, what to do? No doubt you've gone to the authorities?" Amazingly, he could see the look on their faces. "Ha! That's what I thought. The Gate's already been there. Ohhh, yes, I know about The Gate. They came to me first, wanting the system. Sell *them* the system? They'd make worse use of it than the government with their prying, spying, and pirating! I became Filbert Figg and vanished. But Ben was still available, I see. He cut a deal, I suppose, and the deal went sour somehow —" Zedekiah had a sudden revelation. "Ahhh yes! Would you like to hear an excellent guess?"

Brenda and Tank nodded, knowing he could see them.

"Ben struck a deal to sell the technology to The Gate. To show what it could do, he left a Writer earring at a drop point on the beach for The Gate to pick up. Then, wearing the Reader earring himself, he intended to transfer his memory, all the vital information, to The Gate through the system, his Reader to the Writer they supposedly had. Except . . ."

"Except Neville Moore found it first, and Andi got the earring instead!" Tank concluded, sending a pleased look at Brenda.

"And so The Gate was out their money and thought Ben had swindled them, so Ben met an ignominious end, and now . . ." Zedekiah laughed, either at the trickery of the events or at his own cleverness. "And now, it is not The Gate who has all of Ben's knowledge and the technology, and it's not Thatch and his pirates, either; it is Andi who has it all in her head!" Then he stopped laughing. "Oh dear. That doesn't bode well for her, does it?"

Chapter 15
The Wild Man

"We've been good to your friend the prof," the captain told Andi. "Each day, each hour he's still breathing, he'll have you to thank for it. Remember that."

Andi was seated before the computer screen again, looking through screens, menus, and drop-downs, with the captain and Sparks looking over her shoulder. "It all looks familiar."

His hand was on her shoulder. "We need the numbers, the passcodes to access the bank accounts."

"Don't you have them written down somewhere?"

"Ben did, and now he's gone and the records with him."

"So . . ." Andi kept looking. "Looks like you can't always have it your way after all."

His grip on her shoulder tightened. It hurt. "Don't let that thought cross your mind. I'll have what I want."

Well, everyone has their tipping point. Andi was reaching hers. Even while grimacing through the pain she told him, "As if brute force is going to make you right in the grand scheme of things?" She twisted in her chair to look him in the eye, batting away his grip. "You may be captain of this ship, but it's a mighty big ocean. You may scoff at God and truth, but this system runs on truth, on rules of physics and mathematics that must be obeyed whether you like it or not, and if I'm going to solve this problem it's going to be according to those rules, not yours. Now *back off!*"

As if grudgingly conceding her point, he straightened, giving her space, and crossed his arms, removing physical threat. "Well then. Where do we stand according to these . . . *rules*?"

As if the momentary distraction had freed up her mind, she thought of using another path to the files. "Oh, oh, ohhh, looky here!"

"Ah!"

"Recognize them?"

"Yes!" He chuckled and this time patted her shoulder gently.

Sparks patted her other shoulder. "These are the bank accounts — with their codes!"

She began to scroll down the screen. "Yes! This is the code for Switzerland . . . and this is the code for France . . . England . . . Japan . . . Germany . . . and this link takes you to the server in New York. Wow!"

"Keep going, lass," said the captain. Then he added chillingly, "Professor McKinney is counting on you."

She rolled her eyes, but he didn't see it.

There was a commotion below, enough to make the beams quiver. Blows, boots, the clatter of a plate, the creak of an old door. There was that scream again! Footsteps thundered up the passage just outside.

The captain bolted to the door. "Scalarag! What's —"

A body collided with the captain, and he stumbled into the passageway. For a terrifying instant, a ragged wraith leaned in the doorway, eyes white and crazy, hair an explosion, squeaking out a laugh and babbling gibberish as the air carried the stench of feces and urine. Andi cowered in the corner. Sparks grabbed up a chair to shield himself.

With a maniacal cry, the creature bolted, leaped over the fallen captain, and ran up the passage, and it was only now that Andi realized who it was — Jean-Pierre DuBois, the flamboyant French buccaneer! He'd not been seen since the captain handed him Andi's gold earring and he took it below decks.

Moments after that came the first scream, undoubtedly from this same wretch who was now clearly out of his mind.

"Spikenose!" the captain bellowed.

The little cook, nose bleeding, bounded up the passageway. "He jumped me! I was bringing him his dinner and he jumped me!"

"All hands!" yelled the captain. "Lay hold of that madman!"

"Captain!"

Thatch looked at Spikenose impatiently.

"He has my pistol!"

Both men thundered up the passageway, and Sparks followed as the whole ship came alive with shouts, stomps, and footsteps.

Andi, overwhelmed with curiosity, hurried topside in time to see Norwig the Bean and Sparks sprawled on the deck, bested in a tangle with DuBois the maniac, who now scrambled about the deck and up to the forecastle, chased by Rock and Scalarag. DuBois was swinging from the shrouds, hurling things, screaming, laughing. Finally, with Rock and Norwig guarding one set of steps and Scalarag and Sparks the other, he was trapped on the forecastle. The captain stepped forward and tried to talk sense, but DuBois drew Spikenose's pistol from his belt and took aim. The captain ducked just as the weapon went off with a loud report and a puff of blue smoke. A lead ball blasted a splinter out of the mainmast, ricocheted off the deck, and broke out a window of the Captain's Quarters.

At that, Captain Thatch drew his own pistol even as DuBois drew a sizable knife. Stepping up on the rail, DuBois leaped at the captain.

The captain fired. DuBois took a lead ball through the neck and tumbled onto the deck, squirting blood. Andi looked away.

When she looked again, the captain stood over DuBois, cursing. Scalarag knelt by the Frenchman, trying to stop the bleeding, but the damage was done — exceedingly. Rock looked at DuBois, at the captain. "Those . . . those were live rounds!"

The captain slowly replaced his pistol. "Spare me the act, Rock. You're not surprised." He looked around the horrified circle, eyeing their pistols. "Nor any of the rest of you, I'll wager!"

Scalarag stood, blood all over him. DuBois was dead.

"He was my friend," said the captain. "It was Ben who did this to him, but we've made it square."

"What . . ." Norwig was trembling. "What are we gonna do?"

The captain started for his quarters. "Think it through, mates. I have. We hold course for St. Clemens. There's big money to be made."

"But . . ." said Rock, "what about — ?"

"Tie him to some weights and throw him over the side."

CHAPTER 16
TAKING THE *RIQUEZA*

At Zedekiah and Audrey's insistence, Brenda, Tank, and Daniel had dinner and spent the night. Brenda crashed on the couch, Tank on the floor, Daniel on the floor next to Tank and close to Brenda. Sleep, at least for Tank, was a little difficult with the frequent vibrations coming through the floor as a bothered Zedekiah paced back and forth from his bedroom to his computer room and back again.

In the morning, over bagels and fresh-brewed coffee, he shared his musings. "A kidnapping from a lonely beach and a boat rowed out to sea? Not The Gate's style, but definitely the style of Thatch and his pirates. Also, the murders tell me The Gate doesn't yet have the technology, while we know Thatch and his pirates do. Therefore . . ."

With Audrey as his eyes, he led them into his computer room, a chaotic jumble of keyboards, screens, wires, control panels, and papers, all labeled with Post-it notes for Audrey's sake. "If we assume the Read/Write technology interfaces wirelessly with either a satellite or the Internet, I might be able to hack into the system aboard that ship. If we can pick up a signal from any Reader, the GPS inside the Reader will tell us where the ship is, and if . . ." He hesitated.

"If . . . what?" Brenda asked.

Zedekiah opened a drawer and produced a gold earring exactly like the one Andi had bought and worn. "Yes, Ben and I made several of these, both Readers and Writers. This one is a Writer, and if one of us can wear it, we could possibly connect with a Reader aboard the *Predator* and . . . uh . . . receive mental impressions of the surroundings, maybe even overhear conversations, see who and what we're dealing with."

"Can we do that?" Tank asked.

"Well, in a perfect world, yes. But someone on the *Predator* would have to be wearing the Reader in order for us to receive their mental images. We'd be fishing a bit."

Brenda could hear the uneasiness in his voice. "Okay, what else?"

"I have no control over the system on the ship. If Ben or anyone else has scrambled or encrypted the system to prevent invasion, this Writer could, uh, scramble the brain of the wearer." He nervously cleared his throat. "The damage would be irreparable."

I awoke that morning to a new sensation: the rumble of engines! So much for the seventeenth century.

I had little time to wonder about it before Scalarag ducked through the compartment door. "Up and about, you knave! We've a show to do today! Deck yourself out as befits a seaman." He produced the key to the leg irons and set me free. "Cap wants all men on deck. We've set course to overtake the *Riqueza.*"

Ah yes, the *Riqueza* — the colorful and completely fake Spanish galleon I and the team had climbed aboard less than a week ago. Within hours it would be loaded with laughing, gawking tourists with cameras and piña coladas, all ready to be boarded and raided by make-believe pirates. Oh, if those hapless flower shirts only knew!

Donning my seaman's blouse and pirate's scarf, I followed Scalarag topside, emerging on the deck to find the sails unfurling, the crew hauling and trimming to wring out the utmost knot.

"You!" hollered Rock, pointing at me. "On the mizzen!"

"The third mast," Scalarag advised me.

I hurried to join the crew, taking hold of the sheets and letting them out to open the sails fully to the wind. The *Predator* heeled to port, the waves dashing and foaming against her sides. We were motoring *and* sailing, in a hurry.

Thatch stood by the rail at the bow, sighting ahead with a spyglass. "There she lies!"

I could see the three-masted *Riqueza* on the horizon, only half her sails unfurled, poking along to be taken by the likes of us.

"Look alive, men! Cast loose the guns!"

There were six lashed, tied, and chocked cannons on the main deck. The gunners let them loose.

Scalarag led me to a locker beneath the quarterdeck where we found folding chairs. We formed a chain with some of the crew and set them up on the quarterdeck, twenty in all. These would be the choice seats for the tourists with red wristbands.

"Load your guns!"

With practice and polish, the gunners put the powder cartridges and wadding down each bore and rammed them home. No cannonballs; this was just smoke and noise.

We were closing on the galleon, and dead ahead of us both was Pirate Island, a green bump in the ocean where a Disneyesque

Port Royal awaited with costumed staff, souvenir stores, and pirate dinner show.

"Fire!"

From the deck of the *Riqueza* the cannon fire had been exciting and theatrical. From where I stood on the *Predator,* it was a fusillade of thunders that shook the boat and made Jell-O of my insides.

"Reload!"

I could see the *Riqueza* was laden with brightly clad, sun-blocked tourists who were no doubt wealthy — the admission price for this fantasy made sure of that.

The cannons fired again. This time I unabashedly covered my ears.

Zedekiah tapped the keys while Audrey watched the computer monitor. "We'll send out an inquiry and see if we get a reply from any Readers aboard the *Predator.* I'd like to go around the ship's system so nobody notices, but . . . well, here goes anyway."

"I think there was a show scheduled for today," said Audrey.

"Oo-hoo, then we might see quite a spectacle . . . or somebody will."

Audrey looked at Tank; he just wondered why. She looked at Brenda, who cringed a bit.

Zedekiah muttered to himself, kept tapping the keys, moving the mouse around. "Elusive little devils . . ."

Andi sat at the console, letting one memory lead to another as she strived to get the system working.

Sparks sat in a chair beside her, more a snoop and a nuisance than a help. "Come on, we have to get the Readers linked up before we dock." He pointed at a small blinking box near the top corner of the screen. "Is that an inquiry?"

The moment Andi saw it, she knew what it was. "Shouldn't be. Is there a Writer energized somewhere?"

Sparks checked the cabinet where the Writers — some earrings, a hat, a very modern headset — were kept. Just then the whole ship quaked as the boom of the cannons rang through the timbers. Sparks braced himself. He was looking away.

With a quick sequence of clicks, Andi consigned the blinking box to another screen that she minimized out of sight. "No, forget it, looks like we're clear. Must have been something else."

"What?"

"When I remember, I'll tell you."

It was the finest entertainment, really.

Muscular men in pirate garb, swords flashing, pistols popping, swinging on ropes like acrobats, swarming aboard the *Riqueza* and playfully taking captive the extra-paying tourists with a red wristband. I joined in the fun, blending, as it were, helping the hapless souls across the gangplank and aboard the *Predator.* With roguish decorum, I showed a jolly couple to their chairs.

"Oh," said the lady, "I'll bet you have fun being a pirate!"

"M'lady," I said as I took their drink orders, "you have no idea!"

Zedekiah Snow shook his head as Audrey, his eyes, scanned the computer screen. "No, no, we aren't getting through. This has to be the ship's system. It's framed just the way Ben would have done it, but it won't let us past the initial inquiry. It can hear us knocking at the door, but it's waiting for the password to let us in."

"Wait a minute," said Tank, pulling a notepad from his pocket. "What about what Andi said that first time, the aardvark thing?" He flipped through the pages until he found it. "Uh, Aardvark Basil Crustacean 233 —"

"Hold on, hold on!" said Snow, tapping away at the keys. "Now, is that just A, B, C, or the whole words?"

"I don't know."

"We'll try the whole words." He tapped them in. "Now, you have numbers?"

"233 997 417709."

Snow tapped them in. "Mmm. Ben always liked big entry codes. Here goes." He tapped Execute.

They waited.

Chapter 17
An Inquiry

Thatch was in full character, strutting about the deck, sword waving above his head, wild-eyed and savage. "You'll be taking your seats and causing us no grief, or we'll sever the tendons behind your knees, roll you up in squid guts, and throw you to the sharks!"

Our captives laughed. Context was everything.

I brought up the last couple, definitely high rollers judging by the man's watch.

Rock took his turn letting the chosen twenty know where the restrooms and life jackets were, and from that point, as both ships eased into the lagoon and toward the wharf at Pirate Island, there were songs, demonstrations, and even a member of the crew who could juggle knives with his ankles behind his neck. I would never be able to do that.

Andi knew, thanks to Ben's memory, that

another system was trying to link up with the system on the ship. She also knew such a fact could be an advantage if Sparks didn't know about it. "Okay, this must be the codes and frequencies for the Readers. Where are they?"

"In the Captain's Quarters," said Sparks. "They go ashore when we dock."

"Well, I need the identifier for each one so I can keep track of what I'm monitoring."

"Should be on your screen."

"I can't find it."

"We're pulling up to the wharf!"

She faced him and shrugged with palms up, at a loss.

That got him to move. "I'll get the info off the units. Hold on." He hurried out of the room, heading topside.

She had her chance, a window of mere minutes. Hurriedly, she brought up the blinking box. One click and it became a menu, and within that menu was an inquiry. Somewhere, someone was requesting access to the Readers — and with that request was the access code, the words *Aardvark, Basil, Crustacean,* and the numerical sequence.

Oh! It was like being able to breathe again, to live just one more moment. This was the outside world calling, the only people who would know this access code: Tank, Brenda, Daniel!

Come on, come on, she pleaded with Ben's memory, *how do I accept?*

All she had to do was ask, and the memory came to her. She clicked here, entered a command there, assigned a path, and clicked Execute.

"We're in!" said Zedekiah Snow with a clap of his hands.

Tank let out a whoop.

Brenda asked, "What does that mean?"

"It means," said Zedekiah, "that now we can use a Writer at this end to receive brainwaves from a Reader at their end, to tap into what's going on."

"Great!" said Tank.

Brenda was rather quiet.

Zedekiah got a little quiet himself. "And the fact that user input was necessary to complete the access tells me that someone running the system let us in."

"Andi!" said Daniel.

Andi could see the code going through, the system responding —

"Are we ready?" came the captain's voice behind her.

It made her jump. She rose from the chair,

fumbled for the mouse, blocked the screen with her body. "Uh . . . uh, yeah, I think so. Uh, Sparks has gone up to get the identifiers from the Readers."

How long had he been standing there? Did he see the inquiry, the access code? Were they still on the screen?

Well of course they were! She was dead. Fried.

What was he holding? Some oversized green, feathery outfit. "Try this on."

"Uh, right, right. Just let me make sure . . ." Her hand trembled as she moved and clicked the mouse. The menu closed, but the system was acknowledging the inquiry, opening up all the Readers — both on the ship and . . . wherever else. Sparks was sure to notice.

Speak of the devil. Sparks came back in with a list in his hand. "Okay, here are the identifiers —" He spotted the screen and pushed her aside. "Well, looks like you found them."

"Uh, yeah. Up and running as far as I can tell."

He sat in the chair. "Okay, Readers are online, ready to go ashore."

"Aye, and in good time," said the captain. "Norwig will set them up. Got my Writer?"

Sparks reached for a gold earring hanging

on a hook and handed it to the captain. "Grand enough. Tell me when I can listen in."

"Will do."

The captain addressed Andi, "And as for you . . ." He handed her the green, feathery thing. "You, m'lady, will accompany me."

"What's this?" had just escaped her lips when she saw the cartoonish parrot head and realized it was a costume.

"Being the parrot always falls to Spikenose, but not today," said the captain. "Today, it falls to you. I'll not be leaving you aboard the ship unwatched, nor can I let your face be seen, so today you're the parrot."

"Happy squawking, shipmate," said Sparks, his glee all too evident as he turned to the console. "I'll take it from here."

"Yes, yes, of course," said Zedekiah, still clicking and tapping for information. "The *Predator*'s GPS locator places the ship at Pirate Island. No surprise there. You were right, Audrey, they must have a show today."

"But that just proves you're in the *Predator*'s system!" said Tank.

"With the help of someone who recognized the access code, and that it could only come from you. Now if we can just pick up a Reader. Maybe your friend Andi will see to that . . ."

Daniel always meant well, and I imagine he could discern Brenda's misgivings about the magical earring. While all the others were focused on what was happening on Pirate Island, he gently took the earring from the table and looked it over.

"I think I'm finding some of the Readers . . ." Zedekiah said.

The screen went crazy!

"Oh!" said Audrey.

"Oh no, no, no!" said Zedekiah.

Daniel didn't have pierced ears. He may have thought he would hear something by pressing the earring to his ear.

"Someone's scrambled the system!" said Zedekiah, and perhaps the one great fear that came with that made Audrey scan the room for the earring. "Daniel!" she cried.

"Daniel, stop!" Zedekiah screamed.

Brenda's hand grabbed Daniel's wrist when the earring was only inches from his head and plucked the earring from his hand. As if it were red hot, she tossed the earring to the floor. Daniel was terribly frightened, of course, on the verge of tears, but she pulled him close. "It's okay, baby, it's okay. . . ."

Zedekiah settled, shaking, into his chair.

He had to clear his throat before he could say, "Audrey, if you please, the screen."

She returned to her post beside him and looked at the screen.

Zedekiah slumped in his chair. "Where we once had a friend, we now have an enemy. Don't touch that earring."

CHAPTER 18
PIRATE ISLAND

Pirate Island. It was pure fantasy, a seaport in miniature harking back to the Caribbean of the seventeenth century with its colonialism and rowdy decadence. As a tourist, I'd found it amusing. Now, save for my perilous situation, I could have been a part of it. Even as Scalarag and I helped secure the dock lines to moor the *Predator* safely against the wharf, I was enchanted by the village, the costumed populace, the seafaring music, the smell of the sea, and the majestic sailing ships. If I'd not been a captive, I could have been living in another time, caught up in the euphoria of make-believe.

As were the tourists, I suppose, coming down the gangways and flooding the place, cell phones and cameras already clicking at the sights: the wenches peddling their goods, the jugglers, the fire eater, the traditional dancers, and Captain Thatch in full regalia accompanied by his costumed parrot.

Andi did her best to be a parrot, waddling on her parrot feet and looking out through the cartoonish, two-way eyes, but her mind was on the system, the inquiry, Sparks sitting there watching that screen.

The captain drew the gold earring from his pocket as he strutted, and Andi waddled up to the Pirate Island photo booth next to the wharf. Here the tourists could don the pirate hats, scarves, and earrings from the rack and get a souvenir photo with the captain and the *Predator* in the background. Norwig the Bean was running the booth; Harry the Scar was the photographer.

And right now, they were idle.

"Well?" asked the captain.

"Ready when you are," said Norwig.

"Before the show, then. We'll —" Thatch winced and put his finger to his ear. "What? Say again?" He was wearing an earbud to keep in radio contact with Sparks. It appeared Sparks was talking to him. "Why? We're not taking any pictures yet. All the Readers are hanging on the rack in a dead calm." He glanced at the earring in his hand and told Norwig, "Sparks says to put on the earring. We're getting a signal."

Norwig and Harry looked again at the rack of scarves, hats, and earrings, which were all the Readers they had. "From what?" asked Norwig.

Thatch radioed back, "All the Readers are right here, doing nothing . . . well, you give me a Read and I'll put on the Writer!" He shoved the earring back in his pocket. "Keeps telling me to put on the earring. I hate that thing, and what's to monitor?"

"But have you noticed," said Harry, "how many scarves and hats there are already?"

The captain looked about, and so did Andi. Harry had a point. All along the wharf, across the dining plaza, and up the length of the cobblestone street, heads without a scarf or pirate hat of some kind were few and far between.

"So why should they wear one of ours?" asked Norwig.

"What about the mark?"

"Aye, we met him. Mr. Ling. Cold as ice and not to be tangled with."

The captain gave that pill time to go down. "Ling, you say? And where might he be?"

"Scarfing some grub." Norwig jerked his thumb toward the dining plaza.

The captain, with the parrot in tow, hurried back onto the wharf. "Gentlemen!"

Scalarag and I snapped to a ragged attention. "You'll return to the ship. Scalarag, we'll be about a new business now. Have the prof lend a hand, and keep him under your watchful eye." He turned to me. "Sorry, Prof. Still need to keep your pretty assistant in the right frame of mind, and . . . can't have you talking or passing notes to anyone, now can we?"

The parrot gave me a little wave and a lingering look as it walked beside the captain toward the village. Well. Of course Thatch would want her under his control at all times. Andi was falling into the role, waving, squawking, posing for pictures beside her flamboyant master.

And what could I do as a prisoner? A hostage? Insurance to keep Andi in line? As Scalarag escorted me up the gangplank, my anger was getting the better of me. "So what now? Leg irons again? More humiliation while the silly game goes on?"

"No," Scalarag answered.

"And to think at one time you had a conscience!"

"I said *No.* No leg irons. Plan B."

I looked back at him. He nudged me onto the deck where we were unseen by those ashore. "The cap has a nose for trouble, and we might be in it. We have to load the cannons."

"What?!"

He led the way below, toward the front of the hold. "You told me to do the right thing. Well, this is the right thing." He stopped and faced me. "To my way of thinking, anyway."

He hurried onward; I followed. He came to a secure door, unlocked it, and flung it open. Inside were barrels upon barrels neatly stacked, each bearing the label National Munitions, Inc.

I'd seen a few of these barrels topside during the mock cannon firing. "Gunpowder?"

He gazed at the huge cache with visible awe and nodded. "Let's each grab one."

"But . . . you're not going to . . ."

He hefted one into my arms. "If the captain says so."

"But what puts *him* in the right?"

"The guns, I suppose."

We loaded the cannons on the landward side — they were aimed right at the plaza where most of the crowds had gathered.

Of course I wondered what the devil I was doing, aiding and abetting a pack of scoundrels — or at least one scoundrel and his accomplice — but then again, Andi was out there in the company of the captain, and if any plan to save the captain would save *her . . .*

There had to be something right about that.

Regardless, pragmatically speaking, whatever action we took had to be preset without delay if it were to succeed when the time came, so having no time to fret about moralities, I helped fill the powder bags and rammed them down the bores.

Where was our ammunition? Blast Scalarag! He drew a blank and left finding that up to me.

Andi could smell barbecue even through her parrot head. The dining plaza was a town square with a clear view of the wharf and the ships tied there. Folks sat at tables while the serving wenches scurried about with trays of drinks and sandwiches.

At a lone table on the edge of the plaza, two men sat having lunch and a beer. Thatch made a beeline for that table. "Keep up," he told Andi, "and have a good look at these two." He circled around the table to face the two men, with her beside him.

And she walked right into her nightmare, right into *that night:* the wrinkly blonde with death in his eyes. The stone-faced Asian with the gleaming knife. Running for her life as Ben Cardiff ran for his, her body, his body, pummeled and thrown to a slow, drowning death.

There they sat, the blond man, the big Asian man, looking so casual, nibbling on sandwiches, sipping beer. Thatch engaged the blond man in conversation about booking tour groups for the pirate show, how well the season was going, where all these extra hats and scarves came from. She couldn't concentrate on the words, only on not shaking, not fainting, not screaming.

The blond man introduced Mr. Ling, a big investment banker from Hong Kong. Ling looked just as Norwig described him: cold as ice and ruthless. He looked at Andi only once and, seeing only a silly parrot, looked back at the captain. The captain was suggesting a group picture, perhaps with an official *Predator* captain's hat. The killer smiled as if he knew something.

The blond man smiled, too. "Lots of tour groups lined up," he said. "Very good gate this weekend." He had a shirt with ST. CLEMENS TOURS embossed over the pocket, and above the embossing he wore a name badge: Bennett Piel.

Bennett Piel!

Her legs lost their strength. She stumbled backward a few waddled steps, reached out and found a palm tree to steady herself.

Banana Peel!

Chapter 19
Mutiny

A sound, something like a cry, escaped Andi's mouth before she could contain it. She disguised it with a parrot squawk. She flapped her arms a little. It drew a look and an impatient smile from Bennett Piel.

The captain brought up future plans and recovered Piel's attention.

Come on, act like a parrot. With all she had within her she stayed in character, squawked a little, and sidled away to give them space, to come up with a plan . . .

To get to a buffet table and a bowl of fruit.

She squawked a greeting to two dining couples — the women were the ugliest she'd seen in a while — and helped herself to a banana.

She waddled back, moving behind the two men and facing the captain.

Thatch talked with the men about the *Predator.* A good ship, she was. Ready for haul out next month. He had improvements in mind, budget allowing.

She held up the banana hoping he would see it.

He may have. Apparently he was getting another message from Sparks. He took the earring out of his pocket.

She grappled and fumbled with the banana. It was hard to get the peeling started with feathery parrot wing-hands.

The captain pulled his hair back to expose his ear and then began to open the loop on the earring.

She got the peeling started and frantically pulled the segments down.

He looked at her.

With the banana peeled halfway down, she pointed at it while pointing at Bennett Piel with the feathery finger of her other hand. *That's the guy!*

The captain stayed in character, smiling, listening to the two men, looking from one to the other as the color drained from his face. He put the earring back in his pocket, and managing a weak flourish, said, "Gentlemen, the tide waits for no man. Adieu, and fair winds!"

He beckoned to Andi with a glance and started walking back toward the ship. Andi was glad enough to follow.

They didn't get far.

"Thatch!" Piel shouted from behind them. With that came the clicking of a gun.

Click! Clack! Clicklick Clatter! Like dozens of traps springing, the tourists, male and female, sprang from their chairs and trained their guns on Thatch's crew. Others on the rim of the plaza formed a closed circle, brandishing weapons. The ugly women turned out to be men, their hairy arms holding pistols.

"You won't be walking off that easy," said Bennett Piel.

Thatch and Andi turned slowly. Piel stood gloating. So did Mr. Ling.

The captain didn't seem surprised. "So it is as I hear: 'We laugh at honor and are shocked to find traitors in our midst.' "

"Honor can't stand up to a lucrative arrangement," said Piel. "The smart ones know a better deal when it's offered."

"Smart and a murderin' scum! A big money man from Hong Kong, is he? 'Twas you and Ling pitched Ben Cardiff to the brine!"

"If it's any consolation, we didn't mean to kill him. But he did take us for a million!" He nodded toward Mr. Ling. "Nevertheless, my friend here has promised me a fat future to finish this business any way we can. Mr. Ling wants your ship, Thatch, and all that gadgetry you have onboard!"

The captain studied Mr. Ling a moment. "The Gate, I presume? I've heard tell of you around St. Clemens, and oh, you can persuade, I'll lay to that." The captain met the eyes of his men, then looked at Piel and Ling. "But will you leave a bloodied island for the law to find?" The captain slowly drew his pistol. "That we'll try." He looked around. "I'd find cover inside," he drolly advised the costumed servers and staff.

He didn't have to tell them twice.

Thatch's crew drew their period weapons, clicking back the hammers all around, their muzzles mirroring the ones aimed at them.

From the deck of the *Predator,* Scalarag and I could see the frozen tableau of some fifty mock tourists brandishing weapons and Thatch's crew brandishing weapons right back.

"This is insane!" I said.

"This is money," said Scalarag. "Thatch guessed right. Someone made Piel a better offer."

The Gate, I thought. This was their sneaky style. "They . . . they can't just kill each other!"

"Neither has a winning hand, so who knows where it goes from here?"

Oh, Andi! She had such a gift for being caught in the middle. "Cheerios," I said.

"What?"

"Ammunition for the cannons. We have Cheerios."

Mr. Ling broke into a smile. "So now we parlay, eh? And what have you to bargain with, Thatch?" He spoke loudly so all could hear, "Men of the *Predator*! Whatever Thatch is paying, I'll make it double. All I want is that ship and what's aboard. Hand it over and walk away alive — and richer!"

There was a telling pause. Both sides still aimed their weapons, but Thatch's men were thinking about it.

"Mutiny . . ." a crewman muttered.

"Mutiny?" bellowed the captain, striding before them. "And go home lesser men? Can honor be bought that easily?"

Rock leaped to the first large limb of a tree, waved his sword, and hollered out, "Why stand you all tangled in the stays? Was it honor filled your purses? The *gold's* the thing, mateys, and gold buys the wiser! Take it now, live to tell it, and live happy! Mutiny!"

There was a cheer, but it was halfhearted.

■ ■ ■ ■

A knife came from somewhere and pinned Rock's sleeve to the tree! That drew everyone's attention to none other than Norwig the Bean, standing near the captain. He jerked his head at Piel and Ling. "And you'll believe the word of scum like these, when the first word is pistols up your nose? What do you know, mates, if it ain't the captain and *his* word? I say we stick by the old man and let tomorrow come as always! Mutiny against the mutiny!"

Another cheer, but that was halfhearted, too.

Oof! Spikenose, like a wiry little spider on a web, swung in on a rope and kicked Norwig aside, taking his place in the center. He had a pistol in one hand and a saber in the other and twirled them both to get everyone's attention. "Come on, guys, get a clue! Thatch has been using all of us to make himself rich, and The Gate only wants to kill us and take what's ours! Can't you see this whole thing is falling apart? This whole pirate thing, it's over, and I'm sick of it anyway! Listen! I'm the purser with signatory rights on the bank account. Let's split the company assets and get out. Let Thatch and The Gate fight over the rest! Mutiny against the mutiny against the mutiny!"

That brought an intelligent murmur.

Harry the Scar stepped into the center and gave a shrill whistle. The murmuring stopped. "Just walk away with the money, is that it? That simple? Any of you want to lay me odds the Feds aren't onto us by now? They've gotta be tracking these Gate guys and they've got to know where most of our money's come from. You don't think they're all over us, too? Listen, we didn't invent the technology, right? We were just working the ship, doing the shows, right? But we know about the captain and now we know about The Gate, so let's go to the Feds, turn 'em in, and cut a deal." He had to count on his fingers as he said, "Mutiny against the mutiny against the mutiny against the mutiny!"

What was this, *parlay ad absurdum*? Andi looked around, wondering who was going to speak next when —

SQUAWK! A huge hand from behind grabbed her by the scruff of her costume.

It was Sparks's voice! "All this blabbering

and you don't know what's right under your nose!"

He held her up, half hanging by her costume, her parrot feet barely touching the ground. He yanked the goofy parrot head off her and tossed it aside. Her unconstrained hair exploded from her head like a red firework.

Most everyone gave a little gasp or mutter at the sight of her, but Piel and Ling stood silent as lights came on behind their eyes. Piel even mouthed the words, *The red-headed girl!*

"Ah," said Sparks, "so you know what I'm holding!" He put a knife to her neck. "Here's the real prize: Everything Ben knew and you paid for, it's in her head — and that includes where your million dollars went. So here's my offer: Make me captain. Give me the crew and the *Predator,* and we'll come over to your side and hand you the girl." He dragged her around a little, making sure all the crew could see the prize and his knife to her throat. "Can't make up your minds? Take a good look at her! Follow me, I follow them, they get the girl, we keep the *Predator,* and we all get richer."

Spikenose looked into space, counting, "A mutiny against the mutiny against the mu-

tiny . . ."
"Shut up!"

There must have been something about a knife to her throat that Andi found disagreeable. With abandon and bravado she must have learned from Ben, she burst out, "By the powers, ya swab, you're as sharp as paint, you are! Be the captain? Is that why you scrambled the system and Jean-Pierre's brain? You were hoping the cap would put on that earring as always, but Jean-Pierre wore it that day, and 'twas his bad fortune!"

He tightened his grip. "Hold your tongue, or I'll cut it out."

"And toss it to Piel and Ling? Oh, they'll pay you well for that!"

Click! Oh, how she hated that sound!

Sparks spun around, dragging her with him.

The captain was pointing his pistol at Sparks, steady, steely-eyed. In his free hand he held the earring. "So that's why you hoped I'd put on the earring today. You were planning for me what fell to Jean-Pierre." He shouted to the men of the *Predator,* "This man's killed one of your own hoping to finish me! Would you have him wearing the captain's hat?"

Sparks sneered. "This from the man who

scoffs at truth?"

"The cap's speaking straight and I be the one that knows," cried Andi. " 'Twas Ben left the system running when he jumped ship so he could send his mind to Piel and Ling. The system was ticking like a fine clock when I bought the earring and it sent Ben's mind to me along with his killing." She nodded toward Piel and Ling. "And the faces of his killers!"

Piel and Ling were watching, listening. Ling said matter-of-factly, "We *will* want the girl."

"Aye, you hear that, Sparks? So put a thought to it! You cut my neck, you kill the head that's on it, and what do you know but half the system? It's Ben's in my head, and Ben knows the whole of it."

"Meaning . . ." said the captain, "take away the girl and the whole matter ends." The captain shifted his aim so Andi could see right down the bore. "You know half the system, Sparks, but she knows all of it. You know how to scramble it, but she knows how to fix it. Without her, the system's no good . . . and neither is your deal, and what does The Gate go away with?"

Sparks tightened his grip on her. "Give it up, Thatch. You can't do it."

"Ask Jean-Pierre." The captain's voice was

low and even. "You were there. You know I can. You know I will."

CHAPTER 20
THE BATTLE

Lighter in hand, I reached to ignite the vent hole of the cannon.

Scalarag blocked me. "This isn't it."

I nearly struck him. "Isn't what?"

"The moment."

"*What* moment?"

"You'll know. Keep an eye on 'em. Gotta go below, fire up the engines."

I'll know?

The captain called out to his men as he aimed his pistol at Andi's head. "You've all sailed with me, so what say you? What rule's to stop me? From what truth comes the shame?"

He waited, looked them in the eyes. Not a single man gave an answer. Andi began to tremble.

The captain called again, "Can you not tell me? Where's the wrong in taking the girl's life?"

One wimpy little swab offered, "We don't get the money . . ." and a whiny murmur of agreement passed through the crew.

The captain watched them a moment, gave them time, but all he got was silence.

At last, with resignation, he raised the muzzle of his pistol toward the sky and uncocked the hammer. "So . . . if there be a truth, it's of a truth that you have none, and *I* took it from you. Very well, then. Let the truth fall to me, and *I'll* be the man." He tucked the pistol into his belt, then removed his hat and held it high. "Sparks is your captain!"

No one cheered.

"Hip! Hip!"

Two said *Hurray.*

"Hip! Hip!"

Same two.

Sparks's hands were occupied holding and threatening Andi. Thatch did the honors, placing the hat on Sparks's head. He then took hold of Andi and pulled her gently away . . . just as Sparks went berserk.

He screamed, his eyes rolled, he held his head as if it were bursting; he toppled, rolled on the ground. The hat came off, but it had done its work. Sparks would never be clever or conniving again.

Captain Thatch snatched up the hat and,

before putting it back on, surreptitiously removed the earring he'd concealed in the lining. He dropped the earring, crushed it under his boot, and replaced his hat.

This was it! The moment!

Running along, I touched fire to the vent hole of Cannon One, then Two, then Three. Each gun unleashed a fiery, percussive thunder, recoiling against its tethers. The explosions quaked my insides; the whole ship rocked under my feet.

The town square disappeared behind a cloud of blue smoke and oat-colored haze.

The captain knew the moment as well. He held Andi tightly against him, his back to the blast, as five hundred boxes' worth of Cheerios, reduced to crumbles and dust, blasted the whole village like a sandstorm. The stuff got into eyes, stung faces, and threw everyone into a panic.

Which was just what Thatch wanted. "Run, lass, run!"

Andi kicked off her parrot feet and sprinted for the wharf, winged arms covering her face through the rain of oats. The captain, face sheltered under his hat, stayed right on her heels. Passing the photo booth, Andi grabbed a scarf from the rack of Readers, then dashed onto the wharf and up the gangplank.

"Cast off! Cast off!" Thatch shouted, stomping up the gangplank behind her.

I cast off the last stern line even as Andi and the captain landed on the deck.

"The system's yours, lass," I heard the captain say as he threw off the gangplank.

Andi ran up to me and handed me the scarf. "Here, put this one on!" Then she dashed below.

A Reader, no doubt. A signal for help? I took off my old scarf and put on the new one.

The smoke was clearing. Some of Thatch's crew were occupied with Sparks, who was leaping on the tables, waving his knife around, and throwing things. The others were scattered like windfall about the town square, bereft of a leader — or a moral imperative.

Ling was filled with purpose, however. I could see all of his rogues running our way, some squinting and teary-eyed from the powdered oats, some clear-eyed enough to fire their weapons. Bullets pinged and chipped the bulwarks, the companion. I crawled for any cover I could find as the engines below rumbled and the big hull lurched away from the wharf.

Below, Andi tapped out lines of command and code at the console. Once again, the computer beeped, drives whirred to life, and the very attractive lady pirate appeared on the screen, presenting a menu of links and sub-pages.

Ready.

"Oh!" said Audrey Snow, viewing the screen in Key West.

"Oh my word," said Zedekiah, seeing what she saw. "Oh my word!"

Tank, Brenda, and Daniel came running from different parts of the house.

Zedekiah was ecstatic. "The system has unscrambled, and not only that, it's let us in! We're getting a signal from one of the Readers!"

"Way cool!" said Tank.

And that was the last thing said before they all stared at each other, thinking the same thing.

Tank looked at Brenda, then Daniel. "I'll do it."

Audrey picked up the earring. "How can we be sure?"

"Everything looks stable," said Zedekiah. "Only . . . good heavens! The Reader must be aboard a speedboat. I've never seen a sailing ship go so fast!"

Tank didn't have pierced ears. He just pressed the earring against his ear. His eyes widened with shock. "Whoa! WHOA!" He backed off, staring at the earring in his hand.

Zedekiah got quite a scare. "Hello? Are you still with us? What is your name? Do you know where you are?"

"I'm Matt Damon," he answered. "Just kidding. I'm okay, but boy, what a ride!" He pressed the earring against his head again. "Man oh MAN!" He almost lost his balance. Audrey and Brenda guided him to a chair. He jerked, he leaned, he ducked as if the chair were a toboggan at the Olympics. "Woo-hooo! We are *flying*!"

Well, of course Tank was inside my head, standing next to Captain Thatch aboard the *Predator* as the ship defied its design and anyone's good sense, plowing through the water at reckless, breakneck speed, lurching with nauseating power over the swells and kicking up a violent wake. The shrouds were humming, the masts and yards groaning.

Thatch gripped the wheel, a strange, gleeful look on his face as he pointed the bow toward a small island a mile away. "Bindy's

Mayday, they call it! Very nice channel on the other side with little room for ships to pass. Let 'em follow us there!"

I looked astern. Not more than a mile back, the *Riqueza* was giving chase. Apparently, it had oversized engine power as well since it was gaining on us.

"This ain't real!" said Tank, seeing one three-masted ship from the deck of another, plowing along with a bone in its teeth though its sails were furled. "It's the pirate show, but we didn't see this part."

"Whose thoughts and impressions are you receiving?" Zedekiah Snow wanted to know.

Meanwhile, I was trying to talk some sense to that loony captain before he got us all killed, all the while gaining new insight into where the stereotypical sailor got his language.

"Uh . . . angry, scolding, kind of know-it-all . . ." said Tank. "Big words . . . whoa! Bad words, too." He grinned with recognition. "It's the professor."

Thatch grabbed me. "Take the wheel."

Horrors! The man was daffy! "I will do no such thing!"

"Trust your captain!" He pulled me over and put my hands on the wheel. "She likes to bear away to starboard without her sails. Make her mind. Circle to the right of that rock sticking up, just to the right of Bindy's, you see it?"

I was holding the reins of a bucking monster, fighting for control. I nodded as if we were having a reasonable conversation.

"Stay clear of it, then duck behind the island and into the channel. Scalarag's giving you full throttle."

"Full — ?!"

"Whoa!" Tank laughed. "He is scared poopless! Sorry . . ."

The captain raised his spyglass to his eye. "Aye, it's Ling's men, all right. They won't let us get away, no way in heaven or hell." He set the spyglass aside and headed for the companion, leaving me alone at the wheel.

"What are you going to do?" I hollered over my shoulder, my hands welded to the wheel.

"The right thing, if God be my Judge" was all he said as he went down the stairs to his quarters.

The rock to the right of Bindy's Mayday was a black, jagged tooth, a perfect hull opener. I veered farther to the right to be sure we missed it, then cut a gradual turn to port to head around the island. Now I could see another island beyond this one, and between them, a narrow channel. I steered for the channel and, looking back, saw the *Riqueza* had veered to port to circle the island from the other direction.

They were going to head us off.

Zedekiah Snow activated another computer, another program, and a real time map of the Caribbean appeared with a tiny blip representing the location of the Reader. "Well, folks, there it is."

Tank remained in the chair, eyes closed, experiencing the lurching and dashing of the *Predator,* the wind in my face, the salt spray in my eyes, the roar of the wind in the rigging — and the *Riqueza* rounding the other end of the island to intercept us. "He's not having fun. There's something really heavy going down."

Brenda stood. "We've got to get down there!"

Tank pulled the earring away from his head, blinked to get his own senses back, and said, "Andi's grandpa! He's got a jet or a chopper — probably has a boat, too!"

Brenda grabbed her cell phone.

■ ■ ■ ■

"So you've found your friends, whoever they be?"

Andi was startled to hear the captain's voice behind her, but not alarmed. By now it was clear the captain knew it all: the inquiry from another system, the access code, her responding, and of course her fitting me with a Reader scarf to send a signal to whoever it was. "I think it's them."

The captain stepped up and looked over her shoulder. "Look at the tag on the inquiry. You've been queried by someone in Florida." He laughed. "And I can name that party in one guess: Zedekiah Snow! Your friends are in good hands. Come to think of it, so are you! Be assured, lass, they know where you are. Here." He offered her an inflatable life vest.

The way the ship was rocking and pounding, the vest seemed to her an entirely good idea. She put it on.

"Now I need you topside."

"For you, Professor" came the captain's voice over the roar of the wind.

The captain had returned with Andi and was offering an inflatable life vest. As he took the wheel, I slipped on the vest and clipped it tight.

"Ah!" he laughed, sighting the *Riqueza* at the far end of the channel and closing fast. "Piel's thinking hasn't changed. He's at the helm of that boat with Ling at his side, no doubt, and doing what I thought! So how's your honor, professor? How's your truth?"

The face I made must have been hideous. "I fail to see how that pertains to our situation."

The captain grinned, which I did not find amusing. "So we never talked about it, or you weren't listening? It has all come down to the rules, and it's time to face it: Wherever it comes from, we'll need a little honor . . . in our situation."

"I would prefer a level head and better driving."

"Oh, would you now?"

He reached for the engine telegraph and signaled Scalarag to ease the engines back to Dead Slow Ahead, the first sane choice he'd made thus far, in my estimation. The *Predator* slowed, although I noticed the *Riqueza* did not.

"Well," I started to say, still eyeing the *Riqueza,* "a reasonable first step —"

Andi screamed. I turned just in time to see the captain make his way to the rail, holding her aloft as she kicked and struggled.

What — ?

No! I ran, with no other thought than to get her out of his hands.

Too late! I reached the railing only to see her splash into the waves. Her life vest triggered and inflated, bearing her back to the surface where she splashed helplessly, the moving ship leaving her in its wake.

I was about to leap in after her when something bumped me. "I suppose you'll be wanting this?" said the captain.

He was offering me a bulky package, rather heavy. The label read *Life Raft.* With no hesitation I clutched the package to my chest, swung my legs over the rail, and dropped into the sea.

I was still beneath the surface, eyes shut in a grimace and breath held, when the water triggered my life vest and the raft and they inflated, the life vest hugging me as I popped to the surface and the life raft unfolding and forming within my reach. I grabbed on and clambered in, blinking the sting of salt from my eyes as I searched the expansive waters for Andi.

There! I could see the yellow flotation around her neck, the red of her hair. She was so distant, so minuscule, bobbing, intermittently vanishing between the swells. But she was waving. She was safe.

The roar of the *Predator,* again at full throttle, was fading in the distance. I turned to see Thatch looking back and giving a farewell wave, satisfied, no doubt, that we would be all right. Then he looked ahead, closing on the *Riqueza* as if he fully intended to ram her.

Which, I still marvel to report, he did. I suppose Piel, at the helm of the *Riqueza,* expected him to turn tail and run, or perhaps shoot it out, or surrender, being so outgunned. But Thatch would not turn away, nor would he slow down. With cunning and skill, he even anticipated every evasive maneuver the *Riqueza* made, staying in her path no matter what she did.

First came the ball of fire and the flying debris — lumber, sails, canvas, and rigging exploding skyward — and then, a second or two later, the roar and shock of the explosion. I was transfixed. Stunned.

"Hey!" Andi called. She was kicking and paddling my way.

I assembled a plastic oar that came with the life raft and paddled toward her, all the while staring over my shoulder, trying to fathom what I'd just seen, even when nothing remained but steaming embers on the water.

Epilogue

With both of us paddling the life raft, Andi and I easily made the sandy beach of Bindy's Mayday, and it was the need to depressurize, I imagine, to make some sense of all that had happened, that launched us back into the discussion we started on the *Barbee Jay* but never finished: Was there an ultimate truth and therefore a basis for right and wrong, and was the existence of God necessary for such a truth to exist? What happened aboard the *Predator* — everything from our being kidnapped to the horrendous destruction we barely avoided in the channel — amounted to a practical experiment. The devil was in the data, of course, and our differing interpretations. As a result, three hours passed as mere minutes, the intensity of our debate broken only by the sound of an approaching airplane.

"Hey!" Andi cried. "It's the *Silver Lady*!"

It was the nickname given to her grandfather's floatplane. We could see Tank, Brenda, and Daniel waving from the plane's windows as it set down in the channel like a big aluminum goose.

I thought it best to wrap up our discussion before we rowed out to meet it. I granted her the possibility — since it brought her comfort — that nature, physics, and morality could make sense because there was a Superior Mind behind it all; she granted me the fact that, despite the danger and with no thought of what a supposed God might require, I still jumped into the sea to save her.

As for the captain . . . though I assumed he'd acted upon a spark of good in his own nature, Andi preferred to think our being there may have fanned that spark to life. Well . . . either way, I suppose.

But most of all, I summarized feelings I felt no need to explain. "All things considered," I said to my assistant, "I am boundlessly glad and relieved that you're safe."

She smiled and nodded. "Same here."

I'll close my recounting of the tale with a certainty and an *un*certainty.

The certainty: Zedekiah Snow was a decent fellow — at least, as one such as myself might measure such a quality as "decent" — and knew his own technology well enough to isolate memories and impressions in any brain that were not native to that brain. In Andi's case, he quickly identified the memories and impressions of Ben Cardiff and neutralized them in a two-second treatment. Andi is well again, no longer plagued by any past tampering with her mind.

The *un*certainty: While we were lifting off from the channel, we flew over the blackened debris where the two ships had collided and saw on the nearest shore a familiar little craft: the *Predator*'s wooden boat that first carried Andi and I to the ship. It couldn't have gotten there unless someone had rowed it. Had the captain granted Scalarag a dismissal to safety as he had granted us? To add to that, the ships were quite a distance away, too far to tell if Captain Horatio Thatch was still on board when they exploded.

At any rate, to our knowledge, neither man has ever been found . . . and perhaps that was the whole intention.

A strange thing, honor. I'm sure more discussions will follow.

Fair winds.

■ ■ ■ ■

HYBRIDS

ANGELA HUNT

■ ■ ■ ■

CHAPTER 1

I stood at the bottom of the Tampa airport's escalator and searched for Tank with an odd mingling of excitement and dread. Excitement, because I hadn't seen him, Brenda, or Daniel in several weeks, not since we parted after our adventure in the Caribbean. Dread, because each time I met Tank after a separation, his face lit up like Times Square on New Year's and I didn't know what to do about that. I loved him like a brother, but clearly, he felt something more for me . . . feelings I didn't think I could ever reciprocate.

I blew out a breath and studied the passengers on the escalator. Most wore the look of people who'd spent too much time in a cramped space, but a few faces were smiling, probably because they were meeting the pretty young women who held welcome signs for the various cruise lines. Tampa was a major port, and who wouldn't look forward to a few days at sea? As long as we didn't encounter pirates, even I might be tempted to board a sailboat again.

"Andi!"

I smiled up at Tank, who seemed to span the entire width of the escalator as he waved. I pointed to the baggage carousel for his airline, then walked toward it. Tank was loud, enthusiastic, and eager — not exactly the sort of person I wanted to meet in front of all those people coming down the escalator.

I had no sooner arrived at the baggage area than I felt my feet leave the ground. Tank had come up from behind and wrapped me in a bear hug, and his overly rambunctious greeting lifted me at least two feet off the floor. "Andi, it's so good to see you," he said. "I didn't think we'd ever land."

"I'm glad you did. Now, will you please put me down?"

He lowered me gently, then stepped to my side, arms extended as if he planned to hug me again. I lifted my hand and patted his chest in an effort to hold him off. "Brenda and Daniel came in yesterday and spent today at Disney World. They'll probably be back around dinner time."

"Sure was nice of your grandparents to let

us use their house again." Tank picked up the gym bag he'd dropped behind me. "After our last visit, I wasn't sure they'd want to have us again."

I smiled, not needing to be reminded of the last time we'd gathered at the beach house. In the space of a few days, we encountered dead fish and birds, alien creatures, and a green slime that ended up nearly killing me. I hoped *this* little vaycay would bring nothing but the rest and relaxation I'd promised the others.

"How's the professor?" Tank asked.

I glanced up to see if he was asking out of concern or mere politeness, but honest curiosity shone from Tank's eyes. I had to admit — whatever else he was, Tank was a genuinely good guy. He cared about people, even the professor, who seemed to try everyone else's patience.

"He's good," I said, tempering my voice. "Working hard on a presentation he's supposed to deliver tomorrow at the University of Tampa."

Tank frowned. "What's wrong? Something's bothering you, I can tell."

I hesitated. I hadn't mentioned my concerns to Brenda because I didn't want to ruin her plans for Disney *and* because I was hoping my worries were only the result of a hyperactive imagination. But I couldn't get anything by Tank. . . .

"I'm a little worried about the professor, to tell you the truth. His paper is supposed to be on dimensionality and quantum mechanics, with an emphasis on multiple universes. He finished his first draft weeks ago, but he keeps muttering and tinkering with it." I shrugged. "I don't know. He just seems . . . unsatisfied, and that's not like him."

"Ain't he a perfectionist?"

"He is . . . but this dissatisfaction seems different. I can't quite put my finger on why, but something's going on in his head, something he's not sharing with me. And that's not like him, either."

Tank's brow furrowed for a moment, then he grinned. "Don't worry. When the team is together, we always seem to figure things out." He draped his arm casually over my shoulder, then nodded to the bulky mountain coming down the conveyor belt. "That's my bag."

"Good grief." I gawked at the long case. "What is that, a trombone case?"

"Metal detector." Tank grinned. "I've heard that you can find a fortune on the beach — rings, coins, all kinds of stuff. Since we're just gonna be hangin' out at your grandparents' place, I thought I might pick up a new hobby."

I resisted the urge to roll my eyes. "Whatever. Grab your new toy, and I'll meet you on the curb."

Brenda's rental car was parked in the driveway when Tank and I pulled up. Daniel bounded out of the house as I got out of the car. "Space Mountain!" he said, his eyes as wide as saucers. "And more pirates!"

Brenda grinned as she stepped onto the front porch. "I see you had no trouble finding Cowboy."

"Hard to miss him," I quipped, then I bent to Daniel's eye level. "I didn't expect to see you so soon. I thought you'd stay at the Magic Kingdom all day."

Brenda gave Tank a firm slug to the upper arm, then threw me a look. "Can you say *overstimulation*? I figured we should leave before Daniel short-circuited. If the weather looks good and I can stretch my budget, maybe we'll go back another day this week. But we had a great time."

I glanced toward the front door. "Is the professor . . . ?"

"Locked in his room." Brenda lifted a brow. "I don't know what he's doin' in there, but I can hear him muttering behind the door. Kinda creepy, if you want to know the truth. I know he tends to be antisocial, but today he's taking *grumpy* to a whole new level."

I sighed. "Let's all give him some space. I think he's worried about his presentation tomorrow. When it's over, he'll relax. Maybe."

I didn't tell her about my frustrations — about how he'd taken to locking himself in his office and hadn't let me read his latest paper. I didn't want to invade his privacy and confess that I'd pressed my ear to his office door and heard him sobbing. Cursing, too, at times, and at least twice I'd heard the sound of heavy objects being thrown across the room.

I thought the professor and I were close, but apparently we weren't close enough to share whatever secrets he'd been hiding. But how was I supposed to do my job if he closed himself off from me?

I opened the trunk and looked around to make sure I hadn't forgotten anything, as Tank had grabbed his bag and his metal detector and headed into the house. I turned to follow, but couldn't help noticing a pair of children on the sidewalk across the street. They appeared to be about nine or ten, and they were standing motionless, neither of them speaking. They were staring at me.

Something about them sent a chill up the ladder of my spine. I couldn't remember the last time I'd seen kids of that age who weren't fidgeting, running, or talking a mile a minute. We saw a lot of children on this street, most of them tourists whose families had come to enjoy Florida's sandy beaches. But I'd never seen any kids like these.

I stepped forward to study them more closely. Something else about them seemed odd — their clothes. Most kids in the area wore tee shirts, baggy shorts, and flip-flops or sneakers. These children were wearing long dark pants, oversized long-sleeved shirts, and dark shoes. Like children from some reclusive sect that didn't believe in showing too much skin. . . .

I lifted my chin, forced a smile, and wiggled my fingers at them, then turned and walked toward the front door. But before going inside, I threw a glance over my shoulder. The children had gone. Moved on, I supposed, to explore some other neighborhood.

And with their disappearance, I felt an overwhelming wave of relief.

CHAPTER 2

The kid from Perfect Pasta had just delivered orders of spaghetti, lasagna, and pepperoni pizza when I spotted my grandparents' neighbor, Mrs. Diaz, waddling toward our front door.

"Tank!" I called, struggling to handle the bag of food and a large pizza box while Abby, my chocolate Lab, danced at my feet. "Will you take these while I pay for this stuff?"

Tank came to my aid in a flash, and after paying the delivery guy, I walked to the edge of the porch to greet Mrs. Diaz.

"Andi, so good to see you." She smiled, then handed me a small package. "This was delivered to our house by mistake. I think it's your grandfather's medicine."

I checked the label — sure enough, the mail carrier had left it in the wrong box. "Very nice of you to bring it over, Mrs. Diaz. Especially —" I grinned — "in your condition."

"What are neighbors for?" She smiled, then rubbed her very pregnant belly. "The walking does me good. I'm trying to convince this baby to make an early appearance."

"When are you due?"

"Two more weeks." She gave me a rueful smile. "But he's strong and healthy, so he can come any time. Fine with me."

"I hope he comes soon, then. And I'll bet your husband is thrilled."

"He's always wanted a boy. Machismo, you know." She rolled her eyes, then turned toward her house. "Tell your grandparents I said hello."

"They're in New York for the week, but I'll tell them," I called. "And I hope that baby comes soon."

I went back inside the house, dropped Sabba's package onto the foyer table, then joined the others in the dining room. Tank, Brenda, Daniel, and even the professor had already gathered around the table. Brenda had taken charge, which was fine with me, and was passing out silverware, paper plates, and napkins. Daniel had sunk into the chair at the head of the table, leaving the professor to take the empty chair at the other end.

I smothered a smile. He might be nervous

about his speech, but the professor was not so preoccupied that he'd let a ten-year-old challenge his right to sit at the head of the table.

"Sorry," I told them, dropping into an empty chair. "Let's eat."

"Just a minute." Tank bowed his head as he always did. "Lord, thanks for this food, and keep us safe during this time together. Amen."

The professor cleared his throat as we began to pass dishes and serve ourselves. "Before the conversation drifts into mundane topics, I'd like to welcome everyone. And while I certainly won't demand that you attend my lecture tomorrow, I thought you all might like to come — especially since we've had firsthand experience with other dimensions and universes."

"We'll be there," I said, shooting a sharp glance around the table in case anyone was thinking of sleeping in. "We'll be cheering you on."

"Thank you, Andi, but this group's quiet, polite, and discreet presence will be more than enough."

"Are you sure Daniel can handle it?" A line trenched the center of Brenda's forehead. "He's still a little amped up from seeing Mickey Mouse. That stuffy atmosphere might be too much for him."

"Nice try, Barnick, but you're not getting out of this one," the professor answered. "I think you might actually profit from learning a few things you obviously skipped in high school."

Brenda scowled at the professor, then grinned at me. "Actually, I skipped most of high school. And I get along just fine."

"Be that as it may," the professor continued, pressing his hands together, "I thought I might take a few minutes tonight to acquaint you with a few elementary principles so you won't be totally lost at the symposium."

"Professor, I'm not sure —" I began, but Tank cut me off.

"I'm listenin'," Tank said, one side of his mouth bulging with pizza. "I don't know nothin' about that stuff, but if you can help me feel like less of a fool, I'm up for it."

I picked up my fork and cut a bite of lasagna. If the others were willing to endure a lecture with their meal, how could I object?

"I know you understand the idea of three dimensions," the professor began. "Objects in our world — like that salt shaker there — have width, height, and breadth. A line, however, has only one dimension — length."

"Flatland," Brenda said. "I don't remember much about high school, but I do remember that book. Some characters in the book were lines, and if you looked at them sideways, they were long. If you looked at them straight on, they looked like little dots." She snorted. "Crazy stuff."

"Um — yes. Exactly." The professor nodded. "Flatland was a two-dimensional world. We are most familiar with three dimensions."

"I remember something," Tank said. "I forget what movie it was, but Superman takes the bad guys and puts them in these flat things and spins them into space. They're trapped and can't get out."

The professor gave Tank a quizzical look — clearly, he wasn't a Superman fan — then sighed. "Actually, tomorrow I'll be talking about dimensions that exist beyond the three we know."

"Hang on." Brenda's dark eyes gleamed with interest. "Are you going to be talkin' about the beings Daniel can see? Angels and such?"

The professor shifted his gaze to Daniel, who was focused on plucking pepperoni from his pizza. "Not exactly. First, I'm going to discuss the fourth dimension, which is time. We are accustomed to living moment by moment, existing for a certain time in a certain place. But if you could exist in the fourth dimension of time, you might look like a long worm that snaked through all the spaces where you've ever spent even a single second. The worm would be small at one end, where you occupied a smaller space because you were a child, and it would grow to the size of your adult body until the place where your lifeline ends."

Tank sucked at the inside of his cheek for a moment, then shook his head. "Unless your lifeline doesn't end. Maybe it just transfers out of one dimension and moves to a higher one. Maybe it moves to a place where angels and demons live, or maybe it goes to a place even higher than that. You don't really know where a soul goes after death, do you? And you can't prove anything, because no one has really died — I mean, *really* died — and come back to tell us about it." A confident grin spread across his face. "Well, except for the one guy, but the professor doesn't wanna believe in Him."

The professor threw me a glance of helpless appeal, then sighed and picked up his fork. "I think I've prepared you enough," he said, sliding his fork into a mound of spaghetti. "Just remember — tomorrow's lecture is not a forum for discussion. If you have questions" — he glared at Tank — "keep them to yourself. We can talk about them at dinner tomorrow night."

I shot Tank a warning look. Why was he trying to rattle the professor's cage on the night before his big speech? But Tank only gave me a wide-eyed look of innocence as the professor spun spaghetti onto his fork.

CHAPTER 3

Tank stopped halfway into the row of padded seats and turned to me. "Are you sure they don't serve popcorn at these things?"

"I'm sure." I pushed him forward. "You're supposed to take notes, not feed your face. So keep moving, please."

Tank sighed heavily, but I had a feeling he was actually looking forward to the professor's presentation. Brenda and Daniel filed in after me, then we made ourselves comfortable in the big, comfy chairs of the university's auditorium.

I took advantage of the house lights and looked around. Lots of scholarly-looking men and women in the audience, lots of jeans and elbow-patched jackets on people who looked as though they spent a lot of time reading. More men than women. Brenda and I actually stood out. So did Daniel.

Daniel pulled his iPhone out of his pocket

and began to play one of his games. "Okay," Brenda said, "but you have to mute the sound."

Daniel grunted, then pressed the mute button and kept playing. Someone lowered the house lights and a hush fell over the crowd. An expectant atmosphere filled the room, the same sort of anticipation you might experience at a beauty pageant, a concert, or a play . . . except this would be a presentation on the relationship between dimensionality and quantum mechanics.

My fingertips began to tingle as vicarious stage fright triggered my adrenal glands.

"Is this speech any good?" Brenda whispered.

I shook my head. "No idea."

A man I didn't recognize walked onto the stage and smiled at the audience. "It is my very great pleasure," he said, "to introduce one of our nation's leading voices in scientific thought, philosophy, and sociology. Our guest this morning has more advanced degrees than I have time to read, so let me get out of the way and allow our speaker to take the stage. Ladies and gentlemen, Dr. James McKinney."

Polite applause filled the auditorium as the professor stepped onto the stage and blinked in the bright lights. Instead of proceeding immediately to the lectern as he usually did, he walked to a stool in the middle of the stage and took a seat.

"In a few months I will be sixty-one years old," he said, not even glancing at the typed pages in his hand, "and as a man enters the final seasons of his life, he has a tendency to look over the road he has traveled and question his choices — the job not taken, the pregnancy terminated, the shift in careers. The woman left behind."

Though I kept my gaze on the professor, from the corner of my eye I saw Tank look at me, his brow lifted. He wanted to know what the professor meant, but I knew no more about the professor's unusual approach than Tank did.

"Imagine," the professor continued, "that you are holding a strip of paper only one atom high and several microns long." The professor got up and set his notes on a lectern, then spread his hands as if indicating a long strip of paper. "You are holding an object that exists, for all practical purposes, in only two dimensions: height and length. Agreed?"

He looked out at the audience, and as one, we nodded.

The professor smiled. "Now take one end of your imaginary paper and join it to the other so it makes a circle. If you were a tiny sugar ant, you could travel on that paper — over its length — without ever leaving the second dimension. But if you twisted the paper, so that the upper side joined the lower side at the junction point, a sugar ant could literally cross over to the underside of that paper and enter a world of three dimensions — height, length, and width, because you would be able to travel on the *front* and *back* of the one-atom width. Correct?"

We nodded again, but less collectively this time. I glanced at Tank, whose forehead had crinkled. Brenda was thinking hard, too, and even Daniel had looked up from his electronic game.

At least no one was bored.

"Einstein said time travel should be possible," the professor went on. "All we have to do is find a way to fold dimensions so we can move from one to the other. If we discover a way to do that, a man ought to be able to choose a point early in his life and revisit it, making new choices the second time."

The professor smiled as a murmur rippled through the crowd. "Ah, now I have your attention. Yes, time is the fourth dimension, and the fifth and sixth dimensions are planes of possibilities. If I left my current starting point and moved to the sixth dimension, I could find myself in an auditorium like this and face vastly different options. If I could fold over to the seventh dimension, I could find myself in a jungle or on a different planet, because the seventh dimension is composed of possibilities that merge not from my *current* starting point, but from the beginning of time. The eighth dimension includes the histories of all possible universes, and the ninth, all possible everythings. The tenth dimension is limitless, and includes every possible thing anyone could imagine."

The professor stood, his eyes wide with the infinite variety of alternatives he was imagining. I found myself caught up in his fervor, and I barely heard him as he went on to compare dimensionality with inflationary cosmology and our expanding universe, which theoretically creates room for more universes. I was familiar with the cosmology material because my friends and I had met people and creatures from other universes, but I still found the concept mind-boggling.

"Snogg . . . rmph." I elbowed Tank, who was contentedly snoring beside me.

I tried to follow the rest of the professor's presentation, but his idea of time travel through folded dimensions had opened a door, and I spent the rest of the hour imagining the possibilities.

Chapter 4

"Honestly, Professor." I caught his arm as Tank, Brenda, and Daniel scooted past us into the house. "You did a great job. That may have been the best presentation I've ever heard on the subject of time travel and dimensionality."

I expected him to brush me off — after all, the professor has never been one to easily pocket praise. But he held my gaze and the corner of his mouth wobbled. "You really think so?"

"I wouldn't say it if I didn't mean it." I released his arm and jerked my thumb toward the narrow path next to the house. "Want to join us down on the beach? I think you deserve to relax a little now that your big speech is over."

"Maybe later." He smiled, then walked into the house and down the hall. I followed, on the way to my room, but lifted a brow when the professor went into his room and pointedly closed the door.

Okay, then. Maybe he needed some time to decompress.

I blew out a breath. I was hoping the professor would snap out of his preoccupation once he'd finished his presentation, but he seemed just as distracted as he had when we left the house. Was something else bothering him? Something I hadn't even guessed?

"Hey, Andi!"

I turned at the sound of Tank's voice and found him in the living room . . . all wrapped up in a metal detector. Headphones covered his ears, a harness and elbow brace supported some kind of screen/joystick apparatus, and a circular disk on the end of a stick hovered above the carpeted floor.

I gave the contraption a skeptical look. "So that's it, huh? You're serious about this?"

He grinned. "I thought you might want a demonstration. Happy to show you the ropes."

"Maybe later." I forced a smile. "Let me change into shorts, then I'll come outside."

"See you later, then." He went through the kitchen, then out the sliding glass doors and onto the deck. Maybe Daniel would enjoy helping him look for buried treasure or whatever. I wasn't particularly thrilled by the idea.

I was about to go back to my room, but the overabundance of light in the foyer reminded me that I'd left the door partly open. I stepped forward to close it, and through the opening I glimpsed the two odd children I'd noticed yesterday. They were coming up the driveway, staring straight ahead, their arms hanging stiffly at their sides, neither of them smiling. Their dead-pan expressions sent a cold hand down my spine — if they meant to creep me out, they were doing a good job of it.

But they were just *kids,* for heaven's sake.

Abby, who stood by my side looking out the sidelights, saw the kids and stiffened. Then she began to growl.

"Easy, Abs." I pasted on a bright smile and stepped onto the front porch, closing the door firmly behind me. "Can I help you with something?"

They halted in unison, then the boy swiveled his head and met my gaze. "Will you let us come in?" he asked, his voice flat and matter-of-fact.

I looked at the girl, who had also turned her head to look at me. "Is this some kind of joke? Maybe a dare?" I asked. I softened my smile. "Are you two lost or something?"

They didn't answer. The girl stared at me, and something in her unwavering gaze lifted the hair at the back of my neck. "Will you let us in?" she asked in the same dull tone as the boy. "It will only take a minute."

"*What* will only take a minute?"

"We need to use the telephone," the boy said, staring at me without even blinking.

I hesitated. Most kids in this neighborhood carried cell phones that served as invisible leashes connecting them to their parents. With all the tourist traffic on this street, I couldn't imagine any parent sending their kids out without one.

And something — some atavistic alarm signal — warned me not to let these kids in the house.

"Um . . . I'll call someone for you, if you want to give me a number."

Nothing flickered in their eyes — not interest, not gratitude, not even curiosity. "Will you let us in?" the boy repeated. "It will only take a minute."

My heart hammered in my chest as I stepped back toward the door.

"Let us in," the girl echoed, stepping forward in lockstep with the boy. "It will only take a minute."

That's when I smelled it — a scent of

death and dying things, an odor so repulsive that my gag reflex kicked in. I made an effort to look away, then took another step backward. When I felt the threshold beneath the sole of my shoe, I spun and moved inside, slamming the door behind me. I flipped the deadbolt, then leaned against the solid wood, relishing its strength beneath my clammy palms. Abby stood next to me, her nose pressed to the crack between the door and the doorframe, hair lifted along her spine.

Only when my heart had calmed did I move to the peephole and look outside.

No one stood on the porch. No kids walked down the driveway. Since our porch faced the side of the property, I could see the Diaz house, where a giant sabal palm rattled its leaves in the breeze.

I was about to turn away when I saw them again — the boy and girl were walking up the sidewalk that led to the Diaz front door.

This was not good. I don't know how I knew it, but I knew that if I did nothing, I would feel like I had walked away from someone drowning. . . .

"Andi! Aren't you coming?"

I turned, dry-mouthed, and saw Brenda and Daniel standing behind me in bathing suits, beach towels slung over their shoulders. I could smell coconut-scented sunscreen from where I stood — a far cry from the nauseating odor I'd inhaled a few minutes before.

"I'll be right out," I said, rummaging in my purse for my cell phone. "I just have to make a quick call."

I dialed 9-1-1, then hesitated when the operator answered. How was I supposed to explain the panic I felt around those kids?

"I'm not sure this is an emergency," I finally told her, "but two kids are wandering down the street and asking people to let them into their homes. They seem sort of — I don't know, maybe shell-shocked, and I'm afraid they may have been involved in something —"

"Ma'am? What are you saying?"

"I think they've been involved in something really bad. Maybe you could send someone to check on them?"

The woman took my name and address, then thanked me and promised to send a patrol car.

Feeling that I'd done my duty, I moved on down the hall, ready to put on my bathing suit and join the others. Before going to my room, though, I peeked into the others' bedrooms to make sure they had plenty of towels.

I paused in the room Brenda was using — her sketchbook lay on her bed, open to a drawing that immediately caught my attention. On the page I saw the two children, and in the stark lines of a number two pencil I finally realized what had alarmed me most about those kids.

Their eyes. Their eyes were solid black — no white, no iris, no color at all. Just solid orbs as dark as a starless night sky.

I caught Brenda down on the beach. "Your sketch," I said, dropping to the towel I'd spread on the sand. "Forgive me for snooping, but I couldn't help seeing your sketchbook on the bed. When did you draw those kids?"

She frowned. "The image came to me during the professor's presentation. But don't tell him I was sketching during his talk. I'll never hear the end of it."

"Wait — did you see them at the university?"

She looked at me as if I'd been out in the sun too long. "I didn't see them with my *eyes.* I just *saw* them, so I drew them." She snorted softly. "Why? You got spooky kids hidden in the attic or something?"

"They walked up to the house while you

and Daniel were changing into your bathing suits."

Her arched brows lifted. "Shut. Up. You're kiddin', right?"

I shook my head. "I wish. Because they are every bit as creepy as they look in your picture. But I didn't realize why they creeped me out until I saw your sketch — it's those eyes. But not only their eyes — everything about them is somehow *off*. Their speech, their posture, their clothing — it's like they're from the back side of the moon."

Brenda's eyes narrowed. "Maybe they are."

"And they stink. I've never smelled a dead body, but something tells me it would smell just like those kids." I shifted my gaze to the surf, where Tank and Daniel were walking around with the metal detector and studying the sand. "Here we go again. I was really hoping we'd have some time to relax. The professor could certainly use some downtime."

"Ditto," Brenda said. "I love takin' care of Daniel, but I tell ya — being a full-time parent is a lot harder than I thought. And Daniel's not exactly a regular kid."

"Is he giving you problems?"

"Nothing I can't work out. Trouble is, I'm

so busy bouncing between work and taking care of him that my time, patience, and creativity are in short supply. So I was glad when you invited us to come for some beach time. Even if we have to deal with crazy stuff, it's good to be with you guys. I know you love Daniel, too, and that takes some of the pressure off."

I gave her a sympathetic smile and remained silent while she rolled onto her stomach and pillowed her head on her hands. The beach was quiet, probably because it was a weekday and as hot as blazes. Maybe the rest of the week would be quiet and peaceful. After all, we hadn't received any directions or plane tickets from the mysterious people who usually sent us on strange ventures. But Brenda had received a vision of those kids, and I had actually met them, so the odds that we were about to be caught up in some bizarre situation were growing greater all the time —

"Andi!"

Uh oh. What now?

I turned at the sound of the professor's voice. He stood on the edge of the back deck, and when I caught his gaze, he pointed to the house. "Someone here to see you!"

Who knew I was home?

Grumbling under my breath, I stood,

picked up my towel, and shook it carefully so it wouldn't spray sand all over Brenda. "Looks like I gotta go. You think we should grill hamburgers for dinner?"

"Whatever," Brenda murmured, her eyes closed. "Let me know when, and I'll help."

"Okay."

I wrapped my towel around my chest and started toward the house.

By the time I reached the house, I remembered that I'd given my address to the 9-1-1 dispatcher. I was expecting to find an officer or two in the living room, but instead I found Mr. Diaz distractedly petting Abby in the foyer. Perspiration dotted his forehead, his thinning hair was disheveled, and his eyes were wide with fear.

I regretted taking my time coming up the hill. "Mr. Diaz." I tucked my towel more firmly under my arm and hurried toward him. "Is everything okay?"

His face suddenly rippled with anguish. "Have you seen Maria? I came home and the door was standing open. She's not in the house. I've been through it twice, looking everywhere, and she's not there."

"Maybe" — I spoke slowly in an effort to counter his increasing panic — "maybe she went to the store to pick up something for dinner."

"Her car's still in the driveway. Her purse is still on the counter with her keys inside."

I frowned. "Could she have gone down to the beach?"

"She hates the beach, especially now that she's pregnant. She says she can't see her feet anymore, let alone get sand off them."

He was pacing now, moving toward the front door, then striding back to me. "I hoped she'd come over here to borrow something, or to talk to your grandmother —"

"Sabba and Safta are in New York for the week."

"So have you seen Maria at all?"

"Not today." I patted his arm. "I saw her yesterday, and she was fine. But we were at the university this morning and got back about an hour ago."

"Did you see anything? Any strangers? A prowler? A salesman?"

I wanted to say no, but I *had* seen someone — the black-eyed children. And every instinct in my body had warned me against them.

"I did see two kids I didn't recognize. And about twenty minutes ago they were walking toward your house."

"Kids? Like from the neighborhood?"

I bit my lip. "I don't think so. They were . . . odd. They came to our door and asked if they could come inside."

Mr. Diaz blinked. "Why? What did they want?"

"They said they wanted to use the phone, but something about them put me off so much that I called the police when they left. I watched them cross our driveway and head for your house."

Mr. Diaz went pale and might have collapsed if the professor hadn't stepped out of the dining room and slid a chair beneath the panicked husband. "I know my wife," Mr. Diaz said, his voice trembling. "If two kids asked her for help, she'd give them whatever they wanted."

"They didn't exactly ask for help," I clarified. "They asked if they could use the telephone."

Mr. Diaz blinked several times. "Why didn't you let them?"

I shifted my weight beneath a load of unexpected guilt. "It . . . felt wrong to let them in. And Abby was growling, so I didn't think it'd be a good idea."

"Were they some kind of gypsies? Do you think they were part of a gang? Could they be runners for some kind of drug cartel —"

"Relax, man, I'm sure your wife is fine,"

the professor said.

I shot him a grateful smile, glad that he'd stepped in to help.

"This isn't like Maria." Mr. Diaz shook his head. "I'm worried sick. The baby could come at any time. What if she's hurt or something?"

Whirling blue lights appeared in the window, so I gestured to the vehicle outside. "The police have arrived. Why don't we go see if they have any news?"

CHAPTER 5

Brenda, Daniel, Tank, the professor, and I stood at the window and watched as two police officers questioned Mr. Diaz. The poor man was in tears, his hands flying in frustrated gestures, his face taut with fear and worry.

"They always suspect the spouse," Brenda said, eyeing Mr. Diaz with a narrowed gaze. "Seems like nine times out of ten, the husband did it."

"We don't know for sure if anybody did anything," I pointed out. "And I was talking to Mrs. Diaz just yesterday, while Mr. Diaz was at work. She seemed very happy and was excited about the coming baby."

The professor said nothing, but slowly ran his fingers over his silver beard.

"Dear Lord." For a moment I thought Tank was using a figure of speech, then I realized he was praying. "Lord," he continued, not bothering to close his eyes, "please lead the police to Mrs. Diaz, and keep her safe. Place your angels around her —"

"Anoił," Daniel interrupted.

"— and keep her safe from the evil one."

"Duch," Daniel said.

"Daniel," I asked, following a sudden whim, "look around outside. Do you see . . . anyone or anything we should know about?"

Though Daniel can sometimes adopt autistic behaviors when it comes to interaction with others, he seemed to understand what I meant. He moved closer to the window, pressed his hands to the glass, and peered out at the Diaz house, even tilting his head to look upward in case any unseen entities hovered nearby.

Finally he shook his head, and Brenda drew him closer in a protective embrace. "Good to know," she said simply. "Your neighbor probably went out for coffee."

"Would you go out for coffee and leave your purse behind?" I asked.

Brenda shrugged. "Sure would. If my friend was paying."

I wanted to believe her, but a dark foreboding had settled into my gut and refused to go away. One by one, the others left the window — the professor went back to his room, Brenda and Daniel went into the kitchen, and Tank curled up for a nap on the sofa with Abby.

But I couldn't rest while Mrs. Diaz was missing. I went outside and sat on the steps of the front porch, watching quietly as the police went into my neighbor's house with Mr. Diaz. When they came out a few minutes later, I overheard their parting remarks. "We can't file an official missing persons report until she has been missing twenty-four hours," the older officer said. "But given her condition and your neighbor's observation of those kids, we'll issue a bulletin to the officers on patrol. If they see her, they'll radio in."

Mr. Diaz thanked them, then waited on the porch, his hands in his pockets, while the officers drove away.

Before he went into the house, Mr. Diaz lifted his head and caught my gaze. His eyes, so filled with despair and anxiety, sent a wave of melancholy rushing over me, and in that moment I wished I felt free to pray aloud like Tank often did. He summoned supernatural help in a voice that reassured and comforted, whereas my prayer would sound more like a whimper.

Mr. Diaz turned and went into his house, and from where I sat I heard the click of his deadbolt.

But I didn't think a deadbolt could thwart

the sort of evil we were about to encounter.

After dinner, Brenda came over and dropped her sketchbook into my lap. "No idea what this means," she said, folding her arms. "But I saw it clear as day, which means it's probably gonna happen."

I picked up the paper and stared at an image of myself. I was standing in the center of what looked like a crop circle, and I was staring up at the sky as I held a bundle in my arms. My eyes were wide and my lips parted — as if I'd just seen something that scared me spitless.

"Any idea where that could be?" Brenda asked.

I shook my head. "This is the coast — no one grows crops around here."

"Then I guess you'd better get ready to take a trip."

I glanced across the room, where Tank was watching with concern in his eyes. "Are you in danger, Andi?"

"I don't see how." I shrugged. "Maybe we're all just a little confused."

"Yeah, right." Brenda snorted, then went back to the jigsaw puzzle she and Daniel were working on. I tried to pick up my book and resume reading, but the image of that sketch keep floating across my mind.

Chapter 6

A shrill ringing blasted me from bed at 7:00 a.m. I reached for the house phone on a tide of dread, afraid something had happened to one of my grandparents, but Mr. Diaz was on the line, his words coming at double-speed and mixing with Spanish. "They found Maria. She's at Suncoast Hospital, though they won't tell me anything else. Can you come? The police will be there, and they want to ask more questions about *los niños.*"

"They want to ask *me* questions?" I shook my head to clear away the fog of sleep. "About those kids?"

"Por favor, Andi, ¿puede venir?"

"I'll come," I promised. "As soon as I get dressed, I'll meet you at the hospital. Oh — and I'm glad they found your wife."

I hung up before fully considering the implication of Mr. Diaz's words — his wife was in the *hospital* and the police had questions to ask. So Maria Diaz had definitely not slipped out for coffee with a friend.

Maybe I should have headed out quietly, but by the time I'd dressed and left my room, Tank, Brenda, Daniel, and the professor were munching on cereal and Pop-Tarts at the breakfast table. I explained that I was going to the hospital to see Mrs. Diaz, and, either out of curiosity or *esprit de corps,* everyone else decided to come along.

When we arrived at the hospital, we found Mr. Diaz in the waiting room outside the elevator. To my surprise, he appeared nearly as upset as he had been yesterday.

"Your wife," I said, grasping his clenched hand when he stood to greet us. "She's okay, right?"

His eyes filled with tears. "She is fine. But the baby — our baby is missing."

I blinked. "What?"

Words spilled from his mouth. "The police are in there now with the doctor. The baby is gone, but the doctors say Maria did not give birth. There are no marks of surgery, no tearing, no evidence the baby was born. The doctors say the — what is the word? — placenta? It is still in place. They will have to go in and remove it or Maria could get sick."

"That's impossible," Brenda said, her

voice flat. "If the baby's been born, the placenta should be gone, too."

"That's what the doctors say." Mr. Diaz's wide eyes met Brenda's. "But the baby is gone! It has been stolen from her —"

"Wait a minute, let's remain in the realm of actual realities." The professor put a steadying arm on Mr. Diaz's shoulder. "Where was your wife found?"

"In a field, just off the main road, lying in the grass like cast-off garbage." Mr. Diaz sank into a chair as his voice trembled. "An officer called for an ambulance, and they brought her here, to the hospital. The doctors examined her and right away, they said they could not hear a heartbeat. And then they discovered that the baby was gone. But they do not know who took it, or even how they took it, and she will not wake up to tell us anything —"

He buried his face in his hands, silently shutting us out. I looked at the others, who appeared as confused and bewildered as I felt.

"She's not waking up?" The professor arched a brow. "She must have been drugged."

"With what?" I asked. "If she has, surely something would show up in a blood test."

The professor glanced at his watch. "They

probably haven't had time to run a tox screen. Maybe we'll get an answer to that question later."

"We're missing something obvious here," Brenda insisted. "Babies don't just disappear from the womb. Someone's missing evidence that ought to be clearly visible —"

I held my finger across my lips, then gestured to Mr. Diaz, who didn't need to hear our wild speculations. "Let's go to the cafeteria and talk. I can do some Internet searches to see if anything like this has ever happened before. But before we go, I need to know something."

I knelt in front of Mr. Diaz and squeezed his arm. "Mr. Diaz, did the police tell you anything about those strange kids?"

Mr. Diaz blinked as if my question didn't register, then he shook his head. With his baby missing and his wife unresponsive, those kids were the furthest thing from his mind.

I released his arm and stood, then followed the others to the elevator.

Because the cafeteria was crowded, we gathered in a small group of chairs near the snack machines. Brenda fished quarters out of her purse to buy Daniel a carton of juice while I sank into a chair and pulled out my phone to do some Googling. Tank sat next to me, his hands in his pockets, looking uncomfortable and completely out of his element. I think he'd been ready to bolt ever since Brenda uttered the word *placenta.*

"Pregnant woman's baby disappears," I murmured as I typed the phrase into the search engine. I pressed the search key, then caught my breath. "Yikes! Several links here."

"I'll bet most of them are associated with conspiracy websites," Brenda said, sitting across from me. "Seems like I saw something like that in a movie — or am I thinking of the monster who laid its eggs inside the woman's belly?"

I clicked on a link and skimmed the article. "This report is purely scientific. According to this, a woman pregnant with twins might find that one of the twins has been absorbed into the other. Apparently that's rare, but it happens."

"But your neighbor wasn't carrying twins," Tank pointed out. "And she was huge."

"She *was* far along in her pregnancy," I said, amending his statement because no woman, especially a pregnant one, wants to be called *huge.* "And yeah, Brenda, you're right — I see several pages about unborn babies being stolen by aliens."

"Told you," Brenda said. "Kooks rule the Internet."

"But we've seen unbelievable things, and we're not kooks," I reminded her. "I mean, we've seen houses that disappear and re-appear, happy nuns that escort us from one universe to another, monsters in fog, killer slime —"

"Daniel and I came here for a *vacation,*" Brenda said, practically glaring at me. "This wasn't supposed to be another romp in the twilight zone."

Tank grinned at her. "Can we help it if the twilight zone keeps drawing us in?" He nudged me with his elbow. "What about those alien reports? Anything that sounds like your neighbor's story?"

I skimmed several posts on an electronic bulletin board. "Okay, here's a guy who says a woman he knows lost her baby when aliens abducted her. She was found the next day, but she wasn't pregnant anymore. And doctors couldn't tell how the baby was re-moved."

"Bingo," Tank said.

I was about to argue, but my mouth went dry when someone down the hall released a bloodcurdling scream.

Brenda started toward the sound. "Isn't

that near —"

Drawn by the horrific wail, we stood and walked toward the commotion, which proved to be coming from Maria Diaz's room. A couple of cops waited outside the open door, and they looked helpless. I peered around the doorframe and saw that Maria had regained consciousness, but she was flailing and screaming, her eyes wide with terror. "No, no!" she screamed. *"¡No me toquen! ¡No vienen cerca de mí!"*

The nurse was trying to wrap Maria's arms in restraints, but she was no match for the panicked woman. The doctor kept barking the name of some drug, but the nurse had her hands full with the restraints —

Another nurse and an orderly ran past us and attempted to help. But while a nurse injected a drug into the IV line, Maria's gaze fell on her husband and her chin trembled. *"Tomaron nuestro bebé,"* she said, her voice breaking. "They said they were going to take the baby."

"¿Quien?" Mr. Diaz stroked his wife's hair. "Honey, who are you talking about?"

"Los monstruos," she said, her eyelids drooping as the drug took effect. *"Los grises.* The ones . . . the *chicos . . . esos chicos me llevaron a ellos."* Her eyes closed and she stopped speaking.

Mr. Diaz looked at the doctor, who shook his head. "She's obviously not herself," the doctor said. "Probably hallucinating. Does your wife use any sort of recreational drugs?"

"No!" Mr. Diaz recoiled from the question. "She never has, and she never would, not with the baby! She'd never do anything to hurt our child."

Mr. Diaz stepped away from the doctor, and his gaze crossed mine as he looked toward the door. Then he set his jaw and strode toward us, meeting me and the others out in the hallway.

"Where's that detective?" he asked, looking around. "She said those kids" — he swallowed hard — "took her to monsters who took our baby. I want to know who they are, and I want them found. I don't know what they're up to, but I want them found and arrested."

As he stalked off in search of the police, I turned to the others. *"Los grises,"* I repeated. "Anybody know what that means?"

Tank shrugged, then we all looked at the professor, who cleared his throat before answering: "The gray ones."

Brenda, Daniel, Tank, and I went back to the house, leaving the professor with Mr.

Diaz. For some reason my neighbor seemed to take comfort from the professor's calm demeanor, and for the first time I began to see why James McKinney might have been an effective priest in his former profession. When he wasn't arguing, he could be a compassionate listener, and that's what he was doing with Mr. Diaz — listening.

When the professor finally arrived back at the house, he sat in the living room and we gathered around him. "Typical abduction story," he said, glancing up at me as he propped his feet on the ottoman. "Could have been scripted from *The X-Files.* Woman is home, kids knock on the door, she lets them in. Next thing she knows, she wakes up in the hospital bed and she's not pregnant anymore."

"What about the things she was saying?" I asked. "Talking about the gray ones and telling them to stay away from her?"

The professor shrugged. "If those are actual memories, they're buried somewhere in her subconscious. She may recall them in dreams or while under the influence of drugs or hypnosis, but I was there when the police questioned her, and she couldn't remember anything."

"They still got her tied down?" Brenda's eyes narrowed. "I hate it when doctors tie people up like dangerous animals."

"She's calm now, so they removed the restraints. She'll be able to come home tomorrow if there are no complications."

"But what about the baby?" I asked. "She was really pregnant, nearly full term. You can't tell me *that* baby somehow got reabsorbed into her body."

"The attending physician thought it might be a hysterical pregnancy," the professor said, "until Mrs. Diaz's obstetrician arrived. She opened her laptop and pulled up ultrasounds that showed a normal, healthy baby in the womb."

"What about those strange kids?" I asked. "Have the police found *them*? What did Maria remember about them?"

The professor's mouth quirked. "Not much, and no, the police haven't found them. No one else has even seen them." He glanced around. "Is anyone else ready for dinner? I'm starving. I didn't lower myself to raiding the snack machines like you guys did."

I went off to dig through Sabba's collection of take-out menus, but I couldn't get Mrs. Diaz and those kids out of my mind.

After dinner, the conversation turned to weird kids. I tried to do an Internet search, but the terms “strange kids” and “odd children” didn’t bring up anything other than stories about parents contemplating the difficulty of child-rearing.

But then I remembered the oddest thing about those kids, the thing Brenda caught in her sketch: the black eyes. And my first search for “black-eyed kids” brought up exactly what I was searching for.

“Listen to this entry about black-eyed children,” I said, interrupting Tank’s story about a toddler who could throw a football fifty yards. “ ‘According to an urban legend, unusual children with completely black eyes have been spotted in various neighborhoods around the world. These children — called BEKs — reportedly knock on strangers’ doors, usually at night, and ask to be let in. Most people report feeling an unusual sense of dread or fear in the presence of these children, and evil is supposed to befall the hapless person who falls for their disguise and lets them in.’ ”

“Disguise?” Brenda interrupted. “If they’re not kids, what are they?”

I held up a finger and kept reading. “ ‘Explanations of these and other strange appearances go back through the ages. In China and Japan, folklore reveals stories of vengeful ghosts, hungry apparitions that appear and demand to be fed. Those who do not submit to the ghosts' demands meet with bad luck or illness. Europe compares them to vampires, tales from the Middle East offer stories of the Djinn, supernaturally empowered beings from which we get the word *genie*. Some say the BEKs are manifestations of dark thoughts; in the Middle Ages, they might have been considered changelings, soulless children substituted for real children by the fairies. Stories of these black-eyed children, who seem poorly adapted to contemporary social situations and skills, have been around since the 1990s.' "

"Urban legend, huh?" Tank smiled a humorless smile. "That means the story's not true, right?"

"Sometimes," I answered, "but sometimes not. Sometimes people label stories as urban legends just because there doesn't appear to be a logical explanation for the story's events. But sometimes the answers to those stories lie beyond our current understanding."

"Some people," the professor inserted, "believe that aliens seek human babies in order to create hybrids that are half-human, half-alien. Others say that the culprits are human beings — government-types who are using alien DNA to create hybrids for military purposes."

"Sounds like something The Gate would be interested in," I said. "Human-alien hybrids to colonize another planet —"

"Or live under the sea," the professor interjected. "Who knows what they're planning?"

"That makes no sense," Brenda said. "Why would anyone want to mix our races?"

"Our *species,*" I corrected. "Our races are already mixed — people on this planet have become so mingled that we're all human mutts. If you're talking about mingling humans and aliens, you'd be talking about two different species."

"Still." She shook her head. "If aliens are so superior, why don't they just wipe us out and take over the planet? That's what they want in all those sci-fi movies."

"Hang on a minute." Tank's eyes had taken on a thoughtful look. "I know I usually don't add much to these conversations, but bear with me, okay? I don't believe in aliens — not from outer space, anyway. I mean, if alien beings lived on Mars or even the moon, don't you think we would have seen some evidence of their existence? We've sent cameras up there. We've filled the galaxy with space junk — if there were other civilized species in space, don't you think we would have seen some of *their* space junk floating around? Something? We've sent cameras pretty doggone far into space, and they haven't been able to prove that anything's out there."

"A lot of people have seen UFOs," Brenda pointed out. "And a lot of other people claim to have been abducted by aliens. They can't all be crazy."

"I don't think they're crazy," Tank said. "I think maybe these creatures, whatever they are, aren't from other planets. Maybe they're coming from other dimensions, or other worlds — like Littlefoot or the monsters in the fog. We know the other worlds exist, and we know they can come through certain portals. So maybe these other things are plenty real, they're just not what we think they are."

Brenda crossed her arms. "That still doesn't answer the question about why they'd want a hybrid species."

Tank shifted his weight and sighed heavily. "I thought of something," he said slowly, "but I'm not sure I want to tell you. Might be like casting pearls before swine."

Brenda stiffened. "Are you calling us *pigs*?"

Tank's face went the color of a tomato.

"No, no — it's just an expression. But I've got an uncle who's a preacher, and he says that the devil has always been trying to thwart God's plan to redeem the human race. So back in the old days, he sent demons to make babies with human women — it's in the Bible. Those babies grew up to be giants, and they were around even after the flood. Some of them had six fingers and six toes, so I guess you could say they were hybrids."

I blinked. Being Jewish, I'd heard Torah stories all my life, but I'd never heard anything about demonic hybrids. "Where in the Bible?" I asked, staring hard at Tank. "That sounds crazy."

"Genesis," Tank answered. "The story of the Nephilim."

"That story," the professor said in a soothing voice, "has been interpreted in various ways. Some say those who fathered the giants were merely exalted men, not spiritual beings like angels or demons. I would cast my vote in that direction."

Tank shrugged, leaving the professor with the last word, but I wasn't convinced the professor was right. Since leaving the priesthood, he had a tendency to automatically reject any explanation that had to do with God, but his explanation of the Nephilim did not explain how "exalted men" could create a race of giants.

"Maybe we don't have to know all the answers — at least not yet," I said. "Seems to me the most important thing is helping Mrs. Diaz find her baby."

"If the kid has been whisked into another dimension," Brenda said, frowning, "good luck with that."

Chapter 7

Later that day I sat at the desk in the study, searching the Internet for stories of fetal abductions. Rain had been falling since before sunrise, so none of us were in the mood to go outside. I kept looking out the window at the Diaz house, hoping to see Mr. Diaz bringing his wife home, but apparently they were still at the hospital.

I looked up when I heard a soft cough from the hallway. The professor was standing in the doorway, a strange look on his face.

"Andi," he said softly, his face blanketed by a peaceful expression I rarely saw him wear, "if I take a picture on my phone, can you print it for me?"

"Sure." I gestured toward the machine in the corner. "That printer does a pretty good job with photos. How big do you want it?"

"Small. Pocket-size." He flashed a smile, then tilted his head. "Join me in the other room, will you?"

Curious, I followed him to the family room, where Daniel was playing a video game, Brenda was sitting on the carpeted floor and looking at magazines, and Tank was snoring on the sofa. The professor stood in the center of the room and cleared his throat. When Tank didn't stop snoring, Brenda punched his shoe.

"If I may have your attention," the professor said, casting his gaze around the room, "I'd like to commemorate this occasion with a group photo. You'll all have to gather around and squeeze in tightly for this selfie to work."

Brenda frowned. "You want a picture now? I don't have my eyelashes on."

"Just something to remember this little trip," the professor answered. "I'm not expecting black tie and full makeup."

Tank threw me a questioning look, and so did Brenda. I shrugged, not having the faintest clue what the professor was up to. He wasn't sentimental, and this trip wasn't exactly worth commemorating, in my view. But if he wanted to do something to remember this trip, why not humor him?

"Come on," I said, stepping to the professor's side. "You too, Daniel. You're gonna have to leave your game for a minute."

Feeling awkward and clumsy, we all gathered around the professor and smiled at the phone in his hand. He, of course, didn't smile, but carefully adjusted the phone until we were all visible on the screen, then he pressed the button. We heard the sound of a shutter click, then the professor nodded. "Resume whatever you were doing," he said, stepping out of the huddle. "Andi, can you print this image for me?"

I led the way back to my grandfather's study. "What's this about?" I asked, glancing at the professor. "Are you doing some kind of experiment, or getting sentimental in your old age?"

"Neither." He gave me a tight-lipped smile and pressed keys on his phone. "I've just sent the image to your e-mail account, so if you could print it . . ."

"Pocket-sized?"

"Correct. Just slip it beneath my door after you've trimmed it. Thank you."

He turned toward his room, but before leaving he caught my shoulder, stepped closer, and planted a kiss on my forehead. "Dear Andi," he whispered, his voice growing rough. "You are the daughter I might have had . . . if I'd made different choices along the way."

I blinked, my thoughts stuttering in surprise, while he released me and returned to his room, closing the door behind him.

CHAPTER 8

The next morning I rose early and made waffles — my grandmother's recipe, complete with the secret ingredient of almond extract — which filled the kitchen with a scrumptious aroma. I wanted the team to be in a good mood because I hoped to enlist them in my search for Mrs. Diaz's missing baby.

The scent of waffles and sizzling bacon did the trick. Tank came into the kitchen right after I'd finished cooking, and Daniel and Brenda followed soon after. Brenda went outside and brought in the newspaper, then we all sat down to eat. The professor's seat, however, remained empty, and I kept glancing at it, wondering if he was working or had decided to sleep late.

"Look at these shoes," Brenda said, holding up the front of the Lifestyle section. "Ten-inch platforms. I'd need a ladder to climb into those things."

"I don't think they're meant to be walked in." I shrugged. "Aren't those things just for fashion shows?"

"The Reds traded for a new first baseman," Tank announced. "They have several good infielders on their farm teams. Wonder why they didn't just move one of them up?"

I blew out a breath, not knowing how to respond to Tank because I knew next to nothing about baseball or to Brenda, since I knew nothing about fashion. I looked at Daniel, who had put down his handheld video game and allowed his gaze to drift over the abandoned local news section on the table. Then he put his finger on the paper and slid it over, across the table, until it rested in front of me. "Read," he said, not meeting my gaze.

I picked up the paper and scanned the largest headline: *Local Youth Contracts Mysterious Illness.* My pulse skittered.

With increasing alarm, I read the story. According to the newspaper article, Georgia Hanson had run into a mini-market while her son, Jax, waited in the family van. When she returned, another child was sitting in the van with her son. Alarmed, she opened the back door to see who the child was. She asked for his name, but he kept his head down and didn't answer. Instead Jax said,

"He wanted to come in, so I let him."

Alarmed, Mrs. Hanson ordered the unknown boy out of the car. He obeyed, not speaking, but when he left the car, he looked directly at her, and that's when she panicked — the boy appeared unusually pale and wan. She instinctively glanced at her son, who was still sitting in the back seat, and when she shifted to look again at the strange boy, he had vanished.

Almost immediately, Jax doubled over in pain, then passed out. Mrs. Hanson drove him to the emergency room, where the doctors examined him and could find nothing wrong. But Jax remained unconscious and would stay in the hospital until he came out of his coma.

"Guys, listen to this." With a quaver in my voice, I read the news story to Brenda, Daniel, and Tank, pausing only long enough to look at the professor's empty seat and wish he'd hurry out to join us. I could sense a pattern in the odd events apparently precipitated by the black-eyed children, but I was too close to the story to see it. What did it all mean?

"Daniel," I said, lowering the newspaper, "would you go knock on the professor's door? Tell him we need him."

Daniel tilted his head and gave me a

strange little smile. "He's gone."

"Gone?" Brenda blinked. "Gone where?"

Daniel held up his hand, pointed upward, and then rotated his hand as if he were pointing in all directions.

"This isn't a good time for guessing games," Brenda said, an edge to her voice. "If this is a joke, Daniel —"

I sincerely hoped it was. I left the table and walked down the hallway that led to the bedrooms, trying my best to ignore the ominous feeling in my gut.

I knocked on the professor's door and heard no answer. Gathering my courage, I turned the doorknob . . . and realized that Daniel was right. The professor *was* gone, but he couldn't have gone far because his briefcase, his glasses, his laptop, and his current notebooks were still on the desk. But what I couldn't find, even when I searched the desktop and opened the lid of his suitcase, was the small photograph I had printed for him last night.

Abby, who had followed me into the room, sniffed the floor around the desk, then sniffed the professor's pajamas. Then she sat politely and tilted her head as if asking, "Well? Where'd he go?"

"I wish I knew, Abs."

Brenda came into the room as I was opening the professor's laptop. "Do you think he went out for coffee or something?"

I shook my head. "I was up early this morning, so I would have heard the alarm beep if anyone opened a door."

"Have you tried calling his cell phone?"

"Yeah. His phone is right over there, on the nightstand."

Brenda leaned against the doorframe. "Have you searched the house? Maybe he wanted a quiet place to think . . . or maybe he wanted to walk along the beach."

I gave her a you've-got-to-be-kidding look. "Have you ever known him to willingly walk on the beach?"

"Well . . . there's a first time for everything, right?"

"Yeah, but something tells me that this is a far bigger first time than we realize." I sank to the edge of the bed, where the blankets and pillow were neat and unrumpled. "Didn't his behavior yesterday strike you as odd?"

Brenda smirked. "The professor's always odd."

"But he's never asked for a group picture before. And there's more — last night, before he went into his room, he kissed my forehead. It was . . . almost like he was saying good-bye."

Brenda's brow creased, then she shrugged. "I'll admit that he's seemed really preoccupied the last couple of days. But he'd be lost without you, Andi, so I hardly think he'd take off without telling you where he was going. And where would he go? Unless —" Her frown deepened. "You . . . you don't think he was thinkin' of offin' himself, do you?"

"No — no, definitely not. He wouldn't want a printed photo of our group if he was suicidal. He kept saying he wanted a pocket-sized copy of that image —"

"Maybe he wanted the cops to know who to contact . . . in case his body was mangled in a car crash or something."

"A list of names and phone number would be more helpful than a photo. Still, something's not right. I'm going to call the police."

Brenda sighed, then turned toward the hallway. "Honestly? The man's too stubborn to kill himself. But if you call the police, you're gonna feel really stupid when he comes in and yells at you for involving the cops."

"That's okay." I stood and moved toward the phone on the desk. "If I'm wrong, he can be as mad as he wants to be."

■ ■ ■ ■

The police showed up within an hour of my call. Because I'd heard the cops tell Mr. Diaz that they couldn't file a missing persons report until twenty-four hours had passed, I was careful not to say that we wanted to report a missing person. Instead I told them that we'd awakened this morning and suspected that something had happened to the professor — foul play, perhaps. So could they please investigate, especially since something had also happened to the woman who lived next door . . .

My thoughts kept returning to the creepy kids. What if they had managed to get into the house? What if they'd met the professor?

The young cop leading the investigation, Officer Chad Edwards, suddenly stopped writing on his notepad and looked at me. "Haven't I seen you before?"

I felt an unwelcome blush creep onto my cheeks. "At the hospital, I think. I was there to see Mrs. Diaz."

"Yours is an easy face to remember." He smiled. "And what is your relationship to Dr. McKinney?"

"I'm his assistant. And before you ask, our

relationship is strictly professional."

"Noted." His smile deepened as he made a note on his pad.

From the sofa, Tank glowered at the cop. "Don't you want to dust for fingerprints or something? If someone broke in and kidnapped him —"

"No sign of forced entry," Edwards said. "And there's nothing missing or out of place, so an abduction is unlikely."

"Maybe," Brenda said. "But we're only guests here, so how would we know if something was missing?"

Officer Edwards ignored Brenda and smiled at me again. "Why don't you show me around and point out anything that seems odd to you?"

Brenda sighed dramatically and Tank stood, pulling himself upright and thrusting his sizable chest forward. I'd studied enough zoology to recognize male dominance behavior when I saw it, so more than anything I wanted Tank to calm down and behave himself. But if the professor was with those black-eyed kids, he might be sick or dying or in serious trouble. . . .

I led the way to the bedroom the professor had been using. Everything was just as I'd left it — the laptop and notebooks on the table, his watch and phone on the nightstand, his pajamas still folded on the bed.

The cop's gaze fell on the pajamas. "Do you think he slept here last night?"

"Doesn't look like it."

"So maybe he went out. Could he have gone to a bar, someplace that stays open late?"

"No. I set the house alarm before I went to bed, which was right after the professor went into his room. Dr. McKinney didn't know how to disarm the system. If he had opened a door or a window, the alarm would have gone off."

"Anyone else know how to disarm the security system?"

"My grandparents, but they're in New York. So I'm sure the professor didn't go out last night or this morning."

Edwards flipped his notebook closed and narrowed his eyes as he looked around. "If everything you say is true, then your missing professor vanished into thin air. We're missing something . . . because nobody ever vanishes without a trace."

I bit my lip, restraining the impulse to tell him about some of the things we had experienced as a group. "Sometimes they do," I whispered.

My house phone rang just after I escorted

the two police officers to the front door. My heart leapt in anticipation — maybe it was the professor — but caller ID identified the caller as Reuben Diaz, my neighbor.

"Andi," he said, after I greeted him, "I thought you should know that someone else has run into one of those kids. There's a family at the hospital now; their little boy is upstairs in a coma. The wife saw a strange kid in her van and —"

"I read the story in the paper," I told him.

"Not all the story," Mr. Diaz said. "They didn't report everything. I talked to the mother myself. The kid in her van had black eyes."

I turned to face the others, who had gathered in the living room. Brenda, Tank, and Daniel were all looking at me, doubtless alarmed by the expression on my face.

"We're coming," I told him. "We'll meet you outside your wife's room."

After talking to Reuben Diaz, we found the Hanson family in the pediatric wing on the third floor. Jax Hanson lay in a hospital bed, his face still and pale as a heart monitor beeped and an IV line kept him hydrated.

Mrs. Hanson sat in a chair behind her son's bed, and Mr. Hanson was pacing in the narrow space between the end of the bed and the wall. A TV hung from the ceiling, but it was dark.

"Mr. and Mrs. Hanson?" I asked, timidly stepping into the room. "My name is Andi Goldstein, and these are my friends Brenda, Tank, and Daniel."

The Hansons looked at us without reaction, but their gazes lingered on Daniel. "Is he — does he know Jax?" Mrs. Hanson asked. "Is he in Jax's class at school?"

I shook my head. "Daniel lives in California. We are here because . . . well, because the other day I had an encounter with two children with solid black eyes. I wondered if maybe we had . . . something in common."

Mrs. Hanson gasped and gripped the sheets on her son's bed. Her husband looked from her to me, then his face went a shade paler. "I wasn't sure . . . her story seemed so farfetched."

"It's true," I said, meeting his gaze. "I've seen those kids twice, and there's something sinister about them. I can't explain it, and I can understand why other people don't believe it —"

"The reporter didn't believe me," Mrs. Hanson said, her chin quivering. "I told her about that boy's eyes and she looked at me like I was crazy. She wrote down what I said, but she didn't put it in the paper. What good is a newspaper unless reporters are willing to tell the whole truth?"

I didn't have an answer to that, so I tried to change the subject. "Did the strange kid speak to you at all?"

"Not a word," she said. "He got out of the car when I told him to, though. Then he just disappeared. I glanced away only for a second, and he just vanished. I haven't stopped shaking since." She lifted her hand so we could all see the tremor that quavered her fingertips.

"Has there been any change in your son?" Brenda asked, taking a step closer to the bed. She reached for Daniel's hand and held it tight as she looked down on the unconscious boy.

"None," Mr. Hanson answered. "He just lies there, and the doctors don't know why he won't wake up. They've done all kinds of scans and blood tests, but it's like something's got ahold of him and won't let go —"

Without saying a word, Tank stepped between me and Brenda, his gaze fixed on the boy's face. "Would you mind," he asked, not looking at either of the boy's parents, "if I prayed for your son?"

Mr. Hanson looked at his wife, but Mrs. Hanson kept her gaze focused on Tank. "I wish you would," she said, her voice heavy with unshed tears. "I don't know how to pray . . . for something like this."

I stepped back so Tank could move closer to the head of the bed, then we all watched as he placed his palm on the boy's forehead. "Lord," he prayed, "we know you are sovereign over all creation, over angels and demons, over all kinds of forces everywhere. We ask that you return this boy to his folks, binding whatever forces are keepin' him from wakin' up. Bring him back, Father, and wash his mind so that he don't have any memories of anything bad or evil. I ask these things humbly, but in the mighty name of Jesus, who holds authority over everything on and above and under the earth."

Silence fell over the room. Tank remained motionless, his hand on the boy's forehead, and no one spoke. Tears glistened on Mrs. Hanson's cheeks, and Mr. Hanson stared at his son as though he could bring his son back by the sheer force of his will. Brenda had bowed her head, too, though she might have been trying to hide her skepticism.

Daniel, on the other hand, was looking at the ceiling, his gaze traveling the width and breadth of the room as if he were watching creatures from other dimensions, forces who might be trying to steal this boy's soul . . . or return it.

I lowered my eyes as someone took a sharp breath. Jax Hanson's eyelids fluttered and color returned to his cheeks. His lower lip trembled, then his tongue darted over his lips and his eyes opened. "Mama? Dad?"

Tank lifted his hand and stepped back as a flush reddened his face and neck.

"Jax?" Mrs. Hanson rose and hovered over her son, her hands feeling his forehead, his cheeks. "Are you okay?"

"Where — what am I doing here?"

Jax attempted to sit up, but his father, who had rushed to his wife's side, held him back with a restraining hand. "Easy, son, you don't want to rush it."

"I feel fine. What's going on?"

Pssst.

I turned to see Tank in the doorway, already slinking away. Brenda stood behind him with Daniel, and they were waiting for me.

Leaving the Hansons alone with their son, I followed my friends down the hallway. "Wow," I said, completely at a loss for words. "Tank, what you did —"

"I didn't do anything," he said, gesturing toward the elevators. "Come on, we should get going."

"If you didn't do it," Brenda countered, "then how in the heck did that kid get better?"

Tank didn't answer, but smiled as he pressed the elevator call button.

Chapter 9

My thoughts raced as I drove out of the hospital parking lot. I wasn't exactly sure what had happened in that hospital room, but I knew two things for certain: one, strong forces of evil were afoot in my neighborhood, and they seemed to emanate from two weird, smelly kids with black eyes; and two, forces of good were also at work, and they were even stronger, especially when wielded by men like Tank.

"I don't get it," Brenda mumbled in the back seat. "If those kids are stealing babies from pregnant women, what did they want with the Hanson kid? Are the two situations even connected? And what does any of this have to do with the professor?"

I shook my head and slowed for a red light. "I don't know."

"The situations don't have to be connected," Tank said, rubbing his temple as if he felt the approach of a headache. "Evil goes after innocence. Why would evil beings mess around with people who are already on a road to ruin? Evil wants to destroy the innocent — animals, babies, children. It takes little pleasure in bringing down someone whose life is already ruined."

In the rearview mirror, I saw Brenda glare at Tank. "Feeling a little judgmental, aren't we? Who are you talking about?"

Tank shrugged. "I think you know what I mean. God wants to lift people up, bring them out of addiction, crime, dangerous lifestyles. The forces that oppose God want to bring people down — keep them addicted, drunk, and sick. Most of all, evil wants to keep people ignorant. They think they're partying and having fun, but all they're doing is setting themselves up for disaster. Evil demands a high price. It destroys people."

Brenda crossed her arms and looked out the window, and when I glimpsed the pained look on her face I wondered if Tank's words had awakened some painful memory from her past. We knew each other pretty well, but Brenda had kept a tight grip on some chapters of her history.

"I get what you're saying," I told Tank, "but right now all I can think about is the professor. If he's not there when we get back —"

My mouth went dry when my gaze focused on the path beside the road. Walking along the edge of the sidewalk, dangerously close to cars whizzing by, were the two creepy kids. I recognized them instantly, even from the back, because something was obviously *wrong* about them. They walked together, their arms hanging straight down, their heads facing the road ahead, moving like two small automatons with no sense of life about them.

"Hey," Brenda said. "Isn't that —"

"Yes," I answered, stepping on the gas. I sped up and passed the kids, then pulled onto the side of the road and shoved the gearshift into park. Without thinking I opened the door, stepped out, and crossed in front of the vehicle. Upon seeing me the kids stopped and stared. But when Tank stepped out of the car, the kids made a sharp right turn and hurried into an empty lot where weeds grew knee-high and broken bottles glimmered among the wild grasses.

I bent and caught Brenda's gaze through the car window. "Keep an eye on Daniel," I warned. Tank's warning about evil and innocence had given me the feeling that Daniel might be in more danger than any of us.

Then I took off after those kids.

With Tank beside me, we tore through the empty field, picking up sandspurs and narrowly avoiding a couple of red ant hills and areas sprinkled with broken glass and rusty debris. I could see the horizontal strip of blue water on the horizon and beneath it, the swaying sprays of the sea oats. The sinister siblings — if that's what they were — were nowhere in sight, but surely they had to be just past the dune that served as a windbreak between the beach and the waterfront houses on this road.

Tank and I reached a narrow walkway through the dunes and followed it, reaching the beach at the same time. Breathless, we looked north and south . . . no black-eyed kids in sight.

Lots of people were on the beach — older people, tanned as leather, reclining on beach towels or reading books beneath umbrellas. Young mothers with their little ones, playing in the wave wash and looking for seashells. Lots of children, lots of innocents — only the active, loud, normal variety.

The BEKs had disappeared again.

I heaved a sigh and crossed my arms. Tank gave me a sympathetic look, then gestured toward the beach. "If you want, I'll walk south a little way to see if I can spot them —"

"They're gone," I said. "They have a way of disappearing when they don't want to be found."

I turned, my heart feeling like lead in my chest, and followed the path we'd created in the tall weeds. "What is this stuff?" Tank asked. "Wheat?"

I gave him a smile, but only because I knew he was trying to lighten my mood. "It's just weeds," I said, "but I'd admit it does look a little like wheat —"

I stopped. "Hold up. Look how we flattened these weeds when we ran through here. Why didn't the kids leave any kind of trail?"

Tank scratched his head and looked around. The weedy stalks around us stood straight and unbroken, stirring slightly in the wind. I couldn't see any other places where they'd been stomped or broken, except for one small area about twenty feet away.

I walked toward that spot, wondering if the kids could be hiding in the weeds. That'd be a good trick, hiding right in front of us.

I caught my breath as we drew closer. The flattened area was circular in shape, reminding me of . . .

"A crop circle," Tank said, staring at the field with wide eyes. "Just like Brenda's picture."

I quickened my step. Brenda hadn't drawn *just* a crop circle, she'd shown me holding something inside that circle —

I froze when I heard an unexpected sound among the snap and crackle of weeds beneath our footsteps. "Shh," I said, holding up my hand. "Listen."

I heard it again, a soft mewing sound, almost like a kitten. I rose on tiptoe, trying to see above the line of stalks along the edge of the circle, and what I saw turned my blood cold.

A baby. A pale, motionless infant, still shiny and wet with fluid and a smear of blood.

"Tank, call 9-1-1," I told him, my heart rising to my throat. I didn't dare voice my next thought: *We might have found Mrs. Diaz's missing baby.*

CHAPTER 10

We followed the ambulance to the hospital, of course, and waited in a lobby while doctors checked the baby to be sure it was healthy and unharmed. I knew they'd also take blood and try to determine whether or not the child belonged to Mrs. Diaz. DNA tests took time, so we wouldn't know anything for certain today, but with every passing moment I felt more certain that we'd found the missing child.

"Yay for us," I murmured under my breath as Tank bought a candy bar from the vending machine. "We might have found the baby, but I don't have any idea why or how."

Tank grinned and offered me the candy bar. "Sure I can't tempt you?"

"Not right now." I shook my head. "I can't focus on food when I'm upset."

"That's when I find myself craving sweets." Tank fed another handful of quarters into the machine. "I think sugar fuels my brain cells."

I sank into a plastic chair and closed my eyes, forcing myself to think. Where was the professor when we needed him? If he were here, he'd point out some connection I'd missed, something that tied the baby to the kids and that spot on the beach. If those kids had been responsible for taking the baby — somehow — then why had they brought him back? Had they been walking on that road to bait me? Had they purposefully lured me to that beach so I'd find that baby? Unexpectedly decent of them, if that was their intention — at least the infant wouldn't die of dehydration or exposure.

And how could anyone explain the time factor? That baby was still wet with fluids, but someone had removed it from its mother's womb at least two days before. Of course, the baby could have come from someone else . . . but I didn't even want to consider it.

"Didn't expect to find you here." I looked up at the sound of a familiar voice. Officer Chad Edwards stood across from me, his notepad in his hand. "The doctor said you were the one to find the baby."

"We found him," I corrected, pointing at Tank. "We saw those odd kids again, and followed them onto the beach. The kids disappeared, but on our walk back to the car we found the baby."

"In the middle of a crop circle," Tank said, eyeing Edwards. "As strange as that sounds."

"Strange is right," Edwards said, "considering that no one grows crops along the beach. *Legal* crops, that is."

I smiled at his little joke, knowing that it wasn't uncommon for locals to be busted for growing marijuana plants in their backyards. "Is the baby okay?" I asked.

Edwards nodded. "The doctor said he's in remarkably good condition, considering where you found him. Odd, though — he said the kid was still covered in amniotic fluid, which rules out Mrs. Diaz as the mother. We're treating the case as an abandoned baby."

"I wouldn't —" I hesitated, not wanting to reveal too much about our world of bizarre and impossible situations — "I wouldn't make the usual assumptions in this case. I have a feeling that you may encounter evidence that runs counter to the usual laws of science."

"And reality," Tank added. He gave the cop a deliberate smile. "We could tell you stories you wouldn't believe."

The cop gave us a skeptical look, then

leaned against the wall. "The doctor did uncover something unusual in Baby Doe's case. Seems they found a metallic implant near the base of the child's skull. Would you two happen to know anything about *that*?"

I shivered with a chill that was not from the air. An *implant*?

"What, like a microchip?" Tank asked, eyes wide. "Like a tracking device?"

The cop shrugged. "I don't know what it is, and neither does the doc. He's never seen anything like it."

"Are they gonna take it out?" Tank asked.

The cop pressed his lips together. "Not right now. Something about its position between two nerves — too risky to remove it."

I stood and walked to the candy machine, suddenly possessed of a nervous energy that made me want to run screaming through the halls. Where was the professor? If he were here, he would have answers. If he couldn't think of an answer, he'd at least point us in the right direction. He was the calm we depended on, the voice of reason, the one who was never swayed by emotion or whim or —

As if he'd read my mind, the cop tapped my shoulder. "Any word from your missing professor?"

"None."

"Maybe he'll be waiting when you get home. If he is, give us a call, okay? Otherwise, we're sending an officer over. Since your guy's been gone twenty-four hours, you can file an official missing persons report now."

I thanked him, then gestured to Tank. "Let's go find Brenda and Daniel. And let's hope Officer Edwards is right about the professor coming back."

We walked into a quiet house that seemed to be waiting for us. Even Abby, who was waiting for us in the foyer, skipped her usual canine fandango and greeted us with small licks on our hands.

I dropped my house key on the foyer table, then listened for sounds of life. I heard nothing but the slam of car doors outside as Brenda and Daniel brought up the rear. Dust motes danced in a beam of sunlight from the open door, but nothing else moved.

"Professor?" I called out, clinging to the slim hope that he would answer.

No reply.

I knew I ought to go to the professor's room and start looking for clues, but something in me was not at all comfortable with going through his things. We had been good friends, yes, and co-workers, but he had never intruded in my private life and I never wanted to intrude in his. I felt free to go through his professional papers and to open any documents he placed in our shared dropbox, but I would never have dared to snoop among his personal files, paper or digital.

"Anyone hungry?" I asked, heading toward the kitchen. "I could make a bowl of tuna salad for sandwiches. There are cold cuts in the fridge, and maybe some hot dogs, if anyone wants to nuke a couple of them. . . ."

Brenda made *tsk*ing noises with her tongue, her way of rebuking my lack of attention to proper nutrition, but I had more important things on my mind. My boss had gone missing from my home, and I felt personally responsible. Plus, he was *my* boss. . . .

I stopped, my hand on the kitchen counter, as a memory suddenly surfaced. That night, after he'd made me promise to print that group selfie, he had kissed my forehead . . . the first and only time he'd ever shown that kind of affection. What was that about? I had assumed he was only feeling nostalgic, but what if he'd known something was about to happen to him? What if he'd been receiving messages or threats, and didn't tell me or the others because he didn't want to worry us?

I turned to Brenda, who was pulling cheese and mayonnaise out of the fridge. "Has the professor said anything unusual to you lately? Anything about threats or anyone who might want to hurt him?"

Brenda scowled. "Are you kidding? If I knew someone wanted to hurt him, I'd tell them to go for it. Put the man in his place."

I ignored her barb and looked at Tank, who had already taken a seat at the table. "How about you, Tank? Did the professor mention anything odd to you?"

His brow wrinkled, then he shook his head. "I don't understand half of what he says, but none of it seemed any stranger than usual."

I drew a deep breath. "I miss him," I confessed. "It feels strange for us to be together without him. I feel like we're kids bumbling around in confusion because our father's been taken away."

Brenda rolled her eyes. "He ain't no father of mine. And if he decided to walk out on us, that's fine with me. Maybe we can finally get a little peace and quiet around here."

I dropped to one knee so I could look Daniel in the eye. "Little buddy," I said, gripping his hands, "can you see anyone else in the room? Anyone besides me and you and Brenda and Tank?"

He lifted his gaze and scanned the space around us, then checked out the corners of the ceiling. "No," he said finally, lowering his gaze to meet mine. "Just us."

"No professor?"

He shook his head as the doorbell rang.

Officer Edwards stood outside, along with a man and woman in plain clothes. "Hello," Edwards said. "Ms. Goldstein, meet Lewis and Brandolini, crime-scene techs. If you could show us to the professor's room . . ."

I nodded, then led the way to the bedroom the professor had been using. "Everything's just as he left it," I said. "I looked around in here, but didn't want to mess anything up in case — well, you know. So you might find my fingerprints, and my grandparents', but —"

"I doubt we'll be fingerprinting," the woman, Lewis, said, "since this doesn't appear to be a crime scene. We're just going to take a look around and see if we can pick up any ideas about where your professor might have gone."

"I don't think he went anywhere," I insisted. "He's not from this area, so where would he go? He wasn't the type to sit in a bar, and as a recovering alcoholic, he didn't drink. He didn't particularly like the beach —"

"What does he like?" Brandolini asked. "Everybody likes something."

"He likes books." I crossed my arms and nodded toward the stack of books on the desk. "He likes to read. He's super intelligent. Committed to academia. He doesn't have hobbies like most people."

"We'll keep that in mind." Lewis pulled a pair of rubber gloves from her pocket, then drew them on. "We'll call you if we need you."

Taking the hint, I went back to the kitchen.

By the time the police had finished in the professor's room, Brenda, Daniel, Tank, and I had cleared out the kitchen and gone to the living room. Officer Edwards led the two techs down the hallway, then stood by the fireplace and kept his head down as he held a sheet of paper with two fingers.

"I'm glad you're all together," he said, lifting the paper. "I found this document on Professor McKinney's computer and saw that his laptop had been wirelessly connected."

"Yeah," I said. "I set it up so he could

print the speech he gave at UT."

Officer Edwards looked directly at me. "The file was saved as 'For Andrea,' but this letter seems to be addressed to everyone. Maybe you should read it."

I tried to stand, but my legs suddenly felt as solid as marshmallows and I sank back into the sofa. Edwards saw my predicament and stepped forward, handing me the note.

I skimmed the heading, saw that the letter had been dated on the day he took our group photo, and began to read:

Dear friends,

I have come to feel a profound respect for all of you, even you, Ms. Barnick, so perhaps you should consider this my tribute to the courage that resides in each of your hearts.

Tank, you are a prime example of how appearances can be deceiving. Though you look like an overgrown fireplug and have the intellect of a tree stump, you possess a wisdom not often found in more educated and cultured men. I salute you, sir, and give you my respect. And as to that flaming brightness for which you hold great affection, I must warn you — men have been burned by such passions. Do not be like the man who spent all he had on a treasure he could neither hold nor handle.

Daniel, while I was at first unconvinced that a child could be of any practical use in such a motley crew as ours, I have come to appreciate your gifts and your sense of timing in particular. Furthermore, your attachment to Ms. Barnick has proved useful in that it has shut her mouth on more than one occasion. Good lad. Grow in peace, Daniel, and if it is possible for me to peer through space and time in order to keep tabs on you, know that I will do so.

Brenda, my sharp-tongued, nicotine-stained, misanthropic acquaintance: as much as I hate to admit it, your particular gift has saved my shriveled and cynical behind more than once, so for that I thank you. And if the passing years sprinkle your waspish nature with the proverbial spoonful of sugar, be a dear and dust it off, will you? I cannot imagine you other than you are.

Andrea — first, dear girl, please accept my apology for any worry or trouble this has caused you, especially considering that I am writing this in your home. But though you have never pried or queried, you surely must know that I have made many regrettable choices on my journey along the path of life. I have therefore decided to end this path. I have learned all I need to know.

I digress. So sorry. I am giving my old apartment the boot — key inside ceramic ant. Landlord has been busy traveling so don't expect him to repaint. Rent due on seventh. File speech copy under "dimension," please, for others may wish to read. Remember — unlike me, you never needed help. Godspeed.

I bid all of you a fond farewell.

Sincerely,
James McKinney

I lowered the printed page as the professor's words tumbled and leap-frogged in my head. What was this about? The letter read almost like a last will and testament, but the professor had left us no property, and he certainly hadn't —

"We think this may be James McKinney's suicide note," Edwards said, locking his hands.

Suicide? I blinked at Edwards, then turned to the others. "That's impossible . . . isn't it?"

Tank grunted. "The professor wouldn't kill himself. He was too smart for that."

"The big guy is right," Brenda said, thrusting out her chin in the professor's defense. "The professor wasn't the type to off himself. No way."

"There's no proof," I pointed out. "And this letter says nothing about killing himself."

Edwards took the letter from my hand. " 'I have therefore decided to *end this path,*' " he read. "That's the language of suicide."

"He wasn't suicidal," Tank repeated. "No way."

"He was clearly distraught," Edwards said, bracing one arm on the fireplace mantel. "And distraught people often write or say things that don't make much sense. They're confused. They're upset. They ramble, they put down words that don't fit. They're set on checking out."

"But how would he do that?" I challenged. "There's no body. No blood. No empty pill bottle."

"There's an ocean." The female crime tech pointed to the water beyond the sliding doors. "All he had to do was walk across the beach, enter the water, and swim toward the horizon. Eventually he would have gotten tired and drowned."

"But the body —"

"Will wash up eventually . . . or not." Edwards clamped his lips together. "I hate to be indelicate, but sometimes the body is devoured by predators."

I lowered my head as a vein began to throb near my temple. None of this could be happening. Nothing made sense to me, and though I was usually quick to spot a pattern in any series of events, numbers, or diagrams, I couldn't see any pattern in the past few days.

"Thank you," I said, my voice hoarse. "If . . . you find anything —"

"If we have any news, we'll be sure to call or come by," Officer Edwards said, his face grim. "And I'm very sorry for your loss." He looked around the group. "I'm very sorry for all of you."

Chapter 11

After the cops left, I went outside and sat on the deck. The usual ocean breeze had turned into a real wind, riding the edge of an approaching thunderstorm. Dark clouds loomed over the Gulf, and the wind pushed at my cheeks as if urging me to go inside.

Fat chance. I wasn't ready to face the others.

As the professor's assistant, I felt a mantle of responsibility hovering over my shoulders, and I wasn't ready to be the leader, the hostess, or anything else I was expected to be. All I wanted was time alone to sit and feel whatever it was I had to feel as my emotions sorted themselves out.

We were all struggling. Brenda had gone immediately to her room, and soon the sounds of cursing and crashing objects came through the door. Of course she would be angry — she had only begun to open that steel door around her heart, but with this loss, she'd probably slam it shut again.

I worried about Daniel. He didn't respond well when stressed, and I had no idea how he would react to the news that the professor would no longer be with us. But after the police left, Daniel got up and went into the professor's bedroom. I followed, curious about what he might do, and watched from the doorway as Daniel ran his hand over the desk, the laptop, the notebooks, even the professor's pajamas and suitcase. Finally he moved to the nightstand, where he ran his hand over the professor's phone and watch.

Daniel picked up the watch and turned to look at me, a question in his eyes. "Yes," I said. "You can have it."

I helped him strap it on his slender wrist, then watched as Daniel went back down the hallway, his right hand holding the bulky watch securely on his left wrist.

We all mourned in different ways.

I heard the rumble of the sliding doors behind me, but didn't turn to see who was coming out. Maybe if I stayed quiet, the intruder would realize that I didn't want company.

I brushed the wetness off my cheeks and turned my head toward the south, then heard a heavy creak of a board behind me.

Only Tank was heavy enough to creak boards like that.

Next thing I knew he was sitting beside me. I looked at him, about to tell him I wanted to be by myself for a while, but he spoke first. "A person shouldn't have to cry alone."

"No, no — I'm okay. Really. You don't have to babysit me."

"I wasn't talking about you."

And then, while I watched in total astonishment, Tank covered his face with his hands and went completely to pieces.

We wept together, of course — the big lug in my arms and I in his. And when we had cried long enough for the clouds to start weeping in sympathy, we got up and walked onto the beach, both of us ignoring the rain that felt like cold needles on our faces.

I couldn't stand thinking of the professor in the past tense. I'd admired and respected him deeply. I also — though he would not have wanted to hear this — pitied him in many ways. He could be charming, warm, loving, and paternal, but few people ever saw those traits because he hid them beneath a veneer of bitterness and cynicism.

Tank was no longer crying, but those broad shoulders were slumped beneath the weight of grief he carried. We were all feeling the loss, and if we stayed together, we'd feel it for years to come. The professor's absence would be visible every time we sat at the dining room table and every time we rode in a car. No one would sit in his favorite chair when we gathered in my grandparents' living room, and we would still tiptoe past the bedroom he used out of respect for the hours he spent studying there.

Officer Edwards clearly agreed with the crime techs; the professor had committed suicide. He must have seen me punch in the security alarm code, so after kissing me good-night, while I was noisily brushing my teeth, he had disarmed the system, then rearmed it, taking advantage of the thirty-second window in which he could open a door and slip out without sounding the alarm. According to Officer Edwards's theory, the professor had been walking across these sands as I got ready for bed, and he had been swimming for Mexico by the time I fell asleep.

He would have been dead by the time I woke the next morning.

Even though the logical part of my brain understood that scenario and even appreciated that the professor hadn't killed himself in my grandparents' house, something else in me refused to accept that idea. Reason protested that James McKinney was about as likely to kill himself as he was to sprout a fish's tail. Impossible. Unlikely. Categorically out of the question.

"Ummm." Tank paused as if he were fishing for words. "What do we do now?"

I shrugged and blinked up at the rain. "Beats me."

"Do you think we'll keep going . . . as a group, I mean? Whoever's been sending us plane tickets and invitations, do you think they'll keep doing it?"

"I don't know, Tank. I don't know any more than you do." My words came out harsher than I'd intended, and my conscience smacked me when I saw the hurt on Tank's face. "Listen." I turned and took his hands. "I'm sorry. But I'm as confused as you — maybe even more. I've not only lost my boss, I've lost . . . part of who I am. I was his assistant, his right hand, and I could have kept being his right hand forever. Now I don't know what I'm going to do for a job, for a career, for . . . anything."

My voice broke. I started to turn away, but Tank drew me close and patted my back. "It's gonna be okay, Andi," he said, his voice a reassuring growl in my ear.

"Though what the cops said made no sense, I guess maybe suicide never makes much sense. No matter how well you think you know a person, nobody can ever really know what's going on inside someone else's head —"

"But I *did* know," I insisted, pulling away. "I knew him better than anyone! I knew he was fixated on his studies into other dimensions, that he was all excited about that presentation. He kept saying that if we could find a way to bend time, we could go back and repair all the damage we'd done in our past, that we could start over. He wasn't finished with his work, but our encounters with those different universes had given him new ideas and he was just beginning a new phase of —"

I halted as a shard of memory sliced into my thoughts. *I have made many regrettable choices on my journey along the path of life. I have therefore decided to end this path.*

What if the professor hadn't been writing about suicide at all?

"Holy cats." I pulled away from Tank and ran for the house.

CHAPTER 12

"Andi, what *are* you doing?"

"I think —" I pressed my hands to the side of my head in an effort to still my spinning thoughts. "I think he was talking about dimensions, not death. He wanted to end a third-dimension path, that's all. Where's that darn letter?"

Brenda dropped her magazine and searched the room, then pointed to the coffee table. I snatched up the letter and reread the so-called suicide note. No doubt, the letter had been written in the professor's language and style, all except the ending —

"Here." I took the letter and sat at my grandmother's desk, then pulled a highlighter from the drawer. "This paragraph, the one where he talks about his apartment. Notice how it doesn't flow like the rest of the paragraphs?"

Tank peered over my left shoulder as Brenda looked over my right. "Yeah, so? The cop said the professor was losing it at that point."

I snickered. "Have you ever seen the professor lose it? Ever?"

The corner of Brenda's mouth dipped. "Good point."

"It's gotta be a message. Something . . . encrypted. A pattern."

I stared at the page, highlighter in hand, then focused on the paragraphs addressed to me.

> Andrea — first, dear girl, please accept my apology for any worry or trouble this has caused you, especially considering that I am writing this in your home. But though you have never pried or queried, you surely must know that I have made many regrettable choices on my journey along the path of life. I have therefore decided to end this path. I have learned all I need to know.
>
> I digress. So sorry. I am giving my old apartment the boot — key inside ceramic ant. Landlord has been busy traveling so don't expect him to repaint. Rent due on seventh. File speech copy under "dimension," please, for others may wish to read. Remember — unlike me, you never needed help. Godspeed.

"By the way," Brenda drawled, "I can't say that I was pleased to read his comments about me. Even a man who's planning to check out should have better manners."

"He *wants* people to think this is a suicide note," I said. "Because . . ." I waited for an answer to pop into my head.

"Because why?" Brenda asked.

I sighed. "I got nothin'."

"What's that about a ceramic ant?" Tank said, pointing to the paragraph that was nothing like the others. "Some kind of garden statue?"

"He's not a gardener," I said, focusing on that line. "And his landlord isn't a person, it's the university. And he doesn't pay rent, the apartment is faculty housing, provided for tenured professors in residence. . . ." I caught my breath. "That entire paragraph is bogus, but no one who reads this letter would know that except . . . me."

"So —" Brenda twirled one of her dreadlocks around her finger — "what's he trying to tell you?"

I grinned as the light came on. "It's a code, probably a numbered sequence. So what number would he use?"

We looked at each other. "The year?" Brenda suggested.

"His birthday?" Tank said.

"It's gotta be a smaller number," I said, reading the paragraph again. "A number small enough to repeat in this paragraph."

"Five." Daniel appeared beside Brenda. He lifted his hand and counted, pointing to each of us: "One, two, three, four, and" — he pointed to the letter — "five."

"Five of us — makes as much sense as anything. So I'm keeping every fifth word, starting with my name."

> Andrea ~~— first, dear girl, please~~ accept ~~my apology for any~~ worry ~~or trouble this has~~ caused ~~you. But though you~~ have ~~never pried or queried,~~ you ~~surely must know that~~ I ~~have made many regrettable~~ choices ~~on my journey along~~ the ~~path of life. I~~ have ~~therefore decided to end~~ this ~~path.~~

"Andrea accept worry caused have you I choices the have this," Brenda read. "Makes no sense at all."

"So let's try the second paragraph."

> I ~~digress. So sorry. I~~ am ~~giving my old apartment~~ the ~~boot — key inside ceramic~~ ant. ~~Landlord has been busy~~ traveling ~~so don't expect him~~ to ~~repaint. Rent due on~~ seventh. ~~File speech copy under~~ "dimen-

sion," ~~please, for others may~~ wish ~~to read. Remember — unlike~~ me, ~~you never needed help.~~ Godspeed.

" 'I am the ant,' " Tank read, " 'traveling to seventh dimension wish me Godspeed.' " He blinked. "That doesn't make any sense, either."

"Oh, yes it does." I brought my hand to my mouth as the pieces fell into place. "The ant, remember? The sugar ant from his speech, the ant traveling on the thin piece of paper. If you twist the paper, the ant can move from one dimension to another. The professor — somehow — found a way to move into the seventh dimension!"

" 'Wish me Godspeed,' " Brenda whispered, her eyes widening. "How in the world did the old fart manage to do that?"

"I don't know," I answered, laughter rising from my throat, "and no one is going to believe us if we try to tell them where he is. But he's not dead. He has only . . . moved."

Tank stepped backward and rubbed his brow. "I still don't get it."

"You don't have to." I threw him a reassuring smile. "You know how Littlefoot came from another universe? It's kind of like that. The professor's just gonna be out of touch for a while."

"But everyone's going to think he's dead," Brenda pointed out. "And face it, maybe he is. Maybe his technique or whatever he used to zap himself out of here didn't work. Maybe he got to the seventh dimension and a monster ate him. Maybe he transported himself to a Flatland kind of world where he doesn't fit, so he imploded. So many things could have gone wrong —"

"Maybe it doesn't matter," I said. "All of that stuff is out of our control — even out of *his* control. But at least we know he's not floating out in the Gulf. He's not being eaten by sharks. He's . . . he's like an explorer in the new world, conquering unexplored territories."

"He wanted to correct his mistakes," Tank said, his eyes softening. "I get that. And if he can find a way to do it —" He shrugged. "I'd love to hear all about it sometime."

"So what do we do now?" Brenda asked. She glanced toward the empty bedroom. "The man ain't comin' back."

"I guess" — I made a face — "as distasteful as it will be, I guess we have to go along with the suicide scenario. That's how the professor set it up, so I guess that's what he wanted."

"Roger that," Tank said.

"Okay," Brenda echoed.

Daniel just stared at the watch dangling from his wrist.

Chapter 13

As the black-clad mourners milled around the empty coffin, I lifted my gaze to the low-hanging clouds and wondered if the professor had found a way to peel back the curtain and spy on his former dimension. Probably not, considering it had taken him a lifetime to figure out how to engineer a path to wherever he was now.

He would have been pleased by the turn-out at his graveside — lots of faculty, the university president, and dozens of students who had either loved his lectures or hated them, depending on their point of view. Someone in his family had sprung for an expensive spray of roses on the casket. As per the wishes expressed in the professor's will, there had been no funeral or memorial service. There would be no wake, but I knew that most of the university faculty would soon head over to the Thirsty Scholar, where they'd lift a glass in his memory.

I stood in respectful silence as the funeral director murmured, "Ashes to ashes, dust to dust," and the casket lowered into the grave, accompanied by the whine of an electric motor. A couple of mourners tossed carnations into the dark space, then most people wandered away.

I remained, feeling it my duty to see this charade through to the end.

I wasn't the only one who lingered. A woman in a black hat and veil stood on the other side of the open grave. She pressed a tissue to her eyes, and sniffed as she wiped away tears.

Who was she, and where had she been during the professor's final years? She must have loved him, because her tears were genuine. . . .

I stepped closer so I might better see her. Silver hair brushed her shoulders, and when she lifted her head I saw a lovely face marked by the passing of more than a few years. She might have been the professor's age, or even a little younger, and she was still a beautiful woman. Was she one of the professor's regrets? Had he found a way back to her . . . and his younger self?

I was working up the courage to speak to her when the gravediggers approached. One of them lowered his shovel and nodded at me, then he and his partner removed the fake grass that served to disguise the mound of dirt that would fill in the grave. Time to go.

I drew a deep breath and looked up, but the woman had already left the graveside. I saw her walking, not toward the parking lot, but another section of the cemetery. Did she know someone else buried here?

I strode forward, intending to hurry and catch her, but turned my ankle when I stepped in a patch of soft dirt. "Ooof!" I sank to the ground as gracefully as I could, and the gravediggers dropped their shovels and hurried to help.

"Watch your step," one said with a crooked smile. "We wouldn't want you to fall in."

I managed a smile in return. "It's these heels. I don't usually wear shoes this high."

I brushed dirt off my knees and tucked my purse under my arm, intent on catching the dark figure moving through the tombstones and mausoleums.

"Ma'am?" I called, hobbling forward. My ankle was beginning to throb, and if I pushed it, I wouldn't be able to walk tomorrow. I stopped and pulled off my shoes, then hop-skipped forward, lurching left to right as I searched for the woman in black.

I stopped and waved one of my shoes. "Hey, lady!"

She turned and looked at me, and the expression on her face was so heartrending that I nearly wept. My mind supplied a hundred reasons why she would be standing at the professor's grave: she was a former lover, a long-lost sister, an ex-wife, a fellow teacher, a nun he'd known in his days as a priest — and she had loved him, but time and circumstance had kept them apart. But now she'd come here to mourn him . . .

"Will you wait, please?"

The woman didn't answer, but moved behind a wall of marble that blocked my view.

I hurried on. Finally I reached the spot where the woman had disappeared, but when I looked around, I saw nothing but a marble tombstone etched

Marissa Lorena Longworth
1958–1999
She walks in beauty.

No sign of the woman. Only a fence at the eastern boundary of the cemetery and a path that led back to the entrance.

I followed the path, taking my time and placing as little weight on my injured ankle as I could. When I got back to my apartment, I'd put my leg up, cover the ankle with a bag of ice, and call Tank and Brenda. They had wanted to fly up for the graveside service, but I had talked them out of it, promising a full postmortem report.

Knowing that I had my hands full with cleaning out the professor's apartment and office, Tank had volunteered to be my go-to guy for reports on BEKs. He had set up a Google search and was trolling the Internet for new reports of BEK sightings, which, he told me unhappily, were on the rise. Black-eyed kids were being reported in every country, on every continent. A guard at an Arctic outpost had even opened his door one night to find two black-eyed kids outside.

At least the Diaz family had their baby again. While the baby had been confirmed as theirs, according to my grandmother's latest report, the doctors had not yet been able to remove the mysterious implant.

I got to my car, leaned heavily on the back passenger door, and managed to get my door unlocked and opened. Thankfully, I didn't have to use my injured ankle to drive, so I slid in, carefully placed my left leg in a safe position, and pulled my car door closed.

And then, in the side mirror, I saw the

professor, as clear as stark reality. I turned, expecting to see him standing beside the car, but I was alone. I looked at the mirror again. The professor still flickered there, then he pulled something from a coat he wore and held it up — the printed photo, the selfie of our group.

My smile cracked into a sob. The professor's smile softened, and he pressed the photo to his chest and covered it with his hand.

And then he was gone.

Caught in a place between laughter and tears, I leaned my head against the steering wheel and struggled to get a grip on my emotions. He was alive. He was okay. He was just . . . somewhere else.

The Village

ALTON GANSKY

Chapter 1
Arrival

The sun was blinking.

Well, not really blinking. That would be a sign that the end of the world was about to arrive. What it was doing was flashing in my eyes as I did my best to drive the Ford SUV up the narrow mountain road. The real culprits were the trees. It was about an hour from sunset and dogwood trees kept blocking the sun, making it look like it was flickering. Truth be told, it was kinda annoying. Still the forest, the mountains, the clear sky were all very beautiful.

I wished it were that peaceful inside the car.

I shot a glance at Andi sitting in the passenger's seat next to me, then stole a quick look at the back seat. Brenda sat behind Andi, gazing out the window on her right just as she had been doing since we left the airport in Asheville. She hadn't said more than twenty words since we arrived in North

Carolina. If you knew Brenda, then you know how this was not normal for her. Not a single snide remark. Odd, I found myself missing her occasional barbs. Just as well. She hasn't been all that warm and cuddly since —

Well, no need to get into that now.

Seated behind me was Daniel, my ten-year-old buddy. He wasn't himself. I expected to see his young face hovering over the screen of his handheld video game like usual. I hadn't heard a single digital beep out of that game — or a word out of him.

Of course, I had no right to expect anything to be normal.

My friends and I have been living in a "new normal." That's what Andi called it. She's good with words, and the Internet, and research, and just about everything else. She is really good at keeping me on pins and needles. Anyway, she's especially good at seeing patterns no one else can see. She can look at ten unrelated things and see what connects them all. That's our Andi. Now that the professor is gone, Andi Goldstein is the smart one of our group. If I said that out loud I'm sure she'd show me the back of her hand. Brenda might show me the front of her fist.

That's not to say that Brenda Barnick is

any kind of dummy. She's smart in a different kinda way. *Street-smart* is the best way to describe her. She's a gifted artist, although most of her art decorates people's skin. No one can ink a tat like Brenda. She's dynamite with pen and paper, too. The strange thing — not so strange to us these days — is that her drawings somehow show a bit of the future.

Me? Well, if we haven't already met, then all you need to know is that my name is Bjorn Christensen but I go by Tank. It's easier to say. At six-foot-three and 260 pounds, I've been gaining weight, so no one asks, "Why do they call you Tank?" My size is why Daniel sat behind me while I drove. He didn't need as much leg room as Andi and Brenda.

"Much farther?"

Whoo-hoo. Two words from Brenda.

Andi kept her eyes on her smartphone. "GPS says about five minutes, but it's been on-again, off-again. Cell coverage up here is abysmal."

Double whoo-hoo. This was almost a conversation. I decided to risk it and say something myself. "The road is slowing us down. Too narrow. Too many hairpin curves."

"Ya think?" Brenda sounded sour. "I'm

getting carsick." There was a pause, and I redirected the rearview mirror to get a better look at her face. She was staring at me. "And when I get carsick, Cowboy, I tend to vomit forward and to the left. Just about where you're sitting."

Brenda likes to call me "Cowboy." No one else does. "Should I stop and give you a chance to . . . you know . . . let you get some air?"

The three in the car all said, "No!" Even little Daniel.

"Okay, okay. Cool your jets. I'm just trying to keep everyone safe."

"I'm sick of the car," Brenda said. "I'm sick of flying to out-of-the-way places."

"Technically," I said, "Tampa is not out of the way. It's a pretty big city. And when we were in San Diego —"

"Shut up, Bjorn."

Yikes. Brenda never uses my first name.

"Yes, ma'am. Shutting up."

Andi's guess of five minutes was a tad off. Not by much, just a quarter hour. Brenda would have chewed through the car door if she could have managed it, and a big part of me believed she could.

By the time we rolled into town, the sun had dipped below the mountains and what had once been shadows was now full-blown twilight. The streetlights, which looked a hundred years old if they were a day, flickered on and made a brave effort at pushing back the dark of evening. I was glad to pull onto Main Street and leave the twisty two-lane road behind. Newland, North Carolina, wasn't all that far from Asheville, but it was all uphill.

"No cell service, guys," Andi said. "We'll have to find the hotel the old-fashioned way. Look for it."

"You made reservations, right?" Brenda made the question sound like a statement.

Andi shook her head. Her flighty red hair flopped around a little. Some might think it looked funny, but I think she's adorable. As far as I'm concerned, she is gorgeous from the tip-top of her hair down to those tiny things she calls feet.

"I couldn't make reservations. They don't have a website, and when I called all I got was an answering service. And by answering service I mean answering machine. Didn't know those things were still around."

Brenda leaned forward and for a moment I thought there would be three people in the front seat. "You're kidding me, right?"

"C'mon, Brenda. I'm not known for my sense of humor."

That wasn't completely true. I'd seen

Andi laugh many times. She could be witty when she wanted. I'm pretty sure she wasn't feeling it at the moment.

"I'm not spending the night in the car," Brenda said with some heat.

"We shouldn't have to." Andi didn't bother to turn to face Brenda. "You know how this works. We get a message with a destination and information on where to stay. Maybe our keepers made reservations for us."

"They had better."

"Okay, ladies," I said, "let's see what we're dealing with before we start shooting at each other." Of course, for self-protection, I glanced over my shoulder to see if Brenda was coming for me. She wasn't. Instead, I saw little Daniel patting her leg. Daniel might be the only person in the world who can settle Hurricane Brenda. It was working.

I motored slowly down the street, taking in the town. There wasn't much to take in. I've been in a few small towns in my time, and this one was pretty much the same thing. The buildings were old, maybe built in the thirties and forties. Some were made of redbrick, some had wood exteriors. I didn't see any stucco like what I see in California. There were a few shops and one department store, though most would be hard-pressed to call the small two-story building much of a department store. There were two eating establishments that I hoped offered biscuits and gravy, and a bar for those that liked to drink their meals from a beer mug. I slowed when I came to a building with a gold star on the door and a sign that read *Sheriff's Office.*

I pulled to the curb. A second sign hung below: GONE FISHING. We saw a hardware store, a feed store, a shoe store, and a few other stores.

"Anyone else notice the weirdness?" Andi was leaning forward as if by doing so, the town would release its secrets.

"Like what?" Brenda asked.

"Like there's no one on the street. No pedestrians. No cars on the road. I don't even see parked cars. Shouldn't there be a beat-up pickup truck or something?"

"Maybe . . ." I began.

"Maybe what?" Andi said.

I put my brain in high gear, then said, "I got nuthin'."

"Tank's got nothing." Daniel snickered. At least the kid hadn't forgotten how to talk. He was a quiet kid most of the time. *Emotionally challenged* his doctors say, but he's not. He's just different, and since Brenda took over his care, he is more open than ever. Not a chatterbox, but he no longer hesitates to speak. He has a special gift all his own.

"Hey! I thought you were my pal," I said with a big grin.

"I am. Pals. You still got nuthin'."

I caught Brenda and Andi smiling. Sometimes I think the kid could walk into a dark room with no lights and somehow lights would come on anyway. Don't analyze the statement. Just take it at face value.

We reached the end of Main Street and I saw something that gave me hope — a church. A church with a real steeple. It was small, but beautiful. I'm the spiritual one of the group, and I love church. My friends, well, they haven't come around. Yet.

Just as we reached the end of Main Street, Andi piped up. "There. I see the hotel. On the left."

There was movement in the back seat as Daniel and Brenda scooted forward for a look-see.

"I see it." I did and it looked good to me. I was sick of the car. At first it was hard to make out detail in the dim light, but I could see clearly enough to know I was looking at a three-story, wood-framed building with an attractive front porch and shutters on the windows. The place looked very much like a country home on steroids. It wasn't actually in town, but about a hundred yards past the last building on the street. As we drew near, I could see someone had kept the place up. The paint looked new, the shutters hung straight, the furniture — about six or so rocking chairs — was very inviting; although, after a flight and a slow drive, I was looking forward to standing for a bit.

"Looks nice," Andi said. "I like the exterior."

Brenda huffed. "I'm more interested in the interior. I really gotta pee."

With that pressing news, I pulled into the parking lot on the east side of the building, took the first space I could find — which was easy since ours was the only car in the lot — and switched off the SUV.

Brenda's door was open before I could set the parking brake.

CHAPTER 2
GETTING A COLD SHOULDER

"I'm gonna wait to bring in the luggage," I said. "I want to make sure we're staying here tonight."

"It has to be here," Andi said. "This is where we were sent and it's the only place in town, at least as far as I saw."

I agreed with that. I hadn't seen anything that said motel or hotel or boardinghouse, and I mentioned that fact. "Come on, buddy." I put a hand on Daniel's small shoulder. "Let's go see if Brenda made it to the necessary room."

Daniel giggled. "Necessary room." He repeated the phrase then snickered again.

We walked to the front of the old-style hotel, up four steps to the front porch and to a wide green door with stained-glass panels. Light oozed through the colored glass, making me think of the church again.

Andi pushed the door open. It wasn't fully closed. Apparently Brenda's need was real.

The lobby looked like something out of the fifties. The carpet was ornate and decorated with images of flowers. The flowers had faces. I think they were meant to be cute, but they kinda creeped me out. I shut the door behind us, then turned my attention to the front of the lobby. The front desk was made of wood that bore a shiny bar-top finish. It was as pretty as the carpet was disturbing.

A small woman stood behind the front desk. She was short and — I hate to say this — looked like a mouse. I don't mean she had mouse ears; I mean her features were small, her nose slightly pointed, and her hair a light brown that looked like it wanted to be blond. For a moment, I started to look for mouse whiskers. Her eyes were wide, but that was easy to understand. A black woman with dreadlocks had just plunged through the lobby door and made a beeline for — I looked around the lobby — the bathroom next to the stairs. Brenda always made a strong first impression.

I felt a smile might do the lady some good, so I gave her my best we're-not-criminals grin and walked to the desk. "My name is Tank. This is Andi Goldstein, and this little guy is Daniel."

"Um, hello."

She even sounded a little like a mouse. I continued. "I'm guessing you already saw Brenda. She's about the same height as Andi and —"

"The black girl with the funny hair?" the woman squeaked.

"That's her. We've been on the road for a long time and she needed . . . to use the facilities."

"I figured that part out."

Andi moved to my side. "I called and left a message yesterday on your machine but never got a call back."

I heard a flushing sound followed by a door opening. Brenda exited, looking refreshed. "Sorry about that, but when a girl has to go, a girl has to go."

Andi returned to the desk clerk. "Anyway, we would like three rooms, please."

"I-I'm sorry. We're full up."

We stood dumbfounded. I started to say something, but Andi had taken control. "If you were booked up, then why didn't you return my call and tell us that before we drove up here?"

"I didn't get the message. Maybe someone else did." The woman inched back a foot as if she expected Andi to spring over the counter.

I watched as Andi's eyes shifted to a

nameplate on the counter. "Jewel Tarkington, is it? Listen, Ms. Tarkington, I think you're having some fun with us. Maybe Brenda's mad dash in here put you off a little, but we're really nice people and need a place to stay tonight."

"I wish I could help."

"Our money is good," I added.

"I have no doubt that you are wonderful people, but like I say, the hotel is —"

"There are no cars in the parking lot," Brenda said. The temperature in the room dropped at least five degrees.

"We don't use cars much around here —"

"I see you keep your keys on that board behind you," Andi said. "It looks to me like every hook has a key hanging from it. Did everyone leave at the same time?"

"No, of course not, it's just that . . . that . . ."

Daniel spoke to Brenda softly, but I heard him just fine. "Like Tank. She's got nuthin'."

I half expected Brenda to hush my little buddy, but she didn't. I don't think I would have, either.

"Let me see if I have this right, lady. No cars in the lot, no one in their rooms, no noise from people staying here, and you want us to believe that every room in the place is booked. You expecting a bus or somethin'?"

"Please, there's nothing I can do." Jewel began to look a little pale. "I can call another hotel for you. You know. Get you booked there."

"This town has another hotel?" I asked.

"Well, no. I didn't mean in Newland, I meant somewhere else. There's a hotel up the road a piece. I hear it's real nice."

"How far up the road?" Andi's words were coming out a little sharper than usual.

"Not far. Just fifty or sixty miles."

"Fifty or sixty miles!"

I could tell Brenda was about to launch herself over the counter. I put a hand on her shoulder and gave a little squeeze. A second later, Daniel was standing at her side. When I say standing at her side, I mean he had pressed himself against her leg. She put a hand on his shoulder kinda like I had put one of my mitts on her.

She took a ragged breath. "You're going to turn us out onto the street. You're telling us that the only thing we can do is take my son up a winding, narrow mountain road in the dark to some other hotel just so you don't have to bother with us?"

Daniel sniffed. I glanced at the boy. His lower lip quivered. His eyes were wet. He looked at the floor, then leaned his head against Brenda's hip as if sorrow had made it too heavy to hold erect. If I were a member of the group that nominates actors for the Oscars, I would put Daniel's name in for an award.

"Son?" Jewel looked back and forth from Daniel to Brenda.

"What? You don't think a black woman can adopt a white kid? Is that what all this is about? Race?"

"No, of course not."

"Then what is the problem, lady?" Brenda's tone grew hotter. "You gonna throw us back into the dark rather than release three of your precious rooms?"

She looked out the front window. "I can't get you to leave, can I?"

"No, ma'am." I smiled when I said that.

Jewel marched around the front desk, then beat feet to the front door. I watched and then waited for her to tell us to get out. Instead, she locked the door, twisting the deadbolt latch several times to make certain it had engaged. She then checked to make sure the front windows were still battened down. With brisk movements, she closed the curtains over the window, taking a peek out as if expecting a visit from the local pitchfork-and-torch mob.

"Okay, okay. I'll give you three rooms."

She hustled back behind the desk. "Do you mind walking up stairs? Our elevator doesn't work. Never had the money to get the thing fixed."

"Maybe that's because you keep sending paying customers away."

I wish Brenda hadn't said that. Jewel ignored her.

"We don't mind stairs," Andi said as I started to disagree, but settled on being glad that I wouldn't be driving any more tonight.

"Thank you, ma'am." I gave my best smile again, the one I save for special occasions. "It'll only take me a moment to get the luggage from the car."

"No!" the mouse roared. "I mean, leave it. Get it in the morning."

"We have toiletries and clothes in there —"

"I don't care. I've already locked up." She looked at the door. "I don't want any more strangers walking through the door. If I had known you were coming, I would have locked it before you got here."

"Why?" Brenda asked. "Does the boogeyman live in Newland?"

"No. It's too scary for him." Jewel fidgeted with the keys. "Look, I'll let you stay for free. Just don't unlock the door. Got it?"

"No, I don't got it." Brenda's flame was

growing hotter.

"This is the deal. You stay for free, but you don't go out until the sun is up tomorrow. If you're hungry —"

"We are," I said.

She studied me with worried eyes for a moment. "A man your size must be hungry all the time."

"Not all the time . . . okay, you're right."

Jewel pointed to a door in the back near the western corner. "That's the kitchen. Feel free to make a meal for yourself. There's eggs, bacon, and the like. You can have breakfast for dinner." She paused. "There's some leftover fried chicken I made yesterday. Mashed potatoes and gravy, too. You'll have to heat that up, but it should fill the hole."

Fried chicken, potatoes, and gravy. I considered kissing Jewel on her little mouse nose.

"That's very kind of you."

I don't think she heard the compliment. "Stay away from the windows. And by all that is holy, don't open them."

"Until sunup, right?" Andi said. She gave me a knowing look that said *This woman is a couple of sandwiches shy of a picnic.*

"Right."

Andi pressed a little harder. "I don't suppose you want to explain all this. What are you afraid of?"

"You're right, ma'am, I don't want to explain it."

"Leave the woman alone," Brenda said. "We have rooms. Let's be happy about that."

Andi's expression said she wasn't satisfied with the suggestion, but she didn't object. When Brenda was right, Brenda was right.

"Good." Jewel pushed the keys forward. "Third floor. The windows look out the back and onto the mountains. Real pretty in the morning. The rooms don't have bathrooms. Halfway down the hall you'll find a men's and women's facility. Showers are in there, too. It takes a few minutes for the hot water to make its way up to the third floor, so be patient."

She reached beneath the counter and pulled out a handful of toothbrushes, still in their factory wrapping, thank the Lord, four combs, and four tiny hairbrushes. She also retrieved those small bottles of shampoo and conditioner, and soap in a box. She was well stocked for all the people who didn't stay in her hotel.

We each said thank you, some of us more sincerely than others, and started up the stairs. I led the way. From behind me I heard Brenda say, "That wasn't weird at all." Yep, she is still the queen of sarcasm.

Chapter 3
Breakfast for Dinner

The rooms were nice enough. Not grand. Not even business class. I guess most people would call the place quaint. Back in my college football playing days, our football team had better rooms when we were out of town for away games. That was then; this was now. The carpet was brown and looked clean; the bed looked like something dragged out of the fifties but with less style. There was an inexpensive dresser, a side chair, and an end table, all made from oak. The finish had yellowed over time. Still, there was nothing to complain about — except the wallpaper. Like the carpet in the lobby, the wallpaper reminded me of pictures I had seen of homes from the late 1800s. It was gaudy, overdone, and worse, had flowers with faces on them just like the lobby carpet. I didn't know if I could undress in front of all those tiny eyes. No wonder the hotel was empty. To anyone with an active imagination, this was a room designed to raise nightmares.

I also noticed that there was no phone in the room. I guess if you needed to contact the front desk you had to walk down two flights of stairs. In some ways the room was homey . . . if home was an empty old hotel run by a frightened, mousy woman.

Still, the place would do.

We didn't spend much time upstairs. I found the others standing in the hall just a few feet from my door.

"Did you see that wallpaper?" Andi asked. She looked a tad pale.

"Don't tell me," I said, "you want to get some for your place."

"Not a chance." Andi frowned. "Good thing I sleep with my eyes closed."

"I'm hungry." Daniel turned and marched to the stairs. The kid wasn't shy about such things.

"Since we have to go down to the first floor to eat," Brenda said, "I think we should slip out and get our luggage."

I reminded her that a promise was a promise and we had made a promise not to open the doors or windows. She called me a self-righteous side of beef. That was a new one. I didn't waste any brain cells trying to figure out if a side of beef could be righteous. I don't offend easily. "Small brain but thick hide," my father used to say. I suppose that's one reason he never won Father of the Year.

Two flights of stairs later we were back in the lobby and in the kitchen. The kitchen, like the rest of the place, looked like a tribute to the finest appliances of the fifties. The good news was that Jewel had spoken the truth about the food. There was fried chicken and the makings for a decent breakfast. Since there wasn't enough chicken to go around, I offered to whip up some scrambled eggs, bacon, and toast. Daniel liked the idea. Brenda and Andi insisted on helping, but they overruled me on the scrambled eggs, opting for fried.

We're normally a chatty bunch, but there was little conversation while we worked. Brenda kept cutting her eyes to the window behind the heavy curtains.

"Our car is parked just outside that wall, right?" she asked.

"Yep."

"You know, I could slip out the window and —"

"C'mon, Brenda. Let it go." I turned the bacon over. It smelled heavenly. I was a little hungry when we started, but now I was starved.

"She doesn't have the right to make demands like that. It's not like we're related to her. I ain't used to takin' orders from strangers. I ain't used to takin' orders from anybody."

This is where I miss the professor. He had a way of annoying Brenda into submission. He would say stuff like, "Use that brain of yours, Barnick." Of course, she would lash back, but then she would tone down. The two drove each other bonkers and the rest of us had to go along for the ride.

But the professor wasn't here. Dr. James McKinney was a sixty-something walking encyclopedia. In his younger days he had been a Jesuit priest, but something turned him sour on faith. He left the Jesuits, left the Church, left behind any belief he had in God, and adopted a new gospel — one that said there is no God and religion is a poison to society. The fact that I'm one of those evangelical Christians bothered him. It didn't matter. I wasn't going to change. Of course, I always hoped *he* would change. He did — some.

Then he killed himself.

Well, that's what the police said. He left a strange note that we still don't fully understand. Andi carries it with her all the time. She had been his assistant for years. Demanding as he was, he had become a father figure to her. I guess he became a father figure to all of us. We loved the cantankerous, irritable man with his constant I'm-smarter-than-you attitude. And he was right most of the time.

Brenda took his passing harder than she wanted us to know. She is a tough girl. When she gets her mad on, she can frighten rabid dogs. When we first learned the professor had gone missing, we were frightened. Our missions have put us up against some very nasty people, but the professor's note sure made the suicide angle look true. Brenda showed little emotion at first, but we saw signs that the loss of the professor had gutted her like a fish. I caught her crying once, and she threatened my life if I told anyone.

"What's eating you, Brenda?" Andi slipped eight fried eggs onto a platter we found in a cupboard. That's two apiece. I asked for only two eggs because I planned on eating a piece or two of the cold fried chicken in the fridge, so I didn't want to overdo it.

"I didn't say anything was eatin' me."

I noticed she didn't make eye contact with Andi. No two women were more different than Andi and Brenda, and I don't mean the whole black and white thing. Andi was everything Brenda was not: easygoing, book smart, a whiz at research, and sociable. Brenda was everything Andi was not: forceful, opinionated, and creative. They were yin and yang, tomato soup and grilled cheese. We were a better team when they were together.

Andi sighed. "Have it your way, girl. We're just your friends. Who care about you. You don't owe us anything."

That was harsh, and I steeled myself for Brenda to go ballistic. She didn't. And that scared the liver out of me. Instead she whispered one word: "Batman."

It doesn't take much to derail my train of thought, but that was so out of character and made so little sense I didn't know what to say. So I took the easy path. "Batman?"

I pulled the bacon out of the pan and set it on a paper-towel-covered platter. I studied Brenda as she buttered up some toast.

"Can we eat now?" Daniel asked.

"Okay, buddy." I carried my load of fried pig strips to the table, Andi brought the platter of fried eggs, and Brenda delivered the toast. We sat, and I said a silent prayer. The others have gotten used to me doing that and give me a minute or so of quiet at most meals. While I was at it, I prayed for wisdom. I had a feeling I was gonna need it.

We served ourselves, each ate a bite or two. Then Andi said, "Okay, Brenda, dish it. What's this about Batman?"

Brenda pushed her bacon around with her fork but didn't look up. That wasn't like her. Usually she looked you in the eye as if waiting for the right moment to spit in it.

She inhaled. I took a bite of toast. "You know about Batman, right?"

I shrugged. "Who doesn't? You are talking about the guy in the comic books, right?"

"Yes. I used to read them when I was a kid, when I could get them. What do you know about Batman?"

"You mean the character? Not the guys that created him, right?" I clarified.

"Yeah, the character."

Andi looked at me.

"Batman is Bruce Wayne. When Bruce was a kid, he saw his parents get murdered in an alley of Gotham City. He dedicated his life to fighting crime. Studied. Trained. Became a famous superhero — although he's not really a superhero."

"He's not?" Daniel looked surprised.

I explained. "He doesn't have superpowers like Superman. He uses his training and skill to overcome bad guys."

"And?" Brenda prompted.

Clearly I had forgotten something. "Oh, and he had a sidekick named Robin."

"What do you know about Robin?"

I shrugged. I read comics as a kid, and still read them occasionally, but I'm no expert. "He was called the 'Boy Wonder.' I think later he became the 'Teen Wonder.' If you want more detail than that, I'm going to disappoint you."

"I would do some research," Andi said. "If I could get cell service up here."

"No need. I already did that." Brenda cut her egg but didn't eat any of it. She had something to say but didn't want to say it. "I know Batman and Robin aren't real, but I've been thinking about them ever since I became Daniel's guardian. When I was a kid, Batman and Robin were cool. When I became a parent, I began to see Batman as a lousy guardian. I know this is gonna sound crazy, but shouldn't someone have arrested Batman for child endangerment?"

That filled the room with silence, except for Daniel, who crunched his bacon.

"I don't under—" Then I got it. "You mean because Robin was a kid."

"Exactly, Cowboy. The *adult* Batman dragged the *child* Robin into situations where his life was in danger. They faced super-villains, situations filled with guns and knives and all kinds of things meant to kill, and Batman saw no problem putting a minor in the middle of the fight. Today Bruce Wayne would be hauled off to court and Robin — Dick Grayson, I mean — would be put into foster care."

"Brenda," Andi said, "they're not real. That's all imagination and storytelling."

Brenda looked at Daniel. "We're real."

I'm not always the brightest crayon in the box, but I got that connection.

Brenda pushed her plate to the side, and Daniel swiped a slice of bacon off her plate. The kid had been hungry.

I did a quick search of all the closets in my brain, looking for the right thing to say, the thing that would ease her mind. The closets were bare. I looked at Andi. Twice she looked ready to speak, but nothing emerged from her pretty mouth.

Brenda, however, still had things to say. "Think about what we've seen, what we've been through. We've seen things no one would believe. We've all been in danger, and a few times we've come close to being taken out. What happens to Daniel if . . . ?"

Since Daniel was sitting next to her, she didn't finish, but my brain, which was now running at top RPM, finished it for her:

What happens to Daniel if I'm killed while on one of these missions? I was stunned by two things. First, the question knocked me off my pins — then the fact that I had no answer.

Brenda kept at it. "This is — what? The *twelfth* time we've gone on some crazy mission? Eyeless people, dead fish falling from the air, orbs that follow us around, ghostly things, mind-stealing pirates" — she looked at me — "creatures that swim in fog and make meals outta people. Daniel was there. Cowboy, if you hadn't done what you did, we wouldn't be here now, and I wouldn't be yammerin' like a crazy woman."

"You're not crazy, Brenda," I said. "And you're not yammering. We can tell this is important to you."

Boy, could I tell. Her eyes were wet, and she kept biting her lip. A glance at Andi showed she suffered from the same wet eyes.

Brenda took a deep breath but kept her eyes fixed on her plate of half-eaten food. "Now the professor's gone. As big a pain as he was in our corporate fannies, he was the real thinker among us. No offense."

"None taken." Andi and I said that in unison.

"If it was too much for old man McKinney, then I can't figure out how we can do any better."

"He didn't kill himself," Andi said. "I told you I saw him in the mirror —"

"He's still gone, Andi." That was a whisper. Even upset as she was, Brenda couldn't bring herself to add to Andi's misery.

"Where are you going with this?" Andi asked. "What's the punchline?"

Brenda leaned back in the chair but didn't make eye contact. I knew she was serious because Brenda had no problem staring into anyone's eyes, but at the moment she was more vulnerable than I had ever seen her.

"We quit," she said. "Me and Daniel. We're done. I can't be Batman and take a minor —" She looked at Daniel, who had, for some reason, turned in his chair to stare at the curtains over the kitchen window, the one that looked out over the parking lot. "I shouldn't say 'minor.' I should say 'child.' "

After another ragged breath, she continued. "I am Daniel's guardian. What kinda guardian am I when I drag him all over the place to face who-knows-what kind of dangers? Would you drag one of your loved ones into the situations we get into?"

That was a hard question to ask and an even harder one to answer. I couldn't think of a reply. Andi, who always has something to say, remained silent.

If the conversation was upsetting to Daniel, then he didn't show it. He just kept staring at the drapes. Then he stood and moved toward the window.

I wanted to promise, *"Nothing is going to happen to Daniel. I'll see to that,"* but it would have been a stupid thing to say. It was true, Daniel was with us — often helping us — during some pretty hairy situations that could have left us all dead. No one could promise safety to anyone else —

Daniel screamed.

Chapter 4
Tockity

I don't remember running to Daniel's side. I heard his tiny voice cry out, and the next thing I knew I was next to him at the window. A man stood outside the glass, his face no more than an inch from the pane. An ugly man. A real mess of a man with wild hair, a beard that looked like it housed a family of rodents, and missing teeth. He was smiling in a way that kick-started my adrenaline.

I took Daniel by the back of his shirt and pulled him away from the window, turning him around. Brenda had him in her arms a second later. I kept my eyes glued to the face staring in at us. He had one blue eye; the other was covered with an eye patch. The eye patch was made from the top of a cereal box. The first three letters of *Corn,* as in *Corn Flakes,* were easy to read. His hair was a mass of brown and gray, and stuck out from his head in a hair halo, or aura, or something. He wore a kind of overcoat. A *mackintosh* I think they call it. I doubt it had been cleaned anytime this decade. No wonder my little buddy let out a scream. At first I was tempted to do the same.

I stepped closer, but my size didn't seem to bother the guy any. He just stood there with a dog-eating-steak grin. My fists were clenched and every muscle in my body had come alive.

"What do you want?" I used my intimidating voice. He didn't seem to care much.

"Tock-tick, tock-tick, tockity, tockity, tick-tick." He laughed, then shuffled away from the window. He ran, if you could call it running, with a limp.

"What was that?" Andi's words were rife with fear.

I closed the curtains, then turned. Brenda had Daniel behind her. Andi stood beside them, looking ghostly white.

I wanted to make it appear that seeing the man was no big deal, so I shrugged. "Just some poor homeless guy."

"He comes near Daniel I'll put him out of his misery," Brenda said. I had no doubts about her willingness to do so.

"He's gone now. Probably harmless. I think I scared him."

Brenda stared at me. "He didn't look

scared."

She was right about that. I can be intimidating when I need to be. They teach that on the football field, but the Tockity Man looked like he couldn't have cared less.

"Tock-tick?" Daniel said. "Who says tock-tick?"

Sometimes Daniel acted a little older than his ten years — about a decade older. "He has some mental problems, buddy. It probably means something to him even though it doesn't mean anything to us." My heart was pounding, my muscles still ready for flight or fight, and my brain was humming like a jet engine.

Andi said, "If that guy's the reason for keeping the window shades drawn at night, then the hotel clerk should have warned us. I hate being scared like that."

I still wanted to appear calm and put the others at ease, so I started clearing the dishes. I wasn't in the mood for chicken after all.

Sunrise couldn't come fast enough for me. We cleaned up the kitchen, being sure to put everything back where we got it, wiped down the counters and stovetop, and generally left the kitchen cleaner than we found it. Part of the activity was done out of simple courtesy — after all, Jewel didn't have to provide us with food or access to the kitchen, but she did, begrudgingly — and partly because we didn't want to talk anymore. Talking about Brenda's decision or about the Tockity Man was like sticking a hand in a hornet's nest: the hornets don't like it, and neither does the owner of the hand.

Once done with the cleanup, we went to bed. It was an act on my part. I doubted I'd sleep. Instead, I did what I knew I would: I lay in bed listening to every sound the old building made — and it made plenty. Every squeak made me wonder if Brenda and Daniel were sneaking away. Every bump brought images of the Tockity Man sneaking into the place to murder us as we slept. I even spent a good half hour trying to convince myself that I should sleep at the foot of the stairs so I would know if anyone came or went.

I didn't do that. Brenda was a woman who never hesitated to say or do what she thought she should, but she wouldn't take the car and leave us stranded in Newland. Besides, I had the keys.

I did get up a dozen or so times to peer out the window to see if Tockity Man or something worse was messin' about. I didn't see anything. I don't know where a man like that goes in the wee hours, but I was pretty sure he went there.

It was still early. The sun was up, but it was still in a wrestling match with the trees and hills. The scene outside my window was an epic battle of light fighting the dark. The light was winning, but it was going to be a fifteen-round match.

I made my way to the men's shared restroom, made use of the free toothpaste and tiny toothbrush Jewel had given me, took a quick shower, dragged the comb through my hair, and slipped into yesterday's jeans and flannel shirt, then plodded back to my room to put on boat-length sneakers.

I like to read my Bible in the morning and the evening, but it was stowed in the car with my other gear. I checked the nightstand next to the bed, but no dice. Apparently the Gideons didn't travel this deep in the Blue Ridge Mountains.

I did, however, find a notepad and pen. I scratched out a simple note: *Gone for a quick walk. Will bring luggage up when I get back. Then we eat.–Tank*

I folded the notepaper and wedged it in the jamb of the lady's bathroom. No matter how strained things were at the moment, they'd go to that room sooner or later.

I walked down the stairs expecting to find Jewel at the desk. No sign of her. No matter. We promised not to go out until the sun was up and ol' Mr. Sun was showing his face.

I unlocked the front door and walked out.

The fresh air was sweet with dew and the smell of old-growth forest. For a moment, I allowed myself to believe that all was right with the world.

It wasn't.

Chapter 5
A Walk Through Nowhere Land

I'm a pacer. By that I mean that I like to walk when I think. I pace rooms, halls, just about anywhere, but I really enjoy a brisk stroll outside. I know an athlete should jog, but my knees and ankles complain now when I do that, and I like to keep them happy. Besides, I didn't bring a jogging suit, and sweating up a flannel shirt is just plain nasty.

It was quiet outside. The air was cool, bordering on cold. A breeze rolled down Main Street, picking up leaves and bits of trash and scooting them my direction. I wasn't interested in cleaning up the town; I was interested in cleaning up my thinking.

I strolled about fifty steps, then picked up the pace. It felt good. Legs eager to move found a decent pace and soon I was taking in deep breaths. My lungs were having as much fun as my legs.

Of course, having never been to lovely

Newland I had no idea where I was going, so I headed back the way we drove in. That would give me a chance to see more of the town. I passed a barbershop, a beauty shop, hardware store, café one and café two, a bank, and just about every other kind of business you'd expect to find in a small mountain community. The storefronts were quaint but they looked untouched, as if they had been ignored for some time. Of course, what I know about storefronts would fit in a thimble, so I didn't give it any more thought.

When I reached the end of Main Street, I noticed another smaller road. It formed a T-intersection with the main drag, ran west, and looked to be uphill all the way. I couldn't see very far up the street, but I guessed that it led to a residential area. People around here had to live someplace. Walking uphill required more effort than walking flat, and I needed a little more challenge. Before heading up the lane I looked at the street sign. Getting lost would be embarrassing.

It was odd. The street sign topped an ornate black pole, the kind used for streetlights in the old parts of cities. The part of the sign that read Main Street looked okay, but the part indicating the street I was about to walk had been painted over. I could see that once it had read Elm Street, but the shoddy paint job of whitewash and hand-made letters read NOWHERE. I wondered what the local Chamber of Commerce thought of that — if there was a local Chamber of Commerce. I had serious doubts about that possibility.

I headed up the street, my calves informing me that uphill walking hurt more than what I had been doing. No matter. I plodded on.

The sun was still fighting for this territory. I was in shade most of the way, and the shade made things cooler. Increasing my pace allowed me to create my own heat. I listened to my breathing as I hiked, and then something occurred to me. This was prime bird-singing time. Birds like the morning and usually spend some of their morning encouraging the sun on its daily climb in the sky. I hadn't heard a single peep, chirp, caw, or anything else.

About three-quarters of a mile up the grade, I came to another street, this one perpendicular to Nowhere and parallel to Main Street. It was clearly residential. Houses, most of them small cabin-like structures, sat on large lots of an acre or more. Some of the exteriors looked well maintained, and the yards were clear of debris; others, however, looked abandoned. Fences in front of those houses looked worn, and spider webs decorated the slats. Odd. One house looked ready for guests, others looked like something the Munsters would enjoy.

I felt sad for the empty houses and those who had to leave them behind. Small towns this far away from better traveled roads tended to waste away. I've always thought living in a small town like Newland would be wonderful. A great place to raise kids.

That's when something else hit me. I'd walked past a dozen houses that clearly had residents, but hadn't heard a single voice or, worse, a single dog bark. That made me think. I hadn't seen any dogs anywhere. Then I had another thought: I hadn't seen or heard any children. Of course, I told myself, I had only been in town one night, so I shouldn't get too shook up over the lack of kid and dog sightings. And when I coupled that with the weird woman at the hotel and the weirder man outside the window, I knew I was letting my imagination get the best of me. That was the story I was telling myself, but I've seen too much of the strange and the dangerous to believe my own rationalizations. Truth is, I was trying to convince myself that nothing was out of the norm, but even I wasn't having anything to do with that thinking.

I kept up my pace, but my mind raced ahead of me. I started to feel that people were staring at me from their homes. I wondered if whatever lived in the abandoned houses was watching me. Jogging was beginning to look like a good idea, but I kept myself in check. I just kept walking like I was a normal person strolling a normal street in a normal mountain community. I doubted any of that was true.

I reached the end of the street, which I guessed was the same length as Main Street. I found another crossroad, this one with the nonthreatening name of Bass Street. That was something to be thankful for.

Rounding the corner, I continued my hike down the grade to the main drag and found myself at the other end of town, just as I expected. Before going back to the hotel I crossed Main Street and made my way to the pretty little church. It was a true chapel in the woods: white clapboard siding, double-hung windows with dark green trim, and a wide set of steps to the front door. A tall and pointed steeple cast a shadow on the street. The shadow of the steeple's cross fell right in the middle of the roadway. *The cross always leaves an impression.*

I doubted the preacher or the secretary would be in the building this early, but being in, or in this case *near,* a church always eased my mind and settled my heart — something I wish my friends could experience.

At first I felt the usual peace that always came when at a church, but then I noticed something — dust. Dust on the windowsills, dust on the steps — I could see my shoeprints and the prints of someone else who had been exploring the chapel — and dust on the doorknob. And not just a faint powdering. No, sir. There was enough dust to make me think the door to the chapel hadn't been opened in some time — maybe years — and that was depressing to a man like me. Nothing sadder than an empty, unused church. Since I hadn't seen any other churches so far, I grew even sadder. Perhaps, the people went to church in the next town, but if Andi's research was right — and her research was always right — the next town was at least a half hour away, maybe more on the mountain road.

I wasn't looking at a church. I was staring at a used-to-be church, a building in church clothes. I had fought fear and depression all night. This made the depression worse. So much for an uplifting walk.

I slunk back to the hotel and unpacked the car so Andi, Brenda, and Daniel could have fresh clothes and whatnot. The way Brenda had talked last night, I'd be returning the luggage to the car later that day.

CHAPTER 6
BREAKFAST AT TIFFANY'S

It didn't take long for me to carry the luggage into the hotel. The others were glad to see it; Jewel Tarkington wasn't. She was standing on the first tread of the staircase. I think the little mouse was trying to keep me from taking the luggage up.

"I did a little checking for you," Jewel said. Something happened to her face as she spoke. It took me a second or two, but I realized she was forcing a smile. She seemed well outta practice. "I can get you in one of two hotels up in Sugar Hill. It's pretty close. Maybe an hour's drive. I hear it's a nice place."

I set the last bit of luggage down near the others I had already retrieved from the car. Andi, Brenda, and Daniel were going to help cart the stuff up the two flights of stairs even though I said I was happy to do it. My guess is they thought I was moving too slow.

"You hear it's a nice place?" Andi said.

"You've never been there?"

"Well, no, but that doesn't matter." She shifted her weight as if thinking on her feet was taxing her. "I just want you to be comfortable."

Andi wasn't buying it. "Forgive me for such a forward question, Ms. Tarkington, but have you ever been out of this town?"

Jewel deflated like a balloon. "I-I don't see what that has to do with anything."

"It doesn't," Andi said, "and I hope I didn't insult you. I'm just naturally nosy. For example, I used my smartphone to try to find the hotel's wireless so I could check my e-mail. I couldn't find a wireless connection."

"We don't have that sort of thing."

She said it as if Andi had been talking about pornography.

"I guessed that," Andi said, "when I didn't see a computer behind the hotel desk. Everything seems to be recorded by hand."

Andi's observation superpower seemed to be in fine shape.

"I'm a little ol' fashioned."

Brenda gave me a look. She recognized the symptoms of Andi sleuthing. To my surprise, Brenda seemed interested, too. She jumped in. "I notice there are no televisions, no phones, and no radios. This place is a black hole."

"You see there," Jewel said. "That's exactly what I mean. You two are sharp ones. I can see that." I tried not to be offended at being left off the smart list. "That's why you should go on up to Sugar Hill. They have all those things, and I jus' know you'll be much more comfortable."

I gotta admit, I've never seen a business-person try so hard to drive business away. I began to wonder if she was running a gambling den in here or worse.

"Well, we'll talk about it," Andi said, "and we need to change clothes and freshen up."

"And we need to feed my boy, here," Brenda said. "He's a monster if he misses a meal."

"No I'm not," Daniel said. Then he growled.

Funny kid.

I picked up the heaviest bags and started for the stairs. I walked faster than I needed, hoping she'd fear getting run over by — wait for it — a tank. She moved, and I trudged up the stairs. The others followed carrying overnight cases.

It took only a half hour for the ladies to shower and do the stuff ladies do every morning. Daniel came to my room, sat on the bed, and fired up his video game.

Personally, I think my little buddy spends too much time on those games. I guess that makes me old, even though I'm not. I didn't say anything. He had been through enough these last few weeks, and all that was made worse by last night's scare. I used the time to read my Bible, but I couldn't concentrate. My thoughts were bees in a bottle. African killer bees.

Thirty-five minutes later we were all seated in the nearest of the two cafés, a place called Tiffany's.

"Just like the movie," Andi said. "Now we can all say we had breakfast at Tiffany's."

Tiffany's Café looked old on the outside and older on the inside. Tiffany herself was no spring chicken. She was short, round, and sported a double chin that swayed with each step she took. She wore a green-striped waitress uniform with a white apron and frilly collar. I knew she was named Tiffany because she wore a name tag, the kind with a white space to write a name on. It looked like the letters had been penned a long time ago. When we walked in, she was chatting up one of the two customers in the place. She was smiling. That evaporated the moment the little brass bell at the top of the door jingled. She looked at us like we looked at the Tockity Man last night.

"Charming," Brenda said. "We've gone back in time sixty years."

"Maybe it's one of those retro places," I said. "You know, like a fifties diner that serves burgers and malts."

"If it is, they went out of their way to find original fixtures. Look at the booths. They have to be decades old. They have more scars, stains, and tears than I can count." The whole place smelled of bacon grease, burnt toast, and stale tobacco.

We waited for Tiffany to seat us or at least say, "Sit anywhere." That never came. She did telegraph a pretty mean scowl our way.

I sometimes work under the philosophy that forgiveness is easier to get than permission, so I sauntered over to one of the teal and white booths and squeezed into the bench. Clearly, it had been designed for smaller folk than me. Daniel, obviously not put off by the look of the place or the owner, took the space next to me.

"Good call." I elbowed the kid. "Now the wimmin' will be able to look right into our handsome faces while they eat."

Daniel giggled. "Wimmin'."

"The trick will be keeping our breakfast down," Brenda said. She and Andi scooted onto the opposite seat.

Anyone listening to our conversation would think we were happy-go-lucky. We weren't. Dark clouds hovered over us. The team felt incomplete without the professor, coupled with Brenda's revelation about leaving the group, the scary Tockity Man, and the fact that we were in a town that made us feel like we weren't wanted. Of course, the fact that we had no idea why we had been sent here didn't help.

"You folks lost?" It was Tiffany. She had a three-pack-a-day voice.

"Not at all," Brenda said. "We're seated in Tiffany's Café in Newland, North Carolina. Nope, not lost at all." She was getting cranky again.

"We don't get many outsiders in here."

"Maybe we can start a trend." Brenda's face portrayed an innocent spirit I knew wasn't there. It was an act for Miss Tiffany.

"You know, we're just a small-town dive, but up the road —"

"— there's a nice place in Sugar Hill." Apparently Andi had caught the same sarcasm disease as Brenda. "We're here, and we're hungry now."

"Breakfast for breakfast," Daniel said.

Tiffany looked puzzled. I tried to explain. "We had breakfast for dinner last night at the hotel."

"You stayed in town last night?"

"Yes, ma'am," I said. I figured one of the adults needed to be polite.

"At Jewel's place?"

"Yes, ma'am. She let us use the kitchen."

Tiffany's face hardened. "She did, did she?"

"Yes, ma'am. I could really use some coffee. We all could." I needed to change the subject before Brenda got in the woman's face. "Except the boy, of course. Do you have milk?"

"We have milk. I still think —"

I could see Andi tense. Andi was sweet and smart and kind, but she had limits. I was pretty sure Tiffany was about to cross into the danger zone.

"Excuse me, ma'am," Andi said. "It seems you don't want to serve us. Could that be because one of us is black? I'm sure that's not it, but if it were, I think someone would want to know that Tiffany's is still practicing segregation."

Tiffany drew herself up as tall as she could. "Of course not. I ain't got no problem with a person's color. Like I said, we just don't get new people in town, and when we do, they have the good sense to keep moving."

"Now that sounds like a threat." Andi was

pulling out all the stops. I had no doubt she was spoiling for a fight. Too many pent-up emotions can make a person a little crazy.

"No threat, darlin'. I'm just telling you the gospel truth."

I've read the Gospels many times, and I'm sure she wasn't using the word the way the Bible does.

Andi stared at her with innocence on her face and laser beams in her eyes.

Tiffany sighed. "Coffee for three and milk for your boy." She was speaking to me.

"He's not my son," I said.

The woman looked at Andi, who shook her head slowly.

"Daniel's my son," Brenda said.

Tiffany looked at Daniel's white face, then at Brenda's black skin. We get that a lot.

"I'll get the coffee, then take your order."

She walked away. The other two diners stared at us. I sized them up. Both looked to be well into their sixties and in no way threatening. I also noted the cook had come out. He was twice as round as Tiffany and sported the same double chin and dingy clothes.

"Girl," Brenda said, "did you just play the race card?"

"I don't know what you're talking about." The slight grin on Andi's face told me she was lying.

Brenda beamed. It was good to see a smile on her face, even if it only lasted a moment.

Tiffany brought the coffee and a milk for Daniel, we ordered, and she trudged off. I used the time to bring the girls up to date about my walk. It was a short story, but they recognized the weirdness in it. There wasn't much to discuss, but at least they were up to speed.

The food arrived quickly. I guess Tiffany felt the sooner we ate the sooner we'd leave. I dug into a Denver omelet, Andi had a bowl of oatmeal, Brenda had scrambled eggs and hash browns. Daniel wasted no time getting to his pancakes. We ate in silence for a few minutes, then Brenda asked the question we'd all been waiting for: "What are the odds of getting me and Daniel to the Asheville airport?"

I didn't answer. I didn't want to answer. I had been hoping that Brenda would change her mind. She wasn't concerned with her safety; she was worried about Daniel. So was I.

Andi broke the silence. "Since we don't know why we're here, I can't think of a reason not to leave. It's not like our mysterious, invisible handlers have given us any direction. Telling us where to go and funding our trip, putting money in our bank accounts to live on so we can be on call isn't enough. Every situation we walked into we walked into blind. If they want our help, our gifts, then they should give us more than crumbs to follow."

"Amen to that," Brenda said.

I wanted to argue the point, but I had no material to use. Everything Andi said was true. We were sent places, bizarre things happened, we'd get sucked in, we'd fight for our lives and the lives of others, then nothing. We don't know anything about those who send us and fund us. We know they clean up after us, or so it seems. That's it.

"Well, Cowboy?" Brenda was pummeling me with her eyes. "I can drive if you want. I know how to do that."

"I know. I just don't want to lose you and Daniel."

I know it's not possible, but I felt my heart melt. She was leaving to protect Daniel. I was being selfish by resisting her. "I'll load up the car as soon as we're done eating."

Brenda's expression softened. "Thanks, Bjorn. You da man."

"Tank's da man," Daniel said.

Then he sat bolt upright. He looked up and to the area of the door we walked through a short time before. Then he snapped his head around, seeing things only he could see. "Uh oh."

I didn't like Daniel's tone. Too much fear in it.

"What, buddy?"

He didn't answer with words. Instead, he snatched the fork from my hand, then gathered up all the silverware.

"Daniel, what are you doing?" Brenda sounded both irked and frightened at the same time.

He shoved his plate to the floor, then proceeded to do the same with everyone else's plates and cups. The racket hurt my ears.

"Hey! You're gonna pay for that!" Tiffany started our way. I saw the cook come out from the back.

If Daniel was just some other kid, if I hadn't seen him in action before, if we hadn't seen so many unexplainable things, then people would be right to think he was throwing a tantrum. I knew better.

"Hold on," Daniel said, clutching the silverware to his chest. Then his head snapped to the side as he directed his gaze out the window. I followed his example. "Tock-tick."

Just outside the window was the Tockity

Man. The same disheveled, ratty-looking homeless guy. The same freaky eye patch.

He was grinning again, exposing what few teeth he had left.

Through the glass I heard him say, "Tock-tick, tock-tick, tockity, tockity, tick-tick."

Tiffany's shrill voice sounded a mile or two away. "What's he doing in the daylight —"

Then the world went white.

There was pain.

There was fear.

Then there was nothing.

Chapter 7
I Don't Think We're in Kansas Anymore

Once, on the football field, back when I was playing on a junior college team (before I transferred to the University of Washington and made a hash of that), I put a wicked tackle on a running back. I got the worst of the deal. I couldn't breathe, and my head felt like a team of construction workers was trying to knock a hole in my skull using sledgehammers. It was my first and only concussion. One is enough.

When the white went away, I felt the same. I struggled to open my eyes and had to focus just to breathe. The air tasted funny. The light seemed a shade or two off from where it had been. It took less than a second for me to stop thinking about myself and start thinking of the others. With eyes now wide, I looked first at Daniel. He looked pale, slightly green, and more than a little stunned. He clutched the silverware to his chest. He had missed one — a butter knife that Brenda had been using. I found it stuck deep in the backrest of the booth between Daniel and me. Daniel had saved us from becoming pincushions — or silverware cushions.

Andi was in her spot, her hands on the edge of the table as if pushing herself back. Her sometimes wild red hair was wild again. "What . . . was . . . that?"

Brenda looked ready to upchuck her breakfast. Her mouth hung open and she gulped for air like a fish tossed on the dock.

"Are you choking?" I feared her mouth might have been full of food when . . . whatever happened, happened.

She shook her head. She must have had all the wind knocked out of her. Her diaphragm was in a spasm. It's a lousy feeling. I reached across the table and put my hands on the side of her head. "Look at me."

She didn't.

"Brenda, look at me. Right in the eyes."

She did. Those eyes were growing wider.

"Relax. Just look at me and relax. Your breath will come back. Just give it a moment."

I rubbed my thumb on her cheek. Andi slipped an arm around her.

Then Brenda inhaled deeply — and noisily. She sounded like someone who had gone down with the ship and just made the long swim to the surface.

"There it is. There it is." I continued to stroke her cheek. "Keep looking at me. There ya go." Another deep inhalation. Another noisy gasp. "Stay relaxed. You're doing great."

It took a minute or two before she was breathing in a normal fashion.

"Can you speak now?" That would tell me that her airway was clear and everything was working as it should.

She spoke. I won't tell you what she said because it would earn an R rating. I've been around football jocks all my life, and those boys know how to swear. Nonetheless, Brenda could give lessons.

She spoke again. "I don't ever want to feel like that again."

I lowered my hand. "Me neither."

"Cowboy, you healed me. Thanks."

I mentioned earlier that we all have our own special gifts. Andi sees patterns, Brenda draws the future, Daniel sees angels, and I can heal people. Well, *sometimes.* It doesn't work every time. In fact, I never know if it's going to work or not. You can imagine how frustrating that is. If I had full control of that gift, I'd spend my days walking through hospitals putting doctors out of work, if you know what I mean.

"Glad to help, but it wasn't me."

She raised a hand. "I know. You think it was God."

"Well, that too, but I don't think I healed you. You just had the wind knocked out of you. All you needed was a little time for your breathing to reset."

"Is that all? I thought I was dying."

"Me too," Daniel said.

I took a moment to gather my thoughts and tame my emotions when I saw it. I glanced around Tiffany's — or what used to be Tiffany's. "Ummm guys . . ."

While we were blinded by the bright white light, someone had snuck into Tiffany's and repainted the walls. They also added a dozen customers and changed Tiffany's uniform. Except it wasn't Tiffany. The lady moving from table to table filling coffee cups and joking with the patrons was painfully thin, had short black hair, looked to be in her twenties, and stood close to six feet tall if she was an inch.

Other things had changed. In the place we had just been, Tiffany brought us menus. Here the menus were held in a wire holder. I grabbed one. Brenda and Andi did the same.

"This ain't good." Brenda was right.

"This can't be." Andi kept her gaze fixed to the menu. Her eyes darted back and forth. "I-I can't read this."

"Nothin' wrong with your eyes, girlfriend." Brenda touched the printing on the menu as if she could absorb its meaning through her fingertips. "I can't make heads or tales of it myself."

I had noticed the same thing. There were plenty of words, but they were written in some other language. Still, it looked familiar. . . . Something tickled my brain. "The scroll!"

I said that a little too loud. Several people turned to face us. Worse, the waitress came over. I didn't see how that could be a good thing.

Andi nodded. "You're right, Tank. That's where I've seen these letters." She paused just a moment, then asked, "Am I the only one who feels like we just made some kind of trip?"

I wanted to say more, but the waitress arrived. She said — something. I have no idea what. Her tone was light and singsongy. No anger. She did, however, look a little puzzled. I glanced at Andi and Brenda and they looked as lost as I felt. Andi shrugged. Brenda shook her head. She pointed at a particular item on the menu. That made me wonder what happened to the breakfast we had just eaten when we were in Tiffany's. The silverware had made it but not the dirty dishes Daniel had pushed on the floor. That was fine with me. I don't know how I'd explain that. Of course, I didn't know how to explain any of this.

Reaching deep in my gut I brought out what I felt was a pretty convincing smile and held up one index finger. I hoped the universal "Give me a sec" sign would be, well, universal. "Could we have another moment?"

Daniel cranked his head my direction. Brenda slapped her forehead. Andi sat still and looked like I had just undressed in front of everyone. The waitress cocked her head. That's when I realized, in my infinite wisdom, that if I couldn't understand her, she couldn't understand me. I had just proved that we weren't from around these parts.

She studied me for a moment, nodded, and walked away.

"I'm an idiot." I squeezed my eyes shut as if that would back the clock up. It didn't.

"Anyone want to argue with him?" Brenda said.

Andi, who normally was kind, said, "Not me."

"Now that the cat is out of the bag, what

do we do?" Brenda said.

"We need to go somewhere where we can talk." Andi reached for the small purse she carried. "I don't think it's wise to stay here."

"What if what just happened happens again?" The washing machine in my head was set to high speed. "If we move from this spot and the thing happens again, then we'll miss our ride back to our world."

"We can't sit here doing nothing." Andi looked around the café. "People are staring."

I glanced around again. She was right. We had become the morning's entertainment. "Okay, you win. I don't have any better ideas." To Daniel I said, "Scoot on out, buddy. We're gonna blow this popsicle stand."

He set the silverware down and wiggled out of the booth. I slid across the seat. Brenda and Andi were already out and watched me try to work my bulk out of a booth made for thin people.

"Uh oh," Brenda whispered. "Heads up."

The waitress walked in our direction again. I couldn't help noticing that she was looking at us, then looking at the door. At first I thought she was going to block our way out. Then I noticed what she had already noticed. A yellow-and-white sedan had pulled to the side of the street. It had some lettering over a round symbol on the doors. On the top of the car was a globe about the size of a large softball.

"Guys . . ." I nodded out the window. The others turned just in time to see two men get out of the front seat. They wore matching green uniforms. There were yellow patches sewn to their sleeves near the shoulder. My Uncle Bart is the sheriff of Dickerson County in Oregon, so I know a cop car when I see one. And I was seeing one.

"Nuts." It was the best I could manage.

The skinny waitress opened the door, and I was pretty sure she wasn't opening it for us. I was wrong. She smiled. Bowed her head for a moment and waved us out.

Out we went.

The officers were there to greet us, and I mean *greet* us. Both smiled. Both dipped their heads in a slight bow, then the older of the two extended his hand. He either wanted to shake hands or was taking a sneaky approach to clamp on the business end of handcuffs.

It was the former. I extended my hand and he took hold of my wrist, smiling all the time. Just as I was beginning to think the guy was going to twist my arm behind my back, cuff and search me, he gave my wrist a friendly squeeze and shake. I took his wrist and did the same. That broadened his smile. A second later, the junior officer instigated the same kind of greeting. Then they moved to Andi and Brenda. The older of the two mussed Daniel's hair. Just for the record, Daniel hates that. He didn't say anything, but I know the kid well enough to know he was restraining himself.

I did a quick survey of the sedan. It was a cop car, all right. It had something that looked like a shotgun vertically mounted to the dash, and a wire partition between the front and rear seat.

People moved along the walkway. Most looked our way and smiled. A few even waved.

"I gotta say it," Andi said, "but I don't think we're in Kansas anymore, Toto."

Even I caught the reference to *The Wizard of Oz.* Unlike Dorothy, however, this world looked very much like the one we left, except there were more people, it looked cleaner, and folk were friendly.

"Unbelievable," Brenda said. "A half hour ago we were planning on going back to the Asheville airport."

"I've got a feeling that it's a longer drive

now," Andi said.

"Much longer," I said.

Chapter 8
Littlefoot, New and Improved

When we walked out of the café, I wondered how they were going to get three grown adults (in my case, overgrown) and a ten-year-old boy into the yellow-and-white patrol car along with the two police officers. The car was the size of a Prius. I started to ask the officers, but it would do no good. Even if they understood me, I wouldn't understand them.

My question was answered a moment later when another patrol car pulled up. It did so casually. No siren, no red or blue emergency lights — or in this case, green and yellow lights. It took a second for me to realize that the car made almost no noise as it pulled to the curb. I heard the tires on the pavement, but no engine. Electric? That was my guess.

Two additional officers exited the car. They wore the same green uniform as the first two. They approached, each with a wide grin. The older-looking one — I made him to be in his thirties and his partner in his twenties — approached me and shook my hand like a fan meeting his favorite movie star. I half expected him to pull out an autograph book. He did more than shake my hand — he pumped it. He then moved to Andi and Brenda, greeting them in the same way. We did another round of handshaking with the younger officer.

To say I was confused would be downplaying what I felt. We were in a town nearly identical to Newland but different enough to make my head spin. I once read that someone asked Daniel Boone if he had ever been lost in the woods. He said, "No, but I've been bewildered for a couple of weeks." I was that kind of bewildered.

"I'm not leaving Daniel!"

Brenda had pulled the boy to her side. The officers looked at one another. Their faces revealed their confusion.

"What's wrong?" I asked her.

"I think they want to separate us."

I've seen that angry face too many times to not notice it now. One of the officers caught my eye, then pointed at Daniel, then Andi.

"Ah, I get it." I moved to Brenda and Daniel. I put my hand on Daniel's shoulder, then moved it to Brenda's. I did that three times. The officers looked at Brenda, then Daniel, then Andi. Andi caught on. She put one hand on the side of each of their shoulders and pushed them together. There wasn't much movement involved since Brenda already held Daniel close.

Then Andi surprised me — she stepped to my side and took hold of my arm, like we were a couple. That was the first good thing to happen to me that day. As far as I was concerned, Andi could hang on to me as long as she liked. I wouldn't complain a bit.

The first officer we met opened the back door of the police car and motioned for us to enter. Clearly, he didn't mean all of us. A quick glance told me that one of the police officers had opened the back door of the other patrol car.

"You go with Brenda and Daniel," I told Andi.

"She doesn't need to watch over me," Brenda said.

"It's not you I'm worried about." I looked at the two officers by the first car.

"You're a funny man, Tank. A real gut-buster." She climbed into the back of the car and Daniel followed.

"You're right, I'd better ride with them." Andi released my arm, and the world seemed to dim a little.

It only took a few steps to reach the second car. I've never been in the back of a police car; I've been in my uncle's patrol vehicle, just always in the front seat. This car was clean as could be. The interior looked like it had just rolled off the factory floor. It's good to be thankful for small things, especially when you've been transported to some unknown place. So I was thankful.

A few moments later, we were moving down the street, the car purring like a content kitty. What puzzled me now was where they could be taking us. Most of this town was a dead ringer for Newland, North Carolina. Newland was small. My hike earlier led me through town and up into some of the residential streets. In Newland, the sheriff's office was a storefront. It didn't seem to be the kind of place with fancy electric cars and at least four officers on duty.

So the place was similar, but not the same. With that realization I began to think of this place as New Land.

They drove us out of New Land, and I hoped we didn't have an hour's drive to the next town — Sugar Hill, it was called in Newland. For all I knew, there was no Sugar

Hill. Or it could be a major city. Nothing would surprise me now.

The drive turned out to be short, which was a relief. About ten minutes out of town, up a winding road, was a large modern-looking building. It reminded me of an office complex, and maybe it was.

Brenda, Daniel, and Andi were already out of the car when my chauffeur stopped our car. One of the cops had to open the door for me since it couldn't be opened from the inside. At least that was the same as the cop cars back home.

We were escorted to the front entrance, and glass doors opened as we neared. If this was a local police station, then it had to be the fanciest one I'd ever seen.

Inside was a large lobby with a fountain in the middle. A statue stood in the center of the fountain. It was a sculpture of a police officer in uniform and utility belt. In one arm he held a child, and the other arm pointed the way. The way to what? I don't know. Safety? The future? A doughnut shop? My Uncle Bart would have my head for that last thought.

I stepped next to Andi, hoping she'd take my arm again (she didn't). Brenda and Daniel were staring at the statue.

"Cheesy," Daniel said.

That made Brenda chuckle, and I was glad we were the only ones who could understand him.

We had waited for about thirty seconds when a man in a fancy uniform with some in-your-face decorations on the shoulders and sleeves approached. He looked to be in his early sixties. His hair was the color of polished silver and his wrinkles were deep, no doubt earned by a life in law enforcement. Like his officers before him, he beamed, shook our hands, and treated us like foreign dignitaries.

He spoke to us, but I understood none of it. He could have been giving me sport scores for all I could tell. Then he gave me a slap on the shoulder. I took that to mean that he had said something nice, or maybe funny.

He motioned for us to follow him. I noticed that the officers who brought us here didn't follow. Apparently they had done their job. That also told me that the chief — that's what I assumed the older man to be — felt we were no threat to him.

The rest of the building is a bit of a blur. I tried to take everything in, but it was all a little overwhelming. Questions buzzed in my brain.

"Anyone got a guess about what is happening?" Brenda spoke softly.

"Not a clue," Andi said. "I could give a dozen guesses and be wrong on every count."

Brenda looked at Daniel, and her mood darkened. "Batman and Robin. We should have moved on when the lady at the hotel told us."

"You think she knows something?" I asked.

"That'd be my guess."

The chief's office was spacious and dominated by a power desk with photos, file folders, and a half-filled cup.

There was something else in the room. I should say there was *someone* else in the room: a woman. She had long blond hair that was parted down the middle and hypnotic brown eyes. She looked to be in her twenties and wore a green pantsuit. She was tall and gorgeous.

"Hello, Tank," she said. In English.

"You know me?"

"Of course I do, silly. How could I forget you?" Her smile was dazzling.

"I'm sorry, ma'am. I think I'd remember you if we had met before." I couldn't say why at the moment, but I felt like an idiot, like the last person in the room to get the punchline of a joke.

She smiled again. If her smile was any brighter I would need sunglasses. Then she did something weird: she took off her shoes and wiggled her toes.

Still nothing.

I heard her give a playful sigh as she closed her eyes. When she opened them I was staring at the same face but different eyes. Green eyes. Something in my brain came out of hibernation. She closed her lids again, then opened them so we could see what a lovely shade of blue they were.

"Wait."

Daniel charged forward and wrapped his arms around her.

Andi clapped her hands. "Hello, Helsa!"

"Helsa?" I got it. I didn't understand it, but I got it. "Littlefoot!"

It was my turn to embrace her, and she embraced me back. When we parted, I asked the obvious. "I don't get it. When I last saw you, you were just a child."

"That was a long time ago, Tank."

That confused me. "It was less than a year ago."

"It's been a little longer here."

Now I was getting a headache.

Helsa's voice turned dark. "We have a lot to discuss."

"You got that right," Brenda said. "You

can start by telling us how to get home from here."

I didn't like the look on Helsa's face.

CHAPTER 9
FEW ANSWERS, TOO MANY QUESTIONS

After the hugging was done, we sat. I wasn't sure how to feel. To say I was confused wouldn't be going far enough. Not all that long ago, I first met Helsa (her name means *devoted to God* in Hebrew — of course her name just *sounds* like Hebrew, as far as we could figure). It was our fourth adventure, and our team was just getting its legs. Some days that seems a decade ago. And back then, she was less than ten years old.

I'll keep this short. I mentioned my Uncle Bart, the county sheriff, in an area that included Dickerson, Oregon. Every year I go up to Oregon to watch the Rose Bowl with him and his family. While there, he got a call to investigate strange footprints in the snow of a farmer's field. He asked me to go with him, and I did. We found footprints all right. Small ones. Prints of a barefoot child walking through the snow. That image still haunts me.

We found the little girl, and she was as cute as a button. Didn't talk, but she did carry a scroll with strange lettering. That's what Andi recognized back in the café.

"I hope everyone has been well." Helsa was smiling when she said that, but the smile evaporated pretty quick. "Where's the professor?"

"That's hard to say," Andi said.

"He's dead." Brenda didn't mince words. "Police say he committed suicide."

Some people grieve with endless tears. Brenda shed a few of those when she didn't think people were watching. Some people grieve with anger. That was more Brenda's speed.

"There's a lot of doubt about that." Andi's tone wasn't cold, but it was pretty chilly. "Things don't add up. He was looking for a way to access alternate dimensions." She paused and looked at Brenda. "And look where we are: a different universe."

I'm not used to being the reasonable one, but I needed to give it a go. "The whole thing has been a little hard on us, Helsa."

"Either way, he's not with you." Helsa's face darkened with sadness, and her eyes changed color to a pale gray. "It's a loss. I liked him. I felt nothing but love from him."

"That makes you the lucky one," Brenda

said. The professor had always been toughest on Brenda.

"I only got to spend a short time with him, and I had become a child by then."

"This stuff gives me a headache."

To Brenda's credit, she looked like her head hurt.

Andi's curiosity was taking over. I can't say she was as brilliant as the professor, but given the chance, I think she could be. Nothing gets by our Andi.

"When we first met you, you couldn't or wouldn't speak. Now you handle English better than Tank. How is that?"

"Hey" was all I could say.

"No offense." Andi smiled at me and all was right with the world — whatever world this was.

"Come on." Helsa stood. "I'll show you."

We stood, too.

"But first I need to warn you. It might be a little upsetting."

"Cool, just what we need. Something else to upset us." I probably don't need to mention Brenda said that.

Helsa talked as we walked. "I picked up a few things from you, but I've been studying the language ever since."

"They teach English here?" Andi said.

"No. Not at all. But when the Others arrive, I try to learn their language."

That confused me. "Others?"

"That's what you are. You're not from our world, so people here think of you as the Others. That's not bad. My people love the Others — mostly."

She filled us in on how she was a quick study and that English was a simple enough language. I was born in the good-ol' U.S. of A. and I don't find English, proper English, all that easy.

"Some of our team has visited your universe and brought back books for us to study."

"Team?" Andi asked.

"Yes." Helsa slowed to a stop in the wide hallway we had been strolling through. "You know there are other teams, don't you?"

"Wait, wait, wait." Brenda pinched the bridge of her nose as if it would clarify everything. "There are other people like us?"

"Yes. Of course."

"Doing the same thing we do?"

"Again, yes." Helsa looked puzzled, as if this should be common knowledge taught in grade schools. "Not in your universe. You are unique. I'm sure you know that. Only you can do what you do."

I felt good hearing that, but I had serious doubts that Brenda got the same thrill.

"You know, old man McKinney tried to dial us in on the whole extra-dimensions and multiple-universes thing, but he just confused me."

"You don't want to go to any place that has more or fewer dimensions. Nothing would make sense. There are many universes in the greater cosmos. You're in my universe now; I was in yours for a short time. The people you battle are from a universe different from yours or mine."

"The Gate," I said. "We call them The Gate."

"They have many names — most of them less kind."

"They don't deserve kindness," Brenda said.

No one wanted to argue the point.

"No, they don't." Helsa lowered her head and seemed to sink deeper in sadness. "They are smarter, have a better understanding of these things, and use more powerful equipment. They mean your world great harm."

"We gathered that." Andi had had several close calls with death because of them. I figure that gave her the right to be snippy.

Helsa stopped and turned to us. "How much do you know about . . . the people who are helping you fight The Gate?"

"Next to nothing." I offered that bit of revelation. I've noticed that as a group we don't much care to reveal our ignorance. Not many people take me seriously, so I don't mind admitting to not knowing things I should know.

Andi offered more information. "They only contact us through e-mail. They pay for our travels and our bank accounts go up every month — not enough to make us rich, but enough that we don't have to get jobs to survive. They don't talk to us; they just send us tickets to fly or directions to drive to some location. They never tell us the whys and wherefores. They also seem to clean up after us."

"Clean up?" Helsa raised an eyebrow.

"How do I explain this?" Andi furrowed her brow. "We've endured some strange things: killer fungus, creatures that swim in the fog and eat pedestrians, flying orbs — it's a long list. Yet, somehow, most of it is kept out of the media. I don't know how they do it, but when we ride off into the sunset, they send in the janitors."

Helsa nodded. "I'm afraid we don't know any more than you. I hate to admit that. I'm just as confused as you. I'm part of a team here, and what you describe is the same as what we experience."

"You're part of a team?" I couldn't believe what I heard.

"Yes, Tank. It is why I was sent to your universe, to your world. It is why I'm here now. I think it is why *you're* here now. We need you."

She sighed from deep in her soul, then started down the corridor. I had a bazillion questions but didn't ask them. Helsa had something to show us, and she was intent on doing so right now. We fell in line and followed her as she led us to another wing of the building. I noticed the doors had numbers, and many had lights over the door. It reminded me of a hospital. Then it hit me. It *was* a hospital. At least a hospital wing.

Helsa stopped at a pair of doors. A sign was mounted to each of the doors, signs I couldn't read, but if I were a betting man, I would wager they read NO ADMITTANCE. A phone hung next to the doors. Amazing how many things were the same in our two worlds, universes, or whatever. The phone looked like the wall-mounted variety back home but was the color of Red Vines candy and slightly smaller than I would have expected. She said something into the phone that was just as mysterious to me as the words on the sign.

The doors swung open and Helsa walked through. "Brace yourself."

I hate it when someone says that.

I led the others in. They seemed a little hesitant after Helsa's warning.

The place had a distinct smell — a mix of antiseptic, urine, and skin lotion. The room reminded me of an ICU unit, except the patients didn't have private rooms. I guess it was more of a ward than anything else. Nurses dressed in blue uniforms moved from bed to bed. There were, by my estimation, forty or so souls there. I could only guess at the ages of people. Some looked to be in their early sixties. Others looked well beyond the century mark.

For a moment I was certain I had just walked into a sci-fi movie. IV bags hung from metal stands. Some of the patients had fluid flowing into them from more than one IV bag, and the fluids were different colors. It looked as if they were getting a transfusion of rainbow juice.

The patients were quiet. The heart monitors were also silent. Soft classical-sounding music drifted from the ceiling. I scanned the room, then I focused on the patients. Each wore a yellow gown; each had deep wrinkles plowed by years of life.

A thought wormed its way into my brain.

Morgues were places where they kept dead people. This seemed like a morgue for the almost dead. A chill spread through me, freezing me from the inside out. A glance at the girls told me the scene had the same effect on them. Andi was pale. Brenda found something on the floor to look at. Daniel was different. He kept his head up and strolled to an elderly lady reclined in a hospital bed. Her hair was a flat silver, her skin the color of parchment.

He smiled. She smiled back. It reminded me of two children meeting for the first time and becoming friends. Daniel took her hand. The sight of it filled me with pride. My breath caught. My eyes burned.

My heart went out to the old woman in the bed. She clung to a child's doll. She held it up for Daniel to see, then wiggled it so the doll seemed to dance. Just like a child would do. Then the old woman giggled. The giggle was as light as a feather and floated like one through the room. I glanced around the place again and noticed that several of the old folks had a child's toy on the bed with them. The woman giggled again, and she sounded just like a little girl —

My stomach contracted. My knees shook and gave up their strength. I bent forward and fought an almost irresistible urge to vomit on the clean, highly polished floor.

"Oh dear God." I said that so softly that I was surprised to learn that Andi and Brenda heard it.

A hand on my shoulder. "Tank, what's wrong?" I didn't have to look to know it was Andi's hand.

I raised a finger, straightened. Took two deep breaths and walked from the room. Andi and Brenda followed; Daniel did not.

"Tank. Talk to me." Andi was by my side. Brenda stood a few feet in front of me.

I stumbled back a few steps until my back touched the corridor wall, then my legs decided to quit. I slid to the floor.

Brenda tried a more direct approach to get my attention. "Cowboy, so help me, if you don't start talking I'm gonna hit you so hard your grandparents will scream."

"Is it the old people?" Andi said.

I tilted my head up. "They're not old. They're . . . they're young! Dear God, they're kids! Children!"

Chapter 10 The Fountain of Elderliness

Helsa brought a cup of black fluid that I assumed was coffee. It wasn't. I drank it anyway, hoping it would put the steel back in my spine.

"You understand?" Helsa sat beside me. We were in the cafeteria. In the corner. Far from the police officers, nurses, doctors, and other people who worked in this place.

"I don't," Andi said.

"Me neither." Brenda sounded irritated again. "Someone better start talkin' or I'm gonna lose my kind and gentle reputation."

"Tell me I'm wrong, Helsa. For the love of God, tell me I'm wrong."

She sat in the chair next to me and took my hand. "I can't."

After a deep breath, Helsa looked at Andi, Brenda, and Daniel. "What do you remember of my visit to your world?"

Andi rose to the bait. "You were a kid. Your eyes changed color there as they do here —"

"Younger," Daniel said. "You got younger."

Helsa nodded. "That's right."

A few seconds passed and Brenda began to swear. I think she used every profanity she knew. Andi sat like a statue for a few moments, then asked, "So these are kids from our world? How long have they been here?"

"The ones in that room have been on this side — in our universe — for about two weeks. A few longer; a few shorter."

"How do they end up here?"

"We're not sure. Probably the same way you did."

"Can't you send them back?"

"We've tried. . . . We would if we could."

Andi never shied away from asking tough questions. Apparently the steel in my spine had moved to her. "How —" she stopped, then took another running start at the question. "How old was the person Daniel was talking to?"

Helsa had to reach deep for the answer. She pursed her lips, blinked several times. "Eight."

"Eighty?" Brenda jumped in. "You said 'eighty,' right?"

"No. Eight years old. Many have already

died of old age. The older they are when they get here, the faster they age."

I braced myself for another barrage of curses but it never came. Instead, Brenda leaned forward and covered her face.

My turn to ask the difficult question: "How long before we begin to change?"

Helsa gave my hand a squeeze. "It's already started."

One more question from me, but I was already sure of what I was going to hear. "Where are the adults who came over?"

Helsa wasn't the kind to soft-pedal. "Dead."

When a person hears something that doesn't make much sense, it's only natural to call it nonsense and move on. That was my first reaction, but ever since I pushed together with my friends, I'd seen so many things that didn't make sense that I lost my ability to be surprised. Hearing that we would grow old quickly just like Helsa grew younger when she was in our universe was unwelcome news. I wanted to call it nonsense, but I couldn't. Truth was, I was already feeling a little older, but I figured that was due to an admittedly tough day.

There wasn't much conversation after that. Helsa asked us to tell her all the details of what had happened in Newland before we were hijacked out of our own world. She was so different from the child I used to call Littlefoot. Clearly her mind was running at top speed; mine, not so much.

Food arrived. It looked familiar. There were mashed potatoes on my plate, but they weren't white. They weren't the color of sweet potatoes, either. To me they looked gray, like they had been left in the field too long. I'm not a picky eater so I gave it a taste. It was glorious. Slightly sweet. Still weird to look at. Also on the plate were string beans, and thank the good Lord, they were the right shade of green. A nice salad of greens was nestled beside the beans. I usually think of salads as rabbit food, but I had been taught to eat what was on my plate. There were other things, none of which looked like meat. So I asked.

Helsa grinned. "No one eats meat here."

"You're all vegetarians?" I felt like a man who had just been robbed.

"Yes. We don't kill animals for food."

I looked at Andi, who seemed fine with the revelation. I glanced at Daniel; he looked distracted by what had just happened and didn't seem to care about what he ate — and I've seen the kid down his fair share of hotdogs and hamburgers. Then there was Brenda. I studied her as she picked at the stuff on her plate. She looked ready to rebel.

"We gotta find a way home," she said.

Helsa let us eat, then said, "You mentioned a crazy man outside the hotel and the restaurant."

"Yes, probably just some homeless guy."

"He was crazier than an outhouse rat." Brenda didn't bother looking up from her plate. Her description was a tad cruel, but I couldn't argue with it.

"And he had an eye patch?"

"Yep. Handmade. Cut it out of a Corn Flakes box and tied it on with a string."

"Tockity Man," Daniel said. He hadn't done much talking of late, especially since we left the hospital ward. He had that distant look in his eyes. Something was working in the kid's brain.

"Tockity Man?" Helsa asked.

"It was something he said —"

"Ranted," Andi clarified.

I continued. "Both times we saw him, he said, 'Tock-tick, tock-tick, tockity, tockity, tick-tick.' He got some of it backward."

"He didn't get it backward," Helsa said. "That line is from a children's poem." She closed her eyes, then spoke as if reading words printed on the inside of her eyelids:

Tock, tock, tock goes the clock,
Tick, tick, tick, the hands make their pick.
Around the face the hands do move;
Our work the heart does prove.
Tock-tick, tock-tick,
Tockity, tockity, tick-tick,
What life will you pick?

Andi looked puzzled. "I see your children's poems are as confusing and unsettling as ours."

"It is very old, and I'm translating into your language, so it doesn't sound the same aloud as it does in my head. It meant more two hundred years ago than it does today. I haven't heard it since I was a child — I mean, a child in my world."

"Sick minds are attracted to sick ideas," Brenda said. "I once did a tat on a guy that was nothing more than the line 'and down will come baby.' "

"You mean like the line in Rock-a-Bye Baby?" I always hated that lullaby.

"Yes," Brenda said, explaining it for Helsa. "There are variations of the song, but most describe a baby in a cradle, hung in a tree, and when the wind blows it rocks the cradle, then the bough — the tree limb — breaks, and the baby and cradle fall."

Helsa leaned back as if Brenda's word

came with a stench. "That's horrible."

"No one would argue with you," Andi said.

"Mothers still sing it to their babies without knowing what they're singing." Brenda's grumpiness had moved up a level.

I decided to get the conversation back on track. "So why would Tockity Man say those words to us?"

Helsa shrugged. "I don't know. It's the first I've heard of him. . . ." She trailed off, and that made my antennas go up. "Unless . . ."

"Unless what?" I was desperate for answers.

"I need to check on a few things." Helsa stood. "You should rest. You've had a challenging day."

"Challenging?" Brenda said. "That's one word for it."

Helsa patted Brenda on the shoulder. To my relief, she pulled her hand back without a single bite mark. "Brenda, you are very funny."

Helsa said nothing more but pivoted and walked from the cafeteria.

Chapter 11
Useless Hands

Helsa sent someone to show us our rooms, which were in the same building. They reminded me of dorm rooms. My room had a wide bed, a dresser, a small desk, a closet, and a bathroom. I made use of the latter, then stripped down and tried to make use of the bed. The mattress was firm, just the way I liked it. I needed sleep. Nothing is more taxing on mind and body than over-the-top emotions, and my mind and body had had it. The oblivion of sleep was what I wanted.

I was to be deprived. Although the bed was comfortable, my back ached, those gray potatoes weren't sitting right, and my brain was doing jumping jacks. Every time I closed my eyes, images flashed on the movie screen of my brain: Brenda talking about Batman, Tockity Man standing at the hotel and café windows, and — this was the worst of all — the children dressed in old bodies dying in the hospital wing.

I stared at the ceiling through the dim light. Something warm and wet trickled down the sides of my face. They were just children. When that realization hit me, I considered it the worst blow I had ever received.

It took me awhile to admit it, but I was wrestling with a different problem, one that embarrasses me. Me, as I said before, I *occasionally* heal people. I have no control over the when, the why, or the where. It's a great gift when it works, but since I don't know when it works it confuses me and that makes me shy away from trying.

Am I afraid to fail? No. Yes. I don't know. Perhaps this doesn't make sense. When I was still in college, I had to take a class in basic psychology. The professor told us about a study where two monkeys were given a shock. They shocked one monkey on a regular schedule. Same time of day and same number of times. That monkey didn't like it, but learned to live with it. The other monkey was shocked at random. That poor thing went nuts.

I don't admit this often, but with this gift, more and more I feel like the second monkey.

Sleep finally came, but it was loaded with

extra-real dreams, not one of which I liked. I didn't sleep long, maybe a few hours. I didn't know. I didn't care. The bed was done with me and I was done with it.

I swung my feet over the side of the bed, then stopped short. The pain in my back had grown sharper, and a new set of pains had set into my knees and one of my feet, the one I injured playing football. It hurt more now than it did then, and trust me, it hurt a lot back then.

It took two tries for me to hoist my bulk off the mattress. I took a few steps and each one hurt, but as I moved along, the joints loosened up some. My first thought was to blame the mattress. That changed when I hobbled into the bathroom and turned on the light. The image in the mirror made me forget why I had gone into the bathroom in the first place. The man in the mirror was me all right, but I had changed. Not greatly, but I've been looking at my mug for over two decades, and I could tell that my skin seemed a tad looser and my hair a bit thinner. I leaned closer to the mirror. There were wrinkles around the eyes and my hair was longer.

I had aged. I didn't need to think that through. Helsa had told us we would, but I didn't expect it to happen during a short nap. I like to put things in the best possible light, so I told myself how glad I was that I hadn't slept longer. I also realized whatever it was we were supposed to do, we needed to get to it. Tick-tock, tock-tick, the clock. I now somewhat understood what the Tockity Man meant. And I didn't like it.

No more wasting time. I doubted I had any time to waste anyway. I dressed again and left my room. I knew my destination, and I was there in short order — maybe a little slower than I would have made the trip when I first got to this place, but I didn't let any moss grow on me.

I didn't use the communication panel on the side of the doorway to the hospital ward. I just walked in. Nurses looked at me but said nothing. I had a feeling they were thinking, "He'll be in here permanently soon enough."

No lingering for me. I came to work, to lay it all on the line. If I failed, it would be a failure of trying to do something right.

No need to tell the nurses what I intended to do. They wouldn't understand me anyway. I stopped at the nearest bed. A man who looked to be well north of ninety met my gaze. I doubt he saw me. Cataracts covered his eyes. I took one of his hands in mine and laid my other hand on his forehead.

I prayed.

I prayed for all I was worth. Some minutes passed before I could open my eyes. No change. The cataracts were still there, and the old man/kid was still the same as I first saw him. No healing.

I moved to the next bed, then the next. Same result, by which I mean no results. Maybe my gift didn't work in this universe. Maybe I forgot how to do it right. Maybe I had fallen out of favor with God. My eyes grew wet again. Still, I moved from one patient to the next doing absolutely no good at all. The children were all dying of old age.

Time walked by. Tock-tick, tock-tick, tockity, tockity, tick-tick. With each tick I felt more despair and more anger. I didn't think I could slip lower. Turns out, I could.

The door to the room burst open and a familiar-looking young man walked in. He wore a robe and was barefoot. His hair hung to his ears and was styled in the I-just-rolled-outta-bed look. I wondered if he was a new patient, then the ceiling collapsed on me. Daniel.

The young man stepped to the bedside of the eight-year-old kid who looked eighty.

He took her hand and just stood there. A weak giggle rose from the bed, and I stood glued to the floor as Daniel stroked the patient's hair.

If I had died at that moment, I would have considered it a blessing worthy of the highest praise. One of the nurses wheeled a chair over to Daniel so he could sit vigil. He took it. Sat. Then began to weep as the heart monitor next to the bed flatlined.

I limped to his side and put a hand first on his shoulder, then on the dead woman's arm. I needed to speak, but I had no words; I needed to grant comfort but had none to give. I was useless.

Daniel laid his head on the side of the bed, resting it on their clasped hands.

We wept together.

Brenda and Andi walked through the doors. I could see gray in Brenda's hair and wrinkles in Andi's face. They weren't old, but they had definitely aged. Daniel hadn't moved; his head still rested on the bed. The dead girl/woman had been staring at the ceiling until I closed her eyes. I wish I could have done more. All I could do was stand near Daniel until the nurses thought enough time had passed and came to take her away.

Brenda stopped in her tracks. The young

man in the robe must have looked familiar to her, but it was still impossible to believe.

Brenda's eyes shifted from Daniel to the person in the bed, to the heart monitor, to me, then back to Daniel. "Oh, baby boy," she said. She stepped beside Daniel, bent and hugged him. That's when the sniffing started. Andi came to my side, took a look at me, then let the tears flow.

"I couldn't do anything." I whispered the words, which at the moment was the only volume setting I had. "I tried, Andi, I really tried. I prayed for each one. I tried to heal them, but it didn't work. I feel useless."

She took my arm, leaned in, and rested her head on my shoulder. Any other time, any other place, any other universe, I would have been over the moon. I was none of that. I was just heartbroken.

Minutes tock-ticked by, then an idea occurred to me. "We have to get these people back."

"How?" Andi kept squeezing my arm like she feared her legs would give way.

"I don't know. I just know we have to do it. I can't let these kids die one by one, and I can't let . . . others . . . be brought over —"

"Tank?" Andi let go and turned to face me. "What are you thinking?"

"I'm not sure yet. . . ." A fresh thought arrived. It was like someone was dictating directions to me. "Andi, I need your help. You too, Brenda."

Daniel finally raised his head. "What about me?" He wiped his eyes dry.

"I always need you, li— buddy." I started to call him "little buddy," but that didn't seem to fit anymore.

"We have to get Daniel back home." Brenda sounded desperate. "Littlefoot returned to her proper age when she got back to her world; maybe we'll do the same when we get back to ours."

"I was thinking the same thing." My mind was firing on all cylinders. "Andi, talk to the other patients. Ask questions. Find a pattern. We need a pattern."

A motion to my right drew my attention to a nurse on a phone. A few moments later, Helsa walked in.

Chapter 12
Doing Something Even If It's Wrong

My mother used to say that a watched pot never boils. Of course, she meant the water in the pot, but I never corrected her. She used to say that a lot. In our family, she was the one that had all the patience. I'm pretty good at patience, but not great. Especially if lives are at stake, I get positively antsy.

Andi was my watched pot. Brenda, Daniel, and I went to the cafeteria. It was easier to talk around a cafeteria table. More elbow room.

We did very little talking. I didn't know where to start. *"Hey Daniel, what's it feel like to go from kid to teenager overnight? Are you diggin' that?"* That would be as stupid as it sounds. So instead, we played with our drinks and I tried to get my brain to be better than it was. It was wearing me out. I had only been up a few hours and I was already wishing for a nap. Growing older ain't for sissies.

Brenda broke the silence. "You gotta plan, Cowboy?"

"Not really. Just a few thousand questions."

"Me too."

"We have to save the kids." Daniel's voice was nearly an octave deeper. It was interesting to hear, but I wanted my little buddy to be, well, little again.

"I know." I rubbed my eyes. My vision wasn't as sharp as I was used to. No doubt I needed glasses. "I'll do anything I can."

"We got here," Daniel said. "We can get back."

He lifted his eyes and looked around. From time to time Daniel sees angels, and I've been with the kid long enough to know he was looking for his friends. His expression told me he was disappointed.

Through the open door to the cafeteria I saw Andi and Helsa approaching. I was just getting used to seeing Helsa as an adult; it would take longer for me to get used to seeing an older Andi. She still looked pretty.

Andi walked with her head down as if following a line on the floor. Others might look at her and think, "Uh oh, she has bad news." They'd be wrong. Her brain was burning rubber, and I took that to mean something good.

Andi sat across the table and next to Brenda; Helsa sat next to me.

We waited for Andi to speak. I knew she would when she got her thoughts in order. I didn't have to wait long.

Andi said, "Okay, I'm gonna spew."

"Eww," Daniel said.

"I don't mean that. I'm gonna spew what I've learned and then we can try to sort it out. Okay?"

No one objected.

"I've talked to as many of the patients as could speak. A few were showing signs of senility, but even then, I got a few things. Tank, you were right, they are children. The youngest is six and the oldest is twelve. There is no pattern to their ages. It's a mix of those ages and all of the ones in between. There is roughly an even ratio of males to females, but there are a few more girls than guys. Again, no real pattern there. It's what we'd expect if we visited any hospital: girls outnumber boys by a slight margin. So whoever or whatever is doing this is no respecter of persons or genders."

"Is it only children who are dragged into this world?" I felt silly the moment I asked it.

"Think about it, Tank. You, Brenda, and I

are adults and we came over the same as Daniel. The adults have died off already."

"Right. We established that yesterday." I remembered. I just wanted her to know I was listening. Either that or my memory was getting a little wobbly.

Andi went on, her eyes looking around the table but never really seeing us. She was immersed in thought. "All of the children are from Newland. That realization is important. If we had people here from different towns, states, even other parallel universes, it would mean the problem is too large for us to handle. Of course, it might still be too much for us, but at least we're dealing with just one place that is somehow tied to this reality."

She paused. "Remember the mousy hotel manager we met when we came into town?"

"I do," Brenda said. "She needed a good backhand to the face, if you ask me."

"Because . . ." Andi prompted.

"Because she tried to run us off, that's why," Brenda said. "You were there. If she could have shoved us out the door, she would have done it."

"And Tiffany at the café?" Andi said.

"Same thing. She tried to get us to head out of town."

"They don't like strangers," I said.

"Sorry, Tank. You're wrong. So are you, Brenda. And as much as I hate to admit it, so was I. They weren't trying to get us to move on because they didn't like tourists. They were trying to *save* us — to keep us from becoming the next set of victims."

That was a punch to the gut.

"They could have been clearer about that." Brenda was not ready to give up a perfectly good bad mood.

"Not really, Brenda. They couldn't say, 'Enjoy your stay in Newland, North Carolina — oh, and don't let anyone make you disappear.' " Andi took a deep breath, as if revealing this information was wearing her out. "They have lost family members and probably even their own children without the slightest hint of what happened to them. We have the advantage of knowing a little about where we are."

"I misjudged them," I said.

Andi agreed. "We all did."

Helsa said, "When all this began a few months ago, I did some checking. To our knowledge, people from your world only show up here and no place else in our world."

Her eyes turned yellow. That was a new one.

"Not many days ago," Andi said, "we sat

in a university auditorium to listen to the professor talk about alternate dimensions and parallel universes. As you know, I made the PowerPoint slides and helped organize his material just like I've done for the professor over the last few years. He initially planned to include some controversial material but took it out about a week before we went to Tampa. He couldn't provide enough evidence that the events he planned to describe were in fact real and not pure fiction. I helped with that research. Very interesting, but not substantial."

"Like what?" I asked.

"I'll tell you, but just understand that some of this may be real and some of it might be pure baloney." Andi took a deep breath. "There have been reports of people, groups, and even civilizations that have vanished. In 1872, the steamboat *Iron Mountain* disappeared while making its way down the Mississippi. She was never heard from again. Unfortunately, only one newspaper reported the vanishing. So did it really happen? Who knows?

"In 1947, a small plane crashed on Mount Rainier. When searchers found the crash site they discovered evidence of injury, but no people, no bodies, no footprints, and no indication that predators had hauled bodies away. The pilot and passengers were just gone."

Andi fiddled with Brenda's napkin. We gave her a moment to collect her thoughts. "In the late 1800s, on a farm outside Gallatin, Tennessee, a farmer named David Lang went into his field one day and — in full view of his family — disappeared. Some say the family could hear his voice in the field calling for help, but they could never find him. That mystery was never solved.

"It's a long list," Andi continued. "The Eskimo village of Anjikuni was found empty of all its residents, but everything they owned was left behind. A large group of Spanish soldiers vanished in 1711. And don't even get me started on the Bermuda Triangle."

"Are you saying that all these things really happened?" Brenda asked.

"No, I'm not. But we've seen enough in our adventures to make me wonder. The professor, of course, dismissed these stories, but I had a feeling he wondered if he might be wrong about that. But you know him — he was the poster child for logic and the scientific method."

This kind of talk tends to fry my brain, but I had a sense that Andi had more connections to make.

"Man, I could use a cup of coffee," Andi said. She looked worn out.

I started to rise, but Helsa beat me to it. She returned with more coffee for everyone, including Daniel. I still didn't know if it was really coffee, but it looked and smelled close enough.

A couple of sips later, Andi continued. "I tried to nail down exact times when the kids were brought over or sent over or whatever the right verb is, but we're dealing with children and they don't fixate on time like adults do. If some of the adults were still alive, I might have made more progress. Anyway, I learned that there is no clear pattern. It's not like they arrive on a timetable. Helsa confirmed that for me. They keep records of arrival times here. The time between arrivals varies and I can't figure out a pattern on that. For all I know, new folk may show up before lunch or not for a week. I doubt time here is exactly the same as home." She turned to Helsa. "How long does it take for your world to circle the sun?"

"Three hundred and seventy days, of course."

Andi did blink at that. "How long is a day?"

"Twenty-six hours."

Andi turned to the rest of us. "The year here is five days longer, and each day is roughly two hours longer." She rubbed her face. "I imagine a minute here is different than a minute back home. It would take me some time to figure all that out, and there's a good chance I'd fail even if I tried."

"So we got nothin'," Brenda said.

"Very little, I agree, but I did notice that the transition place, if that's a good term for it, was not always the same. We were in Tiffany's Café when we were snatched; others were in front of the café, at the end of town, in their homes, or some other place." Andi slouched in her seat as if telling us all this had drained her. Maybe it did, but I'm pretty sure she was feeling like a failure.

Andi sighed in a way that broke my heart.

"You did good, Andi."

"Thanks, Tank, but I've come up short —"

"Paper." It was Daniel.

I looked at him. He held the watch he had taken from the professor's room as a keepsake. Initially the watch proved too big for the arm of a ten-year-old. Since Daniel's unwelcome growth spurt, the watch almost fit. Not quite, but almost.

"What?" I said.

"Paper. Please." Daniel didn't look at me.

Instead, he gazed at Helsa.

She nodded, rose, and left the cafeteria only to return a few moments later with a couple pads of paper. She also carried a pen and a pencil, covering the bases, I supposed, and set them in front of Daniel.

"Whatcha going to do with that, baby?" Brenda said.

His answer was an action: he pushed the material in front of Brenda. "Draw. The town. Draw the town."

"I'm sorry, Daniel, but I didn't pay much attention to the place."

"Tank did. He took a walk."

Brenda looked at me, then at Andi. "I don't get it."

"Draw." Daniel was insistent. Usually he kept to himself, living much of his life in his own mind, but he had no problem jumping into the middle of things if he had something to contribute.

Brenda took the pencil and started by drawing the main street we used to get into town. I outlined my walk, mentioning buildings I had seen and houses I had passed. Brenda added those to the map. Twenty minutes later we had a pretty decent map of Newland.

The moment Brenda set the pencil down, Daniel grabbed the paper and pushed it in front of Andi. She blinked a few times, looked at me, met Brenda's eyes, then let her gaze settle on Daniel.

"I think I get it," she whispered. With that, Andi picked up the pencil.

Chapter 13
The Wisdom of Daniel

I was pacing, my patience gone. I had a feeling that we were about to cross a threshold of understanding and wanted to pray that we would recognize it.

Andi was putting little circles on the map Brenda had drawn. Each circle represented some child from our world who was dying in this world. Next to each circle Andi wrote two numbers in tiny script: the child's age and the day when the transfer occurred.

I assumed that the circles would be all over the proverbial map, but even I could see a trend. The markers formed a line from Tiffany's Café to the old church. Another line was formed going north from the church and into the residential area I had walked just this morning. Granted, these lines were a bit squiggly, but it was a pattern.

"There may be a time pattern after all." Andi didn't look up from the hand-drawn map. "I've included our event in Tiffany's. It's the most recent event we know of." She let her gaze linger on the paper. I leaned over the table for a closer look. "Odd."

"What's odd?" I leaned even closer to the page.

"I was expecting a straight line, or a clump of events, but I don't see that at all." Andi pointed at the old church with the pretty steeple. "If I . . . can it be that simple?"

"I don't see it, so it's not all that simple to me," I said.

"It looks like all the events fan out from the church building, like spokes from a hub. The earliest events happened in the residential area, the most recent in the heart of town."

"And what does that mean?" Helsa asked.

"Notice how the clumps of circles — people — are associated on one line, then the next taken are a little distance from the first. The same can be said for the other small groups." She scratched her head. "Think of the church as a lighthouse with a beam of light that swings in a big circle. Maybe I can extrapolate the next line — the line along which another abduction might occur."

She didn't have a ruler, so Andi tore a strip of paper from the edge of the page and used it to mark the distance between "spokes" at the same point from the hub, the church.

"The bar," Andi said. "My best guess is that the next group will come from the bar."

"At least there won't be any children in a bar." That was some comfort to me, but it wasn't enough. "This is useful information, but I don't know what to do with it." I began pacing again. "If you're right about the place, Andi, we still don't have a clue about the time."

Andi nodded slowly. "True. I don't know how to figure that out. The times of the previous events seem random."

"I suppose we could move into the place and —"

"Guys?"

It was Brenda. I had been so absorbed in what Andi was doing that I had forgotten about her. One look told me she hadn't been sitting on her hands. She had made use of the pen Helsa had brought after Andi glommed onto the pencil. While we had been talking, Brenda was having a go at one of the other pads of paper, which she pushed to the middle of the table.

She had drawn the front of the bar we had driven past when we came to town and I had walked past on my little hike. "Him.

He's the key. Get him and we get our answers."

In front of the bar stood Tockity Man, and in front of Tockity Man was another figure. A big figure holding the one-eyed man with the cardboard eye patch by the throat, and with his other hand he was holding Tockity's fist. The big man was me.

There was something else in the drawing: a large vehicle.

"What is that?" I tapped the image. It looked like a vehicle of some sort, but Brenda hadn't drawn the whole thing.

"Beats me," Brenda said. "I just draw this stuff."

Helsa took a gander, furrowed her brow a little, squinted, then suddenly straightened. "It's a bus." She blinked a few times. "It's a school bus." Her eyes widened. "That's it."

"What's it?" I asked.

Andi was already dialed in. "That's what's going to tell us when the next event will occur. It's our clock, Tank. School buses run on a schedule."

"It's headed away from the school," Helsa said. "So that means school is out. I'll be right back."

Helsa moved to a phone mounted to the wall about ten feet from us. No one had to tell me what she was doing. She was calling the school.

The thing about Brenda and her drawings is this: she is never wrong.

Chapter 14
A Step of Faith

I had no idea if any of this would work. It was one of those things that looked good on paper but seemed beyond stupid when said out loud. But I was desperate to do something. Too many lives had already been lost, and children who barely knew how to live were facing the death that should be limited to the old. I was older. Okay, fine. Andi and Brenda had aged, but they had already lived a good bit of life. Yet the kids in the ward knew nothing of first loves, hopes, or dreams. Some were just old enough to learn to throw a ball. I had to do something, and I trusted Brenda's and Andi's insights.

The van we were riding in moved down the hill, driven by one of the police officers we had met when we first arrived in New Land. When we first met, he was all smiles. Now he was as sober as an undertaker. Once I told Helsa what I wanted to do, she sprang into action. Clearly, she carried some kind of weight in this strange building. When she spoke, people hopped to it.

Helsa sat next to me in one of the van's rear seats. I leaned toward her. "I haven't asked this before, Littlefoot, because it reminds me of when you left us. Watching you go was as much pain as I've ever felt."

She took my hand. "I still love that name. Littlefoot. I cherish it."

That gave me a grin. "How did you get back here?"

"They brought me back. The people who send you places sent me there; they brought me home."

"How?"

She shook her head. "I don't know. It's beyond me. They know more than we do. They do good for the world — several worlds."

"You really don't know who they are?"

She looked sad. "No, Tank, I don't. I really don't. So much mystery. So many unknowns."

"We feel the same. Still, we've done some good things. How did they send you to our world and bring you back?"

"They set up a machine. I don't think it created an opening between our worlds, but he said it kept the doorway open."

"He?"

She looked away, then said a name that sounded like Shaun or maybe Shane. I don't think it was Shaun, but it was close.

"Where is he now?"

"I don't know. After I got back, he disappeared. It took me a little time to return to my proper age. When I did, he was missing."

"He was part of your team?"

She nodded. "In a way, he was much like your professor. I'm a bit like Andi. When I was my natural age again — that took about three weeks — my team was off doing the work we do. They never came back."

"No idea what happened to them?"

"None, but . . . I can't be sure, but I have a bad feeling about Shaun. I think he might be your Tockity Man."

That was a shocker. "What makes you think that?" I tried to keep all the surprise out of my voice. I doubt that I succeeded.

Tears filled her eyes. "He was the one who operated the device that kept the doorway to your world open long enough for me to pass through. After my team went missing, I went to the building where we kept the device. It's at the end of town. The device was gone."

"The church?" I asked.

"Yes. It is a center for worship. Well, it

was a center for worship. The spiritual ways are not followed here as they once were."

"Same can be said for our world," I said. "It would explain a few things if this guy made off with the equipment and brought it to our world."

"Again, I can't say that's what happened, but I fear it might be as you say."

"Why would he do that?" Brenda asked.

Helsa gazed out the window for a moment. "If it is Shaun, then I think he lost his mind. It's one of the dangers of jumping between universes. It short-circuits our brains."

"Tockity Man is more than a little crazy." That may have been harsh. I patted Helsa's hand. "This isn't easy work. We can only do what we can do."

Helsa's revelation was painful to hear, and I'm sure even more painful to share. I wondered what it was like wondering what happened to a team you had spent so much time with. The thought of losing Andi and Brenda would feel like someone doing surgery on me with a butter knife.

We arrived in front of the building that corresponded to the bar in our Newland, except here, best I could tell, it was more of a juice bar.

Helsa spoke to her driver, who repeated the words over the radio. The patrol cars that had followed us back into town blocked off the road. Other patrol cars, probably teams already on duty, were stationed along the street. Officers slipped from the vehicles and moved to the bar, walked through the door. Moments later patrons exited, looking confused. So did one man who I took to be the owner. He was less than happy.

"You ready to rock and roll, Cowboy?" Brenda sounded confident. I'm pretty sure she was faking it.

"No, but let's do this anyway."

The moment we were outside the van, I heard Helsa. "Tank."

She rushed toward me, threw her arms around my neck, kissed me on both cheeks, then stepped back. "If it is Shaun, and if he has the transport mechanism, then he'll have an activator. It looks like a small red fruit. Don't let him use it, or everything will be for nothing."

I nodded grimly and stepped toward the building. I had been right. It was a juice bar.

Dropping a coil of rope on the floor, I pulled one end up and tied it around my waist. A uniformed officer tied the other end to a stool bolted to the floor. We had a plan. It didn't make a lot of sense, but it was the only plan we could come up with. We had a likely location for the next set of abductees. Andi figured that out. Brenda's future-drawing power had given us a pretty good timeline and placed me at the scene with Tockity. Since Brenda's drawing showed me mixing it up with the one-eyed crazy man in this universe, it meant I somehow needed to bring him here. All we had to do was get to the bar before the event.

"I hope this works," I said. "If it doesn't, then you guys will never let me forget it."

"You got that right, Cowboy." I turned to see Brenda grinning. That did me a lot of good. She could fill a room with laughter or suck all the air out of it with just a few words. Love that girl.

When we were dragged from our world, we were sitting in a café booth. I didn't see anything like a portal or door, but then again I was looking at my breakfast. I hoped I would recognize it when it arrived. I scanned the interior of the juice bar with its blenders, brightly upholstered seats, and artwork of some strange-looking fruit on the walls. We moved the small tables and chairs from the middle of the floor. I figured if I stood in the center of the room I would have the shortest possible distance to anything that appeared in the room.

A light flashed in my eyes, the same kind of light that flashed in my head when we were transported here. Problem. The light didn't form a structure like a door or anything. It was just a glow that filled almost half of the space in the juice bar. I hesitated, wondering where to enter.

Then I got a break: two or three confused and shaken people emerged from the center of the glow. I didn't hesitate. I charged the point where I had seen them materialize. I might have only a moment. I hoped that I wouldn't run through it and slam into the wall.

I didn't.

The light that surrounded me now filled me. And it hurt. Big-time pain. I may have screamed. If I did, I didn't hear it.

Then the light was gone, and I was doubled over but standing on a floor covered in peanut shells.

The bar.

"Tockity, tockity, tick —"

I straightened and saw the scruffy man with the Corn Flakes eye patch. A moment later, I had him by the throat. He had something in his right hand. It looked like the device Helsa described. With my free hand I clamped my big mitt around his hand and squeezed until I was sure I had control of all his fingers. His face twisted in pain and told me I had accomplished that part of my goal.

"Is your name Shaun?"

He looked surprised, then confused, then I drove my forehead into his face. He stopped struggling.

I released his throat and took hold of the front of his filthy coat. The rope around my waist served as my guide back to the portal. All I had to do was make sure that Tockity Man didn't regain consciousness and wiggle his hand with the activator free. If he did, he might close the gateway with me on this side and my friends on the other — my friends and all those old kids who needed help. I dragged him along as if he were a doll. I'll admit, I was a little pumped up on adrenaline and fear. A few steps later we were back in the other universe.

I dragged the unconscious Tockity Man to the side of the juice bar, ordering some patrons who had been snatched from the liquor bar out of the way. It was natural that they would be confused, but the liquor wasn't doing them any favors.

"Back. Go back." Helsa was loud and

forceful. Still they — six men and two women — weren't sure it was a wise idea. Helsa stepped to the spot where I had crossed over and pointed. "Go! Run!"

They stood still, confused.

"NOW!" That was Brenda. She was more convincing. They followed the directions if for no other reason than to save their hearing from another Brenda outburst.

I pinned Tockity to the wall. He was still out of it, but he could come to anytime and I was afraid of letting go of his hand. I wanted the threshold open as long as possible.

Helsa was overseeing the rest of the plan. Officers and nurses poured through the door of the juice bar helping elderly patients into the light. Some were on gurneys, some hobbled, some were carried by police officers. None of the helpers questioned Helsa when she told them to carry their patients into the light, turn around, and come right back.

"Brenda, Daniel, go through. Take charge over there." They exchanged glances and marched through. "You too, Andi."

"I'm not leaving you, Tank."

"Andi, please, just go. I'll be there as soon as I can. Go, those kids need help. Go."

She went.

Moments later helpers were returning, shaken, pale, and a few vomiting, but they kept at it. Time and time again, they carried patients into the white void until every elderly child had crossed over. Helsa spit out orders like a drill sergeant. Based on the way I felt, I guessed those brave souls might need a few days off.

Tockity came to in a fury. His fingernails dug into my face. His knee caught me in the groin. I was already half out of sorts from traveling through the opening twice in short order. I didn't need such treatment.

Some of the officers came to my aid. We took him to the floor, pinned his right arm, and slowly pried his fingers back until I held what looked like a small, glowing red apple. It had a switch on it. Tockity had it pressed when I grabbed his hand, so I kept it pressed.

"Easy with that, Tank. It's your only way home."

I released Tockity to the cops. Stood. Wobbled a little and did my best to keep the contents of my stomach right where they were.

"Go, Tank," Helsa said.

"I need a minute with you."

"No. The activator could stop working. It's not in the same universe as the device it controls. Go. Go now."

I had already watched Helsa — Littlefoot — fade in front of my eyes. I didn't want to say good-bye again.

"Helsa —"

"Shut up. I can't go with you and you can't stay here. If either one of us tries, then we die. Go. Your friends need you."

I walked to the light and looked back.

"Keep up the good work, Tank," she said. "You're a hero. You're my hero."

My vision blurred. My face was hot.

I walked through the light.

I was weeping when I emerged back in my own world. I don't care who saw.

Epilogue

It took several tries, but we were able to take the door to the church down. The sledgehammers we carried made it easy. With me were several townsfolk from Newland. Each had a sledgehammer that he or she either brought from home or had been given by the owner of the hardware store, who was with us, too. After all, he had lost his wife but got his eight-year-old daughter back. It was a little difficult to explain all that happened to the others, but since we had brought many of their children back they would have believed us if we had said the moon was made of chocolate.

I felt a little bad about breaking into a church, even one that had been abandoned a long time ago. Still, a church is a group of believers, not a building, so I put my reservations aside and helped knock the door in.

We found the device that bridged the two universes. The sanctuary had no pews. It was a wide-open space with the device. It was an odd-looking thing. It reminded me a bit of some abstract sculpture. I don't know what I expected. Maybe something sleek and shiny. It wasn't sleek. It looked like an oversized golf ball, but instead of all those little indentations it was covered in little metal bumps. It wasn't shiny, either. I could tell it was metal but it lacked the luster of aluminum. It looked a tad corroded. I doubt Tockity Man took care of his toys.

It rested on a set of wood blocks. High tech meets low tech. An electrical line ran from the bottom of the sphere and had been wired into a junction box in one of the walls. I wondered how it worked but only for a few moments. We had other plans for the thing.

We waited as Walter, the local electrician, disengaged the power to the unit. It was no secret that we had come to destroy it, but it needed to be done with some dignity, not like a crazed mob. Everyone needed to have a hand in ending the problem. This was the best idea I could come up with. Tiffany knew everyone who had lost loved ones and put us in contact with them. When I told them what I had in mind, not a person said no.

I wanted to make sure everyone got a

good whack at the thing. So, I wrote their names on slips of paper, got a brown paper lunch bag, dumped them in, and created my own little lottery.

"Gerald Ames."

Gerald grinned, but he did so with tears in his eyes. He got his son back but was shaken to the core to see what had happened to the boy. They were all shaken. It took awhile, but we convinced them that the impossible would happen and their children would grow young again. Those who didn't get their kids back, well, we couldn't do anything but weep with them. And we did a lot of that.

The group stepped away to give Gerald a little room, and Gerald gave it all he had. He was in his forties but looked to me like he was well acquainted with hard work. The business end of the sledge struck a devastating first blow.

A cheer went up.

Gerald folded over in tears and remorse. Several men went to his side while I pulled another name from the bag. "Jensen P. Monroe. You ready, brother?"

"More ready than I can say." He recited the name of his two children who had been returned to him, then the names of his neighbor's children who were forever gone, then he put every fiber of this body into his swing. The sound of it hurt my ears.

"Lucy Morris . . ."

The children were housed in the hotel at the end of the street. Two entire floors had been converted to a hospital wing. The local doctor, a young man not long out of med school, and a few nurses he called in to help, tended to the children. I can't say enough good about them.

We stayed a week. Daniel began to look a couple of years younger and was having trouble finding the right size clothing. I guess it's true — you can't keep kids in clothes no matter if they're growing up or down.

As for the adults, we were returning to our proper ages, more slowly than I liked, but I could be patient. At least I was in the right universe.

Each night I spent a little time looking at the stars and wondering about Littlefoot. I guess I will always do that.

Once the car was packed, we said our good-byes to Jewel and thanked her for making her place available for the kids to recuperate in. We also thanked her for trying to save our necks by sending us packing.

Before we entered the car, Brenda called us close. "We saved a lot of children," she said. "That makes me feel pretty good. And Daniel was a big part of that. We might not have learned what we needed to know if he didn't insist on some paper and start bossing us around."

We all agreed to that. I waited, figured there was more Brenda wanted to say.

"Daniel and me had a chat. Okay, he did the chatting and I did the listening. You know him, he's not much on conversation, but he did make it clear that he's part of the team and even though he's only ten, he's very different from other boys."

"That's a fact," I said.

Brenda looked at the ground. "Anyway, forget all that Batman stuff I was throwin' around." Except she didn't use the word *stuff.*

"Oh, man, and here I was thinking we finally got rid of you."

She punched me in the arm. It hurt in a wonderful way. "I will take you down, Cowboy. You know I will."

"Yes, ma'am, I do know that."

Then I hugged her. That led to a group hug.

And a prayer of thanksgiving from me.

ABOUT THE AUTHORS

Bill Myers is a youth worker, creative writer, and film director who co-created the "McGee and Me!" book and video series; his work has received over forty national and international awards. His many books include *Hot Topics*, *Tough Questions*, and *The Dark Side of the Supernatural*.

Frank E. Peretti is one of American Christianity's best-known authors. His novels, including *This Present Darkness*, have sold more than 10 million copies. He makes his home in Idaho. Learn more at www.frankperetti.com.

The author of more than 100 published books and with nearly 5 million copies of her books sold worldwide, **Angela Hunt** is the *New York Times* bestselling author of *The Note*, *The Nativity Story*, and *Esther: Royal Beauty*. *Romantic Times* Book Club presented Angela with a Lifetime Achievement Award in 2006. In 2008, Angela completed her PhD in Biblical Studies in Theology. She and her husband live in Florida with their mastiffs. She can be found online at www.angelahuntbooks.com.

Alton Gansky is the author of twenty-four novels and eight nonfiction books. He is a Carol Award winner and an Angel Award winner, and has been a Christy Award finalist. He holds a BA and an MA in biblical studies and has been awarded a Doctor of Literature degree. Director of the Blue Ridge Mountains Christian Writers Conference, Gansky also serves as an editor and collaborative writer for top tier authors. He lives in California.

The employees of Thorndike Press hope you have enjoyed this Large Print book. All our Thorndike, Wheeler, and Kennebec Large Print titles are designed for easy reading, and all our books are made to last. Other Thorndike Press Large Print books are available at your library, through selected bookstores, or directly from us.

For information about titles, please call:
(800) 223-1244

or visit our website at:
gale.com/thorndike

To share your comments, please write:

Publisher
Thorndike Press
10 Water St., Suite 310
Waterville, ME 04901